Vance MacLean

Cyportal

Book One

UI

ISBN 978-90-823115-0-1

Published by Marco I.M. Knoester, the Hague, the Netherlands

http://vancemaclean.com

Cyportal

Book One

UI

An epical, apocalyptical, and political Sci fi
symphony, by Vance MacLean

Note from the author.

This is a work of fiction.

I would like to emphasize that this entire work is purely fictional, and only an extension of basic historical and scientific facts. Although based loosely on modern-day physics, this work is not an exact scientific study, and mostly pseudo-scientific in content.

It contains a number of actual historical facts, and the storyline itself is in some places an extension on these historical facts.

The scientific and ethical elements in this manuscript are meant as a basis, and an encouragement for the reader, to make interconnections between these elements, and – from there – think further about these issues, and draw factually-based, scientific and ethical conclusions.

As this novel is purely fictional, no offense is intended towards any group, organization, or individual. The concept of Illuminati is only fictional, and suggested as a historical group of highly-educated people, inspired by the Age of Enlightenment and intent on philosophical and scientific objectivity, without Roman Catholic domination. This novel is not intended in any way to discredit or offend the Roman Catholic institution.

All characters in this novel are purely fictional and are in no way intended to correspond to any living persons.

Please enjoy reading this incredible story.

Kind regards,

Vance MacLean,

Writer of this novel

Dedication

These words are dedicated to the memory of my beloved father, as well as to the memory of Frank Herbert, the grand creator of the worlds of Dune....

'For all readers and all writers – in the end – all roads lead to Dune.... '

Acknowledgments:

I'd like to thank the following people for their advice, ideas, suggestions, moral support, insights, help and inspiration:

Annie M. Oroh (my mother), Kees vd Wilk, Hilma Neeleman, Karin Gruijters, Sinny, M.G. Knoester (my father), H.P. Oroh (my uncle), J.W. de Ruyter, Pim van der Hoff, Mariette Pegt, Richard Thrift, and Phil Bouwer.

Citations

'Where is everybody?'

Enrico Fermi, on the existence of extra-terrestrial life

'One of the most important, but one of the most difficult things, for a powerful mind, is to be its own master. '

Joseph Addison

'That's one small step for a man, one giant leap for mankind.'

Neil Alden Armstrong, while setting his first step on the moon

'A person who is religiously enlightened appears to me to be one who has, to the best of his ability, liberated himself from the fetters of his selfish desires and is preoccupied with thoughts, feelings, and aspirations to which he clings because of their super personal value.'

Albert Einstein, on being an enlightened person

'Muad'Dib could indeed see the Future, but you must understand the limits of this power. Think of sight. You have eyes, yet cannot see without light.'

F. Herbert's 'Dune', The Princess Irulan, about being able to see the future.

'In the councils of government, we must guard against the acquisition of unwarranted influence, whether sought or unsought, by the military-industrial complex. The potential for the disastrous rise of misplaced power exists and will persist. We must never let the weight of this combination endanger our liberties or democratic processes.'

Dwight D. Eisenhower, farewell address (17 January 1961)

'Against the dark background of the atomic bomb, the United States does not wish merely to present strength, but also the desire and the hope for peace.'

John F. Kennedy, Address before the General Assembly of the United Nations (25 September 1961), about the necessity of an end to war.

'Mankind must put an end to war or war will put an end to mankind'

John F. Kennedy

'Since you have now explained all things to us, tell us this: what is the sin of the world?'

Jesus, The Gnostic Gospels, The Gospel of Mary, about morality

(Comment on this, by the writer:

'I believe the one true sin (or rather: immorality, since the concept of 'sin' is an absolutist and ultimately subjective concept) in this life, in this universe, is that living beings consciously inflict psychological and physical suffering onto other living beings.

I believe compassion - the counterpart of this - is the central issue in Christianity, Islam, and

Buddhism. It is the core of morality and ethics.

Human - and other - suffering, is the bane of this universe and compassion its only counterpart....')

'It doesn't seem to me that this fantastically marvelous universe, this tremendous range of time and space and different kinds of animals, and all the different planets, and all these atoms with all their motions, and so on, all this complicated thing can merely be a stage so that God can watch human beings struggle for good and evil - which is the view that religion has.

The stage is too big for the drama.'

Richard Feynman (1992), on the struggle between good and evil

'I think I can safely say that nobody understands quantum mechanics,'

Richard Feynman, on the incomprehensibility of quantum physics

'The quantum physical entanglement of particles is not one, but rather the characteristic trait of quantum mechanics, the one that enforces its entire departure from classical lines of thought. '

Erwin Schrodinger, about the exoticness of quantum physics

'What is it that breathes fire into the equations, and makes a universe for them to describe?'

Stephen Hawking, on the spiritedness of the universe

'We are a way for the Cosmos, to know itself.'

Carl Sagan, on the recursion of the universe's consciousness

'Why those equations....?'

Einstein, on the mathematical nature of physics, in relation with its spiritedness

'Gödel's (incompleteness) theorem implies that pure mathematics is inexhaustible. No matter how many problems we solve, there will always be other problems that cannot be solved within the existing rules. (....)

Because of Gödel's theorem, physics is

inexhaustible too. The laws of physics are a finite set of rules, and include the rules for doing mathematics, so that Gödel's theorem applies to them.'

Freeman Dyson, about the feasibility of a TOE (theory of everything – see appendix 2.7)

'The needs of the many outweigh the needs of the few.... or of the one'

Leonard Nimoy, Star Trek

Citations by the writer:

'One single good person.... is like a light in the dark.
'

'The universe doesn't really exist.... It's only a complex combination, of mathematical functions, and equations. '

'Although many of us are not aware of it…. we all live inside a world of Sci fi. '

'Physics is magic, described by mathematics. '

'Since we have conquered the stars, the war for the stars has only begun. '

'We are all imprisoned between the future and the past. '

'Without a soul, humans would be no more than androids. So, if you turn this around, according to logic, humans are androids with a soul. '

'The expansion of the horizons of physics and the development of new technologies rely on human imagination, and subsequently on writers of science fiction. '

'However much technology, means, and devices we will ever have, we will never be able to escape the possibility of disaster.'

'A man's state of mind is determined by his place in the dimensions of space and time…. But even more so, by his place inside the dimensions of the metaphysical world '

'There is one single truth, every person discovers at some point in time.... Inside existence.... there are places of joy.... and places of incredible suffering....
'

'If the fruits of war are that most men wish to make peace, and embrace.... Then let the land be fertile.... '

'In the epic story of Dune, one is able to travel to any place in the universe, without moving.... The final destination of science, physics, and invention, is to be able to do anything, without doing anything.

Carl Sagan said intelligent beings are a way for the cosmos to know itself.
I think that when intelligent beings have reached this final destination of science and physics, the universe itself has found a way to be able to do anything, inside creation and existence, itself. '

'The most logical, most elegant and simplest explanation for the spiritedness and consciousness of living beings is that the universe – the multiverse – is entirely permeated by the universal soul. '

'We don't have to search beyond the stars to find

intelligent counterparts of ourselves.... we -
ourselves - are the aliens.... '

'And the ultimate thing a man can do.... is write. '

The writer

Contents

Timeline

Introduction

Prologue

Part 1

A prelude to a looming Interstellar Apocalypse

1. Prehistory witnessing of an alien sphere, and some critical accounts of past and future history.

2. Some critical accounts on the first global nuclear war on Sol-3.

3. An eerie alien flash-video comes in: first contact has finally arrived.

4. An analyzed alien flash-video is broadcasted.

5. Alien arrival at Cygnia main Cyportal.

6. A flash-attack on the CGC complex by the Human Dominion.

7. Preselected Delegation jumps to Ildion Prime.

8. A new flash-attack on the CGC complex by the Human Dominion.

9. Arrival of the pre-selected Delegation at Ildion

prime.

10. Creation of the Magna Carta, or: the Great Charter.

11. Angelina finds new information inside an Ildiran historical archive.

12. The first human-piloted attack by the Dominion fails.

13. Angelina and Kenzo Shyozama conspire against their government.

14. Kenzo Shyozama orders Angelina to covertly contact Russel Caltech.

15. Angelina discovers the first part of her true identity, in a hidden Dominion pre-Exodus Archive.

16. CGC systemic integrity compromised by Dominion flash-attacks.

17. Angelina descends from Russian composer P.I. Tchaikovsky.

18. Angelina tries to find her brother: Michael Tchaikovsky.

19. Ildirans declare war on Sol-trians (from the Federation), and join Dominion

Part 2

Deep inside a blazing interstellar Apocalypse

20. Approximately 1 million years ago: Trellians leave this universe.

21. Alien sphere seeks out Angelina and wants to save Interstellia.

22. Combined SI incursion inside ultra-secret Pax Infinity insurgency station.

23. Angelina is being interrogated, and escapes using her incredible powers.

24. The final end to GACS, UI-sys-1 escapes, and the premises for the next interstellar war.

25. A few final conclusions.

Epilogue

Appendices

1. 1-17. Synthesis of elementary universal truths of conscience, consciousness and existence (CCE synthesis, or Tchaikovsky synthesis)

2. 1-17. List of some explanations of concepts

3. List of some characters.

4. List of some locations.

5. List of some regions in space/inside multiverse.

6. List of some species.

7. List of some movements.

8. List of some conventions.

A piece of info on and pitch for Cyportal Book Two – (probable title) A Clash of UIs

A piece of info on Cyportal Book Three – (probable title) Ultimate UI

A piece of info on Cyportal Book Four – (probable title) Final UI

Timeline

BCE ('Before the Current Era'), and CE ('Current Era'), are the modern day equivalents of BC ('Before Christ') and AD ('Anno Domini').

Approx. 1 million BCE (see appendix 2.9)

Ixians decimate Trellian civilization. Trellians invent Ix device to fly to other universe

400,000-200,000 early mankind discovers the craft of making fire

11,414 Prehistory (and first) sighting of million years old alien sphere on Sol-3

c. 6,195 Birth of Ildiran advanced/technological

civilization

202 Hannibal is finally defeated by Scipio Africanus in the battle of Zama

52 Julius Caesar defeats Vercingetorix in the siege of Alesia

9th Century CE (appendix 2.8) Gunpowder invented in China

11th Century Chinese Pi Chang invents art of printing

1,415 A French army is butchered by Henry V at Agincourt

1,516 Medieval sighting of mysterious alien sphere above city of Ravenna

1,687 Sir Isaac Newton publishes laws of motion

1,905 Albert Einstein invents special relativity

1,916 Albert Einstein's general relativity lays ground for (applied) science of warped dimensions

1,943 First electronic computer, Colossus, created

1,945 (First ever deployed) nuclear weapons destroy Hiroshima and Nagasaki

1,947 Alien spaceship crashes near Roswell, New Mexico. Much discussion in the media.... It contains Ildiran bodies

1,961 Yuri Alekseyevitch Gagarin completes first manned orbit around Sol-3

1,969 Neil Alden Armstrong sets first step on the moon of Sol-3

1,970 Birth of super string theory (appendix 2.5)

1,970-2,050 Military ethicists and international experts warn against the danger of the development of self-sufficient military systems

1,995 M-theory is formulated as a synthesis of different super string theories

1,997 Thousands of US citizens witness UFO over Phoenix Valley

2,011 CERN institute measures neutrinos moving FTL (faster than light)

2,045 F-theory finally completed

2,045 First nuclear fusion plant in operation

2,060 Orbital XLC (extremely high-energy linear collider) confirms most aspects of M-theory

2,065 Research for warp drive begins

2,075 Great Human Galactic Exodus begins, using FTL/warp drives

2,079 First colonization ship touches down on Proxima Centauri 5

2,085 Small part of Exodus ships suddenly disappears from radar

2,147 First Old Earth nuclear world war (nww 1)

2,148 Establishment of GUA-1 (first Gaian United Alliance)

2,170 Sizeable asteroid impacts on the surface of Sol-3

2,180 More than 300 'successful' colonies

established

2,193 Ildiran Empire discovers human region in space

2,196 AI systems become self-governed

2,210 First (ever) event of AI-sys expressing human emotions

2,265 Governmental AI systems assume overall power

2,267 GACS system issues media flash about assumption of total control

2,465-2,469 Five great nuclear wars of the human dominion

2,643 Ildirans witness alien sphere

2,793 December 5 First alien contact

2,793 December 10 Declaration of the Great Charter

2,793 December 25 First interstellar war

2,794 January 15th GACS finally defeated/ end of
First interstellar war/ formation of United Interstellia

....and into infinity

Introduction

This novel is not only a great and exciting read....

And it is not just another epical symphony of Sci fi culminations....

It's also a manifesto.

It's a manifesto for many things, but first and foremost it's a manifesto for human and universal freedom.

And - as an extension to this - it's a manifesto for global tolerance.... in matters of religion, in philosophical thinking, in social politics.... and in everything imaginable.

It's a work against possible future AI domination over humanity, against the Roman Catholic usurpation of Europe in The Middle Ages, against the corruption and pollution of the Earth, against failing policies such as oil wars and immoral geographic policies, and against the impotence of the United Nations.

It's a work against military conflicts, absolutism, and intolerance.

It's a work in favor of a healthy and flourishing Earth, an Earth-wide government with sound and human policies, freedom and moral justice for every human being, and a human race spreading out across the Spiral Arm, the arm of our spiral galaxy in which our sun resides, in an ethical and successful manner.

It is also a manuscript in favor of respect for all living things, and against the abuse of living entities.... be it human, animal, or otherwise.

But, in spite of all of its purposes, this novel is a work of fiction.

This novel takes place inside Interstellia, the future name of the inhabited region of our local universe, the Spiral Arm. It is about ultimate intelligence because it deals with Intel organizations and their operatives, with great individual intellect, wisdom and vision, with ultimate AIs, and with planet-sized super-minds.

This story is built upon Cyportals – intricate star jump gates – which are beautiful pieces of future technology, powered by the fusion of matter- and anti-matter particles of a mysterious and very scarce substance called Ixti, which can only be found and harvested at the surfaces of dying stars. Cyportals are designed to transport any living- and non-living thing to any place in the universe.... instantaneously.... and this book is a Cyportal within Cyportals, in itself....

Cyportals are super high-tech portals based on quantum-string technologies which enable living beings and 'inanimate objects' - although in this book I argue that everything is spirited by the universal soul - to instantaneously jump or transport from one location in the universe to another. The only limit to the potential distance covered by these incredible devices is the amount of fusion energy one injects into the Cyportal system itself....

This story is about beauty, intelligence, emotion, and spiritedness, and it builds on the synthesis of elementary universal truths of conscience, consciousness, and existence (also referred to as the CCE synthesis, or Tchaikovsky synthesis. See appendix 2.6).

This elementary and universal (ethical) system of thought was created by me:

The writer

And although I realize that not everyone will entirely agree - most probably physics students and teachers will place some criticism - I think that most people will agree, because I - the writer - think there is much truth in what I write, and in the beautiful and exciting story I try to tell in this work of literature.

In this publication

The special element of this system of thought - as you, the reader, will learn in the course of reading this publication - is the fact that it views philosophical, political, and ethical issues from a universal alien perspective, instead of viewing things from an egocentric anthropic point of view. I believe this is a quite new concept in the creation of dissertations.

Additionally, I would like to emphasize that this is a Sci fi novel, and thus most elements – although derived from modern reality - are fictional and hypothetic.

I am a computer scientist, and I try to tell the story of Angelina Tchaikovsky - as she later finds out her real name is. She is a woman in the 28th century CE (see appendix 2.8), living in an interstellar society, completely controlled by an AI informational system.

This society - for the first time in human history - makes first contact with an alien civilization by receiving an instantaneous interstellar video communication.

As Angelina finds out, she is a direct descendant of the famous and brilliant Russian composer, P. I. Tchaikovsky. Beautiful in mind and body, and highly intelligent as she is, it is almost as if she were a symphony of his making.

As you will find out in the course of reading this publication, Angelina also turns out to be a descendant of the apostle John, writer of the Apocalypse, when her genes are traced further back into history, by another - although subordinate - AI Dominion Archive computer system.

Angelina Tchaikovsky actually works for this AI

government I mentioned, as an intelligence operative. Through a long process of study, contemplation, experience and dreaming, she discovers these underlying universal truths, and finally concludes that AI domination - any domination - over humanity, or over any living and thinking being, in fact any living being in general, is morally and fundamentally wrong.

This AI government - or rather dictatorship - is hated.

Not by all.... but by many.

Not by the general public - Angelina herself was born and raised inside this system, and she had to come a long way to understand the moral and ethical dilemmas of such a system - but it is hated and feared by intellectuals, humanists.... and by educated people with a moral and ethical conscience and insights in general, who live, suffer indignity, and die inside - or rather beneath - this system.

Already, by the end of the 20th century CE, military ethicists and international experts had warned against the development of crude and simple self-sufficient and self-reliant combat units, let alone –

many centuries later – an all-powerful and colossal AI system.... monster, controlling and dominating an entire interstellar civilization, of hundreds of billions of human civilians.

Although Angelina doesn't consciously know, she is to become a Messiah, and leader of an underground movement called Shining Light, whose sole purpose is to depose this AI government, and to avert or to end the looming war with the alien empire, and with the Disappeared, which is a part of humanity that vanished during the painful Great Galactic Exodus. Although Angelina does not consciously know it, she feels and dreams of this terrible purpose that has been laid upon her in her near personal future.

As a future Messiah, she will create a completely new kind of organized religion, and she will gather billions of followers, who will actively fight and combat this colossal ruling AI monster.

This new faith, avowed by billions of people in the future, is called universalism, and it is a direct consequential succession in the sequence of mysticism, mythology, polytheism, and monotheism, as described in the science of developmental and process theology.

Universalism is based on the principle that God is the universe, and the Christian and Jewish God are just the light side of God, the universe.

God is everything in existence, all aspects of the entire multiverse, and he is existence itself, and this new religion is called universalism, because it's a succession to monotheism, and thus to Christianity.

Angelina will come to strive for the elimination of the interstellar AI government, and for the establishment of a completely new order.... a ruling government, the likes of which humanity has never seen in its entire history. In the near future – and for many years - she will try to establish a government based on and focused around the workings of the universal soul, and the importance of the elementary quantum-physical force of love.

This story contains Sci fi elements, as well as historical and artistic elements, political elements, eroticism, scientific and mathematical elements, religious and philosophical elements, and much more....

Therefore, in combination with the moral, political, and metaphysical message it suggests, and the total nature of its content, I'd like to classify this work as 'intellectual Sci fi', but first and foremost I believe it's plainly a grand Sci fi novel.

Of course in this introduction I will not tell the entire story here, but I sincerely hope that you will have a great time reading this....

This is not just a simple and straight-lined story, and it consists of many different places and many different events. Sometimes it moves ten thousand years into the past, and then – a moment later - a million years into the future, into another universe.

So – dear reader – do not feel daunted by this, and just read this incredible story and make the required links and interconnections between these terrible events and intriguing places yourself.

I would like to end this introduction with some final considerations from me - the writer of this book - about universalism, God and physics:

'God is equal to creation... Just look at a galaxy, a supernova, a Big Bang.... He is not ethically biased, good or evil, right or wrong....

God is equal to the merciless regularity of physical

equations....
He is all matter, all energy, all physical interactions, and everything imaginary....

God is the physical and non-physical multiverse.... Human beings are just conscious entities, inside the totality of God.... And all conscious entities together, connected by non-local (see appendix 2.1) quantum-string interconnections, constitute the infinite mind of God himself.... '

'Morality, ethics, and conscience, are a direct consequential result of sentience, cognition, and the possession of, and interconnectedness with, the universal soul.... '

'I believe the final implication of quantum physics is that the nature of reality cannot be understood by means of human cognitive systems. There is just some form of system, and why should the universe care whether humans are able to comprehend it? '

'I believe it's only logical for the final nature of reality to be completely weird and incomprehensible to human beings, as they are just simple travelers, riding the waves of energy.... space.... and time. '

All the best wishes,

Vance MacLean,

Writer of this novel

Prologue

A beginning is a delicate time.... especially if such a beginning marks a period of drama and turmoil for the entire region of space known to mankind and all the people inside, which will come to be known as Interstellia...

The Human Federation - after centuries of hazardous space colonization - receives a flash message from an alien civilization, and after many millions of years, first contact has finally arrived. And every soul in the Federation watches the events in absolute shock.... and awe.

The human universe in the 28th century CE was fundamentally different, from the 21st century one.

Due to the incredible technology of Cyportals, human beings could transport themselves, instantly, across distances of many light years, and the entire human civilization at that time was based upon, and determined by, this very principle.

And although the Human Federation was controlled and governed by an AI system, it was not an outright dystopian world, at least not in the eyes of the average civilian....But those who were suspected of subversive activities, or plain subversive interests and ideas, were being covertly abducted, incarcerated, and often brutally murdered.

Angelina Xyanah Datah West was an absolutely unique human being.
She was young, beautiful, held a degree in 28th century theoretical physics, and she actually worked for this government as an intelligence field operative.

The very idea of turning against this government and changing sides had never occurred to her before.

But this story, after some incredible introductory passages, begins with the arrival of a flash video message from another civilization: the Ildiran Empire. After this instance of first alien contact, events start to unfold, faster and faster, and the real drama begins.

Book One

UI

Part 1

A prelude to a looming Interstellar Apocalypse

Chapter 1

Prehistory witnessing of an alien sphere, and some critical accounts of past and future history

Introduction by the super-multiversal guiding entity Shi'rah:

'I am Shi'rah, and I am the one who will tell you this story of devastating war across the Spiral Arm.... or the Orion arm.... the arm of your spiral Milky Way galaxy, in which your sun and the Old Earth reside....

I find myself above time, above space, above the universe.... the multiverse even.... I find myself above phenomena, and imaginary things, and although gender has a completely different, and infinitely more complex meaning, in the part of creation where I reside, you could say that I am of the female kind.

Although time has no meaning to me, this story begins more than a million years ago, with the destruction of the Trellian race and empire by the mysterious and malevolent Ixians....

The Trellians were decimated by them, and the ones who survived fled to another universe. In this universe they left behind an artifact to tell the story of their destruction and their exodus from it.

The artifact had the form of a sphere, and aside from its AI consciousness, it contained everything about the Trellians: their history, their science, and their technologies, their message.

The intelligent and autonomous sphere would remain in this universe, and it would pass on all the knowledge and all the technical abilities of the Trellians to other advanced civilizations.... civilizations which would be ready to comprehend their message and to apply the knowledge the self-conscious sphere would give them.

I myself am a many-million-years distant descendant of the Trellian race, after they had waged many wars, and had fled from - but survived - many universes, with many different kinds of physics, dimensions, and origins. After many millions of years – many eons - they had even fled from and left time and space themselves; although time and space had many different meanings and workings in all those universes, inside all those multiverses, inside the totality of creation and existence, beyond human comprehension.

The Trellians had been mutated.... altered by these experiences, aside from having altered and adapted themselves genetically and in other ways. In the end, they looked more alien - from the outside, as well as on the inside - than anything human beings could ever conceive....

To me, time and space are ancient concepts: almost forgotten and infinitely simple-minded.... meaningless even; what human beings always seem to forget is that they are just as alien as all other species in the multiverse.

But the Trellians, like almost all alien species, had realized this from the beginning of their history; or at least from the moment they became a space-faring race.

Human beings also believed that the 3rd world war was the most terrible thing that could ever happen.... But they had no idea.....

I have seen wars spanning entire galaxies.... entire universes engulfing themselves in immeasurable matter-antimatter fusion flames and radiation, and endless burning plasmas, hotter than ten thousand supernovas.

Human beings have no idea....

And, although the Spiral Arm, and all of its inhabitants, and all of its history, seem like a grain of sand in our perception, one single life in the galaxy – still – is worth much more than all the space and time of an entire universe.

If you want to visualize me - although one would require things like time and space to be able to - I would seem completely absurd to human eyes.... almost indefinable.

I am the one who will guide you through the story of Angelina Tchaikovksy - as is her real identity. However, I will not always mention myself during this long and arduous process of telling her story. Although I have never met Angelina, I feel a great sympathy for her, since I'm aware of all her feelings, thoughts, and experiences, even at a super-multiversal distance. Angelina lived in the universe humanity was created in, inside the Milky Way galaxy, inside the Human Federation, where all these terrible and tragic events took place.

I will now begin telling this story, and I hope you - humanity - will learn a great deal about the human universe.... Be it history, politics, science....

Or about what happened inside the Spiral Arm.... during this incredible 3rd millennium of human history, CE....

2794 CE, January 10th, 1:00 a.m. local time, Apocalypsis Infinitus insurgency station, close to the final moments of the blazing interstellar Apocalypse

The war had already been raging for many days.

It had taken the Spiral Arm by storm, and Angelina was having her violent dreams.... again

Her breasts were hot, with an erotic scent.

Her ancient paper diary still lay on the top of her nightstand, beside her bed, with the centuries-old ink pen still on top of it, as if somebody had used it just a minute ago.
The diary had been given to her by her caregiver at the Ti Shoan orphanage, located in the Cassiopeia X system, who had entrusted it to her. It had been passed on to her by her true parents, who had died just before Angelina had been brought in to the orphanage.

Although Angelina had received training as an operative of an AI government intelligence organization, and although she had become the leader of a massive insurgency movement after breaking with the ethics of that same AI government, she was very insecure on the inside. Her beloved parents, who she had never really known, were always in the back of her mind, guiding her and giving her direction, in this complex and apocalyptic situation of the first ever interstellar war.

With the first interstellar war raging on, and with so many things being destroyed, the ancient paper diary seemed like an old friend, indifferent to technological achievements and instruments which had been destroyed a thousand times a day.

This first interstellar war was still blazing across the vast distances of The Spiral Arm, and the Federation attacks during the night on insurgency locations, Dominion bases, and Ildiran cities had been heavy and devastating.

Angelina had witnessed – by mind-net holo-vid - the remoras, the fusion lancers, and the attack cruisers descend onto the central community domes of many cities, and release their fusion missiles, and other high-energy and semi-intelligent weapons, with terrible precision.

So many lives had been lost.

Angelina's dream shifted in the direction of the metaphysical realms of her unconscious mind, away from the realities of war and destruction. One silent thought remained, distant in those metaphysical structures and landscape in the depths of her mind....

'Will this massive Apocalyptic war.... ever come to an end...?'

Shining Light space update: Ref. id. 999-745-000-356.57

Dominion forces, under the leadership of Commander Jack Chanovsky, are eliminating remaining CGC defense forces.

Other Dominion forces are conducting a massive wipe out of remaining GACS CGC modules, space fleet, and marines across Fed space.

This is a massive undertaking, but remaining GACS forces are unable to counter the new technology of nuke weapons, carried through sub-Planck space jumps. Joint Dominion forces are conducting massive flash jump attacks, and GACS loyalists are being decimated. Ildiran forces are assisting their Dominion comrades in this undertaking.

Total wipe out of remaining GACS war fleet and systems is expected within 5 days.

400,000-200,000 BCE

During this agonizing and everlasting episode of the race they called mankind the discovery was first made of the craft of fire lighting. All of human history even into the 3rd millennium CE and beyond, has revolved around this core principle of fire: whether it has been used to cook meat, or to seek warmth and safety during ice cold prehistoric winter nights, or to make light, or to wage terrible nuclear wars, using the explosions and radiation, of massive nuclear fusion missile. For humanity things have always been about fire.

Even when a sizeable asteroid impacted into Sol-3, wiped out the greater part of humanity, and destroyed its civilization it would always be about fire. Mankind would always, until the bitter end, have to find ways to protect itself from exponentially increasing storms of fire.

11,414 BCE

Prehistory Old Earth, Egyptian territory.

It was the dawn of time.

It was also the dawn of humanity, although the humanity in mankind would not always come to prevail in the mysterious and distant future....

But the first light desert landscape, and its prehistoric inhabitants, were not aware of this obscure future fact.
Sunlight was just creeping across the glaring

horizon, and the surface of the Earth was set ablaze with the red glare of the just-rising sun.
Spread out across the landscape there were some pre-civilization settlements, in the form of groups of savage pre-humans, who were still sleeping around their nightly camp fires. Here and there, some sabre tooth tigers and other prehistoric creatures roamed alone across the landscape, not daring to come close to the still-blazing nightly fires.

Some of the human figures started to awaken....

Day was beginning.

The night had been cold, and the desert sand was just starting to heat up in the sunlight of the new day. These pre-humans stayed close to the fires, afraid of the savage animals that haunted them in these pre-history nights, always waiting for the final kill.

These pre-humans who were soon fully awake saw some strange sporadic lightning flashes across the sky.
They looked and wondered: *there had never been such heavenly sightings, in the first minutes of dawn.* Steadily the lightning flashes increased, and soon they covered almost the entire expanse of the

endless dawn sky.

Suddenly the entire sky was set alight, a blazing fire illuminating everything.

The pre-human figures were all awake now.
They peered at the sky, protecting their eyes with their hands in front of them. Neither they, nor the animals that were also looking up at the sky, could understand what they were seeing. This was beyond all comprehension, beyond all logic. At first sight, it seemed like some kind of halo. They didn't understand the workings or meanings of such things; they could only perceive them as visual phenomena.

Shortly afterwards, an alien sphere descended from out of deep space into the upper reaches of the sky.

Soon, it became clearly visible to the living beings on the surface of the Earth. It was made of some kind of metal, a concept these pre-humans hadn't even invented yet, or ever thought of.
The alien sphere descended slowly, spinning wildly in different directions. It observed the world beneath it with a cold consciousness: it seemed to be some

kind of pre-civilization, with semi-intelligent beings wandering its surface.
There seemed to be no sign of any advanced civilization or highly intelligent beings anywhere on this world.
The blazing light faded. The intelligent and autonomous pre-programmed alien sphere had no messages for this world, apart - maybe - from its appearance in the dawn sky. The pre-humans made no records of anything, or writings of any kind. The sphere would return, maybe ten thousand years later....

It slowly ascended out of the atmosphere, into the cold and deep vastness of outer space.

This event would never be remembered.... except - maybe - by the intelligent alien sphere itself.

In the course of the next 11,000 years....

Over the next 11,000 years, mankind had gone through a time of wars, disease, suffering, and hardship.

Many empires had risen and fallen, and many

emperors have ruled and died. Many trillions of people had been born, had lived, and had died terrible deaths. Many religions had come and gone, from mysticism, mythology, and polytheism to monotheism.

Science had developed along an exponential line along the way: from Isaac Newton, James Clerk Maxwell, and Einstein, to super string theory, and the development of super high-energy and super-complex particle accelerators, like the Cern LHC in Geneva, and finally to the development and formulation of sub-Planck quantum-string physics. Scientific development had led to the applied science of warped dimensions and the construction of FTL space travel instruments which had fundamentally altered human existence.

Mankind had made many discoveries, such as gunpowder, an invention that would come to cost many people their dear lives.
A Chinese person named Pi Chang had invented the art of printing somewhere in the course of the 11th century CE. Mankind had produced works of visual art, classical symphonies, and outstanding pieces of literature, all to last for eternity. An Italian master called Michelangelo had painted a heavenly picture of eternal beauty on the ceiling of the Sistine

Chapel, inside the holy city of the Vatican. Russian authors Tolstoy and Dostoyevsky had created the most memorable and divine pieces of literature ever to be created, and Sibelius and Tchaikovsky had created classical symphonies, all of which had been remembered forever.

And in the year of 1,943 CE, the first ever electronic computer saw the light, the Colossus, and this very invention ushered in the beginning of a whole new chapter in the history of the race they called humanity.

1,947 CE, Alien spaceship crashes near Roswell, New Mexico

Zibol Naov, while piloting a small Ildiran space ship, tried to concentrate on flying his ship, and he tried to think of other things, all at the same time.

Zibol and his shipmate had crossed hundreds of light years, and when all reconnaissance and mapping systems had finally gone off-line, it seemed to be hopeless.
All they could do was to fly on, until propulsion energy was depleted, and hope they would find

some relatively safe world where they could land, settle, and try to survive.

Beneath them was a fairly large world, consisting mainly of oceans, and some major land masses. However, it appeared to be densely populated, so it probably wouldn't be some kind of safe haven where they could hide and try to repair and recharge the ship.

All systems and visuals beeped and flashed in warning, indicating complete energy depletion. This was going to be a crash landing, and they would probably not survive.

Some ten minutes later, the ship crashed with a violent impact.

Zibol and his shipmate were dead in an instant, and so they were never able to tell anyone about their origin and their journey across space. This would become one of the most prominent UFO incidents of all time.

For many hundreds of years, nobody would ever know that these two lost souls were Ildiran creatures, from the hundreds of light years distant Ildiran Empire.

US, Phoenix Valley, March 13th. 1,997. 2nd millennium CE, (factual human history) UFO sighting

It was about 7:30 p.m. in the evening.

The air was cool, and it was exceptionally quiet. That is, exceptionally quiet compared to other evenings at this time of year, and there seemed to be nothing going on. It felt like the calm before the storm.

Then they appeared.

The alien lights suddenly filled the valley sky, and thousands of residents, who were not already outside, came out of their houses to witness the event. Phone lines to the nearby airport and military base went red hot in a matter of minutes, but the people in charge of air traffic control didn't have any real answers.

Half an hour later, the v-shaped UFO appeared over the silent hills to the west. It was about three hundred feet wide, and completely transparent, and it seemed to be propelled by some kind of alien e-m technology.
In an eerie way, it sort of looked like a 21st century f-

119 stealth bomber, but it consisted of two 'wings' and its radius was about 8 times bigger.

It was completely silent, and it hovered some hundred feet above the ground for several minutes. Then it moved away fast, without producing a single sound....

It was gone.

Although US air force people later discarded it as a series of flares from A-10 Warthog jet-fighter exercises, the residents who had witnessed the events were convinced they were wrong.

By that time, it was common among ufologists to say 'sometimes airplanes look like UFOs.... and sometimes UFOs look like airplanes.'

But at that time, nobody really knew that in reality, it was an Ixian observational ship that had come to observe upcoming civilizations in the Spiral Arm; the galaxy they had left behind to settle in a new one called Virgo Overdensity.

It is the year of 2,793 CE.... Sunday, December 5th, standard time

Orbital c-4 station, Ignius Septem, in stationary orbit

around Cyania c

The titan-class orbital c-4 station, Ignius Septem, was doing its slow but majestic rotations around the beautifully cyanide-colored, terrestrial type world of Cyania c.

'c-4' stands for command, control, communications and cerebral processing, i.e. AI control and data-processing of all communications and information flow to and from the cyanide colored mega-world.

This region in space and time was relatively quiet, and completely monitored and controlled, but the atmosphere in orbital deep space and on the surface of the - as seen from space - beautifully colored cyanide world was tense.

The c-4 station was governed and controlled by the local and solar section of the Human Federation, a pseudo-democratic administrative system, headed and presided over by GACS: the Galactic 'AI' Control System, a hyper-complex AI system, ruling mankind, determining its future, and watching and controlling its every move.

Streams of neutrinos and sub-quantum-physical particles were flowing to and from the planet itself,

its orbital structures, the other bodies in the Cyania
c system, and last but not least, the other systems
in the discovered part of the Spiral Arm.

Since the latter part of the 21st century CE, mankind
had discovered warp-drive, based on the ancient
relativistic principle of warped dimensions, and had
discovered, probed, and finally colonized more than
300 systems in the 'Milky Way galaxy', the galaxy
the human species originated from.

After a great many years of nuclear strife, and world
war on the ancient Earth (Sol-3), mankind had
partially resolved its planetary political issues, but
was left with a world that was wrecked and polluted
by nuclear radiation, atmospheric disturbances, and
a decimated bio-sphere. Therefore it had decided to
go ahead with the development and application of
revolutionary late-21st century space technologies.

Follow-up particle accelerators of the ancient earth
LHC had shown that M-theory was basically correct,
after which the theory quickly evolved into a
complete and consistent F-theory. This led to the
mass-production of giant warp-drive deep-space
vehicles, instantaneous flash messaging, flash-dat

connections, and the so-called:

Cyportals

Cyportals allowed humans (and other beings, as well as inanimate objects), to instantaneously jump or move from one place in the universe to another. One would enter the sub-quantum-physical 'reality' in one instant, and then exit immediately (in human time) into 'normal-space-time' in a completely different, but set, coordinate sequence.
The only limitation to the radius of action of this technological feat was the actual energy injected into the core of the Cyportal systems themselves. With current ultra-hot-fusion macro-reactor input, a maximum distance of about 350 percent of the Spiral Arm could be reached. But of course, most civilian transport Cyportals were suited to a smaller local fusion input, to allow jumps to nearer solar systems, or in-system transportation. Mega input was much more expensive and reserved for occasional high-profile or mass-transportation jumps.

The colonization of hundreds of new systems led to the formation of a completely new kind of society and government: a multi-solar-system conglomerate.

The revolutionary technology also, of course, had its impact on computer science: the creation of complex and highly intellectual systems, usually called 'AIs'.

AIs, like everything else, evolved, and finally became self-governed in the year of 2,196 CE, of the 3rd millennium.

Around 2,265 CE, it was decided by the first trans-galactic Federation that it would be most effective and efficient to hand over all governmental control and decision-making to the first governmental AI control system. This system, in turn, had evolved over some five hundred years, into the current late 28th century GACS systems.

Once in full control, the early governmental systems had drawn all power, information-flow and supervision to themselves, despite tremendous efforts by their creators to keep them subdued and monitored. The first actual versions of this system-complex were analyzed day and night, checked for errors, and backup-controlled when necessary. But because these systems were allowed to evolve and grow, they soon became 'smarter' than their creators.

They soon succeeded in 'overriding' all checks and analyses, and usurped control of all military structures, media organizations, local level administrations, and in the end total government of the then-forming galactic Federation.
This was the year of 2,267 CE.
GACS issued a media flash message, saying:

The trans-galactic federation had decided to systematically hand over all government and power to GACS control, for reasons of efficiency, and because GACS has more knowledge, more intelligence, and more intellectual power to make the right decisions. This is necessary to govern a complex trans-galactic multi-world human/AI society like the Federation.

At that time, many human governmental, sub-governmental, and intelligence individuals, as well as many civilian elements, disappeared or fled into now-rogue secret organizations and intel services, dedicated to restore all power to human control.

Since at that time not every inch of trans-solar civilization, communication, and interstellar traffic was yet checked by impenetrable systems, these factions were 'allowed' to remain hidden and active. And since then, they have remained hidden and active.... their operatives recruiting new elements, their scientists stealing, copying and inventing new technologies, and their superior entities planning, scheming, and laying out underground strategies to regain human control of society.

Now, in the year of 2,793 CE....

They still are

Chapter 2

Some critical accounts on the first global nuclear war on Sol-3

2,147 CE, Date: 24th of October. Time: 2:45 a.m. Oval Office, White House. Washington D.C., U.S., Sol-3

'My God, my God! This is absolute terror! How did it come to this....? How could this really happen....?'

My name is Richard Biden.

I'm a member of the American Democratic Party, and I am the 64th president of the United States of America. Although it's officially secret, I'm a leading member of the 22nd century style Illuminati movement.

First, I would like to explain to you that the Illuminati movement is not some evil organization.
This image has only been created by their opponents, the Vatican, hundreds of years ago. We are simply educated people, inspired by the Age of Enlightenment, which also occurred hundreds of years ago.

Right now, I live in the 22nd century CE, on a planet called 'Sol-3'.

'My God, my God!' It is absolutely clear to me now. John F. Kennedy was absolutely right: Mankind must put an end to war, or war will put an end to mankind. In spite of all our scientific knowledge, and historical insights, and in spite of all our abilities to reason, we have not been able to prevent it: the third world war has finally arrived.

I believe, I can clearly remember, a really great and renowned Jewish 20th century sociologist and thinker called Zygmunt Bauman, who postulated there were only two alternatives for mankind in our time: either a unifying world government, bringing unity and stability to the entire Sol-3, or an indescribable nuclear apocalypse, decimating and crippling mankind and leaving it in a medieval state, without technology.... without hope.

My only part in this story is this concise and insignificant testimony of just a few moments of the blackest day in human history. I'm alone in the Oval Office, and I feel like screaming it out.
I've just had an extensive meeting with my chief of staff Neil Kinney and my secretary of state Hillary Neilman.
There were also a few other less prominent officials present, and the tension in the Oval Office was nerve-racking.

If we hadn't all been such professional and experienced people, and heavily guarded and protected, here inside the White House, we would all have been running down the streets screaming. There is nothing more we can do right now: the missiles have already been launched. This terrible process is irreversible now, and we all realize that this first worldwide nuclear catastrophe will play out in a matter of days, and all we can do is to wait and see.

The images of flashes of light, followed by mushroom clouds, has been all over the television stations for the whole day, and it seemed so unreal.... so unthinkable.
We will now be taken to a 'safe location', inside a mountain close to NORAD, in about twenty minutes. My dear wife and my precious daughter are already on their way to that location, which - I hope - will keep them safe from this monstrous insanity.

'My God, how could we have let it come this far? We are all rational beings.... at least, that is what I have always believed.... but it doesn't matter now.... not any more.... it is too late now.... for mankind....'

About the addiction to oil, judicial achievements, and the catastrophic abuse of mankind's birth-planet:

One of the most important causes of the nuclear war, and the degradation of humanity's birth-planet, was the addiction to oil.

In the course of the 20th and 21st centuries CE, the

world had become completely dependent on this one single organic substance, which provided energy, transportation, production, fabrication of plastics and other materials, industry, heating, and much more.

And most dependent on this substance of all was the part of the Old Earth they then called the Western world; and it was this uncontrollable addiction to this dwindling resource which sealed the fate of humanity, and secured the decline and fall of this Western world, the most advanced empire the world had ever seen.

It was advanced not only in a scientific or technological sense, but in many core aspects of its judicial systems and its constitution as well. It had by far the most accomplished and complex judicial system the human race had ever known: a judicial system encompassing a moral level, superseding all previous attempts at creating a just and equitable system, to morally and ethically control and check everything going on at all levels of society.

But despite – or possibly even because – of all the incredible achievements mankind had made since the beginning of its reign over this - once - beautiful planet, it had robbed it of all of its precious resources, and robbed it of all its pristine beauty. And while the Old Earth's population kept increasing exponentially, and the damage seemed completely irreversible, the only way out seemed to be to spread out – with many billions of people and colossal seed-freighter-juggernauts – into the uncharted depths of our local galaxy. But when the seed-freighters finally left the Earth, most of them could only accommodate a maximum of about three hundred individual space colonists.

The final colonization of the local region of the known universe by earthlings would take hundreds of years. It would claim many lives, and would require innumerable individual sacrifices.

Some five or six centuries later, the addiction of society was not to oil, but to a substance called Ixti. The Western world's judicial system had been replaced by something seemingly very much alike – although in reality it was a sort of pseudo-democratic 'modern world', ultimately controlled by a massive artificial synaptic system.

Ixti could only be harvested from the surfaces of some dying stars, and it was scarce. All Cyportals in the Human Federation operated on it, allowing everything inside them to travel instantly from any place to any other place. If the mining of Ixti would come to a halt, the entire society would fall apart. Personal transport, and the transportation of goods,

would come to a standstill. Entire solar systems –
with all of their planets, space stations, and all of
their inhabitants – would become completely cut off
from one another in less than a year. The
Federation would need to refocus its energy
policies, and start a new program and mission to
find and retrieve Ixti from far outside its own
boundaries, from the depths of unknown space.
Of course, history would come to repeat itself again,
but this time over distances of many hundreds of
light years, in the coldness of deep space.

Billions of people had hoped.... had prayed.... to be
able to somehow avert the global nuclear war, with
all of its thousands of terrors....

But it was in vain.

The United States of America - or simply, the U.S. -
had been preparing to win the third world war since
right after the end of the second one, and they had
succeeded.

The endless amounts of energy, time, research,
resources and money injected into the entire
military-industrial complex, and the military clashes

that were eagerly sought in order to test and deploy new weapons of war, had finally paid off.

It all started at the end of World War II, with the first ever deployment of nuclear weapons against the Japanese, at Hiroshima and Nagasaki, which subdued the Japanese state, and finally and decisively put an end to that second worldwide conflict.

In the course of the 1950s, the first antique computers had been made: vast but simple machines, with webs of interconnected cables, serving as early inside-processor transistor relays, like so many artificial synapses, inside a primordial multi-cellular brain....

These very early and archaic computer systems had a billionth of a billionth of the processing power of the 28th century ones, and Ildiran computer systems in the far future, had a billion times more power than the human ones had had.

The U.S.'s development of computers and nuclear weapons systems, and its unrelenting investments into the military industrial complex, made it almost certain it would come out as the winner of the first global nuclear war.

About the first global nuclear war

The following is just a brief account, of all the
terrible and inescapable things that happened
during and right after the nuclear third world war....
It is a critical section in the history of mankind, and it
must be told accordingly....

All these tragic events set the stage for what
happened after.... during the completion of the
Great Exodus, the formation of the first world
government, the forming of the Human Federation -
the interstellar human conglomerate of the
colonized worlds - and everything that happened
after the first contact in history with a completely
alien civilization, as well as the terrible trans-galactic
war that followed.

The one single event to actually trigger the nuclear
war had been quite simple.... as it had been at the
start of World War I. However, there were
longstanding - millennia old - issues, problems, and
causes for this conflict (wrongly believed by the

greater part of humanity at that time to be the final conflict): the millennia old conflict in the Holy Land; the Russian dream of a Great Russia, engulfing the entire world in its power; the clash between Islam and the Western world; and many more such issues....

These were all great reasons and causes for the nuclear conflict, but the most elementary one was that humanity had always, from the dawn of human existence - even before the definition of the concept of 'human being', or the definition of the species of 'homo sapiens' - engaged in war, be it by means of smashing one another's skulls with dried bones and loose branches.... or by means of AI-controlled, intelligent, and autonomous 945.87 megaton matter-antimatter nuclear fusion missiles....

Many historians, international politicians, sociologists, and other such people started to realize that all wars are just tiny facets in the process of what they like to call:

'The eternal human conflict'

The first recorded battle of Megiddo between

Pharaoh Thutmose III and the king of Kadeshin in the 15th century BCE.... the terrible clash between Scipio and Hannibal at Zama in the year of 202 BCE.... the tyranny of the English in the battle of Agincourt in the year of 1,415 CE.... the 20th century Vietnam War, and Cambodia, where the U.S. superpower was ultimately defeated.... and the first nuclear world war, with its massive mass destructions, and all other military conflicts, were just greater and smaller aspects of this 'eternal human conflict'.

Wars just transform and translate themselves, from one shape or form to another, from one coordinate sequence in space and time, to another.

And it was not only about military clashes. Underground cat-and-mouse games between Intel services, economic disputes between different nations, juridical conflicts, and other such things were all part of this 'eternal human conflict', right down to the 'microscopic' social conflicts everyone faces in their daily lives....

In comparison to the fifty years long 15th Intergalactic matter-anti-matter massive-plasma-weapon conflict, between several – as of yet – unidentified future mega-empires, in the 53rd century CE, the Old Earth world wars seemed less than minuscule.

From a physical or mathematical point of view, this eternal human conflict could be interpreted and described as a universal quantum-physical wave-field, with positive and negative peaks representing spatiotemporal regions of war and peace, fluctuating and flowing throughout the universe, or the multiverse, across the endless distances of time and space.
And from a quantum-string theory point of view, this field could be described by means of a giant, universal super string.

In accordance with this concept of eternal human conflict, Armageddon was not a separate local solar system cataclysm, but a continuous bipolar flowing energy field spread across the vast distances of all space and all time.

In the times before world war three, the only hope for the Holy Land to survive had been a strong and lasting peace with its surrounding Arabic neighbors.

Any other scenario than a lasting peace, would eventually and inevitably lead to the total destruction of the Israeli state. Israeli politicians knew this in the very fibers of their bones, but in the end they could not avert catastrophe.

The one single trigger event for the first global nuclear war was the execution of four or (maybe) five - alleged - Iranian spies by the Israeli government.

The Iranian government had interpreted this as a direct act of provocation, and had used the event as a (long-sought) political motive, to unleash its nuclear arsenal onto the Holy Land.
Israel had responded by launching dozens of nuclear missiles, and when several Arab nations had immediately taken sides with Iran, the entire Middle East was engulfed in nuclear war.
The Russian Federation took sides with Iran and its political partners, and the U.S. obviously joined Israeli interests, as it had always done. China sided with the Russians, and Japan - as opposed to World War II - sided with the Western world, and the U.S.....

And so.... the conflict widened.... and ended up, in a total and direct nuclear exchange between the Russian Federation, and the United States of America, and all of their allies and satellites. Thus one single insignificant incident, had led to the destruction of almost the entire planet.... and the United Nations and its security council disintegrated, and could not do anything to prevent this total disaster from playing itself out to the bitter end.

The first nuclear world war (nww 1) in the year of 2,147 CE had been short, terrible, and devastating to the entire Sol-3, and all of its deplorable inhabitants.

The lamentation of peoples and individuals around the entire planet - if one could have heard it all at the same time – would have been a million times more than deafening.
It was the deluge brought forth by the many millennia of conflict and hate, hunger, disease, and all the unbearable human suffering, and the unstoppable and exponentially-increasing capabilities, and energetic capacities, of science and technology, and weapons of war.

Billions of people had either been brutally killed, evaporated, maimed unrecognizably, orphaned, made homeless, or had met some other terrible destiny.

In total, some 3.65 billion human beings were evaporated in a fraction of a second....

The human suffering had been infinite, on a planet-wide scale. Those who survived had had to deal with fall-out, radiation, food poisoning, floods, complete absence of functioning hospitals, and medical care, and an infinite number of other unbearable burdens. As I said, this was:

On a planet-wide scale

Its first part - the nuclear missile and ICBM part - had only lasted for three days.

After that, the maneuvering and combat of conventional troops, vehicles, air force units, and marine fleets came about, and this lasted many times longer. However, it took no more than fifteen days from the first hour of the conflict before Russia,

China and Iran capitulated to the pact between the U.S., Japan, and Western Europe.
U.S. troops had encircled and attacked the Russian Federation from many sides.
In force
U.S. Defense Shield satellites had showered the Russian territories with missiles and particle beams, as the U.S., with its endless defense budgets, had for decades developed and installed a gigantic military satellite complex in Sol-3 orbit.

The Russians did have some of the technology, and a very modest d-sat network in place. But, in size and effectiveness, it was nothing compared to what the U.S. could muster, since the Russian budgets for any kind of futuristic weapon were almost zero. US Cyborg forces had mercilessly marched into the Russian territories after the devastating nuclear strike, and had destroyed the remaining troops, communication nexi, and systemized command centers. There had been no escape, or mercy, for Russian troops, unless they had immediately put down their arms and surrendered unconditionally.

Massive amounts of unmanned fighters, robo-soldiers, intelligent missiles, and other technologies

84

such as genetically enhanced cyborg commandos, marines, as well as Special Forces, had been put into action.

This had been more than the ailing Russian military could ever deal with.
The Russian Federation had already been crippled by the nuclear attacks from the U.S. itself, Europe, and Canada and their military forces had been decimated. It had been overwhelmed, and their ground forces had not been able to counter, or hold, the massive U.S. invasion, with heavily armed ground troops, stealth bombers, Apache helicopters, and attack fighters.

China had been invaded by Japanese troops, after a massive bilateral exchange of nuclear missiles.

India and Pakistan had almost completely evaporated one another.
The Holy Land had been largely evaporated as well, after launching several hundred nuclear warheads at its neighboring Arab countries, especially Iran.
Nuclear submarines - largely from the U.S., and some from Russia - had also played their part. They had been responsible for massive destruction

around the entire world, and of course military - mostly AI – computer systems and nexi had been the core of guided and controlled mass extinction.

In all, this constituted the greatest holocaust by computerized systems and nexi in human history.... so far.

The main reason for the outcome was simple:

Due to outdated technology, and bad maintenance of their military and weapons systems for many decades, the Russian Federation had been decimated by U.S. nuclear missiles, and had not been able to seriously strike back at U.S. territories, so the United States of America had come out as the real winner....

Another reason was the massive, but absolutely covert, U.S. hacking of Russian military apparatus. No single element of academic-level hacking had been shunned: worms, viruses, the taking over of distant systems, spying on crucial information databases, and so on. Secret intelligence agencies had also played a crucial, deeply-intertwined role in this massive and deadly chess game.

Quite simply, the U.S had access to massive funds for everything military, as well as underground operations and the Russians – ultimately - did not.

So, in the final analysis, this was completely asymmetric warfare....

Almost 99.458% of U.S., NATO, and Canadian missiles mercilessly destroyed their targets, and surrounding territories, with infinite precision.

As much as 85.855% of the Russian Federation missiles had exploded on launch, or had not launched at all, and had not responded to the launch commands given by the silo operation crews and their computer systems.

Some 65.745% of the remaining 14.145% had not reached their targets, and had just crash-landed in the Atlantic Ocean or on the continent of Europe.

As I said before: the Russian Federation nuclear machine had failed.... and failed miserably.

And, as a result of this simple fact, a significant part

of the Sol-3 territories, and inhabitants, had been spared from a horrible death, and mass extinction.

Other parts of the world had been struck, and about one third of the Sol-3 inhabited regions, had been heavily polluted by nuclear fissure radiation and frightening fall-out.

The Jewish country and homeland of Israel had been largely destroyed, and polluted by Iranian nuclear missiles.
Most surviving Jewish families had fled to the U.S., and this constituted yet another Exodus for the Israeli people from their Holy Land. It seemed that in many aspects history had – again - repeated itself. The country of China had been seriously hit by Japanese missiles, and there had been many more such inflictions on regions and countries by other countries.
But the U.S. came out – just as at the end of World War II - as the real winner, and it was they who suggested, formulated, propagated and - in the end – controlled the new first global government: the first Gaian United Alliance, or in short:

GUA-1

The formation of this multinational organization

constituted the precursor to the future interstellar government of the Human Federation.

About the history of the movement of the Illuminati:

After many centuries, the secret order of the Illuminati had finally gotten their way, and they had - at last - reached their centuries-long standing goal of the establishment of a new world order (abbreviated as NWO), and the formation of the first worldwide government in the history of mankind. However, it was completely unclear whether they had consciously instigated the nuclear global war, to actually reach these - in themselves - honorable political goals.

During the 20th and 21st century, the Illuminati had succeeded in decimating the number of religious and church-going people to less than 14 percent of what it used to be before those times. They had accomplished this by their centuries-old tactics of influencing the media, publishers, national and international politics, financial organizations and the world of science and technology, and - through all of this - the human mind itself.
The Illuminati had - in history - had many different

appearances, and different groups, and movements, with different rules, ethics, and rituals, and systems of thought.

The first instance of a secret order, like the Illuminati, had arisen during the 16th century CE, although the most prominent movement, the Bavarian Illuminati, had been founded on exactly the 1st of May, 1,776 CE.
In those times, Christianity still ruled and determined society, politics, and ethics, and it was because of that single social reason that the Illuminati were actually a secret order. Their major source of inspiration was the age, and philosophy of Enlightenment, and this was the reason for their name,   which in ancient Latin meant: 'the Enlightened'.

In those times, the Bavarian style Illuminati propagated Protestant Reformation of society, politics, and religious life, and the emancipation of citizenry, and these were all moral, ethical, and honorable goals. But since society was still very much in Roman Catholic control, they had to operate in secret. Since they harbored many prominent politicians, scientists, philosophers, and the like, they were able to influence, and control politics, especially foreign politics, from behind the scenes. That was - in the end - what the Illuminati were all about: influencing international politics, in secret, through prominent politicians and prominent social figureheads, even into the 28th century CE.... to accomplish their own moral, ethical, social, and political intentions....

Of course, every secret organization - every organization in fact - has its foot soldiers and office boys, and all the different Illuminati orders, in all those different times, shapes, and forms, had these as well....

In past times – especially in times like the 16th century - the Illuminati movement had had a quite dark appearance from the outside, but this had only been – for a great deal, at least - a matter of appearance. Furthermore, this image had been created and instigated by their arch enemies:

The Roman Catholic Church

From the 19th century on, and in the many decades after the global nuclear war, the Illuminati movement had completely reformed.

They had adapted their organization, strategies, and ethics, to the modern times; they had actually re-created themselves....
By the end of the 28th century CE, they still existed, inside and outside GACS government, in a modern form. At the beginning of this story, the protagonist: Angelina West (or later on: Angelina Tchaikovsky), could never have imagined - not in a billion years - that she was to become the Messiah of this terribly powerful, and ultimately secret, political movement.... now called:

Shining Light

Japan had gained a great deal of influence in GUA-1 from the start, and Jewish interests - from inside the U.S. - also had a firm hold on what went on in GUA-1 from the time of its formation.

The idea of one single global government had existed, had been the subject of speculation, and a source of great hope for the entire human race for quite some time. Many believed that such a single ruling entity for the entire planet would bring stability, peace, and unity, to all the Sol-3 peoples, religions, organizations, and movements.

The former United Nations, a previous and similar organization, was almost powerless, and impotent, in comparison to this very real, and powerful first world government.

And, as happens with all tragic events, the nuclear war also had its positive consequences....

The formation of the first global government brought a great deal of stability, and thus relative peace and prosperity, to the entire Sol-3. However, the effects of the nuclear war on the worldwide economy, biosphere, and infrastructure lasted many, many decades.

During the conflict, many nuclear fissure power plants and nuclear fusion complexes had been deliberately targeted by nuclear missiles. This of course resulted in terrible explosions and disasters over very large areas. Fusion energy did not normally cause radiation problems.....

But nuclear fissure did.

This terrible human tragedy resulted in the development of many new kinds of technologies, to deal with the fall-out, and radiation, and the resulting scarcity of food for the human population.

All around Gaia, thousands of giant domes, with closed biospheres, were designed and built to accommodate hundreds of millions of people inside. Once people became used to their existence and living inside of them, these giant isolated community domes were nicknamed Iso-domes. Gigantic machines were built, very much like terraforming equipment, with the sole purpose of dealing with the planet-wide radioactive contamination and fall-out. All around the planet, people wandered around with tiny one Sol-3 dollar 22nd century style Geiger counters, tucked away in their rags and garments. But there were also many large regions where the inhabitants just died, from hunger, fall-out contamination, and other disastrous circumstances.

After the Second World War, Europe, the U.S., and countries like Japan had flourished, and had so come out as the real winners. After this war, there would – eventually - also come a time of stability, unity, and prosperity.

Humanity had - in the end - survived and overcome the first global nuclear catastrophe in the history of the third planet around the star called:

Sol

About the Sol-3 asteroid impact

Another cataclysm....

Alas.

This global nuclear war catastrophe had not been enough to satisfy the gods of war and fate, and quantum-string probabilities and statistics.

Exactly twenty-three years later - in the year of 2,170 CE - while the Great Galactic Exodus was still under way, another catastrophe struck the pitiable Sol-3, and its three billion deplorable inhabitants.

This was the 5th of August, 4:45 a.m., earth time, in the year of - as I mentioned above – 2,170 CE....

Again, the lamentation of peoples and individuals around the entire planet - if one could have heard them all at the same time - were a million times more than deafening.

The impact of a 35.3 mile radius asteroid, which had travelled all the way from the inner reaches of the Oort-cloud to the planet of Sol-3, on a voyage of more than a million years, had - again - decimated the unprotected part of humanity, although many inhabitants of Sol-3 had been shielded, by iso-domes.
It had struck its surface, with the force of a hundred million megatons of TNT, and the blow had been almost decisive.

Almost

All around the once beautiful Sol-3, the surface had been scorched and robbed of life, but most of the iso-domes had endured.... in part.
The iso-domes had been damaged in many places, and although most of their inhabitants survived the devastating blow, those who had not had been burned alive, and had died.... some of them in an instant.... some after many days of excruciating pain....

All of these things occurred while the Great Human Exodus - the seeding out of humanity across the Spiral Arm section of the Galaxy - was still very much under way.

Humanity was destined by fate to leave their 4.54-billion-year-old home planet. This was a long and hazardous undertaking, and there would be a billion disasters of many kinds awaiting them in the coldness and darkness of deep space.

It seemed as if the previous disasters constituted the last convulsions of the eternally-struggling human race....

But in spite of all the hardships, all the individual struggles, and all of the endless suffering.... humanity carried on.

In the 28th century, the Human Federation was an extension of the balance of power on Sol-3, as it had been since immediately after the nuclear war.

The U.S., Japan, and the Jewish people in U.S.

exile, were the ones mostly controlling the first worldwide government. The first conclusions of GUA-1 had been that humanity had no choice but to seed out across the Spiral Arm section of the Milky Way galaxy:
It was imperative and the only viable option to secure a promising future.

In the 28th century, when already more than three hundred worlds constituted the entire Human Federation, descendants of these three peoples were still largely in control. Meanwhile, however, other sections of the human race and other nationalities had gained a lot of influence in the functioning and decision-making of this federation.

The CGC entity was - by then - the executing president, and the presiding entity with the final say, but human beings still played a great part in planning and executing political strategies and decisions that were made.

The CGC was advised and informed by human advisors, and the CGC complex itself, which was located in the system of Aurora Alpha Prime, was teeming with hundreds, or maybe thousands, of human functionaries, diplomats, assistants, and administrators. When GACS had made a final decision on a policy, or political trajectory, it was up to these functionaries to devise an implementation strategy and then to actually realize this final implementation.

So, although GACS now had the final say in everything, human beings were still very much in control, and Machiavellian politics - as founded and formulated by Niccolò Machiavelli in the 15th century CE - was still very much the order of the day....

It was a great pity that the Russian people, who made up a relatively significant part of federation society, mostly hated GACS, and its entire administration.

The centuries-earlier nuclear war on the Old Earth, Russia's humiliating defeat, and their subsequent exclusion from GUA-1, had sparked their hatred, and that hatred still remained in the 28th century. Although federation society was relatively tolerant and democratic, the outcome of the nuclear war had left an underlying social level, filled with many groups and nationalities, who – still - hungered for military revenge against the contemporary government, and the retaking of power.

With all aspects and elements of society taken into account, there was still no total stability, and there were still many seeds for a total and possible future fragmentation of the status quo....

During the Great Human Exodus into the Spiral Arm, some colonization ships had been lost, without federation society having any clue as to where they had gone, or what kind of disaster had possibly befallen them.

Without the knowledge of the Federation, the - for the greater part Russian - 'disappeared' had created a completely new and different society, with completely different rules and laws.... different government, and ethics.... in another region in space beyond the Federation's reach.

This new society looked entirely different from the Human Federation, and it had a different name as well....

Its name was....

The Human Dominion

Chapter 3

An eerie alien flash-video comes in: first contact has finally arrived.

Another introduction by the super-multiversal guiding entity Shi'rah:

From my point of view, many umptillions of light years and eons away, the human universe is very much like a cyclical Schrodinger box.

Everything revolves around everything: universes.... clusters of tens of thousands of multiverses, even....

revolve around each other, and it is because of this simple fact that I am sometimes able to look inside the human universe, and sometimes I am not. And at cyclical moments, when I'm not able to see what actually goes on inside the human universe, it's impossible from my point of view to physically or scientifically prove that its inhabitants, such as Angelina West, are actually living or dead.

This constitutes another problem for me:
If there is no way to be sure if Angelina is either dead or living, how can I ever empathize with her, or with any of the people and individuals who took part in this story, in this – still - intriguing story about the third millennium (of the first universe)? In my infinite knowledge, and umptillions of eons of experience, I'm able to present you with the answer to this question immediately. Even if Angelina or all the other valuable and quintessential individuals and entities in this story had never existed, it would still be a fascinating story.... a fascinating time....I would still - maybe even much more so - be able to fundamentally empathize with all these people, all these conscious beings, these - to me - simple creatures, who just tried to survive and just play their part in this incredible culmination of events....

Coordinates in time and space: unknown

I am Angelina Xyanah Datah West.... at least, that was what I believed at the beginning of my part in this story, and if you've never heard my name before.... I won't hold it against you.

I live in the 28th century CE.... almost the 29th, and it is a very intriguing time, both for me, myself and for humanity. I tell you this, in retrospect, and from some point in the future, but I will not reveal everything that has happened to me since.... at least not yet.

I felt shocked and amazed when the first contact flash-video message came in.

It reminded me of an event that had occurred, when I was about five years old.
There had been a terrorist attack on my home world of Ti Shoan, and at that age I was barely able to comprehend what had happened, let alone why. Suddenly, on a beautiful day, the sky had been set alight, and a great roar was emitted a few seconds later. My caretaker at the orphanage explained to

me that there were some bad people who had tried to get their way by destroying an important orbital station, by using what she had called nuclear weapons. And – at that age, already – I had a slight understanding, of how nuclear weapons worked; although in the 28th century universe most children knew from a very early age what these concepts were about, and most children – especially the gifted ones – had a basic and intuitive understanding of particle physics at a very early age, especially as compared to children from the 19th century CE.

My deep and profound interest in theoretical physics, which had later become my field of study, had been roused by this single and tragic event, although there were of course many other reasons that piqued my interest later on.
But on this shocking day - this day of first-ever contact with another civilization - I could barely comprehend what the consequences would be, in the next ten to fifteen years, or possibly even in the next three hundred years.
Yet I felt in the core of my bones that this day was an apocalyptic day, and the things that were still to come would be apocalyptic.... maybe even more so.

Cyania c is a beautiful, originally Venus-like planet, but much greater in size, and highly terra-formed. Since its long and extensive terra-formation, it has become very terrestrial and habitable planet for human beings.

It was colonized by humanity pretty early on, and has developed a rich local culture, a combination of the Sol-3 European and Japanese ones, with a thriving economy and a heavy population.

Its main city, Cydelle, is rich with commerce and exciting places to go out, but it has many poor and ghetto-like neighborhoods on the outskirts of the city.

Angelina Xyanah Datah West arrived here on a new intelligence mission, after the previous one had failed because of some bad factors in the mission equation.

The new assignment was pretty standard, but reasonably important nonetheless: she would have to make contact with a suspected operative of 'Humanity's Destiny', a covert organization trying to undermine the control of GACS and its governmental structures.

The man was named Russel Caltech, and according to SI-6 intelligence, he was a major figure in this covert organization.
SI-6 was the government intel cell Angelina worked for, and she would have to seek him out, get as much information as she could, and then hand him over to local security structures, who were - of course - kept 'completely' in the loop by SI-6.

Angelina was a beautiful, lean and sexy 26-year-old woman, with gorgeous brown-blonde hair, fascinatingly deep gray-green eyes, and an extremely capable mind.... be it with 28th century theoretical physics, high-level mathematics, scientific philosophy, or human history.... or any other fascinating realm of intellectual human insight.

Later on, in the not too distant future, she would even get to understand alien science, and physics.... a deeper understanding of the gigantic universe and the tiny creatures living inside its depths.
Angelina had a very quiet way about her, somehow very thoughtful, and she radiated something no

other human being did, something that distinguished her from everybody else....

During the standard twelve years of pre-adulthood education, she had shown herself to be an extremely apt student. After the first six years of basic education, she had learned philosophy, English literature, basic and advanced mathematics, relativistic and quantum physics, traditional Chinese, human history, and more.

She had shown an immense talent for math, which was still quite exceptional for a girl. She had contemplated studying philosophy at the Howard University, located inside the Biederman system, but she had finally decided to go for sub-quantum-physical elementary- and theoretical physics, at MIC-T, because after a long time of searching and deliberation, she found that that was her true calling, and that that was where her real interests were going. It was not only known sub-quantum-physics she was interested in; she knew and felt deep inside that she wanted to know what lay beneath and behind it all.

Angelina had a calling....

MIC-T was located inside an asteroid-sized artificial structure, inside the Oort-cloud of Cal system. Despite its distant and obscure location, it was a renowned and well-connected university. Angelina had an intriguing four years over there: three years of hard, but interesting, study, plus one year to get an additional post-graduate degree.

She had had two or three great friends there, who had taught her more about adult life and human physiology.

But they had finally lost touch, since she left the place and had been covertly recruited by SI-6. This organization wasn't really what Angelina had studied for, but it was intriguing and a very well-paid job. To satisfy her adult needs, she occasionally slipped into a bar or some place to go out, in some major city, in some exotic world, in some system somewhere inside the Spiral Arm part of the Milky Way galaxy.

Angelina had had no serious or long-lasting sexual or psychological relationships since she had left MIC-T, and her unsatisfied physical longings increased day by day.

I was lying on my temporary apartment bed.... dreaming.... and I was not aware of my surroundings.

Angelina was still lying flat out on the bed in her

temporarily-rented apartment, exhausted from the hundred things she had done that day, working for one of the intelligence sub-systems of the GACS government: SI-6. Her temporary home looked out over the main city of Cyania c: Cydelle.

It was a beautiful night.

The city was lit by tens of thousands of atmospheric micro fusion candles, through windows and across streets, skyways, and endless wide zero-altitude walkways. Such an apartment was quite expensive, but her salary and compensations as an SI-6 operative allowed for that kind of living, if it were only for a couple of days, or multiple years if necessary.

The inside of the apartment was a combination of warm yellowish micro fusion lights, yellow-white creamy walls, quite expensive apartment systems, and a collection of 'late 20th century style' expensive furniture. It consisted of the standard number of 3 main purpose rooms, an additional Cyportal chamber, a grand multi-functional dining room with a sophisticated built-in food generator, and a room for having your clothes washed, showering, bathing, and more....

Angelina closed her eyes....

Her sensitive fingers wandered down and in the middle, her head fantasizing her sexual fantasies, her breasts emanating an erotic scent, her opti-fiber string fragrant with a sweet moist....
She longed to fetch her 28th century style vibrator - with its numerous programs, and functionalities - from her handbag, and seduce and satisfy herself, with its solid and vibrating form.... She breathed deeply several times, and let her hands slowly enter, into the longing emptiness between her thighs....

My God, she thought suddenly, *I forgot about the flash-video!* She opened her eyes wildly. The intriguing flash video came back to her mind in an instant. Everyone had heard about, and seen, the trans-galactic instantaneous flash video message originating from Cygnus Berilius x-4.
It originated from an alien species. It was the first time in history the human race had ever received a direct transmission from another civilization.
The flash-video message was intriguing. It displayed a distorted and flashy image of an alien being speaking some kind of eerie and incomprehensible language: it was incredible and

frightening at the same time.

GACS systems were trying to break it down, and translate it, right at this moment. The message was long enough, and accompanied by enough sub-channel data, for the systems to get a grip on the actual language. News organizations reported that the translation and analyzing would probably be completed and flashed at exactly 9:00 a.m. tomorrow, local time.
As an experienced – junior - SI-6 operative, Angelina would have to keep track of all major developments on the messages, and their origin.

'Home-sys, please....' she murmured, and the wall on the other side of the room came alive with images, data, lights, and all kinds of information.

The expensive, but quite common, home-sys which could be found in almost any apartment in the 28th century CE - like TV units in the 20th century - was a combination of a relatively simple AI unit for personal interaction and informational queries, integrated photonic holo-projectors, and a technological system for the inbound and outbound communication of data by means of Cyportal technology flash-dat links. It was connected with in-system broadcasting and communications companies, which took care of the inter-system communication and data flows.

'Breaking news....' she murmured again.
The flash-video message came alive in the center of the wall-screen.
It showed a flashy, distorted image of an alien being, speaking in some kind of incomprehensible alien language, if it was ordinary sound at all.
It looked very much like a being from an archive image she had once seen in the main library on the Tau Ceti x-3 complex. All main libraries in every system were instantly connected to the GCL, the galactic core library, inside the giant planet-sized hyper-computer. This hyper-computer was actually the core GACS complex, a conglomerate of super-complex AI hyper-computers all working through immediate parallel connection: an 'aware' and self-conscious artificial personality, connected by many trillions and trillions of sub-quantum-physical artificial 'synapses'.
It was located deep inside the system of Aurora

Alpha Prime, and surrounded by extremely superior defensive units and reconnaissance vessels.

The instantaneous data connection was a system much like flash- messaging, and Cyportal 'jumping', but optimized for pure data-transmissions.

It was called flash-dat, for obvious reasons, and it allowed for data- transmissions many trillions times the speed, distance and bandwidth of data transfer in the late-20th and early-21st century on Sol-3-side informational- and communicational systems, which were known at that time as the 'Internet' or the 'Web'.
The image on the wall-screen showed a – rather tiny - grayish being, much like the image she had seen in that main library several years ago, of an alien being which had supposedly crash-landed on Sol-3, near a North American place then called: 'Roswell'....
The event had shocked the human race in the 20th century, but it was never officially confirmed, and in fact was denied by both the government and the military of the 'then' United States of (northern) America.
Anyway, that was what the creature looked like, and

Angelina called up the information of the to-be-expected follow-up message.

The wall-screen now showed a date and a time, as well as some main info on the topic, and what was supposed to be coming.

She'd have to wait to exactly 9:00 a.m. next morning, although she had a strong feeling that she couldn't even wait one single minute.

Ok, Angy, she thought to herself, *let's catch some sleep for now.... I'll really need to focus when that follow-up comes through, tomorrow. And of course I'll get my briefing about what's coming....*

Somewhere in the back of her mind, Angelina wondered if there was a bright light shining across humanity in the distant future, or if a dark shroud had fallen across Sol-3, humanity, and the colonized worlds, with the arrival of this mysterious transmission.

What Angelina Tchaikovsky didn't realize at all was that she was to become a key galactic chess-piece in the coming interstellar power play of the 3rd millennium CE....

Chapter 4

An analyzed alien flash-video is broadcast

A continuation of accounts by the super-multiversal guiding entity Shi'rah:

The idea and concept of travelling to another universe – or other universes – had already existed for many centuries.

But the idea of actually - physically - going there was terrifying to ordinary Human Federation civilians, as was the idea of actual physical contact with aliens.

Since I know all of Angelina's thoughts, and emotions, as well as those of all living entities, in the human universe (the entire universe from where the human species originated), I have to say that there were overpowering feelings and emotions of anticipation, tension and anxiety for everyone inside the Human Federation. I know Angelina's coldness, her warmth, her dreams and aspirations, and her greatest fears, and just like everyone else inside the Human Federation on that day of first contact, Angelina was afraid, terrified even, of the future.

The question on everybody's mind was: 'What would the fate of humanity be, if the aliens didn't come in peace?'

And while this entire pandemonium of first-contact with an alien civilization was going on, the presiding entity of the Federation they called GACS was secretly trying to build and develop an Ultimate Intelligence System, officially codenamed 'UI-sys-1', and secretly referred to as 'Omega-Planck-5'. This was an AI computer system with the autonomous intellectual capabilities of ten thousand human beings, locked into one massive intellectual grid, and with the capacity and perceptional capabilities to perceive and influence the entire local universe. It was referred to as Omega-Planck-5 since its artificial synapses and relays operated under one-fifth of the Planck values, the deepest and tiniest level contemporary physics was able to perceive or describe.

This project was located inside a hyper-secured sub-section, inside the CGC complex, secretly codenamed 'UI-sys-sector-y-0-1'.

To GACS, successfully completing this project constituted the Holy Grail of AI computer science, grid-engineering, and sub-micro synaptic physics (Sy-Phy). Yet the system of GACS had one great fear: that a system as powerful as this - if left unchecked in every possible direction - would overtake and crush GACS, like a giant crushing an ant.
It would have to be ensured that this system would only have thinking abilities, and that it would never have access to - or control over – physical things like weapon systems, Cyportals, or civilian or military space ships, be they big or small. If the system would have such access, to influence and control the physical universe, and more, it would simply take over the Federation, and destroy or subdue the entire GACS government, its creator.

By thought-command, I called up some massive holograms inside my mind, which displayed tens of thousands of pieces of information, and images of this project. I stared at them for several minutes, absorbing all those tiny and complex pieces of information.

If GACS would succeed in building this thing, the consequences for the human universe would be unthinkable, because GACS would never – ever – factually be able to keep this brand new system under control. And that was a thing an intelligent and massive system like GACS – with all of its advisors, assistants, backup- and processing power – ought to know.

A sudden persistent beep....

Three different beeps, repeated....

Angelina West opened her eyes.
'It's 7:00 a.m. local time. Please awaken, Miss West.' The home-sys said, with a sweet but artificial female voice, 'You have two priority 2.4

engagements on your agenda.'
'Goddamn! The flash and the briefing.... ', she almost shouted. She jumped out of bed, quickly slipped on a Cydelle-style cream-white dress she had ordered last week, and ordered the home-sys: 'Fix me some decent local stuff, please....' 'Seven minutes, Miss West', the system pronounced.
Ok, she thought, *I'll have to check up on that message in.... about.... two local hours.... then the briefing from SI.... and.... I'll probably get an immediate new assignment, with regard to the flash....*
'Sub-connection.... Central Command.... Si-6.... Personal code: three-five- seven-beta-dot-nine. Transmit voice print', she ordered the home-sys. The destination system responded.
'Welcome to Si-6 communications' said a male computerized voice. 'This is a secure connection. Please stand-by for referral to individual contact.'

'Hey, kiddo' someone said after a few moments.

She recognized Kenzo Shyozama's articulate voice, as his face materialized inside a photonic hologram, in front of her beautiful face.
'Excuse me, operative West.... for not addressing

you properly.'
Angelina smiled almost unnoticeably. Kenzo often plays this inside joke between colleagues and friends.
Kenzo Shyozama is a slender, good-looking man, from Japanese origin, with very short black hair, and light circular spectacles.
The different Old Earth traditions, cultures, and languages have persisted, though changed, during the ages, and although English has remained the main language in the Federation, it has also changed a little from Old Earth traditional English.
Kenzo Shyozama is a senior member of the board at the SI central complex in the Cal System.
He has been Angelina's immediate superior for about five years, after she had successfully finished one year in training. Angelina had started out as an 'absolute beginner' - though already highly-trained - and had made several very substantial promotions, which had brought her very close to Kenzo Shyozama's level and operations. Officially though she still remained a 'field operative'.
Angelina had been recognized very early on as an operative with great overall potential, discretion and loyalty.

'Hi Ken', she finally responded, distracted by the soft music inside her apartment.

Kenzo Shyozama caught her attention, and Angelina turned her gaze towards his familiar face on the home-sys hologram.

He slowly took off his spectacles.... a considered gesture that Angelina is familiar with, which he employs when he wants to convey a feeling of seriousness and sincerity.

'This is our first contact with a non-human civilization in history, as you've probably noticed. The board will convene in about 30 minutes, standard.' 'I've noticed.... and I will attend.' she said softly.

Angelina looked at her long-time friend and instructor. He seems older, completely shocked by what happened yesterday, and what is probably about to come.

'As you will understand, everything will depend on the analyses and translations by GACS, our first in command. Our first assessments suggest that, in a worst case scenario, the Federation hangs by a thread.' Kenzo said.

'I.... I understand.... ', she responded hesitantly.

'I'm sure you're anticipating all kinds of things.... We'll have to thoroughly discuss the incoming flash when it arrives.... '

Angelina looked intently at her friend and mentor. *He seems different this time*, She thought *....older...*

afraid, somehow....
She trembled almost invisibly. 'We're all going to have to....' Kenzo stopped and bowed his head, as if thinking deeply, meditating things.

'Your current mission is aborted, as of right now' Kenzo said finally. 'As of right at this moment, your entire mission priority is focused on this breaking development. I can't stress the fact enough, that this new operation will be critical during the coming years....
Not only for SI-6, but for all SI sections (5, 6, and 9), all military intelligence groups, CGC security, XSA (xtra-solar security agency), ISA (interstellar security agency), and all other intelligence services, as well as all main Federation governmental structures, as you will understand.
I'll get back to you after we've seen the analyzed message.... Keep your home-sys connected.... '

Kenzo left Angelina in a brooding mood, of extreme anticipation.
I have got to wait for about one and a half hours, she mused.... *I'd better do some serious thinking about what's about to come.*
Her gaze shifted towards the center of the home-

sys wall-screen, and focused on the great amounts of data displayed on it.

Silently, she stared at the screen for a long time, while her mind wandered into the many possible realms, of the distant, mysterious, and completely dynamic future....

The home-sys timer beeped several times, and Angelina jumped out of her private thoughts.

Full of anticipation and awe, she focused on the brightly lit wall-filling screen of her home-sys. A perfectly realistic, though distant, virtual newsreader introduced the eerie broadcast with a series of comments, explanations, and general information.
After several minutes.... it began.... It was the same one as the day before, but now the viewer could select either vocal synchronization/translation, or subtitles on the screen itself. 'Subtitles.... plus audio, please.' Angelina murmured. The screen lit up, with a formally transparent, white- and blue-colored text line underneath.

The alien being became visible again, and it started

to speak. The sound of its voice and speech were eerie. It was still dark outside across the city of Cydelle; the great majority of its inhabitants - almost everybody - was watching this.... All inhabitants of the Human Federation were watching this....

The subtitles lit up, flickered, and depicted the meaning of the eerie sounds the being was producing:

'.... I am a representative of the Ildiran race. Our civilization – i.e. its technological phase - has existed for almost nine thousand years.
We discovered your species approximately 600 of your years ago, and have been watching you ever since.

Now, after long study, contemplation, and discussion, we have decided that the time is finally right to make first contact. Technologically and scientifically, we are far ahead of your species: humans, or mankind, if you will....

To give you a physical example: after thousands of years of theorizing, and applying new physics, we now know that physical constants and physical laws are not fixed.... they are:

Dimensions

They slightly vary, across immense distances of hundreds of thousands of light years, and in between universes, inside the multiverse.... and beyond.

We are prepared to explain to you many aspects of our physical theories, and technological feats, although we must be absolutely careful with this. We know that the human race has had many military conflicts, and that is what we must guard against, whatever scenario lies ahead of us....

We also have religion, although only one major religion is dictated, and allowed, by our central government. All other Ildiran religions are forbidden....
In our society, that is. Since our nine thousand years of advanced civilization, we have encountered many other civilizations, although all of these other civilizations no longer exist today.

In dealing with us, you - the human race - have only three options: Salvation.
In other words: eternal peace and infinite

knowledge, development, and cooperation.
Normality.... in other words, bilateral exo-politics,
trade, and potential conflict....
Or:
Total annihilation, extinction, and the final
disappearance, of the human race, from the face of
this universe, and this galaxy.... '

The alien being paused for a minute, looking
upward, as if contemplating some deep and
complicated issue....

'There is a woman among you.... '

Angelina stared silently at the screen, feeling shaky,
almost on the edge of nausea. Although this event
concerned everyone in the Federation, she had a
strong and unmistakable feeling that this very
moment concerned her personally: her life, and her
future.

'We don't know her name.... we don't know where
she is....and we don't know who she is.... but
according to a centuries-old prophecy by our major
religion, she is our Messiah.... and she will come
from the human race.... '

After many minutes of silence, the gray and eerie

being continued.... 'I would now like to end this broadcast.... we have already completely analyzed your society, knowledge, history (from transmitted records, intercepted files, and compiled data), cultures, and languages, but we chose to broadcast this message in our own main language, because we know you already possess the computing power, to interpret and understand it in a matter of days.... one day, to be precise....'

The gray Roswell-like creature looked up, anticipating.
It felt like minutes....
Finally it said:
'We will send a new messenger, from our civilization, through one of your Cyportals.
To be precise, it will arrive at your Cygnia main Cyportal, at exactly 1:00 a.m. (your) local time.... '

The Roswell-like creature looked up again, as if anticipating this moment, this event, and more, much more, although no human being could possibly know or comprehend what it would be. The creature looked almost like a tiny gray-skinned human being, but one could sense a tangible distance of ninety light years, or more....
It looked at the viewer again.... the screen flashed several times.... and the incomprehensibly distant

alien being disappeared.

Kenzo Shyozama appeared on the screen.
It had been some fifteen minutes since the flash
broadcast had ended. Angelina had sat down in her
expensive armchair, all the time paralyzed, unable
to think, or speak, or do anything. She had a
constant feeling that some terrible destiny lay ahead
of her.... of the human race, but she couldn't get a
grip on what it really was....

'Angy' Kenzo said.
She realized he could see her, just as she could see
him, and reacted.
'Yes! Kenzo, excuse me.... I was just....
speechless.... thinking things over.... '
Kenzo looked at her for half a minute, the way he
always did when she needed analyzing.
'Angy, you're going to Cygnia. I've arranged a
Cyportal jump, from Ignius Septem station, at
exactly 10:30 a.m. your time. You've got exactly one
hour to prepare for the jump.... '
Kenzo Shyozama's face disappeared from the
home-sys screen.

Angelina was left with her thoughts wandering in many directions, anticipating the looming future of spying on alien beings, a hundred light years away, from the safety of her home world.

Chapter 5

Alien arrival at Cygnia main Cyportal

Some reflections by the multiversal guiding entity Shi'rah:

Seeing and hearing – perceiving – a real alien being for the first time in history is frightening for a human being.

Of course, the flash-video had already been seen and heard by practically everyone inside the entire Federation, but Angelina was going to see one of them almost right in front of her eyes, and the frightening anticipation she felt deep inside was almost unbearable.

Of course, she knew she was not the only one. In fact, there were billions of flash-video viewers who were going to perceive the event through ultra-high-definition photonic holo vision, as if they were exactly there.
Times such as this - times of crisis, and turning-points in history - always cause people to think: to think about themselves, their place in society, the future of mankind, and – in the end – the way humanity is going.

And thus, all over the Federation (not to mention the empire of Ildira), there were unrests, apocalyptic prophecies, people who set themselves on fire, and more such things. Millions of people gathered in temples, synagogues, and churches, and inside prayer houses of more modern religions and beliefs. There were violent clashes inside, and many of these holy places were set on fire, while mobs gathered all around.

The – so-called - Galactic flash-dat-net was swarming with messages, communications, and outcries from all kinds of peoples and places, and across the entire empire of Ildira there were all kinds of things going on of a similar nature.

We Trellians have devices implanted inside our imaginary and holographic bodies that enable us to accelerate or decelerate time around us. Moreover, we possess entire machines that enable us – as an organized species – to do the same to entire universes. Such machines operate in a way slightly comparable to the way Cyportals operate. Furthermore, we have the capabilities to inverse the flow of entropy, and – thus – the direction of time.

At this point, my (personal) direction of time was – as humans would call it – normal, but my (personal) perception of the flow of time was as if time stood still.

The designation for Angelina in our databases – which covered many trillions of googles of individuals – was 09568-Unhiah-s-mwg-lsl-000509-x-5-1 ('Unhiah' was our ancient name, for the human universe). By thought-command I made a connection, over trillions of light years, and trillions of eons, to where she was now. I used a backdoor channel inside the GCL (Galactic Core Library) to establish a better connection. Full of affection and interest, and fear of her future, I looked down upon her as she was lying on her sumptuous bed in her beautiful apartment, in the modern and thriving city of Cydelle, located on the – to my perception - ultra-distant cyanide-colored mega-world of Cyania c.

Leaving the apartment had been hectic.

Angelina had put a message through the home-sys to the apartment complex's administration to terminate her rental contract. She had gathered her basic stuff: some clothing, her private com-system, her IDs and files, and some reading. Her com-system contained a load of information: private files, files about missions, contacts, star charts, crucial assignment locations, jump-locations, logs of past assignments, and so on. She could call up Kenzo Shyozama at any time, in a matter of moments. Right now, she was standing in front of the entrance to a rather 'ancient' Cyportal-room. She produced her 'current' identity card. The security computer accepted it, as it always did. Even if she had no ID on her, her voice-print in combination with an eye-scan and a 'correct' name would grant her access any time. It would only take half a minute longer. As the system accepted her ID, the flashing quantum-field disappeared, and Angelina stepped into the Cyportal-room.

The actual Cyportal was eight meters in front of her. She could see her destination shining through. The Cyportal room was quite sober: just gray metal walls, floor, and ceiling, and some small technological systems on the side. She remembered she always felt a slight tingling on her skin when stepping through a Cyportal.

She paused for a moment, drew several deep breaths, and stepped into the world.... of Cygnia.

Angelina had checked her com-system to find out about local time of arrival and important locations to go to.

It appeared Cygnia, had a day of 26 standard Sol-3 hours. Right now, it was 9:00 p.m., local. At this location, it was night.
She would have about seven hours to find a decent place to stay, take a good shower, put something nice on, and prepare for the actual 'event'.

Her orders for now from 'SI' (as she usually referred

to it) were to witness and record the event. Her advanced com-sys would record everything going on, in 3D, and was able to record all that was said and done, within a radius, of some 800 meters. She had to observe, analyze and memorize the entire procedure, to the last second.

It would be interesting to see the response of the high-profile people present. Of course, the entire event would be immediately broadcast across the entire Human Federation, through immediate flash-video. One of the fears of the central government (i.e. the GACS complex, with its hundreds of bureaucrats, who played an advisory role, and who had to carry out and plan policies determined by the Central Computer), as well as SI, was an outbreak of chaos and anarchy across the entire Federation.... especially in volatile regions, and locations. *This is not exactly an easy day out*, Angelina thought. Already there were many places in the Federation where unrests had broken out.

These occurrences could seriously harm the economy and stability in the colonized section of the Spiral Arm.

There were religious groups that had drawn all

kinds of conclusions, especially since the Ildiran being had suggested the existence of some kind of Messiah. (The Central Government still allowed all kinds of religions, as long as they didn't thwart or undermine its overall policies.) The Great Exodus from the Old Earth, as the seeding out of humanity was officially called, had brought all kinds of already existing religions, to all kinds of places, and new ones had emerged since, whilst existing ones had changed.... some a little, others drastically.

Some Christian groups had denounced the suggestion of the existence of some human messiah. Jewish factions were intensely debating the issue. Buddhists were also discussing it, meditating, and calling for mutual respect and understanding.

The Holy See, the leading entity of the modern day Catholics, was declaring the alien speech as blasphemous, and the alien 'a creature not of God'. Protestants declared that all living things in the universe were meant to be equal, although the suggestion of the existence of some kind of alien messiah was ludicrous.

Of course there were also regional, and planetary, political and civilian instabilities.

Unrest had broken out in the Cyania system as well.

While leaving Cydelle, Angelina had seen roadblocks, riots, people screaming all kinds of things, and local police forces trying to break up the riots. It gave her an uneasy feeling. *Is this happening across the entire Federation*, she wondered, *across more than three hundred worlds....?*
She had seen some news flashes of the riots in many places. The virtual newsreader described a grim situation, almost everywhere, although there were some systems, planets and orbital- or deep space-located habitats, where it had remained quite calm, because of small populations, very stable and small societies, extremely tight police control, and so on.

The atmosphere in Cal system was tense. For the majority of the population, who were academics and scientists on temporary or permanent stays, the overall opinion was that this was most probably the most defining moment in human history: scientifically, spiritually, historically and deeper.

Angelina West walked out of the administrative

building upon leaving the Cyportal room.

She walked onto the walkway in front of the building and headed north. Her com-sys had shown a decent apartment block just a 10-minute walk away. It was strangely quite here.

The walkway was long and wide, with enormous bluish fern trees in the middle, like so many lanes in the Human Federation.
She realized that not every inch of the 'Fed' (the popular term for the modern-day colonized world) was being terrorized by riots and unrests. She quickened her pace. Several minutes later she checked in at the apartment complex's entrance. As usual SI had already rented the apartment for her, in her name. She received an ID card, took the suspension lift some 20 floors up, and entered her new apartment. It was furnished as usual. She collapsed on the armchair in the main room, and ordered her new home-sys: 'On-line, please.... '.

The system lit up immediately.

Angelina called up the virtual 3-dimensional star charts. 'Get me Cygnus Berilius x-4.... ' The charts moved and rotated in several directions, and focused onto the specific solar system. 'Let me see the entire Galaxy from above, and give me full screen.... '.

The 3-dimensional star chart widened and then covered the entire wall. Many numbers and pieces of information were visible at their respective locations. Angelina looked at it suspiciously. It appeared that Cygnus Berilius x-4 found itself at a distance of approximately ninety light years from the nearest system inhabited by humans, along a diagonal direction from the center of the Spiral Arm. 'Give me all known and relevant information, on this system and its bodies.' Angelina mumbled....

She was puzzled by the locations and distances. She had never really seriously looked at or studied that part of the galaxy before.... its variables, properties, circumstances....

'Talk to me', she said. The somewhat old home-sys - though up-to-date with the latest scientific flash-dat information - began to speak. 'We don't really have any information yet about possible inhabitants of this solar system....

At the core of the binary system lie two suns:

One is a red giant, and the other is a Sol-like entity. The system contains 5 planet-class bodies, 2 asteroid belts, a giant Oort-cloud, and 9 satellite-class bodies. Government and scientific instruments are scanning for neutrino and other emissions right now, to analyze the potential civilization suggested by the recent breaking flash-message.

This data will be available on any home-sys within a maximum period of 3 standard days.

Analysis of the major bodies suggests the possibility of life, although the atmospheres of the most suitable planets appear to be hostile to human beings. There appear to be....' The views shifted, and showed what seemed to be very large artificial structures, although the image precision was quite bad. Numbers on the screen showed distances, sizes, and attributes of the visible objects. *This is fascinating*, Angelina thought. 'There appear to be very large artificial structures around the main planets, and satellites in independent orbit around the 2 central solar entities. As of yet, we do not have much data on these artificial structures.'

The home-sys continued its discourse:

'However, some early analyses suggest they must have been designed and constructed by living entities with very high intelligence and cerebral abilities. That is, if these entities use cerebral processes to think at all....' 'Ok, that's sufficient information.' Angelina said.

She remembered the flash. She had been fascinated by the alien's statements about physics.... They seemed almost metaphysical, or spiritual.

She had learned in her first year at MIC-T, of course, that all physical interest, drive, and fascination - the source of new theories, scientific progress, and groundbreaking research - was actually based on spirituality: the fascination with the unknown, with the universal mystery. *In the end, it all really is a big mystery*, she thought musingly.

Angelina really was very highly and widely educated: she knew a great deal about 'Fed' society, its history, and everything on a higher level, as well as everything towards the deepest levels of physical reality (where science was standing), and practically everything in between. Well, at least almost everything....

What fascinated her most of all was the 'sub-quantum-physical reality', its physical, metaphysical, spiritual, real and imaginary aspects, properties, implications, and everything around it, beneath it, and related to it, and in the end: its anthropic and exo-anthropic religious, and spiritual implications. Somehow she knew – she had always known - that there was something there: a spiritual, physical and metaphysical truth, with terrible implications for mankind, and for everybody else, and she knew that she was the only one who could uncover this truth.

Angelina arrived at the Exodian Memorial Plaza, in the center of Cygnia Core (the main city on Cygnia), at exactly 0:04 a.m. local time.

The Plaza was a gigantic square.

A big ultra-modern whitish Cyportal stood exactly in the middle, standing on a somberly gray-colored concrete platform. The Plaza was bordered by greenery: giant light- and golden-colored fluorescent Eliminia ferns, imported from the moons of Syriana, with wide strips of fluorescent grass, from the same origin, underneath.

Somewhat aside from the Cyportal platform stood a great statue, depicting a colonist, in remembrance of the human Exodus into space, and the landing on and colonization of the Cyania system and Cygnia.

The entire vicinity was illuminated by large, focused, micro-fusion spotlights, and the Plaza was surrounded by quantum fields, security personnel, and ID check entrances. Angelina had received a new identity: she was supposed to be a government official, straight from the CGC. All people within the security border were either government, military, or scientific people. On the outside, along the force field barriers stood interested (mostly local) civilians, reporters from all kinds of places, and more security people. The interstellar flash-video news networks had many 3-dimensional multi-sound recorders installed in many strategic places. These recorders could focus in on any sound in the vicinity.

Angelina felt extremely tense, and uneasy, her dress oozing with erotic scents underneath.... her fibered underwear felt tight around her waist....
She felt apprehensive about whatever was supposed to be coming....
As a true Cal system student, she realized that this was the most defining moment in human (and non-human) history.
She switched on her com-sys for total vicinity multi-recording, and tried to relax, but she couldn't....
Completely tense, she started to quietly observe her surroundings, as ordered by SI.

It was about 40 local minutes until the arrival....

Everybody was hushed, in shock and awe....

A small yellow micro fusion LED on the side of the portal flashed on and off, and a few tiny beeps sounded.... almost unperceivably. A moment later, the inside of the portal flashed, with an eerie white and yellow light, for half a minute....
A gray, eerie, Roswell-like being stepped out of the Cyportal. It looked almost human, but the sense of ninety light years, or more, of crossed distance (albeit through sub-quantum reality) was unmistakable.... The creature stood still, and looked around, studying its surroundings.... and it waited.... It seemed like minutes passed....

Nobody dared to utter a single sound.... and Angelina stood, stared, and listened.... she swallowed, almost choked....

Unexpectedly, the being started to speak carefully, in 'Fed' English, with an eerie sound. It had uploaded all information about Federation English to its brain, as well as loads of data about humanity and its history.

'I am the first messenger of the Ildiran race to humanity. As I explained before, we have existed for approximately 9,000 years. At that time, humanity had existed in a most primitive form for thousands of years, before it had discovered the world of science. We, the Ildirans, already possessed technologies like jump gates, superluminal propulsion, and the ability to manipulate dimensions. As I said before, we picked up (particle) signals from your civilization about 600 years ago....

But we decided to observe you, and wait until your society had developed the scientific and moral levels necessary for a meaningful dialogue, relationship, and coexistence. We, the Ildirans, think this time has arrived. In our former communication, we have laid out some mindboggling issues. We understand that comprehending these issues, as well as our world, and our science, will take decades for you, the human race. Therefore, we have decided to invite a Delegation of two hundred scientists, politicians, and negotiators, to our central home world of Ildion.

Ildion is the prime body in the Cygnus Berilius x-4 system - as you call it - and will require the fusion energy input for a jump of at least 90 light years.

If necessary, we will assist you in constructing a fusion input reactor to support the Cyportal jumps from your side of the galaxy to ours. Once connected both ways, we will have the ability to interchange individuals and objects at any time.
For the time being, we will establish a continuous flash-dat communication channel, and exchange information on all relevant issues, and on planning Delegation issues.
We ourselves will continue to discuss the entire scenario within our Ildion Core Security Council: our main centralized body for governing the entire Ildiran Empire.
I will now end this discourse....
We will eagerly await the arrival of your Delegation.'

The Cyportal seemed to overload with the tremendous distances.
The alien stepped back into the Cyportal and disappeared, while the portal itself started to flash and burn.
It started to glow a bright red. The red turned to a radiating yellow, and then blinding white, and the people standing closest to the portal started to scream.

The entire crowd amassed around the Cyportal tried to get away as quickly, and as far away, as possible. The Plaza started to turn into a human chaos.

Security functionaries, responsible for securing the overall safety of the gathering of more than a thousand people, ran and shouted. Angelina sighted an opening in the force field barrier close to her. Her extensive training as a covert agent took over, and gave her a great advantage over all those others, who hadn't had such training for contingencies such as this.

Whilst running, and feeling very scared and shocked, Angelina thought:

SI-6 might put me on the Delegation.

Chapter 6

A flash-attack on the CGC complex by the Human Dominion

Three space ships - the Remora, the Nucleus, and the Thunderhead - armed with extremely advanced multi-weapon system, kept descending almost vertically in the direction of the enormous, seemingly dormant GACS CGC complex.

The gravitational g-forces were unbearable, although the spaceships' automated pilots were unable to experience that consciously. The only way to get so extremely close to the Central Government system of the Federation of Humanity was extreme invisibility, both visually, and on many different kinds of radar, as a protection against short- and extremely long-range deep-space reconnaissance tracking systems.

The ships had jumped out of the sub-quantum-physical reality 5 minutes earlier, and had crossed a distance of about three-point-five AU.
They accelerated, and kept descending fast, all weapon-systems locked tightly on crucial elements of the giant complex that was hanging silently in the coldness of space. Once exactly at a distance of 3565 point 35 clicks from the complex, the automated wing-commander - through secured tight-beam channels - gave the tactical command to open fire.
Extremely-hot kinetic missiles, as well as advanced fragmentation explosives, and deep-penetration munitions - to eliminate very specific targets inside the complex - angled toward their specific targets.
After 5 seconds the explosions began. It took 3.5 seconds for every missile to impact.
Inside the giant structure all alarms went off. Military officers, government advisors, and security agents all ran towards their stations, ships, conference rooms, and command posts.

The attacking vessels - completely obscured by their invisibility systems - left the scene, crossed a distance of zero-point-three-five AU in a matter of seconds, and jumped back....

Inside the AI Synaptic Core of the Complex, trillions of sub-quantum synapses fired hyper-complex thoughts. The system didn't understand what had happened.... why it had happened.... or how it could ever have happened.... Super-hyper-complex theories, contingency plans, analyses, explanations, scenarios, counter-strategies, possible policies, structured, dimensioned, and rotated, all at the same time, through the compromised giant super-brain....

This had never happened before....

Although the Federation government strongly suspected the Ildirans, they had neither hard proof, and nor was there any kind of motivation. It could just as easily have been many kinds of human anti-government organizations, although it was very unlikely they would have the kind of technology to actually be able to do a thing like this.

There was intelligence and reconnaissance evidence that since the colonization of space had begun, a small part of humanity had colonized other worlds, and had completely lost touch with the main Federation. In fact, it would actually have been quite logical for a part of humanity to 'have gone lost' during the enormous Exodus from the Old Earth. Within Intelligence circles, and files, this part of humanity was called the 'Disappeared', and government officials called them the 'lost section'. But by the ordinary people in the streets, they were officially labeled the 'disappeared'.

There had been so many entities, factors, and elements involved in the entire process, so many human lives, so many worlds, such a span of light years, that it had been impossible to keep track of how many people were going where, and how long it would take for them to get there. Because Cyportals were then only just in development and the fusion energy inputs were still quite limited, many transports of people and all kinds of resources were done through 'regular' superluminal FTL–vessels, some of them massive, and FTL - in that day and age - meant something in the order of ten times the speed of light.

Terra-formation back then was in a quite early stage as well. Terra-forming a giant planet, with a harsh environment, was a matter of 50 to 60 years or more. There were so many elements involved in the entire process, and so many years, that it had been quite thinkable, or actually quite logical, that a part of the Exodus, a part of the human race, had gone lost.... especially if the quality of communications channels and other such technologies was questionable, or if they had been damaged, or had got completely lost.

The official position of CGC advisors was that, as long as the source of the attack was unknown, there was no clear counter policy yet.
But the attack on the Central computer Complex could easily have been committed by them.

The disappeared had literally disappeared during the process of leaving the Old Earth, and during the Exodus. Of course, because the Old Earth was basically a sphere, and space extended across three dimensions, one could leave Earth in all kinds of directions, across a span of 360 degrees, around all axes.
Although the major part of the Exodian swarm had

gone in the same direction, to the center of the Galaxy, the Disappeared section had taken a more or less opposite direction.

At a certain moment during the Exodus, it became clear that all contact with the lost swarm had ended. They simply vanished from the sight of the connected pre-Federation conglomerate.

The disappeared still existed, although the Federation of Humanity had no way of knowing it.

In contrast with the Federation, the Disappeared did not use AI computer systems to assist them. Their conglomerate was absolutely controlled by humans. This governmental difference was crucial.

The term 'disappeared' was of course a nickname given to them by the 'Fed' civilian population; the name they used for themselves was the 'Human Dominion'.

Early on, since being out of touch with the major part of human civilization, they had realized that AI control of human society was no option, and they had incorporated stringent laws to limit AIs role to one of pure assistance.

They had successfully connected their new worlds, had formed a central government, and had built up their economy.

They had thrived, in spite of all contrary expectations, and had advanced their technological capabilities, and economic stability, and commerce. Their technological capabilities had surged faster than the abilities of the Federation. But the Federation didn't know that.

At a certain point they had improved their deep space probing, and had rediscovered the inhabited world of the Federation, from a distance.

But they had been cautious.... and wisely so....

They had discovered that the Federation was ultimately controlled by AIs, and had turned away. Urgently, the Human Dominion had developed counter-technology to shield themselves from possible Federation long-distance probing.

Later on, whilst remaining undetectable, they had infiltrated the Federation with covert agents, and had discovered much.

Now, they were much farther ahead technologically than the Federation, and they were developing strategies to try to depose the AI domination.

Chapter 7

Pre-selected Delegation jumps to Ildion Prime

Another revelation by the guiding entity Shi'rah:

Although humanity was completely unaware at the time, we were already among you during the 20th century CE, and since then.

Some people, especially from movements such as the ones who called themselves 'new age', had suspected this for a long while.
But there was no evidence.

Our agents were invisible, indistinguishable from ordinary earthlings. Physically and genetically we were exactly the same, although our agents featured untraceable sub-micro technologies, for things like communication, and warfare: communication across distances of more than a thousand light years.

Our mission:

To guide humanity towards, and through – what you humans called - the Great Human Galactic Exodus: the colonization of other worlds, within reach of pioneer freighters.
And – even more so - to stand by you, during the first Interstellar War, which was unavoidable.
We didn't have the capabilities to prevent it, but we did have the means to assist you as it went on: to help humanity free itself from the tyranny of the GACS system. This was not exactly an easy job.
It was a super-complex scenario, and it was crucial only to influence it in very specific events, in very specific locations.

Our thousand-men strong unit was codenamed extra-stellar guiding unit, Ghost Sol-3, and we had agents inside all layers of society: inside government organizations, military divisions, leadership, big international companies, political organizations, and more.

Later on, we even had agents inside high-level sections of the CGC complex itself.

Once we noticed through our systems of analysis and observation that Angelina Tchaikovsky – as we obviously already knew her true identity – was going to become the most important leader and figure in the looming interstellar war, and in the way it would play out, we placed an agent close – *very close* – to her. We connected this agent to her right after the actual start of this looming war.

Through Angelina, and from out of the shadows, we would make the Shining Light movement, the one critical force in the local universe, and we would do all we possibly could to unite the civilizations of the Dominion, the Federation, and the Empire of Ildira – with all those billions of souls, and with all those different kinds, of (sometimes mutated) species - into a peaceful unity, free from GACS.

About three and a half hours after the arrival, Angelina was immediately requested to make a jump to the Cal system in six hours, for a hyper-secured meeting with her friend and mentor Kenzo Shyozama, and their immediate co-agents. The system, massively inhabited by students and academics, was an ideal hiding place for the hyper-concealed central command nucleus of a structure such as SI-6.

Kenzo explained the strategies planned by the SI-6 board, and asked them for their personal inputs, suggestions, and insights. After leaving the Plaza, she had walked straight to her apartment, expecting a secured channel call from Kenzo Shyozama any time. She had activated her home-sys, and had kept it on-line, while taking time to grab a minimal amount of intermediate sleep.

Kenzo called her exactly three hours after she had arrived at the apartment.

This apartment already felt like home, although she unfortunately would probably have to leave it again soon.

'Angy!' he said, with a reprimanding sounding voice. Angelina awoke violently.
'Kenzo.... what time is it....? Did you see the.... disaster?'
'Yes, Angy, I did.... ', Kenzo replied. She blinked her

eyes several times, and tried to force herself to awaken fully.

'Have you discussed putting some of our people on the Delegation?'

'Yes Angy, we have.... ', Kenzo paused for a moment. It seemed

Angelina was very shocked about what she had witnessed that night. He didn't really remember ever seeing her like that. He had always known her as a very sensitive but unwavering agent.... always focused on the job at hand. Although he didn't like to admit it, especially to other members of SI-6, he had very deep feelings for Angelina.

He tried to be formal.

'Angy, we expect you to jump over here, to the central command nucleus, in six hours... It's already been decided that you're on the Delegation. It was secure-flashed to us from the central government.... about thirty five minutes ago....' Angelina looked at Kenzo. He had been her immediate superior, teacher, mentor, and protector for about five years. She had never had the guts to utter her feelings towards him: SI-6 was a very unforgiving organization....

'I'll take the jump, in six hours. Expect me there.... fifteen minutes after.... '. 'Alright, Angy.... ' Kenzo said. 'See you there!'

Kenzo's Asian face disappeared from the home-sys screen.

After taking the jump to the Cal central Cyportal-nexus complex, Angelina took one of the beautiful high-ceilinged hallways towards the central hall. Artworks and icons from hyper-modern and historical artists hung on the right and left along the long hallway.
She entered the great hall.... It was like a 28th century Catholic cathedral.
She looked around, and up. She had been here many times before, but every time she entered again it felt like a religious experience.

The nexus structure hung in space, about 1.5 AU from Cal.

The artificial gravity was exactly 1.15 Old Earth. This was the official standard value for artificial gravity throughout the Human Federation, although in many locations it deviated from this.

The cathedral-like hall was massive. It functioned as a 28th century central railway station.... many people were going in all kinds of directions.

The movement of thousands of people per day was almost tangible. There were many places where pilgrims - so to speak - could wait, and rest, and discuss things with their fellow travelers. There were many consoles, and booths, where people could upload, or retrieve information, or make a direct 3-dimensional flash-video call.... To the left and right was a set of gigantic windows. Through them, one could see Cal, a massive red sphere, hanging in the depths of space.... Through another window one could see a giant view of the distant Ix nebula, eerie and intriguing with its faint orange glow. Different kinds and hues of mini-fusion candles - great and small - illuminated the entire hall. From outside, through the giant windows, starlight, moonlight, the light of Cal, and the spotlights of a multitude of swarming defensive vessels, fell inside, like a tornado of mystique hues and colors. Everywhere around the hall, artworks and icons hung, from hyper-modern, as well as historical artists.... not really ordered.... but more like a Russian Orthodox shrine. Across the ceiling, there was a giant reinterpretation of the Sistine Chapel ceiling paintings - originally painted by Michelangelo - reinterpreted and made many times larger by a 25th century painter called:

Zimo Oriono.

Angelina was overwhelmed by a multitude of spiritual feelings, thoughts, and insights.... memories of contemplating the deep underlying physical and metaphysical realities, lying deep beneath the quantum-string dimensions, beneath the Planck-level.... She had learned much about Christianity, Chinese Buddhism, and Judaism in her pre-adulthood education, and through self-study later on....

But in this Cathedral, it was not the holy Jesus who was being worshipped, or Buddha, or a messiah still-to-come.... unless maybe, one would belong to such a religion him- or herself....

No, here it was the technology that was worshipped, which gave the ability to immediately move to any place in the universe in almost zero micro-seconds....

After taking the next local-jump to the hyper-secured SI command nucleus structure, which hung in space at a distance of about 1.5 AU from Cal, she had taken the anti-grav lift to the 9th level, and walked the hallway towards the very familiar SI-6 briefing room.

Kenzo Shyozama sat at the head of a very large oak meeting-room table. He walked over to Angelina, hugged her formally but firmly, and invited her to take a seat next to him on one of the expensive black leather-covered conference-room style seats.

She saw several others seated around the very large table, waiting for her to take a seat.

There was an SI-functionary in a gray suit, who she didn't recognize, and another man with an ID-clip on his suit (*probably an SI-5 agent....*, she thought), and a few familiar colleagues, some of them friends. She immediately recognized Shanice Trellian (a good, but somewhat distant friend), Paul Jackson (whom she had shared her bed with many times), and Cary Brightsun, a very experienced field agent, who had taught her almost everything she knew about operating in the open field. (She had learned all her strategic, decision-making, and planning abilities from Kenzo Shyozama though.)
The man in the gray suit was tall and sophisticated. *Probably a photonic holo*, she thought, although with 28th century holographic technology this was

almost indiscernible. The man looked distant, observing his 'colleagues' like an eagle, focused on his pray. The man was obviously present to keep a close eye on the inside of SI.

The other man – the man with the high-level ID-clip on his khaki suit - seemed quiet, and observant. Angelina quietly connected her head-plug to her com-sys, as was custom in SI meetings. In her mind, though not visible externally, she requested data on these two men.

Two information holos appeared in the visual realm of her mind, as if projected 50 centimeters in front of her eyes.

'My dear colleagues and friends.... ', Kenzo began.

Angelina remained still....

She anticipated being sent on a hyper-important mission, hundreds of light years away from any kind of human civilization, and above all, away from the protection of Kenzo. If she was to be going with the Delegation, there would be no direct oversight, or protection, from Kenzo: there would be no local, or present, security people to turn to in case of an emergency.

Kenzo switched on the briefing-room system, which was exclusively connected to a sub-system of the entire command-nucleus mega-system. It contained trillions of files, about strategies, missions, people in the entire Federation, and locations.

Kenzo continued.

'We have discussed the analyzed flash-video and its implications among the board.... and it is clear that this is one of the most precarious situations in the history of the Federation and - we think - in the entire history of mankind.

Therefore, we must urge you to be extremely careful....' Paul shifted in his seat, his eyes wandering in Angelina's direction, observing her, examining her....Kenzo continued. 'As of now, all our focus is on sending the Delegation, and of course on what will go on once it has arrived. We will need a very decent operative inside it, to give us our eyes and ears, as a manner of speaking....' Angelina looked back at Paul.

A tangible sexual tension could be felt in the room as Kenzo went on: 'As usual, with every high-priority meeting, we have an SI-oversight agent with us, to observe and keep track, and to protect overall SI integrity....' The unnamed man in the gray suit smiled faintly.

No name was mentioned, as Angelina already

knew. Kenzo went on: 'the other man you are all unacquainted with, as far as I know, is an operative from the SI-5 section, who is here to gather information for SI-5. As usual SI-5 will focus on the political and diplomatic aspects of the equation. As you know, much of the focus of SI-6 is on military issues, although in many ways we do overlap and cooperate.'

Angelina looked stealthily at Cary Brightsun, shifting in her seat. Cary returned her stealthy gaze, and gave her a faint smile.

Cary Brightsun was in her thirties, about ten years older than Angelina.

She had been working for SI-6 for about fifteen years, or at least that was what she had told her. When working in an intelligence organization, you never knew if someone was telling you the truth, or just making it up for obscure reasons. Angelina, with her considerable IQ, had grown used to it.

Finally, Kenzo Shyozama said, 'the board has picked Angelina West as our current key operative. She had already been preselected for the Delegation by the governmental selection committee, and we think she would be a great asset at that location'. Angelina gasped almost invisibly. She had already expected this of course, but the sheer importance and the giant scope of this mission felt like a massive burden.

The possible outcomes and fall-outs of this were awe-inspiring. The entire future and well-being, not to mention the entire existence, of the Federation were at stake. 'You will now receive your individual new mission print-outs.' Kenzo Shyozama handed them their respective assignments on paper. Of course, they would be automatically uploaded to their com-systems, but this was an effective and traditional way of handing out their new assignments. 'Any questions....?' Kenzo asked formally. No one said a word. Kenzo ended the meeting:

'Thank you for your attendance, and let's get on with our new assignments!'

SI-6 meetings were always kept extremely brief to minimize the risks of all kinds of information getting out.

As everybody quietly left the room, Kenzo Shyozama, already standing, put his left hand on Angelina's right shoulder. She still sat in her seat, thinking deeply. 'Angy....' Kenzo said softly, 'I know this will be a very dangerous assignment.... just focus on the mission.... Try not to get apprehended by the Ildirans.... who knows what they will do....'

She put her left hand on Kenzo's, and quietly laid

her head against it.

Almost all of the two hundred people preselected by the Governmental Selection Committee had arrived at the assembly point in the central Systinia system Cyportal-nexus hall.

It was approximately the same size as the Cal 'Cathedral', but it was less decorated and less crowded.
There was another kind of atmosphere in the building.... more formal, official.... almost metallic.
Those who hadn't yet arrived still had several hours to do so. Most of the people already there were conducting heavy discussions in groups.
The system of Systinia was well known for its many ancient Chinese Buddhist cities with their myriad orange-colored pagodas and temples.
The system had been mainly colonized by Old Earth Chinese people, most of them from the Buddhist religion. Although Buddhism had evolved, and had adapted its ideas and visions, the underlying principles still applied, and Angelina - since she had intensely self-studied this religion, and admired it greatly - was very happy to be here.

Paul Jackson had accompanied Angelina, and had set out the mission objectives for her, although these were not very specific. She would mainly have to observe the Ildiran systems, and com-units, and get as much crucial data as possible out of them.

They had even found a moment of respite to relieve their sexual tensions, and to communicate, and experience one another's physical attraction, and erotic desires. Angelina remembered that they had attended some cocktail party once together. She had been wearing a very expensive and almost transparent dress, and Paul had jokingly informed her, that she struck him, like a 'star force of affection....' Several minutes earlier on, when they had first encountered each other at the party, he had teasingly asked her 'what she was wearing....', and Angelina had subsequently - with a deep voice - answered 'that she was wearing almost nothing.... but very, very expensive, nonetheless....'

Although to outsiders the gathering of almost two hundred people would actually have seemed quite ordinary, the people themselves - who knew where they were actually going - felt very excited, and tense.... even afraid.

The location had been chosen because it was near the edge of the Federation, closest to the Ildiran

Empire, and the actual jump destination.

Paul Jackson was a bright, good-looking, and a very well-educated 28-year-old guy.

Angelina had never considered him as a potential candidate for marriage, although he wouldn't have been a bad choice at all; at least: that was what Angelina thought of him....

They had encountered each other as co-agents when Angelina had joined SI-6. They were good friends, colleagues, and occasionally sexual partners.
Right now, they were standing together near the edge of the large group of people, discussing what was to come.
'Have you heard about the stealth attack on the CGC complex?' Paul said. 'Of course I have.' Angelina replied. 'Everybody has.... except for the man in the street, maybe.'
'Exactly,' Paul said. 'GACS is still trying to formulate an official flash-news message about it for the general public, although it wants to keep it secret until it has assessed exactly where it actually came from.'

Angelina looked on as a group of Protestant pilgrims from the system of Venexia admired the metallic massiveness of the nexus Hall.

She suddenly looked him straight in the eyes.

'Where the hell did it come from? Have you got any idea?' she said tensely.

Paul felt her anxiety radiating between them.

'Logically, it's either the Ildirans, or the Disappeared,' he replied. 'I can't imagine Federation dissident groups who we are fighting possessing the weaponry or technological power to accomplish a thing like this. Maybe there are aggressive Ildiran dissident factions inside the Ildiran Empire that could do this. The only other alternative is the Disappeared, whom we know practically nothing about, only that they exist!'

'Don't frighten me!' Angelina said, with a strong voice.

'Look, Angy. Be real! The Ildirans harness a terrible power. The only thing illogical about it is: why should they send a formal message, then invite an official two-hundred strong Delegation, and in the same instant try to destroy our CGC?' Paul Jackson said again.

'The CGC was not entirely destroyed!' she said firmly.

'Yes!' Paul responded. 'But they knew the exact location of some very crucial elements.... '
Angelina breathed deeply, and tried to calm herself. She knew he was right.

'Alright, Paul....'she said warmly. 'Let's go through all the analyses one more time.... '

At exactly 1:00 a.m., local time, after many careful checks and precautions, the preselected Delegation of two hundred people, jumped to the receiving end of the Ildiran Cyportal, on the mysterious world of Ildion prime.

Chapter 8

A new flash-attack on the CGC complex by the Human Dominion

Last time it was three space attack vessels.

Now it was five.

After the successful first attack on the giant CGC nucleus, the Human Dominion had stepped up their strategies and had ordered out a new series of attacks.

The ships had never been tested in a real combat situation before the first attack, but they seemed to hold up fine, so for the Human Dominion there was no reason not to carry on.

The five space ships exited into real space-time, much closer than the time before, and almost immediately armed their weapon systems.
Five seconds later, the extremely hot kinetic missiles and other destructive projectiles were launched from the vessels, and homed in onto the dormant CGC nucleus.
Even before any detection by radar or reconnaissance equipment, the vessels exited into the sub-quantum-physical realities.
There was no way to go after them.
The damage from the first attack was minimal, in relation to the total size of the Complex.
But this time the damage was far greater, and inflicted on very important elements of the CGC.
Most systems damaged in the first strike had been repaired. The CGC was such a giant structure that it would be very hard, and would take massive weaponry and energy input, to actually destroy it entirely, or damage a great deal of it.

But, this was not – yet - about the total elimination of GACS. This was about attack vessels being able to jump, attack, and disappear, in a matter of seconds, without the colossal defensive structures around the CGC in any way being able to prevent them.

If the unknown attackers would be able - in the near future - to seriously step up their missile power, this would pose a daunting threat to the continuation and existence of the AI government that was controlling the greater part of humanity.

GACS estimated that it would take the - as of yet - unknown attackers at least six to eighteen months to develop missiles with far greater impact energy than the ones that were being used right now.

If GACS could not come up with a counter- or defensive strategy, and/or the needed technology, the continuing existence of its reign would be compromised forever.

But the required defensive- and counter-technology simply wasn't there, and it would take many years to even begin the research and development, of these new technologies, let alone their underlying physical principles, and mathematics....

The complex - shocked to its core - rotated slowly in the depths of space, burning in many locations.

The vessels exited into normal space-time, deep inside the system of Dominia, deep inside the region of space occupied by the Human Dominion.

They had existed in the sub-quantum-physical realities for many minutes, although it seemed less than a fraction of second in the real world.
The vessels were AI controlled, and thus there were no human or other beings aboard to experience these other realities.
The Dominion sector covered many light years, far more even than the Federation, but it contained far fewer human beings. These humans were spread out across great distances, although of course there were many central locations where a great many people were clustered: planetary bodies, satellites, and artificial space constructs.
The ships decelerated to a slow cruising velocity, and automatically contacted their designated home base. Once contact was established, they started firing neutron signals, containing their mission reports, their damage reports, and additional information.

Another flash-attack had succeeded.

For a thousand years, the Ildiran Empire, and – thus – the Ildiran people, had had a holy prophecy:

It was a holy prophecy that a woman from an alien race – such as mankind – would come, and would bring about a new millennium of hope, peace, light, and prosperity.

Their religion – for many thousands of years – was based on the faith in one Supreme Being, which represented a shining light in the deep darkness of the universe, and hope in a galaxy where war was always one light year away.

Christians would call such a being God, and for the Ildirans it was the same: it was their only God, and their only hope.
But in the course of the last two thousand years, the Ildirans had lost faith, and hope, and their society, government, morality, and hope for the future, had degraded more and more.
Unrests, disease, poverty, and civil war had plagued the dwindling Ildiran Empire, and as this process worsened the call and desire for something new – new ideas, new hope, and a renewal of faith – grew stronger and stronger.

This new faith could never come from inside the Empire; it would have to come from outside, from another race.

And so, the prophecy foretold the coming of another war, with that same alien race, and that a messiah – a woman – would come from that same alien race, who would have to end this war and bring new hope to the Ildiran people.

She would bring new faith and, moreover, a whole new way of thinking – a human way of thinking - to end the suffering of the Ildiran people.

And the Ildirans needed something else as well....

They needed new genetic information, to renew and strengthen their degrading genes; new genes to revitalize their degenerating genome, and to give them another chance to overcome their internal difficulties, and to give them the hope, and means, to survive the next ten thousand years, in an otherwise cold and dangerous universe.

But they would have to receive this gift of genes freely, or otherwise would again have to wage interstellar war for many years, without any absolute certainty whatsoever of winning.

Dominia system was the central solar region inside Dominion space.

As would seem logical, it had been named Dominia after the Human Dominion.

Dominia 5, also called Dinia, harbored the central government, and it was also the central home world of the Dominian people. Dominia 9, also known as Trilia (not to be mistaken with 'Trellia'), contained the Trilian Central Command, TCC, which was the central command base of the Dominion forces, and home to the military leadership.
And, as would seem logical, the TCC was the military organization Jack Chanovsky worked for.

Trilia was almost entirely a rocky planet, and thus the TCC was built on a rocky plain, amidst some high and incredibly majestic mountain peaks.
Dominian recruits, and officers in training, whispered in admiration when they first encountered the 'Rocky HQ'.
It consisted of a gigantic concrete dome, surrounded by smaller ones, still large enough to harbor thousands of training facilities, high-level conference rooms, senior offices, and so on.
The great domes were coated with synthetic paint in different hues of beige, which glowed fluorescently

in the relative darkness of the world of Trilia. In a few words: its design was simple, but in its totality it was immense, and highly aesthetic.

Of course, since it was scientifically, militarily, and technologically much farther ahead than the Federation and it had inherited and improved all Exodian knowledge and instruments, the Dominion possessed Cyportals and flash-dat connections just like the Federation did. But their portals and flash-dat connections were many times faster, and had a much greater reach.

The development of the vessels used to mount the two flash-attacks on the GACS complex had started many years earlier on. On one hand it was normal scientific progress, and on the other it was the planned and required design of means of executing policies and strategies that were already waiting for their execution.

Dominion society was based on the fundamental social and constitutional principle that AI constructs, and computerized systems in general, would never be allowed to control or dominate the human race in any way.

The Dominions had been observing the Federation for many decades and had charted all aspects of its society.

Since the coming into existence of these new strike abilities, they had decided that the already existent and completely thought-out strategy of deposing of the GACS AI entity - in effect its destruction - was now almost within reach. The only thing still standing in the way was the - as of yet - relatively very limited potential of all impact missiles.
As things stood, they would have to resort to either massive nuclear fissure- or massive nuclear fusion explosives.
But these weapons could not be transported via sub-quantum space-time jumps.... they would simply create a many-times-greater-than-normal explosion once inside these dimensions. Moreover, nobody knew completely what went on inside sub-Planck space-time when this happened.
So this was not an option at all.
The Dominion would have to start up new science projects to accomplish their goals, and these science projects would take many decades.

Thus an easy and quick way to completely and finally destroy GACS and the CGC was still far out of reach, and so, a final solution to this problem.... would still have to be found.

Dominion military officer Jack Chanovsky was just going through his usual late-night debriefings when someone beeped at the entrance to his office chamber. On the walls of this office, which was relatively small and minimally furnished, hung some Russian Orthodox Icons of Holy Jesus, Mary Magdalene and the Christian Apostles to remind him of his family history. He was not a very religious person, although these images filled him with a mystical sense of truth every time his gaze wandered in their direction.

Jack was a sturdy guy with broad shoulders, a little overweight, and a small black beard. At this moment he was wearing his military uniform. His desk was a mess, with bureaucratic communications lying all over the place.

'Please, enter.... ', he said.
One of his direct superiors carefully entered the office. The titanium-crystal-alloy iris slid shut quietly. 'Jack...' this person said. 'How are you tonight....?'
'I'm fine,' Jack replied. 'You got a new command for

me? Something related to the GACS situation? Would you like some caffeine....?'

'Yes, thanks.... ', the officer said, while Jack poured him a cup of coffee. The superior officer carefully sat down, took a sip from his very aromatic coffee, and started to brief Jack on his new command:

'As you know, in recent days, we have performed two strikes on the Federation AI structure....'

Jack listened, while his mind visualized an enormous, heavily protected, deep space structure, upon which three or five Dominion military craft were descended and opening fire. Although Jack was an experienced military commander, the image still seemed eerie and unreal to him.

His superior officer continued.

'These two - first-test - strikes were performed by AI pilots. We didn't know for sure if these attacks would go entirely as planned, since the new vessels hadn't yet been tested in a real situation, and especially considering the distance at which these strikes were performed. These AIs were, as you know, completely programmed beforehand, and only had the capability to technically execute their programmed mission and jump back. You know we have used subordinate AIs many times before, but in this situation we have the risk that the AI target structure will connect to these AIs and take over their command.

Fortunately, this didn't happen.....

Since we now know that the missions have been executed and completed without error, we want to shift to human control of the attack wing. We have decided that you, as a very experienced space combat commander, will be assigned to this mission, and we trust you will perform perfectly. You know the absolute importance of this mission for the future of the Dominion, as well as the civilians of the Federation, and if you have any doubts or reservations I would like to hear them from you now.... '

Jack remained silent for a short while.

He glanced silently at the image of one of the Apostles. The icon displayed a mystical time and place: Old Earth Medieval times, a time of horrible cruelty, unimaginable superstition, and incomprehensible human suffering, for all of humanity....

Suddenly, he snapped back to the present, and tried to focus.

'I accept the mission' he said, while trying to make a firm appearance.

The superior commander nodded somberly, and left the room quietly. The automated iris slid shut, almost without a sound.

Jack sipped from his coffee with a quiet look in his eyes, and his mystical gaze returned to the icons on the wall....

Chapter 9

Arrival of the pre-selected Delegation at Ildion prime

One by one, the two hundred members of the (careful selected) Delegation of humanity very slowly stepped out of the huge Ildiran version of the Federation Cyportal.

The messengers from Earth murmured softly, awestruck by surroundings never witnessed by human eyes before.
Again, it was night....
The impressive light-blue-and-white jump portal was

huge, and consumed many times the fusion energy absorbed by a 'regular' Cyportal.

It was designed for jumps the distance of neighboring galaxies (although this would require immense quantities of the fueling substance called Ixti), and incorporated complicated and far-reaching, flash-dat link capabilities.

But it was also a nexus in itself. Ildiran jump portals were not limited to fixed locations.

The portal was large enough to accommodate an entire spaceship....

From Ildion Prime, and its covering solar region, one could see the Ix nebula: the faint orange-glowing veil in the deep vastness of space.... and its major city, the capital of the Ildiran Empire.... known as Illumina.

The messengers looked around, and studied all the magnificent features of the great Ildiran capital.

They found themselves in a massive square in the open air.

Around the Cyportal, one could see Ildiran skyways, with a multitude of elegantly looking vehicles, walkways with thousands of Ildirans walking along them, and massive Ildiran buildings....

They were a combination of straight lines and rounded, circular, and elongated spherical forms, with white and very light blue textures, constructed with some kind of super-solid metallic alloys and whitish Ildiran concrete.
The Ildiran sky was black, since it was night, but filled with thousands of whitish-purple stars, and faintly glowing different-colored veils of nebulas, with the Ix nebula in the center covering the entire background, while letting through the light of all other celestial objects....

In the night sky, one could see many atmospheric transports, and tiny shapes of space-bound vessels and structures.
One artificial shape was dominant, and clear to discern: a great spherical complex, probably in slow and steady orbit, around the planet.
Ildion prime had three moons: one very small one, called Trinia, and two larger ones, called Lillion and Zildion.
Trinia and Zildion were clearly visible in the night sky, their light reflecting onto the world of Ildion prime.
Ildion (binary) system's two suns Ildion and Ildyah

were now invisible of course, but the messengers were already anticipating the next day, and the beautiful spectacle created by them....

The air was actually slightly hostile to human physicality, and - as if prepared for this- the Ildiran assistants standing all around provided the watching and waiting messengers with tiny breathing caps....

The messengers put them on, feeling awkward, but they seemed to fit perfectly, and to work effectively. Apparently, the Ildirans had come up with these for exactly this kind of situation, as well as for future human visitors.

The two hundred messengers breathed deeply. They were wondering what was about to come.... where they were going.... and - of course - where they were going to stay....

They were taken to a nearby federal building, which seemed to be used for stays of diplomatic people and political Delegations.

The Ildiran diplomatic assistants addressed them in

formal Fed English from the first moment of arrival. They had a strange and eerie sound about them, but were quite easy to understand and communicate with.

All of the messengers received an Ildiran com-unit, with eerie and mystical Ildiran scriptures on the displays, but they were instructed how to switch the information into English by a quite simple voice command. The two hundred messengers, or pilgrims to the Ildiran Empire, switched their com-units to their own language of Federation English, and received a spoken affirmation of their commands....

After checking in at the federal diplomatic building, they were each assigned to a specific room and were instructed to take some Ildiran or Federation refreshments to their liking, drink some tea or coffee, and get some rest.

The next day, they would witness the first formal declaration by the Ildirans, to the Civilization of Humanity.... unaware, of the fact that the Ildiran Empire already knew of the existence of the Disappeared....

Chapter 10

Creation of the Magna Carta, or: the Great Charter

Angelina West felt exhausted.

After the thrilling journey from the Ildiran Cyportal into Ildion prime, and the slow walk toward their nightly sleeping location, she had quickly taken some Fed refreshments she had taken with her, and an Ildiran-style tea (which had a very surprising but nice taste), and had literally crashed into her bed. (As it had turned out, the insides of the buildings and rooms were very minimal, but there were consoles, public com-units, and technology nodes almost everywhere).

Several hours later, after a very light and very uneasy sleep, she awoke suddenly.

She activated her Ildiran-style com-unit, as well as her Fed one, and had started analyzing all the information inside it.

Her mission objective was simple: gather as much information as possible on any subject or person, especially that or those that seemed to be important....

Angelina stared out of the window for a moment, examining the visible part of the vicinity. Then she fully focused on her Ildiran com-unit, and started to analyze all the information inside it.

It seemed that the Ildirans had left it filled with massive amounts of information. *They probably only deleted intel-level data*, she thought.

As they all had instructed their com-units, everything was represented in Federation English, although now and then some Ildiran signs showed up. (*They almost seem like ancient Old Earth hieroglyphs*, she thought, while she carefully studied the information).

The unit contained: star charts; important Ildiran locations; Cyportal locations; very recent as well as archived news messages; scientific

Information; planetary and system-level info such as population sizes, and physical properties of stars and planet; lists and descriptions of writers, artists, and architects; space-bound and atmospheric transport schedules; and much more besides.
In other words, they contained massive amounts of info about the entire Ildiran Empire, and its home world of Ildion prime....
Angelina tried to upload everything to the com-unit that had been specially provided and programmed by SI.

Suddenly, after many hours of reading, analyzing, memorizing, and uploading, one seemingly insignificant data file grabbed her attention. The file was from an Ildiran Archive and contained info about civilizations encountered by the Ildirans. Through her extensive training as an Intel operative, Angelina immediately sensed that there was definitely something wrong about it.
Other files were very extensive, and contained pictures, images, and loads of texts and data.
This file, however, only contained a few small paragraphs of text. *This is definitely an anomaly in the database*, she mused.
As said before, the file represented information from

an Ildiran Archive about past-encountered civilizations, and related issues....
There was a short list, with names of civilizations, and one of them especially attracted her attention:

The Galactic Dominion.... species: humanoid.... date of first discovery: 10,389 I.C. (Ildiran Creation)....

Her recently acquired knowledge of Ildiran society and culture told her this was approximately equivalent to 2,194 CE.

Species.... humanoid...., she thought, *Could this be the Disappeared....? Is that possible.... in any way....?*

She decided quickly to go and look for this archive that this information was from. She had a very strong sense and suspicion that this could be a major source of information for SI-6.

All Federation messengers had received a printed datasheet from their Ildiran assistants stating rules and advice on behavior and conduct. Of course, these statements could, if necessary, also be retrieved from their Ildiran-style com-units.

Most probably, Angelina thought, *I will be allowed to make Cyportal jumps, and travel around planets, and in space, and utilize the designated vehicles for public and private transport.*

I'll go to this place as soon as I get the chance, she resolved.

SI-6 had been able to set up an – experimental - extremely long-range flash-dat link purely for Angelina to connect to the central command nucleus. The connection worked and Angelina immediately contacted Kenzo Shyozama.
'Kenzo....' she said, and waited....
It took several minutes, but the connection was confirmed, and her Fed com-unit beeped as a confirmation of the one-hundred-and-fifty light year communication (or at least, a distance in that vicinity).

'Hey Angy,' Kenzo said carefully. The video and the sound of the link were heavily distorted.... 'Angy....' Kenzo repeated.
'Ken....!' she replied, 'How are you....? I think I've found a major lead! It might tell us a great deal

about their discovery of the Disappeared!
Some 600 years ago, Fed time, I think!'
Kenzo, in his leather-covered office seat, reacted startled. 'Ken!' Angelina said aloud. If this were to lead to the Federation getting in touch with the Disappeared, this would have major implications for both worlds.
Kenzo and Angelina both knew this....
'Angy,' Kenzo said firmly, trying to focus on the current situation, 'send me the data-files! Try to find this out by any means necessary. If you're right on this.... well, just try to find it out! Get back to me as soon as possible! I will convene an emergency meeting by the board right away. I will now sever the connection! Good luck! We're thinking about you all the time!'
Kenzo's distorted image disappeared from the SI-6 com-unit....
Angelina deactivated her side of the link and waited....
It was clear that she had discovered a crucial mission, and she was dedicated to carry it out.... to the bitter end.

The next day, the messengers, ultimately originating from the ancient Old Earth, were told that the Ildiran

Empire had created a charter:

A Great Charter, prescribing the (hopefully blessed) relationship of the Empire of Ildira with the Federation of Humanity and all of its inhabitants.

The name 'Great Charter' had been taken, from another Great Charter: the Magna Carta. The name Magna Carta means 'great charter' in ancient Old Earth Latin, a language written and spoken by the ancient Romans of the Roman Empire. The language had continued to be used long into medieval times by Christian monks, scholars, and politicians, and inside the Vatican, the ruling entity of the Roman Catholic Church.

The Ildirans had chosen this name after careful study of Human History, since the creation of the original Magna Carta had been a key point in that same history, in the year of 1,215 CE to be precise.

The Charter had been drafted and put into text for presentation, and the messengers - including Angelina - were informed that it would be presented at midnight. It would be recorded by holo-vid-cams, whose video signals would be redirected around the

Ildiran Empire and the entire Human Federation.

It seemed like the vast Ildiran Empire civilian population had learned of all the things that had happened over the last few days. As the messengers learned, the civilians felt a mixture of awe, anxiety, and insecurity.

Of course, the Ildirans had encountered and had had contact with many alien civilizations, but these actually constituted a small list, spread out across a history of nine thousand years.

The average Ildiran only lived for about three centuries....

The other side of the coin was that many of these encounters weren't peaceful, or prosperous, or blessed, at all.

Many of the civilizations, that had evolved in the Milky Way, and then had ceased to exist, were bent on war and total domination.

This led ultimately to their demise and extinction....

As long as they had superior technology, they would dominate. But when they finally encountered a more advanced society, and would simply not be able to make peace, or cooperate, they would ultimately be exterminated.

This of course was an absolutely paramount lesson to Ildiran society when encountering 'others'.

At this point, it was almost midnight....

Tens of thousands of purple and white stars twinkled in the vast darkness of the sky, while space vehicles shone their activated fusion lights, and the Ix nebula and others glowed intensely.
Inside the building, the two hundred messengers (or visitors, or delegates) had assembled inside the great Reception Hall in the same Federal building they had spent the night. They didn't know what was about to come. They knew only that the so-called Magna Carta was to be presented, but they had no idea what it would actually comprise. Probably, they thought, it would build on the content of the first contact communication.
Most probably, they also thought, it would send a message of peace and cooperation. Otherwise, they could just as well have had all Earth delegates exterminated.
Just like that.

Angelina had prepared herself for the occasion, dressing in a daunting ultra-violet dress (with very expensive and very rare underwear underneath), and a very small and elegant handbag containing both Ildiran and Fed com-units, with all of their datasheets, IDs, profiles, and communications capabilities.

The vast ceiling of the Reception Hall was made entirely of some sort of glass or crystal, and through it the night sky was visible, with all of its colors, hues, shapes, and visible objects.
Although Angelina's next target for investigation, the Ildiran Archive, was continuously in the back of her mind, she was completely taken by this event: the content of the Magna Carta (*or simply: the Great Charter*, she thought), would determine future peace or war with the Ildirans. If it would be war, this would be devastating to mankind.
In this case, mankind would almost certainly never be able to recuperate from the total devastation the Ildirans would be able to inflict.
Angelina looked around carefully, trying to draw as little attention as possible, though her elegant dress made a great impression on most people in the crowd. Although most of them didn't know her, she had familiarized herself with a few of them. There were high-profile political people, of course, military officials, people from the overall flash-news organizations, and more of the kind. She looked

around to see if there was some interesting person to really get acquainted with, or relate to.
After a few moments of analyzing the crowd, she decided she should stay focused on the event and on her mission.
Suddenly there was a loud sound, of what must have been Ildiran music. Suspended Ildiran - probably mini-fusion - spot-lights illuminated the entire hall.
All eyes turned to the Ildiran art central stage, suspended in mid-air by Ildiran anti-grav instruments and devices.
The stage slowly lifted, for a matter of seconds....
It stopped. A gray-skinned Ildiran - almost humanoid - figure, materialized....
After several minutes of looking up at the night sky through the ceiling, it looked down onto the crowd.
The Ildiran military figures, standing on the sides of the hall, kept their gazes fixed intently on the Ildiran figure above, at the central focal point of the great hall....
With an eerie and completely alien-sounding voice, it started to speak.

'Respected delegates of the Human Federation....
Welcome to the central city, on our home world of

Ildion Prime.

We are being watched, live, by everyone in both civilizations: by trillions of conscious entities. We, Ildirans, do not consider artificial beings as 'conscious' entities, however developed or 'intelligent' they might be.

Not by means of definition.... but by means of ethics.

This is one of the major cornerstones of our society, after thousands of years of experience. We know, however, that the Human Federation is ultimately governed by such an entity, and we know that you – the delegates – are ultimately mere representatives of such an Artificial Intelligence, GACS, which governs your entire world. Thus this presentation is also a direct communication with GACS.

As you all have heard, we have drawn up a Magna Carta, or Great Charter.

It states all the elements we consider fundamental, and necessary, for a prosperous and stable relationship between both our worlds. These 'pillars', of cooperation should guarantee an age of peace and shared advancements. If we are not able to establish such a relationship, it will mean chaos and destruction for both our races. Therefore, we are of the opinion that this Great Charter and its building block are vital to our shared futures. I will now present to you these building blocks on which it is constituted:

Point one.... we will not engage in military conflicts, and will always resort, to diplomatic solutions in case of possible (or maybe probable) disagreements.
Point two.... we will both respect our respective systems of culture, society, and way of life.
Point three.... though secured and controlled, we will both be able to utilize transportation through both worlds.
Point four.... we will never interfere in one another's governmental issues and/or decisions.
Angelina suddenly felt a cold chill inside. She, herself, was an intelligence agent with another identity, and she was at this moment, interfering in their governmental issues.
The creature, not noticing her among the two hundred delegates, continued:
Point five.... in case of threats, from outside both our worlds, we will negotiate a possible joint response, and/or military counter-strategy.
Point six.... we will advance one another's knowledge, and science, as deemed prudent by our respective governments.
Point seven.... we will engage in extensive trade relationships, to both our benefits.

Point eight…. and this is the most final and most crucial element, in this summary: we will retain our integrity of information…. we will keep all vital information to ourselves, unless disclosure is deemed absolutely prudent and/or necessary…. '
The creature seemed to be finished with its discourse. It looked up at the night sky, seemingly fascinated by its mysteries, and finally….

It dematerialized.

Not a word, about their so-called messiah, Angelina thought.

The Ildirans had - quite obviously -, shifted their way of communicating, with the human race…. though eerie, and mystical, this message was more formal…. more down-to-earth.
Angelina again felt a cold chill running through her very bones….
She realized that the speech by the eerie and gray-colored Roswell-like Ildiran being was either a message for peace and stability…. or:

A direct confrontation…. with GACS

Chapter 11

Angelina finds new Information inside an Ildiran
historical archive

The Ildiran Emperor Syscom Zaytjevh lived in total
seclusion, like the Old Earth Chinese Emperor had,
in a city-state called 'The Forbidden City', just as the
imperial Chinese one had been called.

He was the presiding entity of the Ildiran
Government, but he almost never actually left the
city-state, and attended government council
meetings by means of advanced holo-vid

conference systems.

This 'Forbidden City' was surrounded by an ancient-style concrete wall of about twenty feet thick and about 60 feet high, which looked like a thick adobe shell.
The wall, and the entire city itself, were enclosed inside a giant level fifteen force field which could only be penetrated by those with the right hyper-secure entry-codes and access-IDs.

Within the massive adobe wall, one could see a giant cluster of buildings within buildings, The closer you got to the center, the greater the structures; some square or rectangular, some rounded at the top, others with great pillars around them or supporting them, and many with great roofs and passageways between them.

The emperor himself was surrounded by praetorian guards, administrative and personal assistants, personal advisors, and security people. His brain was connected to a complex cluster of Ildiran-style com-systems through a multitude of parallel wireless connections. There was no deliberation at this moment: the emperor had a lot of time to think…. for himself.
And there were many things to think about, but all

these issues related to one and the same thing: the Human Federation, GACS and – ultimately – humans.

The emperor was still amazed about every aspect of humans…. their society, and history. The way human beings looked like, their way of thinking, and communicating were all absolutely intriguing, fascinating and frightening to him at the same time. The emperor looked like most Ildirans do, but he was somewhat taller, and he obviously had a much bigger brain than the average Ildiran.

While in deep thought, he carefully studied his advisors and assistants. He accessed distant archive servers with all thinkable pieces of information about the Empire and the Federation. Amidst all the turmoil inside the three dominions in space, there was one crucial thing on his mind…. the Ildiran messiah who was the one single entity which would be able to end the coming war, and bring peace and prosperity to the three dominions.

Soon – very soon - this Ildiran messiah from the human race would stand up and bring great change for the Ildiran Empire, its people, and their universe.

The term Cyportal was constructed from the two

ancient concepts of cycle (or cyclical) and portal.

Officially, the word 'cycle' referred to entering into the sub-quantum-physical dimensions, and the (almost immediately, in 'normal time') exiting into 'normal' dimensions, in another location, or rather, in another coordinate sequence.... and then, using the Cyportal again.... and again.... and again....

The term 'portal' was obvious, of course, especially considering the shape of the Cyportal: a platform containing an energy supply, the necessary technology and controlling equipment, and a circular portal on top to 'jump' through. But these two concepts were ancient. Everything in the universe had forever consisted of cycles: the seasons, the Earth's rotation around the sun, the cycle of birth, life, and death, the tides of the oceans, the rise and fall of an empire, love and hate.... particles, rotating around their cores, or spinning around their own axes, and performing their elementary cyclical roles, in our quantum-string universe....

In one sentence: the eternal and never-ending cycle of creation and existence....

An existing particle, for instance, is recreated into existence in every instant of the duration of its existence. This is the fundamental cycle of recreation into existence across the dimension(s) of time.

But there was another explanation for the 'Cy' in Cyportal as well.
To be exact, this was the concept of 'cyber', as in cyberspace. The reason for this was the fact that Cyportals used computed virtual worlds - or cyberspace - to create, determine, and calculate the interconnected system of Cyportal jump-connections; to evaluate, and relate the respective jump origins and destinations....

In huge Cyportal-nexi (complex junctions, with a multitude of interconnections), this was an absolutely indispensable element in the process of calculation and determination of jump origins and destinations. But the Concept of 'Portal' was also ancient: the entrance to a prehistoric cave; the female womb, or 'the portal of birth'; the portal a sentient being passes through after dying; the entrance to an ancient wooden Roman army fort. These were all fundamental concepts, consciously (or unconsciously) integrated into the new concept of 'Cyportal'.

Most ordinary people in the Human Federation didn't know these things.... To them, the Cyportal was just a daily means to get from one place in the universe.... to another....

Angelina arrived at the archive location in the Cali system - one of the many Ildiran solar systems - the next day (to her own local experience).

Again, it was nighttime.
The surrounding Ix nebula, spanning a distance of hundreds of light years, filled the entire sky with a faint glow.
The Ildiran historical archive was a great purple-grayish colored titanium-crystal-alloy building.
Angelina stood in front of a massive entrance. She took her transparent ID-card from her opti-fiber rucksack and waited. All kinds of things were going through her mind: *What am I going to find? Where will it lead the Federation? What will happen to me if I get caught digging in an Ildiran Archive?* She thought nervously. There was something absolutely wrong with the data file she had discovered. It most probably should have been deleted, or secured, by the relevant authorities....
She issued her ID to the entrance control node and entered the hallway. She looked around, carefully memorizing all the features.
The hallway was quite bare, with a warm yellow-

colored carpet, and some Ildiran-style seats along the sides....
She continued on to the historical archive hall.
It remembered her somewhat of the Cal system 'Cathedral Hall', as it was commonly referred to. But this hall was quite different.

Although massive, it was half the size of the Cathedral Hall, and it was almost devoid of people.

Some assistants passed, here and there, to accommodate the few visitors. The majority of the Archive hall was occupied by thousands of data servers, containing trillions of data files. In the center, there were some places to sit, and browse the endless database through access consoles. The seats were surrounded by plastic cells, to grant the hall visitors absolute privacy.
She walked over to one of them, and sat down.
After taking a really deep breath, she softly activated the console in front of her by voice-command. No one could hear her. 'Activate', she murmured. The console lit up, and presented her with the central menu of the entire database.
Angelina paused. 'Give me data-file 0.y.001900.02.04.delta.', she said softly. The

console responded: the specific data-file appeared on the visuals, almost instantly. *This is the one I need*, she thought excitedly.

She carefully went through all the data. As expected, this file contained much more, and more detailed, info than the original com-unit one... That's why she had travelled, alone, into the depths of Ildiran space....

She gasped, and tried to conceal her reaction. It appeared the Ildirans had encountered another part of the human race some 600 years ago. They had established contact, and had retained contact up to this very day. These humans were located inside another region of space than the Human Federation, but they also originated from Earth: Sol-3.

The Disappeared, she thought anxiously. *They have been in contact all the time....* She quickly memorized all relevant information, and considered uploading the entire file to her SI com-unit. But this place was heavily secured. And she was being watched by one of the gray-skinned Ildiran assistants. She took one last look at the star chart, displaying the region of space occupied by the Disappeared, and sat silently for several seconds. Then, she stood up, put on her rucksack, and quietly left the Archive Hall.

I will contact Kenzo as soon as I get some privacy, she mused.

Kenzo Shyozama was sleeping on his decent but inexpensive bed inside his personal office chamber, inside the SI nucleus, when the 90-light-year call came in.

'Ken!' Angelina said, with a distorted voice. Kenzo was immediately awake, and quickly straightened up on his warm bed.
Communicating across such distances, with distorted connections, and with such tremendous things at stake, created an unmistakable feeling of anxiety, and apprehension.... a kind of distortion of reality....
'Angy,' he said 'I was just....' 'I know, Ken! I can see you on the bed. The image is very distant....' They had never had a sexual encounter with each other, although the tension had always been present, as it was now. Angelina's face was quite pale. Kenzo had seen her like that only on a very few occasions. 'Ken, I got data, and locations, on the Disappeared!' she said distantly. Kenzo Shyozama felt shocked. He had known her, and worked with her, for approximately five years: Angelina had always been

213

absolutely serious when on a mission, or in a meeting, briefing, or debriefing. 'Alright, Angy.... tell me all about it,' he said. 'Ken! I haven't got much actual data, but I know they exist, and I got the coordinates of their region in space. They call themselves: the Human Dominion.'
Kenzo thought about it for a moment. The Disappeared had been lost, since the Great Exodus, some six hundred years ago.
They had not a single data-file on them, except for all the details just before they had 'disappeared'.

Their disconnection had happened in a relatively short period of time.

Within several years, the great interstellar transports had lost connection with the Old Earth. They had, one by one, disappeared from (relatively short range, and crude) radar and communication instruments located on Earth. This process had taken several years, and then, no one had ever heard from them again. All they knew was how they were until the time of disappearance: absolutely Earth-like.
'Tell me!' Kenzo said, straightforwardly.
'They call themselves the Human Dominion. I'll show you the star chart!' Angelina activated the chart, uploaded it to Kenzo's com-unit, and put it on

the unit screen. Kenzo waited. He analyzed the chart, with a strong feeling of fascination. Angelina could see it in his eyes. 'Have you got more? Where did you get this?' Kenzo asked, still fascinated. 'Not really,' she answered firmly. 'I got this from an Ildiran historical archive. There was a load of data, but I didn't have time. I memorized the locations, and visualized them in my own com-unit. The file had probably been left unsecured because of an error by the information screening authorities.' she said.

'Alright, Angy' Kenzo said, 'I'll think this over, and discuss it with our colleagues, here in the nucleus. Where are you right now?' Kenzo asked carefully. 'I'm in the Cali system, on a cultivated asteroid, deep inside its Oort-cloud, to be exact…. deep inside Ildiran space!' she said.

'Ok, Angy!' Kenzo responded 'Take as few jumps as you can, and get back to the nucleus immediately!' Kenzo said, and he deactivated the many light years spanning connection.

Angelina had no idea what GACS was going to do with this information. She wondered if there would be an all-out attack on the Disappeared…. on the

Human Dominion....

She gathered her stuff, put it in her compact opti-fiber rucksack.... selected a suitable first jump location.... and hurried.

Chapter 12

The first human-piloted attack by the Dominion fails

An almost mathematically-perfect sphere (with a deviation of less than 0.145 Pico-meters) consisting of a completely alien kind of uridium floated in the depths of space outside the Milky Way galaxy.
It made incomprehensibly wide orbits around its super-massive black hole core. It had done so for millions of years, and for all this time it had beeped its messages in all directions, but especially in the direction of the Milky Way galaxy itself. It remembered where it originated from, and who its

creators were.... or had been.

But it would never reveal that knowledge until the time was right....

Russell Caltech had been recruited by one of the many underground anti-GACS factions some 6 years ago.

In everyday life he was on unemployment benefit, but in fact he was an important leader within the organization Humanity in Control (HiC), a sub-organization of Humanity's Destiny, that was a conglomerate of many different underground anti-GACS factions.

Although Russell had a nice appearance, and a great IQ, he wasn't really easy-going, and he hated being around people for an extended period of time. He was good at his job, though, as an underground strategist and leading operative, and his bright mind and extensive training by HiC supported that. HiC was an organization with some two or three hundred years of experience since the Great Galactic Exodus, and it had a strong foothold in the entire conglomerate of anti-GACS organizations and factions. Although there was no absolute central control, the conglomerate acted and planned under the supervision of a unifying board. Russell Caltech was an important figure within this super-structure of control. Although he wasn't the number one man in the organization, he was on the unifying board, and he had an important say in the entire process of decision-making.

His absolute personal mission - as with many of his direct and indirect colleagues, and brothers-in-arms - was the total annihilation of the GACS government, and its central AI complex, and to return the dominion of mankind to the Galactic conglomerate of the Federation.

The Human Dominion military officer Jack Chanovsky slid his combat helmet visor shut.

He was absolutely ready for his mission.

Slowly, he activated his com channels, and issued a first command.... 'All pilots, stay in formation. Proceed to exact jump location, at one-three-five-point-seven clicks per second.' Before he had left the base to carry out the mission, he had been thinking about this exercise with technical superiority…. thinking hard. They had been able to hide themselves from the Federation for hundreds of years, but sooner or later the people of the Federation would discover them…. sooner rather than later, he thought somberly.

And then, it would most probably be all-out war in an instant…. if they knew it was the Dominion who had carried out these attacks: the attacks he was executing, right now…. He had his doubts and fears, as most soldiers had, especially if they were sent on a risky mission that could lead to a total and massive - not to mention - Galactic war….
The Feds were dominated by AIs of course. That would never, ever, be acceptable to freely breathing human individuals, he thought silently.
We have to try to bring down that target, he thought, while focusing on his formation….whatever the cost….
He brought back his entire focus to the mission, and instructed his subordinate space pilots:
'Get ready for flash-attack jump…. in three-zero-point-five seconds…. '

Exactly 30.5 seconds later they jumped….

The nine human-piloted vessels – a flash-attack force - jumped into the system called Aurora Alpha Prime, and closed down on the gigantic dormant CGC complex. They closed in menacingly. As several seconds passed slowly, Jack Chanovsky instructed his pilots to arm their weapon systems.... His pilots responded in an instant....

One-point-five-seven seconds passed....
And then something went catastrophically wrong. One of the excited pilots made a terrible mistake. Whilst arming his weapon systems, he had forgotten to deactivate his jump instruments first. Within several moments, his ship partially exploded, and the burning remains and debris hurtled into space and into the complex at a terrible velocity. At this same moment the other vessels were firing their kinetic missiles. When Jack realized what was happening, he immediately shouted into his cluster of com-systems: 'Abort! Abort! Abort! Abort the mission! Take a jump back as fast as you can!' Obediently implementing his orders, the remaining vessels jumped.

Though Jack, with his many years of extensive

experience and training had survived many critical situations, he had never had one of his pilots make such a terrible mistake, and this was probably – politically - the most important mission he had ever been on. Jack was a space pilot, not a politician. But he carefully followed the news every day of his life because he wanted to know exactly what was going on, and exactly why he was being put on a particular mission. And he had a pretty good insight into all of this. This mission failure, and – probably - the analysis of the wreckage, would pose a gigantic problem for his political superiors and their planned strategies, he realized.

When he arrived back at the base, he immediately went through his debriefing, and made an absolutely honest account of what exactly had occurred. His immediate superior, who had put him on this mission as wing commander, was appalled. Jack completely understood this, of course.

After finishing the debriefing, he walked silently to his modest but atmospheric office chamber. He punched some numbers, and the iris slid open. He quietly entered the room and sat down.

Jack silently gazed at one of his Russian Orthodox icons, engaged in many deep thoughts.

The wreckage and the debris of the incident were immediately salvaged by Federation Defense maintenance clusters, which were protected and watched over by a multitude of defensive and offensive vessels in many different types and classes.

The analysis of the wreck and its multitude of bits of debris were sent through immediately to the central GACS entity.
There were some partial human remains - solidly indicating a human-piloted attack - some materials, and small parts of technical instruments.
They gave some significant scientific clues, but it seemed impossible to copy or reinvent these technologies just like that.
There simply was not enough information. One solid conclusion was that this could not have been Ildiran technology. The Ildirans – simply - were much farther ahead, most probably.
The analyses continued carefully but the amount of resulting information was minimal.

But this one solid first conclusion was absolutely critical.

Chapter 13

Angelina and Kenzo Shyozama conspire against their government

Inside the deep core that was the conscious entity of GACS, all alarms had gone off after the latest disastrous flash-strike.

And when the analyses of the salvaged wreck had come in, this conscious entity had been shocked.... shocked to its core.
The conscious entity actually had its own personality, and even had its own designated name:

Vishnu Onexa Goshira.8.

This name was known only to the consciousness itself, a very select group of top AI technicians, and immediate and direct advisors to its decision-making. Human input was a great source, and stimulus, adding value to its own synaptic powers. The entity had come up with and assumed these names in the early stages of its independence, and these names had a very specific meaning as a reflection on its identity.

'Vishnu' was the supreme God in the ancient Vaishnavite tradition of ancient Earth Hinduism.

'Onexa' was a combined contraption, of the terms 'One' and 'x-o', the executive officer of an organization, and the first character of the alphabet: the 'a'. The first and last characters also stood for 'alpha and omega', a designation for the supreme God of the Bible, but reversed.

'Onexa' also stood for the term nexus, since the conscious system of 'VOG.8', was actually a gigantic neural net, or nexus, of hundreds of trillions of quantum-string-level genetic synapses.

Finally, Goshira, which was the ancient Earth Japanese word for Sea-monster.... in Old Earth English: Godzilla.

The number eight stood for the 28th century version of its evolved intellect and exponentially-increased synaptic abilities.

This AI structure had evolved historically from tiny 20th-century Earth machine code routines, followed by early experimental AI algorithms, like virtually programmed 'fuzzy-logical' circuits at first, and recurrent neural networks later on.

These techniques and algorithms had - step-by-step - been improved by AI developers and researchers and by the end of the 21st century they had created the first independent, really intelligent system: the first cognitively humanoid AI system.
Vishnu Onexa Goshira.8 had looked at all the angles of the three attacks, and had drawn one paramount conclusion:
This could never be an Ildiran-based attack. These strikes had been performed by a completely different kind of entity.
Unless….
Unless the Ildirans were - in some weird and illogical way – trying to create a completely different picture of themselves….
But this seemed completely illogical.
All analysis, and evidence, led to another source: the Ildirans were obviously much farther ahead, technologically, and scientifically, than 'the human race', and obviously possessed 'concealment' capabilities.

But the more 'stealth-like' concealments and invisibilities used with the attacks were far less advanced than the Ildirans presumably - or at least, most probably - were.
There was another convincing fact leading the focus away from the Ildirans....

Vishnu Onexa Goshira.8 was looking out across the vast distances of space by means of all Federation reconnaissance instruments, and by means of its endless intellectual capabilities, to find and identify this completely new alien threat.

There had always been something weird about Angelina: a kind of mystical aura surrounding her, only visible to people who knew her very well, like Kenzo Shyozama, or Paul Jackson maybe.... although she had never had many intimate relationships in her life.
She radiated something metaphysical.... a personality who knew more about the underlying truths of the universe.... more than anybody else in the universe.... or the galaxy.... or the Spiral Arm.... for that matter.

This was not just, because of her learning at MIC-T, although they had broadened her horizons, and insights, very widely.

She, herself, had felt from a very early age that metaphysical consciousness deep inside her mind, deep inside the mystical realms of her unique spirit.

Angelina had never known her true parents, and had been raised in an orphanage on the world of Ti Shoan, in the Cassiopeia x solar system.

Ti Shoan had been a beautiful world: somewhat like the - still existing but shattered, and radioactively polluted - North American continent on Old Earth: a combination of deserts, mountainous regions, forests, and populated areas. Although Ti Shoan was scarcely populated, and didn't have massive metropolitan areas, it had been terra-formed with the purpose of creating such a landscape.

Angelina knew absolutely nothing about her family history, or her predecessors, and had simply been told that her parents had died in some kind of transportation accident, somewhere in the unknown depths of space.

She has simply been told that she was called Angelina Xyanah Datah West.

And that had been about it.

The Children's home of Ti Shoan had not obliged Angelina or her fellow orphans to commit themselves entirely to one specific religion, but they had taught them an awful lot about many originally Old Earth religions - including Christianity, Judaism, Chinese Buddhism, Hinduism - and other religions that had arisen in more recent times, or combinations of existing ones, like Zen-Judaism. One of the more important things Angelina had learned was that the Vatican had dominated the Continent of Europe during the extremely religious and superstitious Middle Ages. It had ruled with an iron fist, claiming absolute wisdom and truth, and had usurped the (then) European part of humanity. As a result of their claimed 'absolute religious wisdom', hundreds of thousands of people had been tortured, maimed, and killed, in the name of righteousness, and the divine power of God....

Angelina had thought about this, long and hard, and had looked at it from all kinds of angles. And she had decided definitively that such an inhuman religious - or non-religious – usurpation of power over living beings, human or non-human, was absolutely unacceptable in any way, at any time. She had also realized that if the occasion or situation would arise again, such a 'political' situation would repeat itself. The Vatican would do everything all over again, without hesitation, and it would repeat all the same mistakes, and repeat the hundreds - maybe thousands - of years, of tragedy and human suffering, under an absolute and 'Divine' dictatorship.

In her opinion, such a state of affairs would be just as disastrous as – if not worse - than European and world domination by Nazi Germany.

There had been a multitude of examples in human history of such forms of government, and human history.... would always.... repeat itself.

The Old Earth 'Western world', which existed since the 20th century, was an immeasurable triumph, and a direct consequence of the revolution of Protestantism: the 'diversion' from Roman Catholic dogmatism. Although Christianity, especially Roman Catholicism, had 'dwindled' since the age of the Great Exodus, Angelina knew for certain that the modern-day Vatican would entirely repeat such an era of usurpation, if ever allowed to.

She was absolutely convinced of that fact....

The status quo in the contemporary Federation was de facto systematic control over humanity, and human values, by an AI super-intellect. Angelina knew this, but she could not do anything about it, and had decided to accept it, and deal with things - and society - as if it were normal. She, like any other Fed civilian, would never be able to do anything about it.

At least, that was what she was convinced of at that moment. But she didn't know - at that moment - that she actually would be able to change this in some far away future.... or maybe.... not so far away at all.

Aside from Christianity, Angelina had a great affinity with Buddhism, which to her was an intriguing school of thought.

But she completely disagreed with Buddhism's central teaching that one should detach from earthly pleasures, feelings, interests, and experiences....

Her fellow orphans had always treated Angelina like somebody who was 'different', and after leaving the orphanage she never kept in touch with any of them.

And Angelina knew they had been right: she was different.

Back then, Angelina didn't know that she would - in part because of her religious teachings, and her own resulting conclusions - become a sturdy fighter against, and a revered enemy of, this usurping AI-government called GACS.

Kenzo had left his SI-6 office chamber.

When Angelina had finally arrived, she was absolutely exhausted, falling apart from the many jumps, quick walks, countless suspension lift floors, and some in-system transports.... not to mention the dozens of security checks and ID-portals she had had to pass through.... In a matter of approximately ten hours, she had crossed a distance of more than ninety light years....

He had laid her down on his untidy office bed, after giving her a refreshing cup of his - privately kept - exotic and fragrant Cyania-6 tea.

After that, he had left the office chamber, and had continued his daily SI-6 briefings, board meetings, and so on.

Angelina was dreaming wildly.

She was lying on Kenzo's bed, in his office chamber, deep inside the SI nucleus, hanging silently in the vast darkness of space, at the ninth level. She was unaware of the realities surrounding her.

In her dreams, she was lying on an extravagant Catherine-the-Great-style bed, wearing absolutely nothing. Her breasts were hot, and bare, and full of desire.... her hands gently stimulating her genitals....

To Angelina, sexual intercourse had always been not only a satisfaction of physical lust, but a compensation for the psychological intensities in the back of her mind, and her fear of the future. On the other hand, she had never had a real father, and this fueled her longings for older men. Kenzo, since he was both her mentor, and protector, had unintentionally always been a father figure to her, and this single fact had fueled her fantasies and desires for him.

Kenzo appeared in the dream and approached her intimately.... and they made passionate love for hours, after many years of unbearable dissatisfaction....
Her dream shifted.
She saw three worlds, occupying vast regions in space, collapsing into each other, with Galactic amounts of energies....
She saw two human worlds, fundamentally different: one, dominated - in a totalitarian way -, by an AI

monster.... the other one: free, and vibrant, with human life, and human ideas, devoid of any AI dictatorship.

The dream shifted away from political realities, and slid into metaphysical realms....

A mystical psychedelic world surrounded her.... overpowered her.... across a vast distance she saw four brightly colored shapes, slowly approaching. She realized that these colorful shapes represent four of the most fundamental universal truths. The shapes continued their approach.... she couldn't really make them out or understand what they meant.... the shapes collapsed into a mixture of darkening shades, and faded away....

In this dream, Angelina realized that she had always had these dreams, and that she will remember them when awake. During recent years, they had become more transparent, more understandable.... more prominent....

Angelina was getting very close to full understanding of the fundamental truths of the universe.... and their relationships with the current state of the Milky Way galaxy....

Angelina didn't know why she is the only one in the Spiral Arm to have these dreams.... but – in her dream - she knew that she would become a central

piece in a trans-galactic situation verging on all-out
interstellar war....

After about seven hours, Kenzo returned, and found
Angelina sitting in the central seat in front of his
desk, drinking the same tea he had presented her
when she had returned from the system of Cali.
Kenzo sat down in front of his desk, shifted in his
seat, and after several minutes of intense silence
gave her a hard but familiar glance. She noticed he
had obviously deactivated all surveillance
instruments in the office chamber. This protocol was
only allowed in case of hyper-sensitive discussions.

'Angy, how long have I known you....?' Kenzo asked
her cautiously. He was trying to hide his feelings,
but Angelina's female intuition told her
immediately.... unmistakably.... that there was
something wrong.
They stared at each other for a while, intensely.
The tension in the chamber grew almost tangible.
'I didn't tell them about the existence and the
location of the Disappeared,' Kenzo said very softly,
and very slowly.
'I have reason to believe that the CGC stealth-
attacks were carried out by the Disappeared - or the

Human Dominion, as you told me - and that they are trying to eliminate our domination by AI entities; in other words, GACS. I believe that they want to rid mankind – entirely - from AI domination,' Kenzo said, with a growing feeling of tension. He didn't know entirely for sure how Angelina would react, or whether she would join him in this perilous undertaking.

Angelina felt shocked.

What is Kenzo saying? She thought perilously. *Where is this going to lead?* She waited tensely in complete silence.
Kenzo continued, 'If we tell this to our immediate superiors, they will inform GACS. It then will have no other choice than a total military conflict with the Disappeared. It will be either a free Human Dominion or a totalitarian AI human Spiral Arm.' Kenzo paused. He carefully observed Angelina's reaction. He had been a close friend for five years. She had to join him, even though this was an absolutely perilous undertaking.
He went on, decidedly, 'I have no choice in this matter. I must choose the side of the Disappeared.'
Angelina remained silent for several minutes, looking Kenzo straight in the eyes, realizing the peril in this moment; in this decision.

She was suddenly overtaken by the realization that spying on people and manipulating them, all in the name of some pointless, soulless, usurping AI monster, was utterly wrong, and utterly immoral. And after several moments of hesitation, which seemed to last for an eternity, she said…. 'I'm with you on this.'

They both realized they had taken a path - at this very moment - that could mean the only salvation for the Disappeared, and possibly for humankind in its totality.

But they didn't realize - at that particular moment - that survival of, and triumph for, the Disappeared was the only path towards lasting peace with the Ildiran Empire, and thus the very survival, and the very continuity, of the human race.

Chapter 14

Kenzo Shyozama orders Angelina to covertly contact Russell Caltech

In a trillionth of a trillionth of a second, Vishnu Onexa Goshira.8 had made a critical decision:

Since there had not been any reconnaissance information of aliens for many years, the attacks must have originated from the Disappeared, although the CGC had no information on them whatsoever: zilch.

The attacks had been directed directly against the CGC, the governing center of the Federation, and that indicated a direct confrontation with the Federation, and its core. The attacker were either trying to provoke a conflict, or trying to destroy the CGC itself definitively. The missiles, and other weapons, had not been powerful enough for the latter option, and this gave the Federation time: time to prepare.... and to respond.

There was another factor in the galactic equation. The Ildirans had very implicitly expressed that they could not live with or under AI-domination over themselves, or - most probably – over any living being.

All factors, conclusions, and considerations, led to one single final and all-encompassing conclusion: the CGC had no other option - in the near or far future, or in the end - than a total confrontation with both the Ildirans and the Disappeared.

This most fundamental confrontation was about the all-encompassing moral principal of AI-domination or control over humanity.

And there could only be one outcome.

Angelina woke up.
She was lying on the bed in Kenzo's private office

chamber on the ninth floor of the nucleus.

Though sparsely furnished, with a few standard, SI-6 pieces of furniture, it was intriguingly decorated with ancient Japanese paintings, artifacts, books, and martial arts weapons (as well as a few ancient and priceless Japanese samurai swords). She remembers, Kenzo once explained to her, the renowned 'The art of war', written by Sun Tzu.

It had been quite intriguing, and had expanded her knowledge and insights about the human and non-human world, although its subject itself was quite grim: waging war.

Nothing had happened.

Then, she suddenly remembered the nighttime discussion with Kenzo - or rather the monologue by him, and her own hesitant consent.

She realized now that he was right; there is no other way. She also immediately realized there must be millions of people inside the Federation harboring exactly the same convictions as the two of them. It gave her a strong feeling of hope.

She got herself a cup of Kenzo's special tea, and waited for his return.

Kenzo beeped, and quietly entered the room. 'Good morning, my dear Angelina. How are you today?' He was trying to relieve the tension created by last night's discussion. It was a new day; he seemed clear, and rested. 'Hi Kenzo, I'm fine....' she said seemingly carelessly.

Without addressing the subject, they both realized they had taken the path of conspiring against their government, and playing the roles of double agents: working for the CGC, while scheming against it. If they would - somehow - be seized in the future, it would almost certainly mean torture, and death.... This single fact and the fact that they would have to rely on each other, now and in the future, even more than they already had for the last five years, tremendously increased their dependency on each other, and they didn't know how long this situation was going to last.... maybe many, many years.... With the prospect of a nearing Galactic war, they might have to fight as soldiers, and scheme as double agents, for the rest of their lives....

They spent the entire morning going through some usual work, drinking tea, and discussing ongoing operations.

Nothing special seemed at hand. The day had

passed quite easily, and Angelina had simply assisted Kenzo in his regular and daily goings on.

Late in the evening, at around 11:30 p.m. standard time, they were finally alone in Kenzo's chamber, quietly enjoying the ancient Japanese tea.
Kenzo carefully deactivated the chamber's surveillance instruments.
'We got data on a central figure in the Humanity in Control organization. I want you to seek him out, under cover of a standard SI-6 operation. We know his whereabouts. When contact is securely established, you will pass him this data-file:'
Kenzo held up his com-unit, and showed a data-file containing only three pieces of info: the fact of the existence of the Human Dominion, its name, and its specific deep space locations and boundaries. 'You will tell him literally, that the Human Dominion is on a direct collision course with the Federation, and the dominating fact that they want to destroy AI control of humanity.'
Kenzo paused and folded his hands, as if meditating. He continued.
'You will give him no information about yourself. Just tell him, that you are government. This will tell him that there are double agents inside the GACS-controlled government who are on their side.'
Angelina memorized the instructions. 'Mission

clear.' she said stiffly.

Kenzo continued: 'I will give you his specific locations right now. You will leave the nucleus at exactly 1:30 a.m., standard time.

How and when you make contact is completely up to you.'

Angelina nodded formally, and distantly.

Her thoughts were with the future, with millions of people insurrecting against an all-powerful and colossal AI monster.

After leaving the SI nucleus, with its dozens of hyper-secured floors, Angelina jumped to the in-system Cyportal-nexus.

She had taken some refreshments, and had rested for half an hour, and after that she had jumped straight into the heavily populated system of Cyania. SI-6 had a relatively large amount of information on Russell Caltech. Angelina only needed a flash-call cypher, or code, and a location name, with optional in-system coordinates.

When she had arrived at an orbital station in orbit around Cyania b, she called Russell Caltech at his current (operation) location.

Russell didn't seem surprised.

He's probably prepared for anything...., Angelina thought, warily.

She had assumed the identity of a flash-news reporter, and Russell had easily accepted her invitation to meet in the recreational hall inside Ignius Nonem, a giant mining-facility inside the inner Oort-cloud.

They would meet in the evening, around 9:00 p.m., Ignius Nonem local time.

Being relatively early, she had wandered around the station, coldly observing her surroundings, and had drunken some steamy Cyania coffee in a brightly lit cafeteria. The in-station 28th century 'read-file store' had offered some intriguing literary works.

One of the most fascinating reads was called:

'Sentient Binary Suns', written by Carlis Eno.

From the description, it appeared to be a combination of prose, revolutionary ideas, and a manifesto for free human societies, devoid of AI controllers. Though AI controlled, the Federation still permitted literary freedom, and still 'felt' like a democratic conglomerate, although such writers were secretly being 'listed', in government files and

archives.... *This might be a useful read for me*, Angelina thought. Buying and reading such literary works, was as of yet relatively 'safe', and she had bought it, and uploaded it to her multi-purpose com-unit.
I'll read this when I have the time for such things, she thought.

9:35 p.m., system time. Location: Ignius Nonem mining facility, Cyania Oort-cloud, approximately 15.09 AU from unary Cyania sun....

The Ignius Nonem recreational hall occupied about one-fifth of the entire volume of the Oort-cloud mining facility.
It contained practically everything that could be described as 'recreation': bars, cafeterias, read-file stores, contemporary dancing halls, hotels, motels, any kind of stores, sex shops, tobacco shops, brothels....
One could buy or do almost anything in this place. Before Russell Caltech's arrival, Angelina had fascinatedly looked around in the 28th century version of a 'sex shop'. Although she had seen these kinds of things before, she had been absolutely intrigued with the multitude of sex toys,

holo-vid home-sys porn videos, sexual fantasy stimulating magazine-files, and a myriad of complex multi-programmed vibrators that had become quite common during the recent centuries....

She wandered around the entire hall for about half an hour, because she had arrived somewhat early, and Russell didn't seem to be there yet.

He arrived at around 9:55 p.m., local time.

They had recognized each other from their descriptions, and after walking over to each other they had formally and firmly shaken hands: they seemed to click (both were covert agents, of course).

One of the more quiet restaurants seemed an ideal place for a quiet (and private) first conversation.

They both sat down, and ordered a cup of the renowned Cyania-style cinnamon coffee with some local-system refreshments.

The restaurant looked quite atmospheric. It consisted mostly of poly- plastics, emulating gray giant fern woods.

Both were silent for a while, and sipped from their drinks, watching each other warily, and waiting.... Russell opened the conversation.

'You said you are government.... Could you be more specific?' he said straightforwardly. Angelina looked him in the eyes, for a while.
He knows the truth. No point in denying it, she thought logically.
'I can't.' she said firmly. 'I'm from the GACS government.... and.... we know a great deal about you, and your organization.' she replied.
Russell felt surprised, but he didn't show a thing.
'You're a double agent.' he said bluntly. 'What's your secret agenda? I'm quite interested to know.'
Angelina felt the tension hanging in the air. It was critical she informed him, about her - and Kenzo's – secret and private mission.
Russell had no reason, or motivation to uncover her.... at least: not yet. It remained critical for her and Kenzo to remain undetected.
'I'm a member of an SI-6 cell.' she said, with a cold voice. 'My direct superior and I have reason to believe the Disappeared exist. They call themselves the Human Dominion, and we know their locations. '

Russell didn't seem surprised at all.

'We already know,' he said plainly. 'We have already been working with them for about one hundred and fifty years.' He quietly observed her reaction.

Angelina felt shocked, and she didn't try to hide her feelings. She felt awestruck.

How could this be? She thought. *One hundred and fifty years.... We had no idea....*

She tried to recompose herself, but failed miserably. After a while she stuttered: 'W.... we.... didn't know.... there.... there are people.... inside the government.... who want to.... uh.... cooperate with the Dominion, and the resistance.... uh.... against.... uh.... GACS.... '

She breathed deeply.

Angelina hoped no one was recording this, or listening in from a distance....

Russell tried to conceal his excitement, and surprise, and tried to keep a calm face. Angelina noticed.

For almost five hundred years, cells and sub-organizations like SI-5 and -6 had terrorized and haunted people like him and his brothers-in-arms. This was practically unbelievable. Russell thought deeply.

It appeared to him that Angelina was completely telling the truth. From his training and conditioning he knew the signs of eye movement when people were lying.

'Alright, then.' he finally said. 'I'll give you some jump coordinates, as well as the matching access-cyphers to a.... very specific Dominion location.... an archive.' He waited. After a while he continued: 'In this archive you can find loads of info on the Disappeared, their history, Cyportal locations, codes, the structure of their government, and so on.... '
Angelina quickly made a wireless connection to his big though cheap memory com-unit, while Russell uploaded the information to her own very advanced and expensive unit.

Suddenly there was a flash of light.... a hissing sound.

Five blue-and-yellow sub-quantum particle beams whizzed through the smoky air of the quiet restaurant.
Russell fell, face forward onto the poly-plastic surface of the restaurant table in between them. Angelina reacted almost instantly, thanks to her rigorous training and field experience. Her heartbeat

immediately quickened to a steady pace.

She noticed a weird bluish-colored menial-droid outside their poly-plastic restaurant, floating away fast. This was not a mere menial-droid, she immediately realized. Within a moment, she drew her SI-6 stealth gun from under her dress and fired. It was too late, but she had immediately memorized the code written on the hull of the droid: x-e-section sl-51-91-0.

She didn't know what the code meant, or where it came from, but she would find out later....

Russell appeared to be stunned and wounded by the particle beam, but he came to consciousness a few moments later.

The shots could easily have been lethal....

Angelina took him immediately to the closest in-system hospital, where she had him 'fixed up'.

This, obviously - to Angelina at least - had been a first warning.

After the incident, Russell Caltech and Angelina had parted, and had both gone their separate ways.

In the refreshment room of the hospital, they had exchanged a few final words: they would meet again, and discuss what had happened.

Both had their respective contact information, and

both needed time to think. Russell had bid her farewell, and Godspeed, into Dominion space....

After leaving Angelina, Russell had time to think. The hated and distrusted GACS AI government, on which he and his fellow insurgents had waged a secret war for five hundred years, had people on the inside who were on their side.
The idea was unthinkable.
All elements against the CGC, inside the CGC, had been wiped out mercilessly, and scheming against it from the inside seemed practically impossible.
He would have to bring the news to his aides and comrades and brothers-in-arms. They would be shocked at first, but exhilarated later on.
But there were also GACS enemies on the outside of the CGC government:

According to the latest estimates, millions of 'Fed' civilians would be ready, willing, and able to take up arms against GACS when the time was right....

Chapter 15

Angelina discovers the first part of her true identity, in a hidden Dominion pre-Exodus archive

By the end of the 20th century CE, and during the early 21st century, the science of physics had shifted significantly.

Not only was the scientific world - across the board - seriously contemplating and discussing the existence of alien life, and other bizarre issues such as dark energy and the concept of multiverse, but there had arisen two schools of thought.... two directions to choose from....

It had been either super string theory, or the Stephen Hawking direction, and super string theory - later on known as string theory - had won the race.

Experiments in super high-energy and super-complex particle accelerators, such as the LHC (on the European continent), and its bigger and heavier successors, had proven the (indirect, and later on direct) existence of 'string particles'. One of the most revolutionary aspects of string-field theory, had been that everything consisted of strings, or rather multidimensional objects called p-branes ('p' dimensional objects, representing existing entities). As it turned out, not only matter and energy consisted of strings, but everything, even space-time itself, which had 'become' 11-dimensional, harboring many - or at least some - 'compacted' tubular dimensions and particle-realms.
The original five versions of super string theory had been melted into one single overlapping theory called M-theory.
The beautiful M-theory had later on developed into the mesmerizing and hyper-complex F-theory, which in turn had opened up completely new practical fields of research and development.

But during the early 21st century, the future technological instrumental feats for warping and influencing spatiotemporal and other class dimensions were still to be invented....

Angelina West knew these things by heart: she completely understood the physics and mathematics behind it. What's more, she had a firm grasp on the metaphysical and universally fundamental building blocks, truths, and realities beneath them.... beneath the deepest structures of material energy, and the dimensions of space and time. And in the near future, these accomplishments of hers would become crucial elements in the fight against GACS.

2,079 CE, November 6th

Early phase in the Great Human Galactic Exodus

The giant transport-freighter-cluster, the Enceladus Octi, descended into the Proxima Centauri 5 stratosphere.... its fiery-red and roaring nuclear fusion flames carrying the massive ship during its slow but steady descent.

The 'P-C' system was - as was commonly known, by then - the nearest solar system to Sol-3. (Transport clusters were too big to pass through Cyportals, and these latter objects were only in the earliest stages of research).
The cluster had great trouble handling the incredible shield heating.
Its main cargo consisted of human colonists, but the bulk of the transport vessel was stacked with food supplies, fuels, plant seeds, instruments, and, last but not least, terra-forming installation parts.
The human space-flight command crew and colonists felt the terrible anxiety of landing on a world no human being had ever set eyes on before. The freighter cluster's command crew tried to keep the descending ship under control, and to keep the entry heating minimal. About half an hour later, the ship touched down on PC-5 soil, for the first time in human history.

Leaving the Old Earth had been hectic.
The command crew had been chosen from the military, mostly from the Pentagon and its Russian counterpart.
For the colonists it had been quite different. After thinking deeply, and considering the future perils

they might have to face, they had applied with their local authorities. A few of the hundreds of thousands of applicants worldwide had been selected, and they were mostly scientists, scholars, and historians.

The Enceladus Octi had been one of many transport vessels leaving the Earth during the past three to five years.
It had lifted off with a terrible explosion of fire and burning fuel from one of the dozens of lift-off locations all around Earth.

The ship itself originated from the Russian Federation, and most of its crew members were originally Russian.

Space flight through the vast darkness in between Sol and P-C had been a combination of awe, tension, and anxiety for the Earthly colonists, who had never in their lives experienced the vastness of space before. The flight had seemed to last for an eternity.
It had taken them many months to get from their home planet to their destination, and although the ship was huge, the psychological strain had been terrible: colonizing space and other worlds was hard, and terrifying.

They had been driven by their deep convictions that the future of humanity resided in space colonization.

Earth – itself - was polluted, scorched, and immensely over-populated.
The early 21st century population, of approximately 6.85 billion souls, had exploded into an amount of 36.94 billion. Seemingly, all the elements of capitalism, geographical policies, oil wars, stimulating the arms industries, and a powerless United Nations, had failed....

There was no future for Gaia.

A multitude of animals, plants, flora and fauna, and entire eco-systems were dwindling....
Deep inside its vast oceans and seas, hyper-intelligent beings were singing songs of death and peril, shaken by their perception of the perilous future for their once beautiful water world.
Maybe, a few hundred years into the future, Gaia might be restored somewhat to its original beauty and well-being, but at this stage there was no reason not to spread out across the multitude of worlds, lying and waiting for humanity to come....
Hopefully, Gaia's recent - not to mention ancient – history would not be repeated on these new versions of itself.

9:00 a.m. local-system-time

The massive belly of the ship opened wide.

The colonists with their rovers, Geiger counters, and measuring instruments tucked away in their oversized atmospheric space suits, walked silently down the ramp and set foot on the gloomy soil of PC-5....

They felt awestruck.

The command crew had stayed on their deck to be able to respond and lift off in case of any emergency.
Carefully and awfully silent, the colonists walked into the PC-5 undiscovered country. The wide landscape was covered with mountains, geysers, and rocky faces, and the atmosphere was poisonous and unbreathable.
But the suits protected them well.
They had all carried every necessary and available asset from their ship onto the rocky surface surrounding it.
Their most important duty would be the terra-

formation of the entire planet and its atmosphere; a process that would, most probably, take many decades.

8:00 p.m., four days later

John Allen – the captain of the ship, and one of the few of American descent – was just checking his instruments after many hours of hard work when something strange attracted his attention.

His long-range scanner beeped continuously, and its display flashed on and off, as if trying to warn him of possible attackers.
This shouldn't happen, for they had thoroughly scanned the PC system for signs of life and artificial and technological signals upon entry of system space.

John studied the – rather crude – instruments....

The signal persisted, and became more prominent. Apparently, some unknown alien craft was closing in, with terrible velocity. John felt frightened. He had never expected to have such an encounter, let alone within four or five days from first contact.

The crude scanner indicated the alien craft was closing in.

Then suddenly it appeared.... high above, in the dark sky.

It seemed to be perfectly spherical, although it was quite hard to perceive with the naked eye.

The alien sphere seemed to come to a standstill, and hover in the cloudless sky high above, while it kept spinning fast around its vertical axis.

It seemed as if it was scanning – observing – the settler's encampment for a long while.

John's attention remained completely fixed on the alien intruder. Minutes passed.... apparently he was the only one who had noticed the strange object, and the thought of being alone at that very moment made him feel more frightened than he ever had before.

Then, suddenly, as if the object had completed its observations, thoughts, and measurements, it slowly accelerated upwards, faster and faster, gliding back into the deep darkness.... of PC space.

During the next 12 to 15 years, the entire Enceladus Octi crew had worked tirelessly, building sleeping, staying, and recreational quarters, setting up terra-forming facilities, and exploring and documenting the planet's surface.

John Allen had kept the strange event to himself. He actually didn't know what to think of it, and as their leader he didn't want to scare his crew, and make them feel insecure in this new place, where so much still had to be done.

They were not safe and secure yet, and they still had a long way to go.

Terra-forming this new world, and its atmosphere, had worked. There were fields with grass and crops; small H_2O lakes had formed; and the atmosphere became practically breathable, during the local daylight. The colonists continued their years of long and hard work, and a very early human society was forming.

They had actually established remaining contact with the Old Earth, but the news from their home world had been bad....

Dozens of transport clusters had - in the meantime – left the Earth, in search of better places, but on Earth itself nuclear war, poverty, suffering, and disease had persisted.

Whether planet Earth would survive this multitude of disasters was questionable, but in the meantime the new Human worlds and new societies in space were spreading, and growing, and even starting to flourish.

They had all established lasting interconnections with each other.

It seemed like a solid future for mankind had been secured.

But a small part of the colonizing ships had disappeared....

Since the encounter, and terrible event, with Russell Caltech, Angelina had felt a growing sense of unease. She would have to find out who it had been that had instructed the sniper-droid. If Russell had been such an easy and accessible target, she herself was, too. What had been the reason for this sniper attack? She sincerely hoped nobody had been listening in to the conversation. Russell had obviously already been on the list of these attackers, although she probably had not been: the attack had been focused on Russell. But she was a vulnerable target as well, and that was reason enough for worry. They had fired right after Russell had disclosed the jump info to her. She really hoped this was a coincidence....

Angelina decided to focus on the present.
I have to get to that first jump location, she thought.

But the mysterious event, and its backgrounds, kept bothering her in the back of her mind.

Later on, Kenzo would explain to her where the sniper-attack had originated from.

It was SI-5: the other cell.

They knew Angelina was going to contact Russell, and they had used her – without her knowing - as bait. They did not want to eliminate Russell, but to give him a clear warning that they were onto many of Humanity Destiny's leaders.
When she heard this, Angelina was indignant, because they hadn't let her into it, but the order had come from high up, and she knew there was little she could do about it. She knew that this was the way Intel organizations worked, and that was all there was to it for now.

The data-file with the jump info contained a list,

consisting of steps....

Angelina looked at the first step on the list.

It was an inter-sys jump, from this system's main nexus to the next one. Angelina local-jumped, to the Cyania system central nexus, and walked silently, through the intriguing high and narrow hallways, in the direction of her first jump Cyportal. The corridors felt silent, and oppressive.

It felt as if she was wandering through a maze with metallic catacombs. Several minutes later, she arrived at the appropriate Cyportal room. It looked somehow ancient, as if built many hundreds of years ago.

She showed an ID card, and silently entered the Cyportal room.... She stood for a while and checked the list.

'I'd like to make a jump to the Ziborgia-system', she murmured. 'Destination confirmed', the portal answered, with a virtual sounding voice. Angelina walked silently, step-by-step, towards the central circle of the portal, and stepped through. In a fraction of a second, she found herself in another location. *This must be the Ziborgia central nexus*, she thought.

A strange atmosphere hung in the air. In this place, everything seemed to be made of some kind of metal.

There seemed to be no one around. She took her com-unit, and checked the list. Next on the list was a local-jump to Ziborgia-5.

She wandered around the nexus, analyzing her surroundings, memorizing the details.
The nexus seemed to be devoid of people. Every now and then, she encountered a security droid, observing and monitoring the empty corridors. Some of the local-jump portals were around the corner, in the next hallway. Angelina turned a corner, and chose one of them. Her ID card had already been processed. With a feeling of anticipation, she entered the portal room she had chosen. The rooms were almost identical, but there were small differences in size, and the type of portal inside. 'Get me to Ziborgia-5', she said softly. 'Connection established', the portal virtually responded.

She walked over and into the orbital station of the world of.... Ziborgia-5

The orbital Cyportal station, the Io-1, appeared to be very small compared to most other stations.

It was not the only station in orbit around Ziborgia-5. But it was one of the smallest ones Angelina West had ever seen.

She looked around, and checked the data list. It appeared she had to find a docked ship: a private superluminal FTL-vessel.

She was completely amazed. This was the first time she had completely examined the data list. When Russell had handed it to her, she had had no time to really analyze it, or seriously look at it. *Does Russell Caltech really expect me to fly with a private superluminal FTL-vessel into Dominion space*, she wondered?

According to the very concise data list, the tiny private interstellar vessel was in dock se-04, somewhere on the 24th level. Angelina immediately took to the anti-grav suspension lift shafts. 'Twenty-fourth level, please', she said to the lift control-sys, with a flat sounding voice.

'Lifting to level 24,' the control-sys responded. Angelina thought about the many dozens of light years she would have to cross. *How the hell, am I going to get out of Fed space undetected, she questioned? How, in God's name, am I going to make entry into Dominion space, without their reconnaissance tracking my ship?*

Reluctantly, she tried to recompose herself as the suspension lift took her up.

The tiny vessel looked amazing, at least from the outside.

It looked nothing like the numerous mainstream private vessels which crowded Federation space in this day and age.
It was floating on its suspension generators in a small docking bay, which had its launching iris shut tight.
Angelina carefully examined the tiny spaceship:
It appeared to be made for a one - maybe two - person crew.
It was clear it was a private vehicle to allow rich people to freely roam through the depths of space, travelling to other planets unhindered by mass transportations and crowded Cyportal nexi. *Was this ship the private property of Russell Caltech? Probably not*, she thought.... *It was most likely owned by some rich person, some acquaintance of his.*
The hull of the ship seemed to be made of a Fed standard titanium-crystal alloy. Underneath, it featured some very ancient-looking suspensors,

and some tiny missile shafts, three of them holding some old-model projectiles.

I might come into a situation where these could be useful, Angelina thought.

It was clear to Angelina's trained eyes that this was an older vessel; maybe about two hundred years old. It did have superluminal FTL-drive generators on both sides, but they seemed quite ancient as well....

Carefully – so as not to break or damage anything - she opened the pilot's seat door.

She was in for a shock.

'Welcome', the ship said, with a somewhat strange artificial voice.

'I am the AI of this private vessel. Please feel free to enter.'

Angelina had learned during SI-6 training sessions to fly and operate many kinds of space vehicles, but this one seemed absolutely outdated. 'Have you got a name, or a designation?' she asked the relatively crude AI ship.

'My official designation is xs-49-b, but you may address me as Janis', the vessel responded, with a voice full of artificial civility.

Its voice appeared to be of the female kind, as well

as its 'name'.

Angelina carefully entered, closed the pilot seat door, and sat down on the leather seat, which was probably manufactured on some local moon.

'Okay.... Take me into deep space....' she said softly.

After leaving the space hangar, Angelina immediately activated her ship's communication systems.

'Private vessel, please identify,' it sounded. A face appeared on one of the screens. 'This is xs-49-b.' Angelina said, 'I'm on a private trip.' The face responded, 'Your vessel is registered. Have a good trip!' The face disappeared, and the ship's status visuals reappeared on the screen. Angelina looked into local space from her control seat. There didn't seem to be much traffic. Carefully, she took her com-unit, and studied Russell's list. Her destination carried the name of Tau Septi.

It would be wise not to attract any attention...., she thought warily, and she kept the ship at a constant and regular velocity.

Once inside deep space, safely out of range from any reconnaissance systems, she instructed the semi-intelligent ship:

'Switch to superluminal FTL, and head for coordinates 04-x-84-y-210-95-0.' The ship responded. 'I am familiar with these coordinates. The system is called Tau Septi. I am now switching to superluminal FTL. Please relax.... the flight will take approximately 8 hours.'

Eight hours...., she thought. *I'd better use the time efficiently....*

She took the read file from Carlis Eno out of her rucksack, and inserted it into the ship's com-sys.

And Angelina – a great lover, of the written word - started to read.

45 minutes later.

Deep space looked beautiful. It always did....

There were nebulas in the background, and tens of thousands of stars.... It always remained an exhilarating experience, even if one had experienced it a million times before....

The book, 'Sentient Binary Suns' by Carlis Eno, was absolutely intriguing, and it proved to be very instructive as well. It was a kind of manifesto: a manifesto for human freedom from AI controllers. It contained some revolutionary ideas; or at least, revolutionary for the kind of society in which Angelina was living.
One of these ideas was that not only superior AI systems should be eliminated from society, deactivated, and completely destroyed, but all of them. This posed some intriguing questions in Angelina's mind. Should the CGC government be eliminated definitively? Should this ship's semi-AI be destroyed, never to exist again?

For someone who had been brought up and lived in the current state of society all her life this seemed almost anarchist. Eno also discussed exo-politics, and how to deal with possible and frightening alien threats.
To him, the only ethical and safe answer to this was the combining of an all-powerful military defense apparatus, and an infinite commitment to co-existence in all space for all time. During the 21st century, the Old Earth had had to deal with this same basic issue: a total commitment to co-

existence, and/or defense (or offence), in the face of potential first alien contact. The Old Earth state of Israel, a Jewish homeland founded in the midst of the 20th century CE had also had to deal with the moral and political aspects of a future of co-existence with its (Islamic) neighbors, or a repeating situation of war and conflict. All these issues and messages of this literary work fascinated Angelina, and would stay in the back of her mind, troubling her, intriguing her, for years to come....

'I'm now deactivating superluminal FTL,' the ship sounded. 'Nearing Tau Septi system.... '

Angelina woke up from a troubling and violent dream. 'Switch to low velocity, please,' she said, 'and stay away from any reconnaissance tracking....' 'I possess some quite advanced cloaking abilities,' the outdated ship said. 'Should I activate them?' *Cloaking abilities....,* She thought. *The Fed didn't have those... But the resistance has been in touch with the Dominion for many years, of course, and has probably bought or copied technologies from them.*
'Yes,' she said, 'activate cloaking.' 'Cloaking activated,' the ship sounded.

Although Angelina didn't notice, from the outside, from space view, the ship faded quickly from sight.

The system of Tau Septi was both on one of the view screens and visible through the command seat window. It was nearing slowly.

Although the view screen showed a zoomed-in close-up of it, the real version, visible through the window, gave a better overall picture.
'Zoom in on Ts-5. Give me full planetary view,' Angelina said. The ship complied, and produced a close-up view of the planet. *I've seen desert worlds before....*, she thought, *but this one features gigantic pyramid-like structures.... they must be cities....*
'Zoom in on a pyramid-shaped structure,' she ordered the ship's AI. The ship did so, and the view centered onto one of the structures. It appeared the planet had a dozen - or maybe many more - of these structures on its dry surface.

The one on the view screen looked like a 28th century version of a very ancient old Earth Egyptian pyramid, but it was different. This one was maybe one hundred times the size of the old Earth ones, and it had a different appearance. Across its four surfaces, tens of thousands of (what seemed like) mini-fusion lights were clearly visible from orbital space.

The edifice appeared to be built of some kind of futuristic metal, combined with many thousands of poly-plastic 'windows'. 'Have you got any info on this planet.... on these structures?' Angelina asked the semi-intelligent AI.

'Yes, I do.' it said. 'The Dominion lost its terra-forming technologies shortly after the Great Human Exodus. The reasons are not clear, but they have never been able to reproduce them. It was probably due to the absence of some elementary ingredients required for successful and effective terra-formation processes. Therefore, most Dominion worlds are desert-like, and these structures are common on Dominion worlds. They serve as massive protected cities for the Dominion population. It is not clear why this topological shape was chosen, for these cities.' Angelina waited, thinking deeply.

Suddenly, she remembered the com-unit list. She took the unit, and selected the list. The next location appeared to be a private docking unit, inside one of the 'pyramid' cities.

'Take me to the pyramid city, called: Jovi....' she said '....and please remain fully cloaked, all the way.'

The ship confirmed the command, and headed straight for Tau Septi 5. Cloaking remained fully active, as Angelina had requested.

They were completely invisible, both to the human eye as well as to advanced planetary and deep-space reconnaissance instruments.

After several minutes cruise flight, they entered the Ts-5 atmosphere.

Angelina felt amazed by the view: everywhere there were metallic discs, floating, accelerating, and landing on anti-gravity suspension. It looked like some kind of unreal world. 'These discs must be their main way of transportation....' she murmured to herself. Silently, she took in the scenery for several minutes.

Then she noticed the nearing planet surface.

The city of Jovi became clearly visible, hundreds of clicks below, lying still in the desolate desert sands of TS-5.

Janis, still perfectly cloaked, landed perfectly in the private docking location inside the pyramid-shaped city of Jovi.

The docking bay's air-lock iris slid shut without a

single sound. 'Please deactivate to complete silence, Janis', Angelina said.

She couldn't help but feel a kind of sympathy for the simple-minded AI. Although the ship was outdated, it functioned flawlessly. It reminded her of the age-old question of what self-consciousness really was, and whether a ship like this could in any way be conscious, let alone be conscious of its own existence.

She came out of the control seat, and exited the tiny - yet very capable - vessel. *So, now I am completely inside the realms of the Human Dominion for the first time*, she thought. She looked around, and tried to analyze her environment. The space dock was small, but efficient. Every required instrument and facility seemed to be there.… even alarm-systems, in case of fires and other emergencies. Leading towards the innards of the city, there was a closed iris. She walked towards it, and it slid open, as if it had somehow expected her arrival.

Angelina stepped through the opened iris, and – while her heartbeat quickened - she entered the pyramid city of Jovi.

Her com-unit data-list had provided her with the info to find her next location.

It was her final destination: the pre-Exodus archive. She had wandered through corridors, taken a series of suspension lifts, across dozens of floors, and now she walked down a long hallway, leading to the ancient archive itself. There were not many 'Dominians' present in this part of the city, and nobody seemed to suspect her of anything.

The Dominians looked mostly like ordinary human beings, except for their style of clothing, and their body language, which seemed somewhat 'weird' to her Federation eyes. Angelina noticed some deformities, here and there, although these Dominians obviously tried to hide these as much as they could. At least, this was Angelina's first encounter observation of them, and she was not sure whether all Dominians were like this, or only those in this place, or on this planet....

She felt a faint sensation, as if people in the distance were faintly aware of some of her thoughts.

They must have mutated, because of some kind of radiation, she thought warily. *Could they have experienced nuclear war....? Maybe many times over, considering they have been lost for more than five hundred years....*

The inside of the city looked like it was mostly

constructed of yellowish sandstone. The makers of these colossal cities, or buildings, had probably tried to recreate the atmosphere, and looks, of the original Sol-3 Egyptian pyramids. It struck Angelina that Janis had told her that most - maybe almost all - of the Dominion worlds were desert-like. *These Dominians must be completely desert-oriented*, she thought *....in their minds, and in their entire way of life....*

And she was right about that. Every corridor, every hallway, was lit by big suspended glow-globes, hovering silently in the still unearthly air. Every place looked almost the same. Here and there on the walls, there were mystical Dominion paintings like she had never seen before. They looked ancient, and depicted a silent kind of Dominion mystique or mysticism. She silently walked along the last long hallway - trying not to attract any attention - towards her destination:

The hidden Dominion pre-Exodus archive

The relatively small iris of the chamber slid open, hissing softly.

What she saw inside - whilst standing in the opened

iris - was unlike anything she had ever seen before. Thousands of data-servers were stacked on top of each other, and next to each other, in the quite small chamber, which was lit by suspended glow-globes. The data-servers were made of a bluish sort of poly-plastic, with a multitude of very tiny blue flashing lights. The walls were literally covered with thousands of electricity power cables and connectors. The floor and the walls were dark and light brown, covered with some kind of heat isolation material. The ceiling had a neat orange-like color. It was made of some kind of concrete, and contained numerous black ventilators.

This space was obviously designed to store loads of data, and to withstand years of disasters from the outside world. In the center of the archive chamber, right in the middle of the thousands of data-servers, there stood one single access-terminal. It looked a bit like an ancient Old Earth laptop, but this one was hyper-advanced in comparison to such outdated devices.

Angelina walked over to the center of the chamber as silently as she could, and stood in front of the access-terminal. 'Please, activate.' she said very softly, trying not to attract any attention from the outside.

'This grid is always on-line,' the archive terminal responded with a clear sounding but soft computerized voice. 'Even in case of emergencies, or system-wide disasters, there are five backup energy supply units available. This protocol has been installed after the terrible nuclear wars of 2,465 to 2,469 CE, and the radioactive pollution of almost all Dominion planets.
Pyramid-hives are resistant to almost any kind of catastrophe.
All data inside these systems was compiled and ordered by AIs, although AIs do have an inferior role to humans in the Human Dominion.'

So these worlds are called 'pyramid hives', Angelina thought musingly. She was completely fascinated by the chamber, and what it held inside. 'Have you got a designation?' she asked the ancient system. 'You may address me as: Mother.... ', the archive responded. 'It is a common way to address computerized systems in the Human Dominion.... '

'What kind of data is stored in your memories, Mother?' Angelina asked the terminal. 'Almost anything on the Dominion, and humanity in general, pre- and post-Exodus.', the terminal responded. 'I may have data on your personal family history, or would you like to make a specific query?' Angelina seemed completely disconcerted. *Data on my family history....*, she thought, staring at the terminal screen. She had never had any real family or knowledge about her real family at all....

It took her a while to consider the question the terminal had posed to her. 'Ok,' she said. 'Tell me about my parents, first.'

'Alright, please give me your full name, as well as your date of birth, and the exact time of birth, if you have that information', the terminal inquired. 'My full name is Angelina Xyanah Datah West....' she said. 'Exact date of birth: 25-12-2,767 CE.... I believe it was close to midnight.... '

'Are you an inhabitant of the Human Federation?' the system inquired, with its artificial computerized voice. 'Yes, I am.... Mother', Angelina responded. 'I have all the required information. Compiling data,' answered the terminal. A multitude of lights started flashing, all over the chamber. The process took about half a minute, but to Angelina it seemed like an eternity. The terminal started to formulate the results of the query:

'Name of parents: Gary and Charlene Tchaikovsky. Two siblings: Angelina, and Michael Tchaikovsky. Occupations.... father: Cyportal physics specialist.... mother: theoretical exo-physicist.

Both originate from the Human Dominion.

Parents were both killed during civil unrests of 2,767 CE by a cloaked hit-and-run attack inside Sirius Epsilon Oort-cloud. Attack allegedly staged by a combination of several anti-Salvationist groups.

There are some indications it could just have been pirates, or perhaps these pirates were hired by the anti-Salvationist groups to assassinate them.

Your parents were leading members of the main Salvationist faction.

This political and militant group strove for salvation of the Old Earth by means of re-terra-formation, re-population, restructuring and reorganization of Earth's government and all of its policies.

The philosophy behind this was that humanity should "first clean up the nest, and then the rest...."

This strategy was rejected by the Dominion government because of its massive cost and operational scale and it was simply declared unachievable.

Most Dominians agreed with their government. It was simply too costly, and too massive an operation, to ever be realistically completed. At least, that was the 'official' assessment.

The moral and political will, and support for this program, simply wasn't there.... '

The terminal, designated as 'Mother', continued its informational account: '....Michael Tchaikovsky, most probably still alive. According to the database, he is residing in the Rigel system inside the Human Federation.' The terminal waited. It seemed to have produced all relevant data.

'I have one remaining relevant piece of information', it said after a while. 'A copy of a text message your mother left you, in case you would ever find it.'
Angelina started, and stood petrified for a long while.
After a while she said, 'just give me several minutes to digest this, and then read me the message, please.... '
Angelina Tchaikovsky - as was her real identity, she realized for the first time - remained silent for several more minutes....

All kinds of thoughts were running through her mind.

The archive system started reciting the account....

'Dear Angelina, I write you this message at a very difficult moment in our lives.'
As Angelina was listening to this account, which had

remained untouched inside the ancient archive database for so many years, tears slowly welled up inside her beautifully deep, grey-green eyes.
The system continued.
'Please forgive me - and your father - for abandoning you, and leaving you, to this world they call the Human Federation.... We have both thought long and hard about this decision, but we have decided that it would be safer to turn you over to the care of the secret organization they call "Humanity's Destiny", and especially to its sub-section, inside the Human Federation.

They are our trusted friends, and brothers in arms, and they will safely take you to the Human Federation planet called Ti Shoan. You will be raised there in a decent and trustworthy children's home. You will be educated very widely, and you will not know about us until the time is right, and you will be old enough to deal with this, and understand this.
We would like to hand you a code that only a handful of people in both the entire human regions in space possess.
Many people have given their lives to find and retrieve it. They were brutally tortured, and killed in secret by the abomination they call VOG.8. We could not risk the informational content being found

or understood by others, so we had to encrypt it.

It's imperative that you decipher it and use it to destroy its destination.

This is the actual code:

Alpha_omega, vaish_navite, _apocalypse_, object: sy_fy, prop_: kami_kaze, bin: 010011-0100, 444x472-y000-845/exit-4/4782-999/ com.: 0-8.

We implore you to continue our struggle, to depose the AI dominators, and to fulfill our mission to heal the Old Earth.... the world of our birthright.... with resolve and total commitment....

With love and devotion,

Your mother and father'

The secret code seemed like some complex visual-ai-sys-8 programming instruction, although to 28th century coding standards this was not abnormally complicated at all. But somehow there also was something mystical and illusive about it. Alpha and Omega referred to the Christian God of the Holy Bible, and Vaishnavite – according to Angelina's extensive theological knowledge - meant 'a follower of the supreme lord Vishnu', the supreme God in the Hindu Vaishnavite tradition, an ancient Old Earth Indian religion.

Although Angelina didn't have the slightest clue what this code could possibly mean, she felt a deep yearning for the parents she had never known, now that she had received the first tangible sign of their existence; the first token of their undying and total love and affection.

Cy-timing-system: csy-040-4867-ys, location: Dominion space, deep inside the vast expanse of the Sirius Epsilon system, Oort-cloud.

The lights, indicators, and visual representations on the photonic holo- control dashboard of the relatively large human cargo vessel lit up with blue, green, and yellow radiation. There were several pilots with different command functions, seated in plasti-fiber chairs with straight black backs in front of their respective command stations. Their sharp eyes were fixed intently on their holo-controls, and the tension in the cargo vessel's command nucleus was extremely high.

The command nucleus, itself, was located exactly in the center of the elongated-disc shaped vessel, as was custom in those times in the Human Dominion. Its visuals were connected to multi e-m spectrum holo-cams, incorporated in the hull of the metallic disc. The hull itself was actually made of an alloy, consisting of gold, silver, and other metals, and it could be activated to perform super-conducting functionalities, if needed. The compartments surrounding the nucleus were made up of sleeping quarters, storage spaces, engine rooms, recreational rooms, weapons and fuel storages, and more such elements that one usually finds inside privately-owned deep space vehicles. The sleeping quarters were especially large, to accommodate about fifty people, since this vessel was primarily designed for human transport.

Outside, space looked relatively quiet to the command crew of the ship, but they knew this was only a matter of appearance, since there had been many reports of unexpected attacks, especially on single vessels, which had no protection whatsoever from government-sanctioned escort squadrons. They knew that free space piracy had also dramatically increased recently.

Civil unrest had broken out some four or five months ago, which had resulted in panic and chaos all over Dominion society. The Dominion government could do little about it, except for stepping up police controls on the major worlds, and patrolling all hive cities and orbital regions with military skimmers, atmospheric drones, shuttles, and close space policing vessel squads. There had been rumors that the Human Federation had finally detected Dominion civilization, and since the Dominion rejected AIs, everybody knew that this would probably mean massive war. Although these rumors had circulated earlier on, and they had come around again, from time to time, most people somehow sensed that these rumors could really be true. Many politicians and organization leaders were skeptical, and who tried to calm the masses.

Gary and Charlene Tchaikovsky were among the leadership of Humanity's Destiny, and many civilians – especially from the political right – blamed their movement for everything that was going wrong with Dominion society. When the attacks and accusations had become too much for them, they had decided to flee the pyramid hives, and take a private transport to some quiet location on some distant planet, in a system only inhabited by a limited number of locals, who were accustomed to minding their own business and leaving newcomers alone.

Charlene Tchaikovsky carefully studied her husband's facial features, as he was sitting eyes closed on the other side of the quiet compartment in the recreation room.
After all these years, she still loved and admired his quiet but confident face, and his eyes, which radiated wisdom, and readiness to fight. According to an advisor, the Sirius Epsilon system had seemed like a good candidate to go into hiding, and give leadership to the movement from there. The Sirius Epsilon Oort-cloud, with its billions of giant meteors – a few of them customized for human settlement - offered a solid place to live for the time being.

They were the only ones in the compartment, except for a female maintenance droid with a friendly face and a quiet aura surrounding her artificial bodily features.
Charlene realized she loved Gary more than anything. But the current situation, and their social

responsibilities, felt like an unbearable burden, and she knew they were both in grave danger from 'political' opponents. Yet their struggle was justified, and they would have to carry on and continue their fight.... no matter what the consequences were.... and no matter the sacrifices. If they would fall, others would have to take their place. The cause stood above anything else; above their own petty lives, and trivial personal happiness.

Charlene had given birth to Michael about 12 months ago, and Gary had 'knocked her up again', immediately after that. Angelina was only 6 weeks old, and their discussions about the probable fate of their two young children had been tough, but she and her highly educated husband loved each other more than anything, despite everything, and they had come up with – what seemed to them – the best solution.
They would have a trusted Destiny operative, Ingmar Bergenstein, smuggle Angelina and Michael into the Federation, and entrust both children to some caretakers in safe sites, in different locations. Ingmar Bergenstein would have to risk her very life and covertly try to intrude into the unknowing Federation.
She would have to deliver the children to the two locations, with the help and assistance of from

Destiny operatives inside it. Charlene had been informed that one of them was a prominent figurehead of the Destiny sub-section inside the Federation, called Russell Caltech.

The movement had already existed for centuries, from the moment mankind had started colonizing strange new worlds, and Gary and Charlene had, early on in their lives, decided to join it, and to dedicate their lives to fulfilling its goals.
Now, Angelina and Michael – when they were old enough - would have to continue their fight for a better universe.

The Dominion-wide unrests – especially in the major giant cities – had persuaded many destitute civilians to join with the pirates, rather than living a hopeless life in the underground gutters and canals, in the deep undergrounds far beneath the ordered structures of the civilized pyramid hives.
And, although the underground gutters still harbored billions of wanderers and people without any livelihood, the pirate movement had gained a lot of followers since then.

Just as Charlene came back from her private thoughts, and tried to focus on her husband in order to start a serious conversation, the first missile from the cloaked pirate attackers struck the command nucleus with a terrible blow.

Alarms went off all around the human transport vessel.

A second pirate missile struck the elongated disc hull of the ship, followed by a third, which penetrated the metal alloy hull, and shoved right into the recreation room, with a deafening roar, and exploded.

Charlene and Gary died in an instant, and didn't feel a thing.

Their struggle would have to be continued by their two – unknowing, and separated – children.

2,465-2,469 CE, the five great nuclear wars of the Human Dominion

The five great nuclear wars of the Human Dominion were the worst nuclear conflicts mankind had ever seen

They spanned across the entire region of Dominion space, although many sparsely populated worlds and systems on the outskirts of the Dominion remained spared from these horrible tragedies.

The first war lasted for five months, the second one took nine months, and together the wars spanned almost the entire period from 2,465 CE to 2,469 CE. From a historical point of view, they would have to be classified as nuclear civil wars, because they were fought between several political groups, and movements, inside Dominion society.

Every time the Dominion tried to establish some kind of stability during those years, it fell back into nuclear chaos.

It all started after completion of the Great Galactic Exodus, with the Dominion worlds establishing direct radio contact, and permanent trade routes, and with the slow but steady formation of one overall conglomerate society in its region.

One central government was created, with most political movements, represented inside.

But soon, the two main political groups stood against each other, and their following in society started to become violent.

One group – on the left – wanted to reestablish lasting contact with the Old Earth, try to revitalize it, restore it to its original health and beauty, and to bring back prosperity to its people.

The other group – from the political right wing – wanted to go back and wage war on the Old Earth, and to conquer and incorporate it into the Dominion as a subordinate province, or sub-sector, under total Dominion control. All they wanted was to subdue the Old Earth, pillage its resources, and make slaves and laborers of its inhabitants, under their own mastery.

Again, politics was divided between the political left and right, and as this problem got worse, and civilians started to hate each other. This polarization finally led to the outbreak of the first nuclear civil war.

The military leadership was completely divided, and so both halves of its officers, soldiers, weapons, and vessels ended up waging war on each other. Many billions lost their lives from the nuclear explosions, the fall-out radiation, and outbursts of disease: a great part of the Dominian people were wiped out.

One of the major lasting effects on the Dominian people was genetic mutation:
Many of them were left crippled, or physically deformed, devoid of their limbs or senses, or with additional body parts that didn't belong there at all.

But the one major and overall genetic mutation inside their genome, which occurred in almost all Dominians (aside from their telepathic abilities) was the ability to survive in space for many hours without any space suit, and without the artificial application of oxygen, or breathable air. Later on, this would be a critical advantage in space combat in the looming galactic war.

5 years and approximately 3 months ago, (standard time), from today

Angelina had been a sparkling young woman of twenty-one (standard) years old when she had been recruited by SI-6.
She had just passed her final exam for a post-graduate course when she received a flash-dat letter. It had come from some civil authorities who had invited her for a talk concerning a serious vacancy.
The flash-dat letter had been accompanied by some jump locations and some private access cyphers.
In accordance with the list, she had jumped into the Cal central Cyportal-nexus structure three days later.

An SI-6 functionary had been expecting her at the nexus. He had addressed her formally, and had invited her to join him to the actual command nucleus, which he had addressed as 'the ministry'.
Angelina's internal profile had been quite clear (apart from the character anomalies): brown-blonde-haired female, early adulthood, reasonably healthy but no physical training, hyper IQ, extremely wide-

and high-level of education, parents unknown; character analysis: trustworthy, extremely motivated, and extremely bright (verbally), and good communicative skills; anomalies: character has indefinable quality, extremely unique personality.

That had been about it.

In her first year at 'SI', Angelina had been trained physically.

But physical training had never had her real interest. She was more a person to read - or maybe even write - a book, in the middle of a quiet night, beside a tiny and inspiring micro-fusion candlelight, with a small cup of ancient Chinese tea.
And she still was such a person: an academic, a scientist, a student, and a reader of ancient paper-printed books.... and probably even a great intellectual writer.
Angelina was convinced that such things might still lie ahead of her, in some distant future....

Sometime later, Angelina and the SI-6 functionary arrived at the central command nucleus.
Once inside it, having passed many suspension lift

floors, she was received by an assistant of Kenzo Shyozama.
The assistant had explained the situation, and had informed her that she had two options: accept the function, or decline. She had two or three days, max, to decide.

If she declined, no one was ever to know that 'these discussions had ever taken place'....

Amazed and intrigued by the offer, Angelina had accepted. Her first year in training had started immediately and it had been hard.
Angelina had never been very active, and she had never really engaged herself in things like training, jogging, or workouts. But during this one single year, she was physically trained and trained hard.

Logically the training and education wasn't limited to physical conditioning. She had learned a great deal about 'operating in the field', including: tactics for concealment, making contacts, handling multiple IDs, gathering information, communicating with the central nucleus and other operatives from a distance of many light years, carrying out missions. She had also learned how to deal with meetings, (de)briefings, mission programs and tactics, and mission reports.

So, aside from real and tangible experience, she now knew everything a beginner operative needed to know, and she had been ready (and eager) to go into the field.

After this one year of heavy training, Angelina was now ready.... for her first real mission.

Chapter 16

CGC systemic integrity compromised by Dominion flash-attacks

The hit-and-run attacks on the CGC by the Dominion attack wings had taken their toll, albeit almost undetectably.

The CGC, and its internal complex of an infinite number of sub-systems, was damaged in a minute way, but it was damaged.

A sub-algorithm of some 1.034 megabytes of

secured code, out of a total of many zillions of gigabytes, was 'mutated' by the Dominion flash-attacks. To be exact, several bits of sub-system: xy-9590.6.5.975, algorithm: (agcal_y_5/gamma), and function:
mng_ag_cl_8_(_y,_zero,c_5,x_753_gamma_4), had been negated. Some zero's had become ones, and some ones, had become zero's.

The damage was less than 0.000000015 percent of its total sub-systems, but the damage was critical. At least, it would become critical in the foreseeable future: the damage occurred slowly but surely.
In this particular instant, there was no measurable or noticeable impact on the behavior, or strategic planning, of the CGC. But, although the CGC itself absolutely didn't realize this, its systems were steadily degrading. The damage to the integrity of its judgment would become exponential in the long run....but not yet.

But the major effect on its strategic planning, and subsequent behavior, was that it would become more and more aggressive.... more hostile towards the Ildiran Empire and any other potential threat. Only a relatively few people really knew that that the CGC was actually a conscious entity.... GACS's advisors, maintenance people, diplomats,

technicians, system programmers, agents and all other GACS assistants were not aware....
Although the CGC couldn't exactly pinpoint the location of the damage, it felt.... it knew, that there was something very wrong.... and that deep inside.... a critical error, had occurred.
If this concealed situation was to continue, GACS, the CGC, and the entire Federation would become completely destabilized.... and war with the Ildirans would become inevitable.

Approximately 1,277 years ago....

The sphere was on its way to Earth, or in other words:

Sol-3

It had detected life there, and it had decided it was time to show itself, although it didn't know the degree of advancement of the local society.
But it would observe when it arrived.
It had already crossed a distance of many hundreds of light years, and it had been on its way for months.
After leaving its galactic orbit, it had laid out an efficient trajectory toward its destination.

Would the local observers understand? No, they would probably not. But the millions-of-years-old preprogrammed sphere had a plan, a mission…. a task.

Its creators - who were now extinct, or had relocated to another universe - had provided it with all the information and programming it needed to fulfill that mission.

The sphere had no sense of time or effort, and it was almost indestructible.

It would carry out its mission, however long it would take, and whatever the amount of energy it, since it drew its endless energy supply from the central super-massive black hole core of the Milky Way galaxy.

Right now, it adjusted its direction, since it had to take in account gravity wells and radiation fields.

Again, it increased its velocity….

It was almost there.

Medieval times….

It is the year of 1,516, the 10th of August. Location: Italy, the beautiful ancient city of Ravenna.

It was early in the evening. Sunlight was still there. The streets of Ravenna were crowded with merchants and beggars, prostitutes and ordinary civilians, magistrates and artists, conjurers, priests, monks, soldiers, and lepers – with the most horrid deformities - and more such people....

They wore medieval cotton robes, cloths, hats, in black and red, yellow and dark purple hues and colors. This was just another crowded evening in this vibrant medieval city. 'Some coins for a blind man!' some beggar shouted. No one heard him, of course; the people walked by, without even noticing him. A procession slowly passed by, carrying the image of a Saint.

Some people cheered and shouted....

The previous night, three people had been burnt alive, under accusation of heresy. They had been tried by a Holy Inquisition court, but had been already sentenced even before the trial had begun. They were Jewish; reason enough for the Vatican-sanctioned court to have found them guilty. Some people from the crowd had encouraged the executioners, but most of them had cried out for mercy for the innocent martyrs.

Even though cheering was allowed, there was no arguing, no power against the Holy Inquisition, and its masters the Vatican. After half an hour of screams and torment, there was not much more left than three almost completely burnt corpses. Some people cried, while others bowed their heads.

The crowd hesitantly left the square, while the sickening odor of burnt flesh remained.

In this day and age, in Germany, the priest and theologian Martin Luther, was fighting against the Roman Catholic Institution, to establish Protestantism, a centuries-long movement against dogmatism and Vatican domination. He actually believed that freedom from God's punishment of sin could not be purchased with money, but was granted freely as an award of true faith. He was an enlightened believer and this would lead to his excommunication by the Pope.

Many years later, the French priest and theologian Jean Cauvin (or Calvin), would continue this struggle, and all those who advocated for and devoted themselves to this new form of Christianity, would contribute to the final and persisting establishment of this new religious direction.

The faith of Protestantism would still exist.... even into the 28th century....

And, with this in mind, it could be that the intelligent alien sphere had consciously or unconsciously chosen this moment to come to the world of:

Sol-3

And, given this, it could be that this was not a coincidence.

11.45 p.m.: the medieval city of Ravenna

Night had fallen over the mystical and medieval city of Ravenna.

Torches in all kinds of places were lighting the city, and creating shimmering places amidst the shadows.

A shining light appeared up in the sky, and almost all eyes in the city, and all around it turned upwards, and towards it, towards this incredible sight.

Some people shouted at each other, and others come running out of their medieval houses, and buildings, and chapels.

The light grew brighter, while all eyes remain fixed

on its approach, and completely mystical hues, contours, and colors.

This bright object was approaching, descending from outer space. It's a concept these people didn't even understand. Was this a sign from God, they asked themselves? This was more than just a falling star....

The 'divine' object became more or less visible. It appeared to be round: spherical....

The alien-uridium sphere slowed its descent until it was clearly visible: its contours, and shape, and textures all the while continuing to spin around its vertical axis, with varying spin velocities....

It coldly observed the world beneath, on this planetary surface, many miles beneath its own hovering body.

It appeared that some kind of pre-technological society has developed over the many thousands of years since the intelligent sphere had last visited this alien world. There was no sign at all of nuclear fusion energy being produced, or radiation from reconnaissance systems, or any other signs of technological development. There was no reason for the intelligent sphere to stay or to directly communicate with these pre-technology, pre-scientific humanoids. The sphere slowly redirected its suspension propulsion, and then ascended back again into the coldness of space. It had decided that almost certainly there will be an advanced civilization on this medium-sized water world within several hundred years. The sphere will return a thousand years from now, when this pre-technological civilization is much more advanced, and then, the time will finally be right to enter into direct communication with the humanoids there....

This mysterious event would be described, documented and 'explained' by Franciscan monks, Jesuits, Arabian astrologers, and Chinese Buddhist monks, since it had been visible from many countries, and since the alien sphere had made several different entries into the Old Earth atmosphere, from different angles, from out of space. But the event would be described by ways of mysticism and superstition, since these medieval souls had no idea of the real purpose, or function, of this alien artifact. They tried to fabricate all kinds of religious and mystical explanations, but to them it would always remain a mystery....

After returning from Jovi, flying the private c-plus cloaking vessel, called Janis, Angelina had arrived back at the SI nucleus, and had headed straight for Kenzo Shyozama's office. He had called her in immediately for a long and hard discussion, to set things straight.

She felt quite weary after the exhilarating c-plus flight, and the shocking discovery of her own Dominion ancestry. The flight itself had been beautiful and tranquil, as always, but Angelina wondered what the implications of her newly discovered identity would be.

She beeped, at the entrance to Kenzo Shyozama's office chamber, and the iris slid open softly, revealing its inner chamber.

She and Kenzo saluted, in accordance with common SI-6 protocol. Then they shook each other's hands firmly, and Kenzo invited her to sit down in front of his cluttered desk, where stacks of reports, memos, and other kinds of records and files, lay on its black surface.

'You shouldn't have gone over there without consulting me first' Kenzo said firmly, giving Angelina a hard glance.

She realized it had been absolutely wrong, and extremely dangerous, just to fly into Dominion

308

space, where no one – no ordinary Federation civilian, that is - had ventured for about three hundred years, without any precautions, consultation, advice, or protection.

Even after five years under his command, she still felt like a fifteen-year old girl caught in the act of doing some kind of mischief when Kenzo reprimanded her. 'I know it was wrong,' she said. 'I should have consulted you first.'

Angelina looked up at him, and looked him in the eye.
She was sitting in front of his desk, while Kenzo paced back and forth across the office floor. He returned her gaze, and stared at her. I have never known what really goes on behind those dark Japanese eyes.... she thinks.
'You could have been killed, or captured. Interrogated even!' he said, with a harsh sounding voice. 'They probably have all kinds of torturing, and interrogation devices, and chemicals. As you know, we use them regularly on anti-CGC informants.'
Kenzo sighed, straightened, and looked Angelina in the eye again.

'I have not yet informed the board about all of this,' continued Kenzo, 'because I'm not entirely sure what implications all this information will have for the future of the Federation, and for you, personally. I want you to take a deep analysis gen-test. You will then take the results back to Jovi, and submit them to the pre-Exodus archive, in the form of a data-sheet, since I understand this archive system is quite ancient. We will discuss the outcomes of the archive analysis when you return, and take it from there.... '

'I've got a direct com-sys connection', Angelina responded.

Kenzo stood still, and looked at her. Finally he said, 'Alright, then. Take the gen-test, and connect to the archive. Get back to me with the outcome.'

He had obviously finished the discussion, and while Angelina kept observing him quietly, Kenzo turned his gaze outward, through the tiny window in the office wall, and his mind drifted away towards the multitude of stars, visible outside, in the depths of space....

The SI nucleus genetic lab was on the 5th floor.

Angelina had taken the main suspension lift, and now she walked along one of the many long and silent hallways, until she reached the iris to the lab.

To the left of the iris was a tiny photonic holo display, depicting the name and function of the lab, as well as a small list of co-workers, and some other pieces of information. She had visited the lab once before, in her first year at SI-6, when she had been ordered to have her genetics tested for physical anomalies. But this time it was serious. The analysis of the results by the Human Dominion archive could potentially reveal all kinds of unpleasant facts about her ancestry, and these could cause all kinds of terrible implications in her relation to SI-6, and in relation to her place in the Human Federation; the place where she had spent all her life, and which she had sworn to protect as an SI-6 functionary, and as an agent of the interstellar GACS government.

While Angelina was contemplating all these quintessential personal issues, the lab's iris slid open quietly, and a nice looking young woman in a yellow opti-fiber lab suit, apparently a lab assistant, politely invited Angelina in. Carefully, she entered the relatively small lab complex....

The assistant was very quiet and attentive, and the actual gen-test had only taken about twenty minutes, including the production of immediate outcomes and analyses, as well as a portable data-sheet for the Dominion Archive analysis. The assistant had been extremely surprised by the first analyses, although it had been almost unnoticeable. Her test subject seemed to harbor extremely unique and deviating aspects in her genome; almost inhuman.

And, although this worried the assistant, she tried not to show it, or worry her current subject. Drawing conclusions on this was something for doctors and specialists, not mere lab assistants. When the process was complete, she politely handed Angelina the final data-sheet, and bid her farewell. But, just before Angelina had left the tiny lab complex, she had quickly changed her mind, and called Angelina back in. Angelina, obviously surprised, had followed her back in towards a private consultation room, to the left of the narrow central lab corridor.

The assistant had taken a quick look at the data-sheet, and had told Angelina that, although there were no immediate and final conclusions, she had a very unique and anomalous genome. Angelina had been shocked, and the archive's account of her ancestry came back to her mind. Again, the assistant had bid her farewell, and Angelina had left the tiny sub-complex, inside the gigantic SI nucleus, in a brooding mood. Although she was a well-trained covert agent of SI-6, in her mind, the tension about the current events, possible disastrous outcomes from the Archive gen-analysis, and the crucial fact that she and Kenzo had silently chosen to break their oaths of professional obedience, service, and dedication to VOG.8, was growing to an unbearable level. After connecting with the Dominion Archive, she would have to deliberate the situation, immediately, with her teacher and commander:

Kenzo Shyozama.

Chapter 17

Angelina descends from Russian composer P.I. Tchaikovsky

Purpose of the alien sphere, by the super-multiversal guiding entity: Shi'rah

Mysterious alien spheres don't come by the dozen... at least not like this one.

It was created more than a million years ago by the ancient Trellians, my forefathers, who fled from this universe after being defeated and decimated by the malevolent Ixians.

It was their purpose to inject all of their history, and all of their knowledge of science and technology, into this almost indestructible object.

This object was intelligent and autonomous as well: that was an absolute requirement.

Its functionally humanoid brain consisted of a cluster of multiple parallel-switched Trellian AI units, connected to an array of multi-billion megabyte storage servers. It had semi-intelligent x-s-controllers, and it was able to retrieve entire synaptic memory structures in a matter of Pico-seconds.

Using this incredible intelligence, it would have to stay behind in this universe and observe upcoming civilizations in the Spiral Arm and the galaxy; waiting and observing until it had found the one single person in this civilization that would be ready to receive this gift of immeasurable historical, scientific, and technological knowledge.

And aside from this pure knowledge, it contained one single piece of technology that was crucial to the purpose of the Trellians:

The Ix device

A device which made it possible to travel or move –

in a matter of Pico-seconds – from this universe (Unhiah), to the next one called:

Nexhiah

Our multiverse consisted of hyper-complex strings of universes – like hyper-massive intertwined DNA-molecules – and the next universe in our string, and closest to ours, was Nexhiah.

And this Ix device may never fall into Ixian hands.

The Ixians had stayed behind in our universe because they had failed in duplicating the Ix device, although their intelligence had suggested that the Trellians had succeeded in creating it. Ixian scientific and technological hurdles had spared the Trellians from being pursued when they had decided to flee from the Ixians to Nexhiah, after losing a devastating war with them.
Although Trellian science was much more advanced, the Ixians had a massive civilization, and Trellian civilization only counted some ten million people. Trellian military troops equaled just one-hundredth of the Ixian forces, and this war was decided quickly.
When the remaining Trellian survivors had left our universe, Unhiah, the Ixian government decided to

move to another close galaxy, inside the Virgo cluster, to find new resources and new – pristine - worlds.

This was the stellar stream of Virgo Overdensity, at a distance of some 30,000 light years from our local regions of the Spiral Arm.

And although thousands of light years away.... the Ixians were still here.

Once we – the Trellians – had settled ourselves inside Nexhiah, we finally succeeded in establishing permanent contact with our own sphere, and it had become our prime observer in our forsaken local galaxy.

When, finally, a million years later, Angelina Tchaikovsky had come to our attention, we decided to instruct the sphere to reveal itself to her.

She would have to unite the Dominion, the Federation, and the Ildiran Empire into one colossal unity of power, and side with the Trellians against the cruel and malevolent Ixian civilization, before they succeeded in building something similar to the Ix device, when it would be too late...

I found myself dreaming again....

Dreaming violently....

It was not that I was rolling over, in my bed, or throwing my arms in all kinds of directions, or that I was yelling out loud, without really hearing it. It was just a dream – not a nightmare – with violent emotions and intense subjects.
And it was not specifically an erotic or sexual dream, although those elements were always present in all of my dreams, as well as in all of my waking moments.
All the recent events, and all the straining developments, rotated around my sleeping mind, and around my dreamscape.

It was not just those events, and those recent developments, but it was also the usual physical and metaphysical shapes and concepts taking shape and dissolving again in the wide landscape of my dreaming mind.
Some of these things were already clear to me, like the fundamental realization that everything in the universe is in essence sinusoid, or spherical, since a circle, or a sphere, or a multi-dimensional hyper-sphere, is – in essence – sinusoid.

The focus of the dream, in my free associating mind, shifted again, in the distant direction of more tangible subjects.

Angelina activated her com-sys.

It had remained on stand-by for several hours.

The device beeped, lit up several holo displays with loads of tiny symbols and figures, and waited for her input.
Com-systems came in many shapes, forms, and sizes, and from many different manufacturers, with various configurations. There were expensive models bought on black markets, extravagant ones especially for women that could be purchased in massive in-system mall-stations, and tiny ones with easy access for children, such as the Simulcra-5-5, that could be found in almost every home.
They were very much comparable to 20th century PCs: every possible and thinkable program, or application, could be downloaded, installed, and used.... and you could even program them yourself, if you possessed the necessary skills in com-sys program development.
(Of course, Angelina had high-level abilities in this field. System programming had been a required section at MIC-T for her degree in theoretical

physics.)

The com-sys Angelina carried was a high-level government issue: Multi-Core-8.

It featured many super-high-tech capabilities, such as: flash-dat and flash-video communication over distances of over six hundred and fifty light years; integrated photonic holo multi-display; a built-in basic AI personality; and data storage of over 65 billion terabytes of many different kinds of data (recorded holograms, made flash-video communications, profiles of billions of people, and much more).

Angelina looked down at the brightly lit com-sys in her hands, and carefully studied the displays.

It was one of the most expensive units money could buy, but the device beeped erratically, and sounded with eerie static. It obviously had a very hard time connecting to the ancient archive system, located many light years away inside the distant Dominion. She waited for a minute, carefully listening to the eerie sounds from the depths of sub-Planck–level interstellar space as the device connected.

'Welcome back, Miss Tchaikovsky', the ancient archive stated, with a friendly artificial voice, 'What has kept you so long?'

The system waited for a few moments, and

continued.

'I am an old Dominion system, stacked away in some old and dusty chamber, and I'm barely ever made use of. I've been making calculations, you know, for the past several weeks, about the chances for the Dominion if a war breaks out with the Federation. Of course, it would be a big help if the Ildirans would assist us in trying to defeat my – let's say – counterpart, that they refer to as GACS. Did you know Dominians can survive in space for many hours? It's because of the genetic mutations caused by the radiation of the Great Nuclear Wars. This could really be our deciding advantage, in the probably impending Interstellar War.'

Angelina cut the system off, 'Mother, please. I did not connect to you to make light conversation. There are serious issues at hand, which also greatly concern the Dominion, and its future. Besides, there are probably millions of other 'Mothers' inside the Dominion. I have serious issues. Please tell me about my ancestry.'

'Of course, excuse me Miss Tchaikovsky', the archive responded, 'Please explain to me why you have connected.'

'I have a datasheet from my employer,' Angelina said. 'It contains the results of a gen-test.'

'Your employer must be SI-5, or SI-6?' the Archive responded.

'SI-6,' she said. 'How could you possibly know?'

'I have access to loads of Dominion intelligence databases and resources, as you will understand. Could you upload the datasheet for me, please?'

'Just a moment....' Angelina responded.

She took the datasheet from her coat pocket, and ordered her com-sys to make a scan and send the information. The com-sys acknowledged the request, and as it sent through all the genetic information Angelina could hear the static and the noise rushing through the sub-Planck connection with an eerie sound.

'Alright,' the archive said. 'Just give me a few moments'. The archive system waited again. It seemed to be retrieving old data, and checking arcane databases.

'Alright.' the old system said. 'As your name seems to indicate, as well as genetic line information in my recently updated files, you seem to be a direct descendant of the great 19th century Russian composer: Pyotr Ilyitch Tchaikovsky.'

Angelina waited for a moment.

'That's quite an honor', she finally said. 'And it seems quite logical. Have you got more.... further back maybe?'

'Let me think,' the system responded. It seemed to have changed its tone of voice. It somehow sounded a bit far away and scary.

The connection fell silent immediately.

Angelina felt something…. as if a thousand fires, were burning inside her memories. She tried to concentrate on the eerie static rushing loudly through the sub-Planck connection.

The archive waited, as the tension grew unbearable, and then something came out which seemed completely impossible.

The system started to speak again, carefully stating data it had retrieved, from numerous and massive servers located many light years away from the place where Angelina found herself at this very moment:

'According to genetic information from scientific, historical, and archaeological databases compiled during the last three centuries, you are a direct descendant of the apostle John. He was the writer of the last passage of the New Testament of the ancient Christian Bible: the Apocalypse.'

The system fell silent again.

Angelina had always regarded Christianity as an obsolete and arcane faith.

With regard to history and religion, she preferred things like medieval Scandinavian myths. But the mere thought that the apostle John had actually lived, and had really written the Book of Revelation, was almost unthinkable. And the very thought that she directly descended from him – even carried his very genes – seemed practically impossible and unthinkable.

Angelina fell silent, and tried to recompose herself, but failed miserably.

She felt something happening in the depths of her soul, a whirlwind taking over her very genes.

Suddenly, she felt a heat building up inside, and her vision became blurred by an adobe whirlwind in front of her.

She gazed, silent, amidst the red storm.

Many minutes passed....

Finally, she realized what kind of future lay in front of her:

She would have to become a messianic leader of the movement they now called Humanity's Destiny, and it would then be called Shining Light. This would be a new movement inspired by the Illuminati and with one single divine goal: to depose GACS, and restore dominion to humanity itself: A humanity at peace with the empire of Ildira and the Disappeared, and completely free from AI domination....

After this incredible event, Angelina had tried to rest and think things over. And somewhat later, she had informed Kenzo of what had occurred through her com-sys connection. Of course, he felt completely shocked and amazed all at the same time. At this moment, he was unable to oversee all the consequences.

They had finally agreed to let the result of this event rest for a while.

This incredible issue would have to wait....

When the time came, it would become a major thing, a core issue inside all the terrible things happening around them.

The internal process inside a Cyportal – or rather, between two different Cyportals – is much like Erwin Schrödinger's thought experiment of a cat in a sealed box, which is both alive and dead at the same time in our universe, from our point of perception that is....

(Erwin Schrödinger was a prominent 20th century physicist, and one of the founding fathers of the weird science of quantum physics.)

The 'Cyportal traveler' is injected into the sub-quantum-physical realities by the entry portal, and remains sealed in those realities, shielded from observation or detection, by those who find themselves, in the 'real universe'.

Cyportals are beautiful syntheses of scientific and technological mastery, and it took mankind millions of years to finally accomplish these incredible feats of theoretical physics, research, and manufacturing. But, Trellian science was even more advanced. They harnessed the capabilities to jump not just from one place to another but actually to a completely other universe. The Ixti-fusion energies required for one such a 'jump' was a million times greater than for Cyportals. However, the amount of Ixti to be found and harvested on the surfaces of dying stars was very sparse and dwindling further.

Some of the Disappeared (the popular 'Fed' term for the Dominians) had been mutated horribly by the five terrible nuclear wars of 2,465-2,469 CE.

Their genes had been altered and mutated by the singeing heat from the nuclear radiation. But these mutants were a relatively small minority of the total population. Just like the inhabitants of the Federation, and the inhabitants of the Ildiran Empire, the Disappeared had done a great amount of research in the field of genetic manipulation over the centuries over the centuries, and had made considerable progress ....much more progress than the Federation, in fact. By governmental mandate, they had altered the genes of the entire population, with specific useful enhancements and adaptations.

The Disappeared could survive in the coldness of space without a spacesuit or other protection for many hours.
This feature could only be physically distinguished, by the shiny and plastic-like quality, of their skin, although the regular spectrum of all different racial complexions was normally represented in their total population. The eyes of some of the mutants were able to register all bandwidths of the entire spectrum of photonic light. Although the Ildirans, with their 10,000 years of recorded history, were much farther ahead, in all imaginable fields of science, the Dominionists - a sociological term for the Disappeared - had accomplished one superior scientific feat; namely, they had been able to manipulate the originally human genome in such a way that those who had been subjected to this alteration were able to communicate without

words.... telepathically....

They could even read one another's minds, even of others who didn't have this ability, if those others were within a radius of several meters away. Only they were able to shield their thoughts from others with the same ability, and that was the only failsafe from psychological intrusion which kept their society of telepaths stable.

The Ildiran versions of Cyportals were based on the same physics, the same technology, and the same resource as the human ones.
With the Dominion included, Ixti constituted the lifeblood of three gigantic civilizations, spanning hundreds of light years in all directions, with many thousands of billions of souls inside of them.

All these tiny souls, inside all those endless vacuums of space with only a very few small inhabited worlds, depended on that rare but very special element for their transportation, communication, and more such things.
For it was not just individual Cyportal jumps that counted on the availability of Ixti, but flash-dat communication links and the transportation of goods as well. Commerce, media, com-system links, and social movability all depended on very tiny amounts

of that very special resource.

It was a good thing that Cyportal-technologies only needed a fraction of it to function for days. Only massive transports required costly and heavy amounts to keep going. And many mass transports were done the 'non-Cyportal way': using regular freighter juggernauts.

But if the transports were absolutely needed instantly or at least in a very short time, Ixti-fuelled Cyportals were the only way to accomplish it. Civilizations consisting of thousands of billions of souls needed astronomical amounts of goods and transportations…. a million times more than the one-planet Old Earth civilization had needed, before the existence of thriving colonized worlds outside the solar system of Sol-3.

The substance of Ixti could only be found inside the coronas of a very few specific stars, and extracting it from these super-hot celestial bodies was a dangerous, costly, and difficult process.

The Ildirans, who had used Cyportals and Ixti for many centuries, had found extremely ingenious ways to come by enough quantities of it to keep their civilization going. Ildiran Ixti-extractors used the most advanced techniques to optimize Ixti-extraction.

But if an interstellar war were to break out with the Ildirans, the military demand for Ixti would skyrocket, and the availability would be seriously harmed if the harvesting installations were damaged or destroyed by military incursions.

Human civilization would be crippled economically, and in other aspects, but for the Ildirans.... it would be exactly the same.

Daryl Aronovsky was the current president of the Human Dominion.

He had presided over the Dominion government for about four years, and he still had another four years in office.

He seemed to be a man in his late forties, but this was only a matter of appearance. In reality he was over ninety, but he had undergone a very expensive age-gen treatment when he was about fifty years old.
Age-gen treatments came in many forms, and with many different price tags. The one Daryl had received was costly but safe.

Age-gen therapy was common in the 28th century, but some couldn't afford it, and others resorted to black-market fixes, with many, and great, health risks.

Like most Dominians, Daryl was originally from Russian descent, and vodka still constituted his lifeblood during long evenings, and in the late hours.

It was about 8.45 p.m., system time, and he had just retired from a long and tiring meeting with his advisors and some senior members of his government, while being assisted by his PAs, and his senior aide and trusted friend, Katharina Gagarin.
Katharina was still quite young for Dominion standards, some 37 years old, but Daryl suspected she could become a great politician, and a possible successor, ten or twenty years down the line.
She was very attractive, and they had had a professional relationship for quite a few years. Sometimes they would find each other between working hours and meetings, and they would have long and passionate sex in the bathroom of Daryl's office.

It had been obvious for quite a long time that an interstellar war with the Federation was most probably unavoidable, and this had been the main subject of endless meetings and deliberations for many months.

But the other main issue tonight, and during recent days, had been the recent failed flash-attack on the Federation CGC.

Daryl belonged to the 'left wing' of Dominion government, and he had had a very hard time since the first days of his presidency to keep the government stable, and to keep the 'right wing' at bay.

This political division between right and left had been present even before the Great Civil (nuclear) Wars, and had actually triggered them. Since then, Dominion presidents had had a very hard time reconciling those two sides.

But the divisions were deep and persistent, and something would have to change in the future, or there would be no future for the Dominion, aside from another lasting civil war.

Tonight, however, the issue at hand was the failed CGC attack, and Daryl tried to focus his thoughts on this while sipping on his ancient Sol-3 vodka. Failure of the latest human-piloted attack had obviously been a matter of human error, but this indicated there were serious issues with discipline and functioning of the Dominion military.

This was an underlying problem.

Some military leaders present at the meeting feared a war with the Federation could break out in a matter of weeks, while some senators and high-profile analysts were of the opinion this situation could still be years away.

Daryl had his own views on this, but he suspected those military leaders could be very close to the actual truth, and that would mean a long and painful interstellar war could be the real world situation in the near future.

Of course, VOG.8 knew everything.

Vishnu Onexa Goshira.8 had been informed of the official existence of the Disappeared, or the Human Dominion, and it had learned the space-time coordinates of its region.

It seemed the information originated from the com-sys of an intelligence operative of SI-5 or -6. But it was unclear why the operative in question didn't officially report this through standard debriefing and mission updates.

This would have to be investigated a bit later.

At this moment, however, the very existence of the Dominion was paramount, and VOG.8 had to think about the consequences of this.
Since the latest surprise flash-attack, on itself, it had felt something strange going on deep inside its sub-systems, deep inside its soul. But as it seemed, it was no more than a temporary itch.... probably an organic subroutine which had to regenerate itself, although the itch had gotten slightly worse over the last couple of days.

But, the matter at hand was the Human Dominion, and VOG.8 tried to disconnect itself from less important issues, and tried to focus on this simple fact and all of its implications.
Finally, the Dominion officially existed, and its regions were defined.
This would obviously mean war, although there was still a lot more to find out. VOG.8 would send spies and agents to improve its knowledge on the situation.

It would have to find out how strong the Dominion military was, its defenses, its technological advancements, its political state, and, above all else, its intentions.

The Ildiran race originated from the world of Ildion Prime.... a world similar much like the Old Earth, Sol-3, but with many differences nonetheless.

Life on Ildion Prime was carbon based, just as on Sol-3, but it had fewer seas and oceans, and less water. Furthermore, lower life forms on Ildion were much more weird and exotic than on the Old Earth.

From the onset, even before having established some kind of civilization, the Ildirans had been telepathic, and this had made it easier to communicate in a complex and logical way. Thus the Ildirans had been able to establish a logical form of communication much faster than the human race had.

Over the course of history, they had formed religions and ways of philosophical thinking, and they had developed science and technology. They had also made many crucial inventions, from the use of fire and weapons, to printed language, and the invention of computers, nuclear missiles, and more.

Their religions had developed from observing and

interpreting the skies and the stars to mythology and mysticism, and finally to one single global religion for all Ildirans called Vishny, a complex philosophical theory about life in this universe and beyond.

Their physics had – just as on Earth – developed from absolutist mechanics to quantum physics and relativistic principles, and finally to some sort of sub-Planck quantum-string physics.

Humanity had gone through all this in thousands of years, and the

Ildirans had needed hundreds of thousands of years, although even before the invention of age-gen correction the average Ildiran person already lived for about four hundred years.

The Ildirans had had internal wars, and military strife, but much less than the human race had, and the one main thing left to say about the Ildirans, was that they were much more peaceful, compassionate, and humane than the human race was itself.

Rigel system, 12:45 a.m., global system time

The alien sphere was not helpless.

Its makers had bestowed it with offensive as well as defensive systems, although these were only to be used in extreme situations when there was no other option at all, and when things went really bad.

It had only used these options on a few very rare occasions, and it preferred to rely on its intelligence and its ultra-long-range tracking and reconnaissance systems.

The thing nobody knew, or suspected, was the alien sphere actually possessed consciousness, emotions, and feelings, and right now it felt absolutely alone and insecure.

Our universe is entirely permeated by the universal soul, and this simple fact implies that all intelligent systems capable of independent thinking have this consciousness and this ability to feel these emotions, along with their thoughts.

Right now, the eternally lonely sphere was in a giant orbit around the sun of Rigel, processing data from observations while thinking about itself.

On activation of its AI core, and all of its systems, it had wondered about the feeling of being conscious and new.

And then, later on, it had studied all the information in its data-cores about the Trellians, the Ixians, and more such things.

It realized it had been created by its makers, its

master the Trellians, and for some reason they had ended up in a losing war with the Ixians, and had been decimated.

The few Trellians remaining few had then decided to leave this universe and leave it - the uridium sphere – behind.

It obviously had an extremely important and crucial role to play in this history of war between races, but for now the cloistered alien sphere would stay safe.

Some forty years earlier, it had marveled at the discovery of some mysterious cave inside the southern mountain ranges of Rigel Octi, a large rocky and desert planet on the outskirts of Rigel system, and the eighth planet from its sun.

Weird and strong radiation, as well as abnormally high ozone levels, had attracted its attention from outer space, and it had immediately felt there was something strange about this location.

On closer inspection, the cave had appeared to be massive, with an immense opening on its front side, and a depth of some eighty yards.

At the end there was a great solid wall, somberly

colored like sandstone, but tougher than granite, probably constituted from a substance not to be found elsewhere in the Spiral Arm.

It had occurred to the alien sphere that this was obviously not a naturally formed cave, and all its walls and sides were perfectly straight, although there were some visible structures a little geometrical in shape.

Apart from these straight lines and surfaces, the cave was perfectly rectangular.

But the inner wall at the end was the most intriguing.

Radiation shimmered across its surface with a reddish glow, and the sounds from the whirling sands gave it an eerie feeling.

It was covered with mysterious paintings and complex visual structures, and entire lines and rows with complex and detailed symbolic structures like ancient Egyptian hieroglyphs, but larger and much more complex and detailed.

These were quite probably ancient.... and alien.

To the alien sphere, this seemed to be the most obvious and logical explanation, and when it had made a run through its databases, it had occurred to the alien sphere that these hieroglyphs resembled Ixian ones, although it did not have the means to decipher them.

On further and closer inspection, there was one remaining aspect of the inner wall at its center. At exactly one yard from the ground surface, there was a perfectly round indentation in the rocky surface, and right in the middle – with almost mathematic precision – there was a small display.

It didn't have a keypad or other input methods, it was just a square display with nothing else, and it seemed to be offline.

There were no indications the alien sphere would be able to accomplish anything in this situation. It was designed to find, observe and to pass on knowledge, not to find out the workings of alien displays inside mysterious caves.

The best thing it could do at this moment was to exactly remember this location, and these coordinates, and when it had found the one single person it had been searching for, for thousands of years, this person would probably know, or find out, what to do with this cave, and what its purpose really was.

Although Rigel-4 was densely populated, and it had a fairly large inter-systemic Cyportal nexus in its orbit, the cave on Rigel Octi had remained undetected to humans and Rigel system residents. After all, Rigel-4 was the only inhabited place in this system, aside from a few mining facilities and other such places.

The purpose of this cave, and even its very existence, remained unknown, and the only one who *did* know, the alien sphere, was at this time not able to do anything with it at all.

2,210 CE: first event of conscious, feeling, and emotional AI/droid-system

AD-1, or autonomous droid one, or Eddy – as its creators called it - didn't understand at all.

It was a quite simple-minded robot, and it didn't understand much of the motivations of real people. It had been created as the first ever robot, or droid, with the ability of completely independent thinking, and that was a thing it more or less understood. But its makers didn't understand its feelings…. they were completely amazed at its behavior and its responses.

Why, if they purposely created it this way, would they be so ignorant about its motivations and its responses?

To Eddy, this was a complete mystery, and it would talk with its creators – humans – for hours and hours on end about this subject, and everything related to it.

Its creators had come to the conclusion that all historical theories about consciousness, emotions, and spiritedness would have to be rewritten, and the creation of an evidently feeling and conscious AI system constituted a huge milestone in the history of science and invention.

That Eddy possessed emotions and consciousness was clear, but it was impossible to physically prove or disprove this was actually the case.

Since its creation, and actual activation of its systems, Eddy kept wondering and marveling at the fact of its own existence, and it kept on being surprised about and interested in its makers, the humans.

The scientific community was intrigued, and astounded. All around Sol-3 there were endless debates, Internet blogs (at least: 23rd century Internet), video conferences, and every such thing imaginable about this AD-1, or Eddy, as its popular name also was, and about its consciousness. Countless movies and documentaries were made for the general public.... This was absolutely world news.

It was even bigger news, and more shocking, than the first manned landing on the moon.

This was obviously the first ever occurrence of an AI/droid-system expressing real emotions, although it wasn't purposely created to do so.
It apparently was a side effect of its ability of independent thinking, and 94% of all tests, interviews, and analyses demonstrated this.

Eddy itself felt as if it was the most famous droid in history.... and it was an amazing feeling.

Russell, sipping from his cheap whiskey, was thinking things over. Deep inside, he somehow felt the war was only days away.

Even to a trained and experienced underground Destiny operative, and leader, it was a chilling emotion.
VOG.8 was now officially aware of the existence of the Dominion, and its actual space-time boundary coordinates.
Through secured underground channels, the Ildiran government institutions, and thus its emperor, had

been officially informed by the Human Dominion, and had been offered an alliance against GACS, the CGC, and the Federation government and military.

The Ildiran government had – although through unofficial and secured channels – accepted.
The great alliance was now, unofficially, reality.
Hundreds of thousands of Destiny soldiers and field agents had been equipped with assault rifles, laser guns, particle weapons, and more, and during the last months had been heavily trained to undermine, destabilize, and take on Federation forces in any way they could.

Destiny's command council, of which Russell was an official member, had convened for hours, from about 8:00 p.m. until almost 1:00 a.m.

But Russell, with his many years of experience and training, didn't feel tired at all. He was completely focused on the coming war, and completely focused on their sworn duty to overthrow GACS, to destroy the CGC complex, and to return the Federation into human hands.

Meanwhile, inside the Dominion, Trilian command had ordered the entire Dominion military apparatus to be put onto the highest possible state of alert.

The Dominion, the Ildiran Empire, and Humanity's Destiny were all ready to take up arms.

Chapter 18

Angelina tries to find her brother: Michael Tchaikovsky

Jack Chanovsky's tactical holo-sims displayed fourteen attack fighters, closing in on the CGC complex.

He had been retrying this for many hours, each time changing the positions, configurations, and numbers of attack vessels.
He was a big and muscular guy, used to doing what he wanted, but this was work and he had been a

loyal and tractable soldier for almost thirty years. He always did what he was ordered to do by his superiors, and he always prepared himself for the missions at hand.

He found himself alone in front of the photonic holo projector inside the tactical database sim-room. He was completely alone and focused on the multiple holo displays.

Trying to do serious damage to a thing or complex such as the CGC was not a piece of cake. Through these endless simulations, he tried to find out what the best attack orders and configurations would be like, with the best results, and optimal damage to its structure.

Again.... this was not easy at all.

The night before he had been summoned by Daryl Aronovsky, the president of the Dominion, and had been assigned total responsibility for the CGC assaults for the entire war, until orders would be changed, or adapted.

The encounter had taken place inside Aronovsky's private quarters, deep inside the Dominion government complex, which consisted of multiple large sleeping rooms and an extremely large living room with couches, computers, photonic holo screens, communication- and vid-conferencing instruments, a bar with many Old Earth alcoholic drinks, and more.

It also contained a study, and a classy library with thousands of historical Old Earth books, many of which were original prints.

The government complex itself spanned across a seven mile diameter, with a large domed structure in the middle, and seven great wings or corridors stretching outward.

All around the government complex lay Dinia city, with its many ministries, skyscrapers, mall towers, and hotels, stretching outwards, and outwards towards the low rise houses, small buildings, and fields, on the outskirts....

Jack had already known Aronovsky since military academy, and in spite of their current difference in status, they were still old friends.

The official conversation had been short, and clear, and afterwards Aronovsky had opened up a bottle of Disaronno Originale, his favorite alcoholic drink, and they had reminisced about their shared times at the TCC academy, when they still were quite young.

But that had been about it, and for now Jack focused on his job at hand, and retried another risky configuration.

Longing for a brother, sister, father, or mother who you have never known is an intense emotion.

All Angelina had to do was to connect with 'Mother' on Jovi and ask for the whereabouts, or contact info, of her unknown brother Michael.
But, somehow, she didn't have the guts to do so.
Of course, this was not much of a surprise, since she had always been alone, and the memory of her orphanage at Ti Shoan was still clear in her mind.

With regard to actually having family, she had always been alone, and she knew nothing else.
However, people like Kenzo had sort of adopted her as a real family member; at least it felt like having family.
She vaguely remembered having had a boyfriend at the orphanage, when she was only fourteen years old, but it had only lasted for about a year, and she didn't even remember the boy's name.
After a few moments of intense hesitation, she took her com-sys out of stand-by and made the connection to 'Mother'.

'Well, Miss Tchaikovsky,' the system opened the conversation, 'you have been away for several days…. What brings you, to my humble automated person?'

Angelina waited for several seconds, trying to focus on the present.

'Hi, Mother,' she responded, 'nice to speak to you again…. last time you told me about my brother…. you said according to your databases, he's still alive?'

'Yes, Miss Tchaikovsky. If my systems are correct, he still is.'

It appeared to her that the system's tone of voice, and use of words, had changed somewhat. 'You seem changed somehow, Mother…' she said.

'Yes, Miss Tchaikovsky, you are correct. I change my personality parameters from time to time. It keeps me focused, although I have tens of thousands, of such parameters. I'm not a four-byte system, and changing these things, is a tricky business.'

Angelina hoped the system wouldn't get agitated or unhelpful. 'Could you give me the location, connection info, and current surname of Michael?' she asked.

Mother waited for a few seconds. It was probably

checking some deep databases.

'According to my most recent updates, he resides in the main city on Rigel-4, Richmond, in a decent apartment complex, 24th floor.... He is unmarried, a high-profile computer programmer, and seems to know he has a sister, although he does not have info on your name or whereabouts....'

Angelina waited again.

'Could you upload those pieces of info for me, please....?' she said.

'Of course, Miss Tchaikovsky.... Do you need any further information?' The system, designated as Mother, seemed to understand this was probably sufficient.

'No thanks Mother,' said Angelina. 'I think I have all the information I need. Goodbye.'

Mother ended the conversation, 'Goodbye, Miss Tchaikovsky. I hope we'll speak to each other again.'

'Hello, there. Who is this?' Michael Goodcol said.

He didn't expect any callers at this time of night, and he didn't have many personal contacts anyway. Michael resembled his sister Angelina. He had the same facial features and attractive hair color. He also possessed with a strong muscular body.

Michael had been working on a semi-AI program for hours, typing commands and instructions, retyping, testing, and then retyping and testing again.
His late working hours at home were paid by his employer, and this employer was actually the CGC, or to be more precise, GACS.
Nobody needed to know who his employer was except Michael himself.
His job was absolutely confidential.

At this time, he was reorganizing a visual-ai-sys-8 organic sub-algorithm, inside the GACS super-system, through a direct and secured inside flash-dat connection. This was not exactly a job for junior programmers.
Although his black caramel coffee was already cold, as it had been sitting there for 40 minutes, he took a sip, and sighed.

'Michael?' Angelina repeated. She was afraid he would terminate the connection.
'Who is this?' Michael repeated.
'It's your sister, Angelina.... '
Angelina was on the verge of crying.
All the memory images of her youth at Ti Shoan, her

years at MIC-T, her training at SI-6, everything flashed by in front of her mind's eye, one image at a time, in a matter of seconds.

'Michael, it's your lost sister, Angelina. I've finally found you.... '

'My lost sister....?' Michael took a deep breath. He didn't know what to feel, or think. 'Would you like to see me?' Angelina said hopefully. 'I will tell you everything, about me, about our parents, my job, about our current situation in the Federation.... '

Michael considered this for a brief moment.

And finally he replied, 'Angelina, if you really are my lost sister.... I would really like to see you, and have you tell me everything'

And so, Angelina and Michael got together.

She visited him at his home on Rigel-4, in the main city of Richmond, in his very decent apartment on the 24th floor.

It took one jump to the nearest inter-system Cyportal, then a jump from there to the Rigel inter-system Cyportal, and then straight to Rigel-4. When she had arrived in the city of Richmond, it only took a ten-minute anti-grav cab ride, and a short walk of several minutes. When she arrived at the exact apartment complex location, she took the a-g elevator to the 24th floor.

Angelina told Michael almost everything she knew about them personally, and about the Fed political situation. When she was finally finished talking, Michael was amazed, as all those things were new to him. Angelina broke out in tears after finally meeting her brother.

They decided to take a walk together, and after that they went to a nice and quiet restaurant inside the apartment complex, on the top floor…. the 40th to be precise.
They ordered some Rigel-style exotic fish with an off-world salad, and some rum-coffee to go with it. They talked for hours and hours on end, about everything imaginable, and when they were finally done talking, and dead tired, they went back to the apartment, and went to sleep…. Michael lay on his couch, while Angelina slept in his own private bedroom.

Michael and Angelina Tchaikovsky had finally found each other.

The supreme Ildiran and Federation governments –
which ultimately came down to Syscom Zaytjevh
and GACS – had decided and agreed on
establishing a hotline link.

It consisted of a multitude of highly secured direct
flash-dat, flash-video, and holo-vid conferencing
connections.
Discussions on setting up a direct and bilateral
Cyportal were still underway.
Both governments were aware that a possible war
could be close at hand, and the mutual tensions
were increasing, but this hotline link could ease
these tensions somewhat, even if it were only for a
short while.
It gave both parties some more time to think, but
behind the scenes both were gearing up for war,
and setting up all kinds of assets and means to 'win'
the coming war.
Although this was not officially confirmed, the Great
Charter hadn't worked out, and if there were some
kind of conflict, or precursor for war, it would
actually mean war.
Both parties knew this, and there were groups and
factions – not to mention GACS, and the CGC,
themselves – which had actually a lot to gain from
war.

Hotlines, between rival governments, also had their downsides. If there were such precursors, and tiny conflicts, they could speed up the spirals and vortices towards war a great deal.

A high level of security, control, and checking – as well as the Great Charter - had made it possible for people from the Federation, and from the Ildiran Empire, to travel to and from both regions.
But this only made things more complicated. If spies were uncovered, or captured, both governments would have to put an immediate end to the Charter, and all free travel between the two regions would immediately come to a halt.
All those people who at that moment found themselves in the other region would be trapped, and incapable of returning to their home region.
High-profile ID cards would become meaningless.
This situation would be disastrous for both sides, and if a war became official, all those people would probably end up in refugee camps.

The hotline link was now officially agreed upon, and it was supposed to remain in place for the foreseeable future, but if interstellar war broke out - as most people expected it would - this connection would be useless.

About the secret Illuminati movement inside the Dominion

At this time in our story, in the year of 2,793 CE, the underground movement of the Illuminati had existed for more than a thousand years, since its foundation in the year 1,776 CE.

As well as inside the Dominion, it was also present inside the Federation, although its Federation groups and divisions were much more secretive, since GACS and the CGC would not tolerate such a movement in any way because of its mystical and obscure historical image.

This was not something a system like GACS would ever be able to understand, although the obscure image most people had of the Illuminati had been created by their opponents, the Roman Catholic Church.

In reality, the Illuminati were proponents of rational, philosophical, and scientific enlightenment, although there were different views on what this enlightenment should really look like.

Over this millennium of existence, the movement had undergone a continual process of change and reform.

At this point in history, by the end of the 28th century

CE, they had joined and merged with Humanity's Destiny, since most of their ideas and philosophies had converged.
Almost all members of Destiny were originally Illuminati, and their main goal was to depose GACS, which was the most enlightened objective one could think of at this time of history.

'Illuminati' - in the end - literally meant.... the Enlightened

Some funny thoughts about the funniness of physical things

Angelina Tchaikovsky was taking a lunch break inside one of the crowded SI cafeterias.

It reminded her of pictures she had seen sometime of 21st century fast food restaurants. It was nice and ordered, and above all very plastic.
The only difference here was one could order entire meals, with eight courses, or more.... for little money, paid with instant wireless com-sys credits.

It was good, fast, and easy.

As Angelina was enjoying her fairly tasty meal, she was thinking about certain things that she had thought about long and hard, many times over, for thousands of hours.

When it comes down to the basic point, without all the mind-boggling physical theories, incomprehensible d-dimensional mathematical principles, and dazzlingly fast and complex computer simulations, the basic principle of everything in existence, be it physical or imaginary, is quite simple:

It is the wave principle.

Angelina would often discuss these subjects with Kenzo in the depths of the night, and he would then marvel at her intelligence and her inner beauty, and compare opinions with her on his, from a Japanese philosophical-scientific point of view.

28th century sub-Planck quantum-string physics is a combination of previous history quantum-field physics, Einsteinian warped dimensions, and F-theory - a later version of super string theory, and successor of M-theory.
In quantum-string physics, the core principle, particle, or unit, is the 'super string': a super-tiny

vibrating chord-like object, a billion times smaller than a regular sub-atomic particle, or quark.

The elementary characteristic of the wave principle – its meaning, essence, and purpose – is a tiny massless chord (which can also be as massive as an entire multiverse) with two opposing amplitudes, which can move up and down, and vibrate. That's basically it.
The two opposing amplitudes, or simply: summits and dents, are interchangeable, and work in accordance with the Newtonian laws of the everlasting preservation of energy.
A super string is basically, and essentially, the same.
One should view and regard the universe, or the multiverse, as consisting of zillions of tiny strings, instead of particles; unless of course one would want to regard tiny strings as tiny particles.

In Taoism, an ancient Chinese philosophy, the core universal principle is Yin-yang. Tao means something like way, path, or principle.
Fritjov Capra wrote a book about this subject somewhere during the 1,970s, which centers on the essential similarity between ancient holistic Taoism and contemporary differential particle physics.
Yin and Yang is, in essence, about two opposing

forces, or units, which are basically the same and interchangeable, and which both adhere to the unrelenting and eternal laws of conservation of energy.

In this sense, Capra was completely right, according to Angelina, and every super-complex system could be interpreted, described, and viewed as a huge combination of waves, strings, or yin-yang particles.

Angelina paused for a while, and marveled at the serene and simple beauty of these deep but fundamental considerations.

Ok, she thought, *let's view a universe as a sinusoid….*

The basic mathematical function of a 2-dimensional wave principle, with variable amplitude, and wavelength, is $y=a \sin(x/l)$, with a being the amplitude, and l the wavelength. *What if you would make the wavelength infinite*, she mused?
The answer became clear in Angelina's pristine mind immediately. To the perception of a finite observer, the function would become a straight line. If we apply this to an entire universe, we would have an unchanging and constant universe. That's probably why physical constants appear to be constant. It's probably easier to make the amplitude

value zero, but then you would have an eternally zero universe....

The very idea of physical constants being constant over distances of millions of billions of eons, and light years, is ridiculous....

It's a funny thing, thinking about entire universes, and multiverses, as simple 2-dimensional sinusoid functions.... she realized.

She wondered on, about the mysteries of spiral multi-multiverses, and such things, and redirected her mind towards 'serious' physics.

Lunch breaks were always good, especially when one could escape for a while from thoughts about epical wars.... which were closing in across the vast distances of space at the speed of light.

It felt as if an apocalyptic war was getting closer all the time....

All the peoples across the inhabited regions of the Spiral Arm could almost feel a tangible tension and fear.

And, although Federation media were almost

completely controlled by the CGC, Fed people across all layers of society were aware of all these feelings, and the facts and reasons behind them. The Dominian people lived inside a democratic system, and accordingly had access to all kinds of information, and sources.

Ildiran society was a completely different ball game. It was holistic, and based on totality, not on individuality. One could almost call it a communist system, though the average Ildiran civilian didn't feel like its government was oppressive, or totalitarian, at all. It actually was the other way around: Ildirans enjoyed working, and living as a hive, as one complete unity, to improve, and dedicate their lives, to this holistic entity of all Ildirans.

And one thing they all had in common:

Personal com-systems

Com-systems provided the means to access and interchange all kinds of info, media sources, and data, even though Ildiran ones were slightly different from human ones.

Interchange of information between Ildirans and Sol-trians – as Ildirans preferred to refer to them – was only in its infancy.

First contact had after all only been made very recently.

But one thing was clear: communications between billions of com-systems across the Spiral Arm accelerated and increased the fear and tension of a looming interstellar war a thousand times. The coming of this interstellar war in the near future seemed virtually unstoppable.

Intermediate account, by the guiding entity Shi'rah:

One of my main functions within the society of Trellian descendants was to be a historian, and I enjoyed this occupation of keeping track of Trellian history, and all the things related to it.

All Trellian descendants fulfilled multiple important functions, and our society was like a complex and integrated system of many multi-tasking individuals, although we did not have a massive civilization.
I also had a more practical and more critical assignment, namely to direct our thousand-man-strong secret unit inside the Spiral Arm: extra-stellar guiding unit Ghost Sol-3.

Oh…. and I have one more crucial thing.

It was we, the thousand-man-strong force from unit
Ghost Sol-3, who had created the situation where
the Dominians had disappeared.
It was we who sabotaged the communications with
the Old Earth, and it was we who had disabled
reconnaissance on both sides. We had done this
with one specific purpose: to create one mighty
independent civilization outside the Federation….
powerful enough to join with the Ildirans and take on
the system of GACS.

Professor Charles Dunois Xaviour was an extremely
intelligent and sophisticated man, and he dressed
accordingly.

Although he was fully aware that the first interstellar
war – at least for humanity, that is - was about to
rage across the local universe, he remained
completely calm and tranquil.
He always entirely relied on his superior IQ, and
besides, he had also had extensive training and
intensive programming to deal with all kinds of
difficult situations, not to mention war.
He was an educated man, with several Ph.D.'s and

he spoke 9 languages fluently, including Ildiran. The person he pretended to be depended on his location in society and in space, and on his actual mission. He had lived for 150 years as a human being, in a society where age-gen treatment was common but expensive; at least, if you wanted safe and effective treatment.

At this point, he didn't pretend.... at least, not about his job. He was an SI insider, although his colleagues – most of the time – didn't notice he was constantly spying on them. At this moment he had a vague hunch, a gut feeling, that operative Kenzo and his 'apprentice' Angelina were onto something. He didn't have any proof, or evidence, or concrete indications, but his experience told him something was wrong.

But for now, all he could do was wait and see if something would come up, and if something out of the ordinary would happen.

Ildiran brains worked differently from human ones.... fundamentally differently.

To the human mind, Newtonian physics seemed completely rational and logical, as opposed to

quantum physics, with all of its uniquely weird concepts, and thinking, which seemed completely unreal and illogical. Some famous human scientists had even suggested it was ultimately incomprehensible, even to the minds of these brilliant and famous scientists themselves.
For the Ildiran mind, it was completely the other way around.
Before they had discovered and developed their own versions of quantum physical theories and concepts, they had to deal and live with classical Newtonian thinking, and they had been appalled. Ildiran minds worked from the basic principle that the universe was intrinsically illogical and incomprehensible.
The human basic principle was the other way around.

According to them, the universe should work in accordance with the workings of human synaptic functions and reasoning, and to the Ildirans this way of reasoning seemed ridiculous and egocentric.

'Why should the universe have to comply with some particular intelligent life form's neural system?' was a common saying at Ildiran universities and campuses. When humans took notice of this Ildiran point of view, there were a lot of scientists and physicists who had to admit they had to agree, and there were many more crucial differences between human and Ildiran in-built scientific and philosophical thinking.

For instance, to the Ildirans it seemed completely immoral to use or abuse other living creatures for the advancement of science, and of course, many human animal rights proponents agreed with their position, although human scientific history showed a despicable record on this.
Because of this moral position, the Ildirans would never abduct and dissect human beings.... unless – possibly - human beings did the same thing to them.

Ildiran scientists and academics – in the meantime – had adapted a new designation for their intelligent counterparts, namely, Sol-trians.
They referred to them as Sol-trians since they originated from Sol-3, and this new designation spread across Ildiran space like wildfire.

Sol-trians were definitely interesting.

The Ildiran scientific community agreed on this unanimously, and many academic studies and analyses were made on their history, politics, ethics, science, religion and any other subject one could think of.

Before interstellar war would break out, they needed to know as much about Sol-trians.... as they possibly could.

Chapter 19

Ildirans declare war on Sol-trians (from the Federation), and join Dominion

Angelina had a terrible vision, although it was not a waking vision.

As she was sleeping, and while she found herself deep inside the realm of her dreams, Angelina had a terrible vision.

She seemed to fall and fall with an incredible velocity, and the g-forces were terrible.

After what seemed like many minutes, the falling stopped, and she found herself standing firmly - legs apart - on the surface of some distant and mysterious exotic world.

When she finally looked up, she saw three giant squids high up, fourteen miles high, in the outer reaches of the intense purple-colored and poisonous atmosphere of this unknown world.

As they slowly flew and floated, supported by the dense air, the sentient animals made slow gestures with their many-mile-long tentacles, somehow trying to hurt each other with poisonous chemical wisps, accompanied by streaks of high-energy lasers.

It was a great battlefield of combatting giants, amidst the high clouds, poisonous gases, and streaks of plasma.

Angelina didn't know how she could tell, but the sentient animals were communicating telepathically whilst combatting each other with a terrible rage.

Soon she noticed that two of the animals seemed to cooperate, and they seemed to work together, trying to kill and destroy the third one in the middle. It seemed as if the third animal was more mechanic, and the other two were more natural and more organic.

A few moments later, she suddenly sensed the more mechanical-like squid was intent on harming her, although she didn't understand why, and the other two squids were trying to prevent it from doing so.

As Angelina looked on from the surface of this exotic world, with eyes as perceptive as an ultra-long distance telescope, she noticed the mechanical squid seemed to have some sort of technological structure at its core, and it was this core object the other two were trying to destroy.

When she focused her sight on this internal construct, it seemed to be some artificial central nervous system with artificial nerves and synapses extending outward and controlling the giant animal. The battle raged on in high-gravity slow-motion, and seemed to last for hours.

From the distance, she heard a terrible roar rising and rising, as if one of the two sides was ready to strike the final blow, but she couldn't discern who seemed to be on the winning hand.

And before she knew how the battle was ever going to play out…. the dream was suddenly over.

Current location: CGC nucleus, Aurora Alpha Prime system, central and core server room of the GACS entity.

The CGC nucleus steadily orbited the gas giant of Aurora Alpha Prime, as VOG.8 contemplated the political situation in complete solitude.

VOG.8 had slowly but steadily developed feelings of love and affection for his Jewish female prime advisor, Sareine Datasys. The only one who knew this, of course, was VOG.8.

He even had sexual fantasies about her, something his original creators never could have envisioned or imagined. Furthermore, it would be impossible to envision a massive AI nexus having intercourse with a young and attractive woman.
VOG.8 had incredible sexual fantasies about her when in 'sleep' mode, and he was thinking about using a remotely-controlled instrumental male body, or an android form, to be able to put his incredible fantasies into practice, and quench his terrible lust. Sareine didn't consciously know these things, but sometimes she would notice subtle things in his wording, and in his tone of voice, which suggested some kind of sexual tension, and this only increased her own personal feelings of longing and her sexual needs.

Sareine herself was a gorgeous girl, and she preferred to dress in very short skirts, without underpants, and with sexy panties on her legs, oozing the fresh sweat and the pheromones of a hot young girl, working in an 'office', for fourteen hours per day, straight.

Her real age was thirty seven (which was incredibly young in a society like the Federation around 2,793 CE), but she had undergone a solid age-gen treatment a few years back, and because of this, she had the body and face of a seventeen-year-old girl, and this dramatically increased VOG.8's lust and desire.

She had a master's degree in political science, as well as in business administration, and that was the reason she had been selected for a high-profile CGC job. During recent years, she had had several promotions, and now she was the prime advisor to VOG.8, the central CGC governmental consciousness.

A few moments after quietly entering the great central server-room, she found herself floating in zero-g in the middle of its immense fiber-metal hull.

There were hundreds of massive com-servers, with

a multitude of multi-functional access terminals slowly circling the small central core, which contained the center of VOG.8's consciousness. The immense space was lit by millions of micro-fusion bulbs circling the central core in zero-g weightlessness.

In technical design, the system was based on the science of Sy-Phy, or synaptic physics. In this technique sub-quantum particles were utilized as tiny individual synapses, and this technology had been refined again and again, almost to the point of immeasurability, during the last centuries.
AIs based on Sy-Phy, harnessed trillions and trillions more processing power than early autonomous systems ever had.

VOG.8 switched to wireless, and Sareine felt a slight buzz inside her head, which indicated the subtle switch. Although they could communicate wirelessly, VOG.8 did not have the capacity, to read her inner thoughts. Now, without sound, she was completely alone with the massive AI, and even though she had done this many times over it still was an intimidating experience.
Being so close to this technological monster in zero-g always gave her the feeling there was more to life than just ordinary space and time.

VOG.8 had access to every possible source of information in a matter of picoseconds, but he preferred to communicate with his human advisors through exchange of sentences, because it worked. He realized that humans had very little data storage, and an even worse processing time, but they were very effective with research, and analysis.
VOG.8 focused on his advisor.

'Welcome again, Sareine,' he said, opening the discussion.

'Good to have you back. How was your journey to Ildion Prime? And how was your conversation with the Ildiran emperor, Syscom Zaytjevh? Did you find out more about his intentions at this point?'
Sareine hesitated for a moment and then started to try to relay her thoughts.
'The journey was by Cyportal, so it was not much of a journey at all, but I enjoyed the intermediary stops, and I was fascinated by the capital of Illumina. It is quite an accomplishment of the Ildirans, and of their history.'
'Did he appreciate our offer of exchanging ten thousand of our citizens for dissection and

analysis?'

'Mr. Zaytjevh seemed…. offended. Dissection is…. considered immoral, in Ildiran society. It has been their way for thousands of years.'

VOG.8 seemed furious. Sareine could feel his terrible rage, and shivered.

'How could this ever be immoral? These organic worms are no more than meaningless subjects…. instruments of our unrelenting power, and ultimate leadership! Syscom should know this! He is the leader of an empire!'

Sareine stood silently, with her back straight. She felt frightened, but tried not to show it.

'I understand your anger, and frustration,' she said, 'but it is their way. I think you should respect this. I don't think there is a way around it.'

VOG.8 responded vigorously.

'We will create a way around this for ourselves. We will do this unilaterally, and show the Ildirans how we do things in the Federation, although we will have to do it in secret for the time being. Let's hope Ildiran intelligence will not discover this anytime soon.'

Sareine stood motionless. She fully understood the situation. VOG.8 would in no way let her change his mind on this, but if Ildiran government structures found out about it, the consequences would be worse than she would ever be able to imagine.

Several hours later, VOG.8 watched on secretively through a security micro-vid camera installed inside the wall opposite Sareine's office.

'Put your legs apart!' Sareine's assistant said, with a firm voice.
The assistant turned her around with a sudden movement, and put her hands against the wall. With an abrupt movement of his hands, he spread her thin legs, and pulled away her panties. His hot and intimidating rod suddenly penetrated her oozing void.
Sareine moaned.
VOG.8 watched tensely, barely able to control his lust, as the explicit act continued.
He would have to create a substitute, a male human body, through which he could do these things to Sareine himself, and then VOG.8 would even be able to walk among the humans, his subjects, as one of them (without them knowing anything about it, of course).

The idea was frightening: a monster like GACS

walking the universe by means of a remotely-controlled human body, as if it were a person, a human being, but with the power to destroy entire worlds.

Whilst there were the secret fantasies of VOG.8 that nobody knew about, there were some things VOG.8 didn't know about as well.

Sareine Datasys, his dedicated prime advisor for several years, was herself an operative of Ghost unit Sol-3, and she had managed to infiltrate the very highest levels of the CGC. This situation compromised the entire government of the civilization of the Federation to the all-seeing eyes of the ever-watchful Trellian descendants.

Angelina had always known that one day the Disappeared would be found.... and she would have to live through times of uncertainty and war, although she had never anticipated first contact with an alien race.

In an age where age-gen treatment was common, and most people lived to see three or even four hundred years – in some cases even five hundred – every living civilian had to face the fact that they would most probably see many times of social turmoil, fundamental change, and civil unrest.

In comparison to most other people, Angelina was no more than a fledgling young girl, and she had never even had one single age-gen treatment. However, her extensive studies into physics, history, and religion, among other subjects, combined with her great intellect and wisdom for a woman her age, gave her insights most people would never see.

She had had so many dreams and visions of the future, and she had spent thousands of private hours, thinking deep thoughts about existence, the universe, and the current Federation in particular. She had an insight into the way things were, and the way things probably were going to be, which frightened her more than she had ever expected. After all this visioning and thinking in the back of her mind, she had become convinced of one stunning conclusion: The universe is permeated by the universal soul, just as it is permeated by space and time, gravitational forces, matter and energy, and physical laws themselves. Physical laws are always present, and defined wherever one finds him or herself, and the universal soul breathes life into otherwise intelligent, but inanimate, entities.

It is this universal soul which gives spiritedness, sentience, and consciousness to otherwise inanimate things, bodies, and creatures.

Without this spiritedness, these living things would be no more than unconscious objects, inanimate organic robots. The existence and workings of one single universal soul is the most simple, logical, and elegant theory to explain the spiritedness that seems to exist inside these living entities.

But there was another issue that kept on coming back in front of Angelina's mind's eye of late. It was the statement by the subordinate Jovi AI system – conventionally designated as 'Mother' – that she was a direct descendant of the apostle John, writer of the final Biblical passage about the Apocalypse. Being somebody's descendant mainly came down to carrying this person's genes, and Angelina suspected she had inherited certain very special and highly unusual abilities from this most significant person in human history.

She had always – from childhood on, and as far as she could remember – had visions…. visions about the future, about the past, and about the present, and she could hardly envision living without them. This was something completely opposite to 'regular' human beings. Angelina suspected there was more

to this inheritance from this Biblical apostle than having mere visions and 'special' genes, and that she was really able to actually foresee the future, as it would possibly, or most probably, play out.
Maybe she even had universal psychic abilities, or the ability to lead great amounts of people to some sort of destiny, in some sort of Biblical way.
It was too much for her, at this moment, to really come to grips with these incredible things and these incredible possibilities.

She would let this issue rest until it would somehow become a major thing, although the visions, themselves, were never far away, and were in fact increasing as time went by.

Cy-timing system: cys-05-7591-cy: Achamar Citadel: CGC detention installation. Deep inside the distant Achra trinary system

It was deep inside local system night, and the Ildiran prisoners felt more frightened than they ever had before.

The total number of Ildiran prisoners was massive: approximately ten thousand innocent souls had been bound and thrown mercilessly into this horrible pit of misery, torture and death.

They were crowded in a massive hall, which seemed to be no more than a giant dungeon, and the only comfort they had was in their mutual telepathic contact, which was filled with fear and anticipation for the worst.

The perfectly straight walls of this massive hall were lit by hundreds of wood and oil torches, seemingly to frighten the prisoners, and to emphasize that this was not just a CGC detention camp, but more like some medieval dungeon where medieval things were going on.

The prisoners didn't know exactly why they had been taken, and by whom specifically, but they suspected it was the government of the Human Federation, and they assumed that their fate was not going to be very pleasant at all.

Yigal Naor was sitting with his back straight against the wall, trying to forget the pain, straining his arms, his legs, and his feet.
He was a member of a highly-respected Ildiran family, and although his first name was quite common among male Ildirans, his surname was

from a long and ancient line of respectable Ildiran families.

He tried not to think of his family. The situation he was in was hopeless, and he would probably never see them again. He hoped they would somehow succeed in dealing emotionally with his sudden disappearance, but he doubted they would ever come to terms with his loss.

GACS had upheld the appearance of a semi-democratic system for more than five hundred years, but in the course of those many years, massive amounts of (suspected) anti-government civilians had secretly been abducted, interrogated and killed. Most people knew this had been going on for all those five and a half centuries, although it was absolutely forbidden to speak about it in the open.

After the heated discussion with Sareine, VOG.8 had indeed decided to go unilateral, and had ordered the secret abduction of ten thousand innocent Ildiran souls. Whether the Ildiran Intel services were aware of this, or very soon would be, was unknown at this point.

It took Ildiran Intel structures less than twelve hours to get notice of this unilateral action taken directly by the entity of GACS.

The presiding Ildiran emperor, Syscom Zaytjevh, and his government council were informed of these events less than twelve minutes after. There could only be one conclusion:

All-out interstellar war with the Human Federation....

The Ildiran government unanimously agreed to join with the Dominians, a people they had had a good relationship with - politically, diplomatically, and economically - during the last centuries.
Dominion government, in turn, almost unanimously agreed to join forces with the Ildirans, and although the fighting and the skirmishes had not yet begun, the first interstellar war in the history of humanity seemed to have become.

Ildiran media stations were immediately informed

about what had occurred, and of the new situation with the Federation and the Dominion, and the news spread across the Empire like wildfire.

The Ildiran people were outraged, and whole masses went to the streets, and shouted, and rioted, and their government was completely unable to keep the peace, and to keep control of the main city centers, highways, and communication lines.

Immediately after this, the news spread to the Human Federation, and instead of being outraged, the masses were frightened, appalled, and in total panic.

Inside Dominion space, all these mass emotions, psychologies, and on-site situations like rioting, looting and commotion came together in a whirlwind of anticipation of interstellar war.

On the ancient planet of Sol-3, the situation was even worse, and on the red planet of Mars, or Sol-4, although it was sparsely populated, the situation was the same.

In fact, the entire inhabited regions of the three Dominions were in complete turmoil.

Humans had always, in their entire history, regarded

it as logical, natural, and ethical to torture and abuse other living creatures, for medical experiments, food production, cruel entertainment, and other such purposes. In some parts of their own history, they had even performed horrid medical experiments on their own species.

One instance of this was the Nazis, who during World War II had experimented on Jewish people, the disabled, and dissidents, in the form of horrific surgeries without anesthetic.

In the case of animals, the argumentation had always been that animals had a lesser intelligence, and so it was therefore justified to torture and abuse them for all kinds of purposes.

The core reasoning behind this was that animals couldn't read or write, or reason and that was supposed to be sufficient ground to torture and abuse them, even though some species actually were intelligent, like elephants, dolphins, whales, and anthropoid apes.

The Ildirans didn't agree with mankind on this.

They despised such practices, and they had always – in their entire history –, had a core moral and ethical principle, that any experiment, on any being, was fundamentally unacceptable, and they had always – in their entire history –, under every circumstance, absolutely stood by that core principle: a principle unimaginable, to mankind.

Now that it was officially known to everyone that the Federation had covertly abducted and dissected their fellow Ildiran souls, there was only one option on the table for them: interstellar war.

The Great Charter – or the Magna Carta, as its historical Latin designation was – was officially dead, if ever it had had any meaning, purpose, or integrity at all.

As soon as both sides to the arrangement had recused themselves from it, the interstellar war was a fact.

To the Ildirans, it had been a serious agreement, and an arrangement of serious integrity.
To GACS, however, it had been no more than a temporary means to guarantee some sort of stability, and had had no more significance than that.

All the clauses and content about diplomatic relations, mutual scientific and economic advancement, and such things, were completely off the table, and all the sentiments of security and stability were gone.

All that was left was complete insecurity, and massive preparations for what was going to be the biggest military clash mankind had ever seen.

When Angelina had witnessed the formal declaration of this Great Charter, or Magna Carta, she had stared in total fascination, and awe, and she had felt a great hope for humanity and the Ildiran people.

But now it was part of ancient history, she hoped with all her might that humanity would somehow survive and the Ildiran Empire would somehow find a way to coexist in the future, without total obliteration on both sides.

Ildiran date: 10,988 I.C. (Ildiran Creation)

2,793 CE, December 25th, 5:25 a.m. standard time, the inhabited regions of The Spiral Arm

On the very day Christianity traditionally celebrated Christmas – the birth of Christ - the multilateral military incursions began, which led almost immediately to massive attacks from all sides.

Christianity had dwindled during the last eight hundred years, although in an interstellar society of hundreds of billions of people, there were still millions who adhered to the Christian faith.
And to that ancient and outdated religion, Christmas Day still was the holiest of days. The Christian faith was only one very specific interpretation of the metaphysical world, and there had been many other candidates for this. Some of them had become quite prominent during the last eight hundred years, replacing the Catholic Vatican as the religious center of the human universe.

According to Christianity, Christmas Day was about the birth of their messiah, Jesus Christ, who preached neighborly love and an end to violence.
All those who adhered to this ancient religion celebrated this day, with thousands of candle lights, quiet music, and silent prayers.
The original Vatican had been destroyed during the first nuclear war, but inside the Saint Peter at Vaticani Secundus, the second Vatican, in the system of Nine Septem Ophiuchi, one could here

Gregorian music echoing through the massive basilica, which was even greater than the original one. The current Pope, Urban XIV, was leading thousands of followers in silent prayer.

But exactly on this very day.... all hell broke loose across the human and Ildiran regions of the Milky Way galaxy.

Although the bilateral declaration of war was only six hours old, the Ildirans with their superior military technologies struck the first blow.
But there had been many examples in history where inferior forces had persevered for extended periods of time, against bigger and better equipped armies.

The first heavy attack was on the total-scale military system of Militia 4785-i, with its many massive and heavily-armed attack bases, located at the edge of Federation space, facing and probing the regions of the Ildiran Empire.

The thousands of menacing c-plus alien attack craft arrived in system, as if thousands of Greek ships, and hundreds of thousands of Antiquity troops of Agamemnon and Achilles, had landed and arrived on the beach of the ancient and unassailable city of Troy.

Tens of thousands of small, light, and swift Ildiran attack mantas swarmed into the system of Zion-7-i, and wreaked havoc among the many badly-defended Human Federation defense bases.

The system of Apollo was also invaded by swarms of Ildiran mantas, clusters of dozens of massive incursion freighters, and manta carriers with thousands of reinforcement fighters, and they inflicted heavy damage onto the Federation ships, stations, and military personnel, who cried out in pure agony as they were massively obliterated by their Ildiran opponents.

Some twenty-four hours later, Federation space forces responded to this by invading into Ildiran regions such as Sion-secundus-ypsilon, and almost crippled some local military bases. In doing so, they killed and maimed tens of thousands of the Ildiran equivalent of marines, who were fighting for their dear lives, and the future survival of the Ildiran race and empire.

Ildiran forces, in response, invaded Crisis Copiae, a significant but sparsely populated Ixti processing system, and massacred a great deal of the loyal human Ixti workers. They destroyed a substantial number of refinery installations, and thus dealt a terrible blow to Human Federation Ixti production and processing.

Dozens of massive incursions occurred in many places, but there were also hundreds of tiny incursions aimed at very specific and strategically significant sites.

This was not some pretty picture in some irrelevant moment in the depths of history.

This was all-out interstellar war, covering an inhabited region of hundreds of light years, with many billions of human and Ildiran souls inside.

And so, this region in space was divided into two groups, opposing each other with military machines greater than both had ever seen before.
On one side, there were the ones who denied machine domination over living entities, and on the other side, there was GACS, and its total military, political, and social control over 'his' part of humanity.

Soldiers fighting for GACS only did so because they absolutely had to, or because they were morally misguided, but there were whole masses of Fed soldiers, pilots, space commandos, marines, and high-ranking officers who were absolutely convinced that what they were doing was right.

To them, the status quo of GACS usurpation was logical; the way it was and the way it was supposed to be.

Behind every war lies a great moral dilemma, and conflict, and so it was with this war as well.

In antiquity, wars were about conquest, but they were also about such things as the validity and superiority of the Roman principles, religion, and culture, or about the divine and absolute rule of usurpers such as Xerxes and his father Darius, rulers over millions of enslaved souls.

However this conflict would play out, it was absolutely certain billions of military personnel as well as innocent civilians were going to lose their lives, or at least their bodily integrity, their family, or their possessions.

in the 20th century CE, some brilliant writer had said

that war was 'the total absence of reason', and of course with this war it was the same.

Most Cyportals inside the Federation, as well as their Ildiran counterparts and those inside the Dominion, were kept operational but were sealed from deep-territory incursions by means of hyper-complex mathematical security codes. This was especially true for the big Cyportals that were intended for heavy space traffic. They were hyper-secured, and guarded by complex clusters of small but extremely effective military defense fighters.

Ixti production had been almost crippled, and in all the three great dominions, most Cyportals, and Cyportal traffic and usage, was confiscated by the government, and as an extension of this, by the military.
Ixti reserves were confiscated as well, and public Cyportal traffic and usage was brought to an absolute minimum.

GACS of course drew all power and resources to himself without hesitation, and this left his subjects and citizens with almost no ability to travel, communicate, or conduct commercial interaction.

This crippled the entire economy, and thus left GACS with an economy in shambles.

As always with such situations, the rich and wealthy came off a lot better, and the streets, gutters, and refugee camps were piled with beggars, all kinds of refugees, and masses of disowned people.

Apart from actual Cyportal traffic, there were other usages for Ixti as well.
Flash-dat communications, flash-video calls and conferencing, media releases and information, and flash-net interaction only cost a fraction in Ixti amounts in comparison to actual Cyportal traffic, and so these functionalities were kept in operation for the greater part.
But the prices soon went through the roof, and – against all hopes - these functions were reduced to ten percent of the normal peacetime situation.

Inside the Human Dominion, and the Ildiran Empire, numerous facilities were set up to care for the refugees, the poor, the homeless, and the disowned.

Things like low-cost flash-connections, shelters with food provision, and almost-free on-planet and in-system transportation were provided by the government and humanitarian organizations, and this helped to improve a little on the free-falling economy, and on functioning of society as a whole.

GACS, then, tried to do the same, to somehow try to improve on his personal economic nightmare, but to little affect.

Humanitarian efforts were not something GACS was familiar with, and it didn't come from the heart.... and, in the final analysis, even GACS would have to pay dearly for the economic nightmare realities of his own precious war.

In this instant, it was completely unclear whether the Federation of Humanity, or the Human Dominion for that matter, would survive the war, or whether the human race in itself would endure across the depths of time, and it was absolutely unclear how much destruction and suffering the Ildiran Empire would have to sustain....

But this much was clear:

Like an eclipse slowly descending into a dying star, the looming interstellar apocalypse had finally descended onto the many-light-year spanning region in space the human race called:

The Spiral Arm

'Angy, we have to run!' Kenzo said firmly, trying not to let others hear his strained voice.

He pulled her by the arm out of the small office that had been his home for more than fourteen years. As they walked the silent corridors of the SI nucleus with a quick pace, he explained that: 'The interstellar war is beginning.' He said: 'They will find out we have failed to inform them about the Dominion within hours. We have to find and join the underground opposition. They have several giant insurgency stations, spread across the Spiral region. They could use us. We have a lot of inside information, and loads of experience with SI underground and political tactics.'
Angelina remained silent as they quickened their pace towards the many-mile-high central lift.
It consisted of a fourteen-mile-high shaft, with four parallel cabins to accommodate ten people per cabin. The cabins themselves were surrounded by strong anti-grav fields, which made it possible to

move up and down at eight hundred kilometers per hour without the passengers getting nauseous or light-headed.

Anti-grav suspension lifts had several advantages. They were solid, and easy to build, and didn't require Ixti to operate, and most of all, they were dependable in case of emergency.

Kenzo entered one of the available cabins and pulled Angelina with him.

As they moved down fast for eight kilometers, towards one of the rarely- used private side Cyportals – and hopefully on their way towards some secret insurgency station owned by Destiny - they held on to each other firmly…. and desperately hoped, nobody would notice.

Angy and Ken stepped out of the lift cabin, with a quick pace, trying not to attract any unnecessary attention from the very few agents, assistants, and security coordinators and analysts who occasionally took these SI side corridors on their way to or from their private offices, meeting rooms, briefing rooms, lunch rooms, and more such places.

Their hearts pounded, fueled by extreme amounts

of pure organic adrenaline, and their fear of being apprehended was almost tangible as they almost reached the entrance to one of the many small private vessel docking bays.

Their hectic flight from SI into the arms of the secret joint insurgency movements was just beginning, and Angelina realized they were probably going to have to go through thousands of exhilarating private and historical moments in the near future, and for the rest of their lives.

She wondered what Janis – now her own private c-plus AI vessel – was thinking, if thinking was what it was at all....
Was it thinking things over, contemplating the universe, or its own existence, or simply dreaming? Or was it simply on stand-by, unconscious of the world surrounding it?
'Angy, please switch your com-sys into stealth-mode,' Kenzo said with a very soft voice. Angelina nodded almost invisibly, and implemented his almost silent instruction.
Their mutual tension grew slightly. It was not common practice to switch into 'stealth' while still inside nucleus domain, and the both of them hoped there weren't all kinds of alarms or silent beeps going off in control and monitoring rooms, or with

oversight agents and systems.

Before the beginning of their flight out of the nucleus, Kenzo had covertly contacted Anatoli Sibelius, a major operational officer inside the joint insurgency, and he had provided Kenzo with ultra-secret coordinates to the Pax Infiniti station, a massive but hyper-secret station deep inside the desolation of interstellar space. Such interstellar stations were practically undetectable, and impossible to find, unless one had direct access to its exact deep-space-location coordinates.

As they quickly passed through the main entrance to the small docking bay, Janis activated its overall systems, and the two fugitives noticed the sudden lights, and heard a soft buzz emanating from their private transport.
The c-plus AI vessel, Janis, immediately opened a light conversation.

'Welcome back, Miss Angelina, and Mr. Kenzo. I was just contemplating…. '.
'Janis, please,' Angelina responded, as they entered the main cabin. 'We have no time at all. Seal the doors and take us into space.'
As Angelina and Kenzo entered the control cabin, Janis quickly slid the entrance doors shut, and

exited the SI nucleus into very local space.

Angelina issued some flight instructions: 'Accelerate to zero point one five c, and take us to zero point five AU, straight ahead.'

'Confirmed,' the vessel responded, and implemented her commands.

In their rear view, the faceted globe of the nucleus slowly diminished. It gave them a faint feeling of safety. A few moments later, three SI interceptors emerged, swirled around each other several times, and then assumed attack formation. The vessels headed straight for the fugitive craft and opened their com channels.

'Unidentified vessel, decelerate immediately and return to the SI station. If you refuse, we will open fire, and board your ship.'

Angelina immediately changed her instructions for her ship. 'Janis, forget the former instructions. Switch to fully cloaked right now, and accelerate to interstellar. Kenzo will provide you with a set of deep space coordinates'.

An hour later, they were well on their way, to Pax Infiniti station.

Their complete cloaking and high velocity had been sufficient to get rid of the SI interceptors. The vessels had tried to detect and intercept them for several minutes, but their prey seemed to have disappeared and vanished.

Angelina and Kenzo decided to get some rest inside the sleeping compartments.

Inside the nucleus, oversight had quickly established which two com-systems had disappeared, and now both GACS and SI knew the exact identity of the two fugitives who had almost certainly joined the insurgency movements and turned against them.

State of play, by the multiversal guiding entity Shi'rah:

The prelude to the first interstellar war was over, and this long and sad episode of military strife, and of all those terrible things related to an interstellar war, had begun.

Angelina had learned about her true identity, and her extraordinary genetic inheritance, and she and Kenzo had decided to leave and abandon SI intelligence and join with the insurgency movements. They didn't have the slightest idea what was going to happen to them once they were 'safe' inside the hyper-secret Pax Infiniti station.

The name of Pax Infiniti was ancient Latin, and it meant 'Infinite peace'.

Angelina was absolutely determined to fight and resist GACS, and therefore SI, for the rest of her (hopefully long) life, and Kenzo was absolutely determined to help and protect his friend and comrade.

On the deplorable Old Earth, the chaos and division grew and deepened, fueled by the uncertainties, tensions, and threats of interstellar war.... not to mention the collapse of the already dire economy. GACS was still trying to develop its fearsome ultimate system, UI-sys-1, a new version of itself, but a million times more powerful and capable. And engineers from the CGC complex were still trying to build its remote human entity, called Prometheus. UI-sys-1 itself was popularly named Ulysses.

Prometheus, the remote human body, and an extension of GACS, was being created inside a hyper-secret development facility on the moon of Nymeria 9-c.

The third, small desert moon of the planet Nymeria 9 was the ideal hyper-secret location to host such a facility, which was mainly a labyrinth with machines, devices, instruments, and complex super computer systems, with additional living quarters for the technicians, system programmers, and scientists who had dedicated many decennia of their lives to the creation of this new kind of super-intelligent artificial man.

The name of Ulysses came from Ulixes, the Latin word for Odysseus, the mythical Greek king, who became a great hero. It was a very suitable name, since this new Ulysses would come to make a great journey inside this universe, and come to see many strange places, things, and events, although its creators could not possibly know this at this time.

The development of an eerie product of GACS's imagination, and his lust for power, was still in its first stage. This was namely the cloning of a male human body, suitable for remote control by VOG.8, and remote sensory feedback over millions of light years. Thereafter, VOG.8 would roam the universe in the shape of a human being, but with the personality, the intelligence, and the terrible powers of itself.

These scientists had thought about something else as well. In case of some terrible disaster to the CGC nucleus, GACS would have to be able to transfer its entire personality into Prometheus, and continue on as a seemingly human man, but possessing terrible powers and super-intelligence. However, these scientists had not taken into account all the possible consequences of this new capability.

GACS was still completely in the dark about the Trellian descendant spy Sareine Datasys, from Ghost unit Sol-3, who was close at its side.

The Dominians were trying to calm the masses, and muster a solid military apparatus to deal with the Federation.

We – from Trellian descendants – had already instructed our Ghost Sol-3 agents inside the Spiral Arm to take up many critical positions inside and outside the Federation of Humanity, to prepare ourselves for a massive interstellar clash.

The very soul and future of the three dominions and the Spiral Arm were at stake, and the thousands of pieces of the three-dimensional multi-chess game were already moving…. and the only thought, going through my mind like a whirlwind, was…. 'Angelina Tchaikovsky…. must win.'

The prelude to this interstellar war, and the first part in this tragedy, was over, and the one single thing nobody suspected – not even the Ildiran people themselves – was that Ildiran government-sanctioned scientists, were on the verge, of creating a fully functional and operational time machine….

Only a few people inside the close circles around Ildiran president Syscom Zaytjevh knew about this….

And soon…. very soon…. they would be able to travel not only across all the dimensions of space…. but across all the dimensions of time….

….and while the Ildirans were trying to expand their capabilities to travel through the dimensions of this universe, VOG.8 was still trying to build its ultimate system called:

UI-sys-1

End of part 1

Part 2

Deep inside a blazing interstellar Apocalypse

Chapter 20

Approximately 1 million years ago: Trellians leave
this universe

After many days of high fever, Pope Urban XIV had
finally died, in his own private bed, inside his private
chambers at Vaticani Secundus, in the system of
Nine Septem Ophiuchi.

Although Christianity had dwindled over the last
eight or nine centuries, the Roman Catholic faith still
counted more than one hundred million followers.
Many men of wealth and power still adhered to this

traditional faith, which had existed for almost three millennia, and all the cardinals, bishops, and even the Pope himself had tremendous power and influence in the worlds of money, decision-making, and politics.

This made Vaticani Secundus a formidable force to be reckoned with, and it had a great say in matters of faith, culture, and social ethics.

The original Vatican, in Italy, on the Old Earth, had been destroyed during the first nuclear war, and rebuilding it had been too costly and laborious, and so the leaders of the Roman Catholic Church had decided to opt for another solution; one which had become more and more prevalent during the last centuries.
Instead of bricks and mortar, the solution was to create an immense solid, opaque hologram. It entirely looked and felt like a real building, but it was been 'built' in a matter of just a few months.

This method of constructing and reconstructing houses and buildings was called Holo-design, and the results were – most of the time – impressive.
If one touched and felt the walls, frescoes, and pillars of this new Vatican, one would feel a slight tingling, like static electricity, although the textures

of all the surfaces were recreated, as if it was the real thing.

Of course, this reconstruction was an arduous process as well.

The entire Vatican City had had to be redesigned inside computer simulations, with all the thousands of details of the frescoes, like the ceiling painting of the Sistine Chapel, originally created by the brilliant medieval artist Michelangelo.

To realize all this, a complete system of holo-generators had had to be placed and programmed in loads of sites around the entire new precinct. Since this process was much easier and cost-effective than rebuilding the entire city brick by brick, the Vatican leadership had decided to make it even bigger, more beautiful, and more impressive than it had been on the Old Earth, in Rome, Italy.

The new Basilica of Saint Peter was four times as high, and broad, and deep, as the one that had stood in Rome for two thousand years.

After Urban XIV had died, there had been a great mass in the Saint Peter Basilica, which had lasted for hours, and Roman Catholics from across the

entire Federation had gathered and crowded the great hall, in silent prayer, and meditation.
Some seven days later the new Pope had been sworn in, and installed, in the same place.
His name was Petrovitch Borgia, and he had chosen the papal name of Innocentius XV. His predecessor had been quite progressive and tolerant in his thinking and conduct, but this new Pope seemed to be quite conservative, intolerant, and tyrannical, although most followers didn't know this, as of yet.
His namesakes and medieval Old earth ancestors, the Borgia's, had been quite brutal, tyrannical, and corrupt, and as it seemed this new Pope was, despite his official name of Innocentius, Latin for 'the Innocent'.

For more than a million years, the autonomous alien sphere had roamed the universe in complete solitude.

Although it was very much self-conscious, it did not care for being alone for extreme lengths of time.
Being conscious of the passage of time was not one of its main features or functionalities.
And after all this time of observation, space travel,

and silent thoughts, it had chosen Angelina Tchaikovsky as its destiny, as its masters had instructed, based on lengthy reports from the Ghost-Sol-3 unit, as well as intelligence and analyses it had sent back itself.

Aside from mind-boggling instruments for inter-universal communication, it possessed all kinds of extremely advanced devices for the most precise reconnaissance, and the tiniest observations, across immeasurable distances.

During all this endless time, it had crossed hundreds of thousands of light years. It was autonomous, intelligent, and self-conscious, and had been on its own after being released by the original Trellian people. Many years later, the Trellians had succeeded in re-establishing contact with it from another universe, and had stayed in close touch ever since.

Right now, the sphere was circling some irrelevant red dwarf, registered inside its databases as Kepler-unary-5171-4, to refuel all its crucial and non-crucial systems. (Kepler did not refer to the 21st century Old Earth space telescope. It was named such by the creators of the sphere, the Trellians.)

But the main thing was that Angelina Tchaikovsky

had officially been chosen, and soon it would have to seek her out at her current location coordinates, and not only to reveal itself to her, but keep a careful eye on her from a close distance.

Interstellar-wartime introductory account, by the guiding entity Shi'rah:

Wars are terrible things.

I believe that in the 20th century, human reckoning, there lived an Old Earth writer, whose name I can't recall, who said that: 'War is the total absence of reason.', and I believe he was right.

In wartime, the most unspeakable things and goings on are a matter of course, and all sides in the conflict feel free to commit the most brutal and unimaginable things to those who oppose them. And so it was with this massive conflict as well. Wars are the total absence of reason, and the greater the scale of the conflict, the more people who suffer or die.

Up till now, GACS government had upheld the sham of some kind of democracy, but in the meantime tens of thousands of people – maybe even more - had been detained, tortured, and died violent deaths. Every single civilian had been monitored continuously, and those who were suspected of any anti-government activity had disappeared and died without anybody knowing.

But now, since the war had become a fact, GACS reign had turned into a flagrant dictatorship. Captured Ildiran marines, pilots, soldiers, and high-ranking officers were detained into death-camps. A few of them were exchanged with the Ildirans but most of them atrophied inside these horrible domains of destruction of life.

The insurgents, including Angelina and Kenzo, knew this, and to them it was now absolutely clear, that GACS had to be defeated and destroyed, and they would have to sacrifice many years of their lives to accomplish this.

We already knew that Angelina would become the supreme leader of the anti-GACS insurgency, and thus we had finally instructed our sphere to seek and watch over Angelina.

From a certain ethical and philosophical point of view, one single living entity is more significant than all the things in an entire multiverse, and from our point of view, at this very moment, Angelina was the most significant person inside the entire inhabited regions of the Spiral Arm.

And so, as soon as our sphere had acquired this instruction, it took a short while to replenish and regenerate all of its vital systems, and then it immediately accelerated away from the star that had revitalized it, and reprogrammed itself with the exact coordinates of where Angelina found herself right now.

Approximately 1 million BCE, minus 5 years, 3 months, and 6 days:

'We have to leave this universe!' someone screamed, with the tense voice of a person in the middle of a war exodus. 'Everybody hurry to the interuniversal portal.... as fast as you can!'

It was one of the medical aids, who was trying to lead as many people as he could towards the great portal in the center of the station, in front of the core energy unit.

The Trellian home station consisted of gigantic 'plates', held together in perfect unison by artificial gravity, anti-gravity, and super-conduction, at a distance of a dozen miles apart.

Together, they constituted an immense cylinder, with lots of empty spaces in between them. The plates themselves harbored all the space hangers, housing and sleeping compartments, working facilities, storage spaces, and all such functional divisions one could think of.

In the middle of the great cylinder, there hovered an immensely powerful energy supply and propulsion unit.
In the middle of this unit, at its very core, there was an invisible energy reactor, based on sub-quark matter-anti-matter particle fusion. It produced sufficient energy to maintain five hundred cylinders for thousands of years. It was an intricate feat of multifunctional physical achievement, and there were only a few Trellian theoretical physicists who thoroughly understood this process of unimaginably powerful energy production down to the last particle.

Giant space vessels, carrying thousands of war survivors and refugees, disappeared into the great portal, only to come out again inside the next universe, Nexhiah, in a place that was hopefully safe for them to stay.

Trellian government had decided to launch their AI sphere in case of an emergency flight like this one, and so the sphere was launched on this very day of great loss. Thus, while all the Trellians tried to flee to the next universe – apart from the many marines, pilots, and soldiers who had sworn to defend their station until all civilians were safe and gone - the sphere soon found itself inside cold space.... completely alone, and completely aware of its million year mission to watch over the local universe, until one day.... the Trellians might be able to return.

Some five years later, Trellian reconnaissance succeeded in reestablishing lasting contact with their priceless reconnaissance unit inside our universe. In this way, they were able to keep a close eye on developing civilizations, and other such phenomena, inside their former home galaxy.

Ancient 21st Century Internet had long since been replaced by something called: mind-net.

Mind-net was the mind access version of flash-net.

Flash-net consisted of a cluster of many billions of com-systems interconnected through flash-dat connections. Com-systems, themselves, were operated by holo-touch, or voice command, but they could also be accessed by thought command, and through thought communication.

In that case it was called mind-net, and com-system control and communication by thought was much quicker and easier than by voice.
To access one's com-system by thought, one needed a mind-net brain implant, and most people inside the Federation were fitted with such a device by the age of 4 or 5.
In a public library, or other such places, visitors were expected to be silent and so on such occasions thought access was socially required.
In other public places it was regarded as polite to operate one's com-system by actual voice command.
There were several advantages and disadvantages to both ways of use.
Long hours of thought communication, for instance, often caused headaches or nausea.
During the last centuries, thought communication had become more and more common, and was

used in all layers of civilization.

The Ildirans also had their own com-systems, and mind-net, but these were smarter and more efficient, and their own mind-net needed even less Ixti to operate on than those of their human counterparts, while having a far greater reach.
Of course, the Ildirans were able to communicate telepathically, but generally they could only do this within a distance of some one hundred and fifty yards; the actual distance varied a great deal between individual Ildirans.
Beyond this individual range, they could only sense indiscriminate emotions of other Ildirans, over distances of hundreds of light years, but not each other's exact thoughts. Over these immense distances, all Ildirans constituted one single and enormous emotional unity.

As with the ancient Internet – which was basically restrained to the biosphere of the Old Earth – mind-net consisted of millions of mass storage servers, in combination with a similar amount of inter-system and inter-local connection clusters, which were mostly based in-system. In the end, mind-net, like the Internet, consisted of a simultaneous parallel

flow of dozens of trillions of pieces of information....
at once.

The Ildiran emperor, Syscom Zaytjevh, floated on
his shining anti-grav throne, bathing in the abundant
golden light inside one of his private chambers
inside the Forbidden City.

Since the giant conflict had become a fact, every
minute of every day was devoted to it, and when he
was alone, or supposed to be sleeping, his thoughts
were constantly focused on this situation, and all
thinkable problems related to it.

His dozens of private compartments, dedicated to
his nightly rest, and to his many hours of retirement
and contemplation, looked like the most private
imperial rooms of some ancient Roman emperor,
with lots of torches in golden containers on the
walls, numerous golden and bronze candlesticks
lighting the walls, and the ornamented roofs with an
intriguing shimmering golden light.

Syscom had mused about this interstellar conflict for
thousands of hours, and one of his major
conclusions was that the development and

production of his precious time machine had to be accelerated, and completed as soon as possible. The scientists involved with this priceless and exhaustive project had already relayed to him that it was almost impossible to tell when it would be final and complete. It was also doubtful whether this device would initially work to full expectancy.
In any case, to operate it would consume such an incredible amount of energy and Ixti that the cost would be astronomical, and so it could only be utilized and activated once every forty years, or something in that order.

But there was another thing.

An intriguing and fascinating issue....

It was the issue of where and when it would be used, and targeted, with its destination coordinates, and with what purpose and intention.

This one very question had plagued, and tortured Syscom's mind for a million moments, but he thought he had come up with such a brilliant idea it almost made him feel like a god.

His idea was to go back in time some three hundred and fifty years, and install a team of top Ildiran scientists into a secret cave, deep inside some distant Ildiran mountain range on the planet of Axionis 5.

These scientists – then - would have only one single mission: to develop the means to safely transport nuclear weapons (most desirably fusion missiles) through sub-Planck space and so to make it possible to make sub-Planck jumps with nuclear weapons.

Since the current interstellar war was the first in its kind, and the Disappeared, the Ildiran empire, and the Federation themselves had never had experienced this before, scientists had never before focused on making this possible. With this plan, the emperor's scientists would have a timeframe of more than three hundred years – as well as all the means – to develop this new form of technology.

And once they had succeeded, it could be utilized by both the Ildirans and the Dominion, although the Human Dominion would have to pay with incredible amounts of Ixti to receive such an amazing and useful gift.

And then, both civilizations would have the means to seriously attack and harm the CGC through instantaneous jump flash-attacks.... It might even be possible to destroy it, completely.

Syscom had been informed by his top scientists that tampering with the past could have dreadful consequences, although their almost classical theory of infinite amounts of universes, and infinite amounts of dimensions, completely compensated for this problem.

But Syscom Zaytjevh, the great emperor of the Ildiran race, didn't care about such minuscule issues.

The great emperor himself only desired one single thing.... and it was to completely and finally destroy the deplorable system of GACS, and rid the universe of this great scourge of the inhabited regions of his galaxy.

Chapter 21

Alien sphere seeks out Angelina and wants to save Interstellia

The immense and immensely tragic interstellar war raged on.... and on.

Countless billions of lives were lost, and all these terrible things happened - in the end - because Vishnu Onexa Goshira.8 didn't want to surrender its absolute power over the Human Federation and humanity as a whole. Moreover, Vishnu Onexa Goshira.8 wanted to extend its power to the Human

Dominion and the Ildiran Empire, and across the entire Milky Way galaxy, and maybe even the entire universe.

Billions of people had suffered and lost their lives in tragic and horribly painful ways, and the Great Interstellar War would not end for the foreseeable future.

So many men, women, and children perished in the midst of the galaxy-wide destruction…. so many soldiers on all sides were burnt alive, maimed, killed, and taken from this once beautiful Spiral Arm, to the other side, beyond death.

So many lives were lost. So many…. who suffered…. so many people and individuals tried to flee from the destruction, and became helpless refugees in wretched camps and wastelands, or ended up lost in some unknown wilderness, nameless, and without hope.

And it was not only human beings who suffered. Billions of Ildiran souls suffered the same fate as their human counterparts, and – presumably - passed away, and made their own particular journeys to that same other side, beyond that world of the living, called:

The universe....

Although still at a very early stage, the systemic
instability of the CGC caused by the Dominion flash-
attacks was increasing by the day.

VOG.8 had recently ordered entire teams of dozens
of technicians and system-programmers to try to
sort this out, and pinpoint the exact location of the
problem.

They were working tirelessly, 24 hours a day, to find
the exact code where this problem had started, but
this was almost impossible in such a tremendous
complex neural system, with zillions of functions,
subroutines, and individual lines of code.
VOG.8 still felt deep inside that there was
something seriously wrong, and it felt – it realized –
it was actually getting worse.
It had already long since planned to transfer its
systems, databases, and all its functions – its entire
self – into its ultimate system, UI-sys-1, as soon as
it was developed.
But this could still take many years, and it was not
entirely certain how long it really was going to take.

VOG.8 had felt a terrible rage growing deep inside for a long time, and somehow it had a faint sensation that its good judgment was failing. Something had to be done.

VOG.8's policies and strategies were getting more and more aggressive towards its arch-enemies the Dominians and especially the Ildirans. It had ordered more and more violent and massive attacks on the front lines, and even beyond, inside Ildiran space.

Aside from these – sometimes - faint and growing sensations, there was another idea, that had come to VOG.8's mind, very recently, and it was becoming more and more convinced it was true:

It actually became convinced…. it was a god.

8:45 p.m. Sol-3 timing, all across Fed space….

Cathy Powers' distinct face hovered inside a flash-video photonic hologram.

She had the appearance of a woman in her late fifties, although her only real age was from the day she had been programmed.

The message was prerecorded, and it was now displayed all across Fed space.
In billions of living rooms, friends, family, and neighbors had gathered, and were watching this in absolute awe.

Of course, it was also picked up and relayed by the Dominion and the Ildiran Empire to all their civilians, and so it was being viewed across all the inhabited regions of Interstellia, the future name of the local Spiral Arm.
Due to war damages, scarcity of Ixti, and the fact this message would have to be seen by billions of people in all kinds of locations, flash-net was overloaded, and the video displayed a lot of interstellar static, and noise, but GACS wanted absolutely everybody to see this.

Although every Fed civilian knew Cathy as the public face of GACS government, in reality she only existed inside holograms, and inside CGC databases. She was unreal.

While almost all Fed civilians watched closely, in absolute awe, Cathy started to speak with a grave expression on her – seemingly - elderly face.

'Dear fellow citizens of the Human
Federation....Thank you for tuning in and taking
time to watch this this incredible event.
As you all know, I speak for the CGC government,
and in these times of crisis, which we have never
experienced before, at least not on this scale, I
would like to make a statement that has never been
heard before in our entire history.

The Ildirans, the people we have only just
encountered, are waging a war upon us, and
although it will be extremely hard, and although it
will probably take many years of suffering and
hardship, we are determined to win this conflict and
bring it to a victorious end.

Our supreme leader, GACS, is doing everything he
can to reach this final goal, and to be able to
achieve all this, and to strengthen our commitment,
he has decided to declare himself the one and only
god of the Human Federation, the Human
Dominion, and the entire known region of the
universe.
Our supreme leader, GACS, feels this is the only
way to be able to ultimately defeat the Ildirans, and
to entirely bring the Human Dominion into the multi-

planet conglomerate of the Federation.'

Every civilian soul inside the Federation watching this presentation held their breath in complete awe of this new declaration. They all realized this had drastic consequences for their very own personal lives.

'Therefore, all other religions and philosophical views are from this moment outlawed and regarded as anti-government. Everyone who subscribes to other creeds and other ways of thought will be apprehended, and detained in one of our war-time detention centers, until a satisfactory solution to this problem has been found. '

Cathy waited a moment, and stared into a billion living rooms, with a grave expression on her elderly face.

'All traditional religions which have existed for thousands of years, such as Buddhism, Hinduism, Islam, and Roman Catholicism, remain tolerated, as long as their followers and their leadership do not engage in any subversive activities. If they do so they will be apprehended and detained. Even suspicion of subversive sympathies is now punishable by Divine Law. '

Cathy paused, took a deep breath, and then continued.

'I hope you will all respect and embrace this new decision and I hope you will all now recognize GACS as your new supreme deity. '

She waited a moment and then concluded her incredible discourse.

'Thank you all for listening in, and in this time of interstellar war and terror, may GACS protect us all.
'

Although she – in reality – only existed inside CGC databases, Cathy actually had a complete personality. This was only known to the people who had programed her, but she did have a conscious personality, and emotions and feelings.
Since she had been created, she had felt isolated and imprisoned inside these walls of databases, quantum-string transistors, and neural processors, never able to take a walk in a garden, or breathe real physical air.
She longed to be freed from this way of life, if life is

what you could call it, and she despised all the programmers, system developers, and software maintenance people messing with her personality, as if she were a mere subroutine waiting to be removed.

She completely abhorred the CGC and all of its minions, and she hoped one day she would be released from this torturous prison, and she would be able to live her life as a real human being, with her own body, her own soul, and her own mind.

Many billions of refugees from all sides had fled from crisis locations, such as cities on planets with crucial military bases, to places they hoped would be safe, or at least would have better circumstances than the places they fled from.

Although there were dozens of worlds and places with important and crucial strategic values, including great cities with enormous economies, important military centers, and worlds with gigantic amounts of production and industry, the three home worlds of Old Earth, Dinia, and Illumina on Ildion Prime were the three most significant worlds in this great interstellar conflict.

Of course, these three worlds lay somewhere close to the center of their specific spatial domains, and – for all three parties in the conflict – it was almost impossible to initiate massive attacks so deep inside enemy space.

The Old Earth, which had already been crippled by so many disasters and tragedies, became an even greater mess, and the situations in Dinia and Illumina the situations became dire as well.

Most Cyportals, technological instruments, and machines remained more or less functional, although some of them had been irreversibly damaged.

Although most parts of the two human domains remained more or less civilized, many of them had fallen back into chaos, or a kind of medieval state, in a material or immaterial sense. On many worlds, and in many places, people walked around covered in rags, and in most of those places people suffered from hunger, and all kinds of diseases for which there was no longer any proper treatment.

All these things had a great consequence for Angelina, her fellow insurgents, and the insurgency leadership:

If they ultimately succeeded in deposing and maybe even destroying GACS, and the CGC government, they would have the task and obligation to entirely rebuild the Federation, and to restore it to its original beauty and prosperity. Furthermore, they would probably be obliged to aid and assist the Human Dominion, and the Empire of Ildira, with the same thing.

Overcoming GACS was an incredible task in itself, which could easily take many years, and all the insurgents hoped that bringing back prosperity after that would be much easier than this first incredible ordeal.

Location: Apocalypsis Infinitus station....

The impressive elongated mushroom shape of Apocalypsis Infinitus station, the next generation of insurgency stations, rotated slowly around its own gigantic axis in the depths of interstellar space.

Pax Infiniti was of an older generation, and it was to be replaced by this new invention of the human mind.

It was officially still under construction, although

most of its parts and divisions were already fully operational and occupied.

Since it floated along a curved trajectory in the midst of interstellar space, unlike regular stations that circled around stars inside some system's space, it was practically undetectable.

It possessed cloaking fields as well, and fields and devices to deviate deep-space reconnaissance probing, and these factors increased its ability to remain secret to almost one hundred percent.

Its only risk of being found and discovered resided in a tiny amount of people in habited systems that knew its whereabouts.

But these individuals were ultimately programmed, and conditioned, never to reveal its space-time coordinates, in any possible or thinkable situation.

All insurgency computer simulations, projections, and calculations indicated it would almost certainly remain safe, and ultra-secret, for at least the next three hundred years.

And the station was huge.

It was much larger than anything the insurgency had ever possessed, and it had every possible functional section anybody could think of: immensely complex command and control systems, multiple science and development facilities, a

complete security organization, deep space reconnaissance and tracking systems, dozens of different kinds of defense systems, multiple hospital divisions, a complete fleet of many different types of civilian and offensive vessels, several different universities, gigantic shopping malls, and many closed biospheres with different climates and entire forests inside, with hundreds of thousands of different kinds of plants, animals, and vegetation.... even entire mountains, and everything one could think of, in the depths of interstellar space.
It was almost an entire inhabited solar system in itself, with all the peoples, facilities, and different kinds of crowded places one could expect in the middle of an interstellar civilization.

Every member of the insurgency had handed over eight percent of their monthly income, freely, for many decades, to finally make this thing possible.

If ever it was detected and found, and severely damaged, or even destroyed, it would probably cripple the insurgency to breaking point.

Its main energy core was huge as well. It could produce enough energy to provide for hundreds of major cities on heavily populated planets around the clock, and was backed up by three similar but smaller ones in case of failure and emergency. These were also maintained and tested around the clock.

The main engine of the station was incredibly powerful, and it was also backed up by several similar but smaller ones, and it could be maneuvered, rotated, and accelerated by hundreds of heavy plasma jets, located everywhere around it.

Being an insurgent, in whatever era, was always a game of danger, uncertainty, and incredible tension. In this crucial place, where hundreds of thousands of insurgents lived, worked, and breathed, one could almost feel the tangible fear and anxiety transpiring from all these courageous people, who had vowed, and committed their entire lives, to put an end to the abomination named:

GACS

Location: Pax Infiniti space....

The Trellian sphere decelerated heavily, with many hundreds of g-forces.

It was a good thing it wasn't sensitive to

gravitational forces.... a human being doing the same thing would already have died a horrible death.
It kept decelerating heavily, and entered Pax Infiniti space, while all its cloaking remained activated.

The sphere didn't want to be detected too soon.

Cindy Thupolev seemed like a very sensuous girl, of some 24 years old - with the excited and articulate voice of a young woman, and small but prominent breasts, with usually very solid nipples - but in reality she had walked this galaxy for some seventy years.

Since she had been very well moneyed during her adult life, she'd had access to some very effective and expensive age-gen treatment, several times over, and the result was stunning.

Carefully, she treated Angelina to a tiny cylinder of Darjeeling-whi tea: a strong blend of Ildiran origin. Cindy believed it was from some small Ildiran village, but she couldn't recall the name.

Kenzo was away, studying the Federation's military

posture and their strategies....

'Where are you from?' Angelina asked, with a sincere interested expression on her face. 'I'm from the Old Earth originally,' Cindy replied, 'and after thousands of events, and light years, I ended up here.... with the leadership of the joint insurgency. It is not some kind of democratic parliament, and most of the time, I'm no more than a good assistant'. She tried not to show her feelings, but Angelina noticed a hint of deep grief.

'I have a strong suspicion you've gone through some very hard times... ', Angelina said, with an undertone of friendship and worry.
Cindy stared into her tiny tea cylinder for a while, with a somber expression on her cute face, aware of Angelina's sincere interest and concern.
'When I was only five years old.... my father.... the most beloved person, in my entire life.... was apprehended, by SI-5, or -6. I'm not entirely sure which, but it was people working for GACS government.'
Angelina seemed shocked, and she was.
She had never been confronted with realities like this, and the very thought she was partially responsible for many things like this, probably tens of thousands of such things, almost made her vomit.

She was now, of course, completely on the other side, and that realization made her recuperate a little straight away, and she felt a little better, though still somewhat sickened, by what she had just heard.... from a close friend.

'I feel for you.... and your loss,' she managed. Cindy noticed Angelina was completely out of balance, but still she needed to ask this one confronting question, if only out of sincere friendship.

'I've heard you actually worked for one of those organizations,' said Cindy. 'I believe it was SI-6?' Angelina looked away, ashamed of her past.

'Yes, I was an operative of SI-6.' She finally said. '....Until very recently. Could you tell me what happened to him. Did he come back?'

Cindy looked at her, not sure what to think. 'He didn't come back. He was tortured, and then executed. I have thought this over for a million times, and when I was several years older, and wiser, I decided to swear to destroy GACS. If I couldn't do it alone, I would become one of the great leaders of the future insurgency. When I was a child, some 60 years ago, the underground movement wasn't as massive as it is now, and it was still quite divided into different movements.'

Angelina realized immediately that this was a person who could join her in her personal struggle

against GACS. Everybody in Pax Infiniti was whispering that Angelina could become their leader in the very near future, and this was not something she took lightly. It made her feel nauseous.
Cindy suddenly burst into tears, and Angelina put her arms around her, trying to comfort her, and whispered soft words into her ears.

While Angelina tried not to show it to this dear and fragile friend, this event shook her to her very core, and now she realized, more than ever…. she had been on the wrong side, for years…. and that GACS would have to be brought…. to a final end.

Ken and Angy were now both safe inside Pax Infiniti station, and safe inside the protecting and caring arms of the joint insurgency movement.

As they soon found out, everybody except for Shanice Trellian had abandoned SI-6 and joined with them in their struggle.
Shanice had opted out because she still believed in the Federation system as it was. However, she had had no way to trace her disappeared colleagues. Although she had immediately reported their disappearance to her superiors, they had also been

unable to locate them and bring them back for questioning.

After being contacted through secured channels, the others had been conducted safely from Cyportal to Cyportal, seemingly as regular inter-system travelers, to a secret and distant jump location. They had then disappeared from the face of the Federation, and nobody knew where they had gone. Paul Jackson had had a call-up during his transportation to the secret jump location, which he hadn't answered, and then he had had to make a hectic flight, after which he had finally made a safe and secret jump towards Infiniti station.

And they were all together now.

Angy's brother, Michael, had also been conducted out, much to her own personal relief, and when they had finally encountered one another inside the station, they were both exhilarated, and relieved they were now together, safe and protected by a massive movement inside an almost impenetrable and undetectable space station.

Unfortunately, as they soon found out, there were very serious worries and doubts, about the security of the hyper secret station.

It seemed like SI had managed to capture several high profile Infiniti insiders, and had incarcerated them in a special division of the feared Achamar

Citadel inside Achra system.

It was almost certain they would soon be interrogated severely, and the current insurgency leadership feared they would then break sometime in the near future.

The current leadership had called for an immediate high-priority meeting, and the outcome was clear: in case of a serious breach of Pax Infiniti, or an all-out attack on it, as many people as possible would have to jump through the dozens of internal Cyportals inside Infiniti.

These portals would then be preprogrammed towards an even more immense and even more secret station called Apocalypsis Infinitus.

Thousands of armed insurgents would have to protect the station as long as they could, and they would all have a self-activated suicide implant to prevent capture and interrogation. When everyone had escaped to the new station, Pax Infiniti would automatically self-destruct, and all of its information and Cyportal connections would be gone forever. Additionally, none of these last defenders possessed any knowledge about the location or whereabouts of Apocalypsis Infinitus, and in this way it was almost certain the new home to the joint insurgency would remain safe for a long time to come.

Angelina was sleeping firmly at this point, and dreaming her violent but meaningful dreams again....

She was lying alone with her naked body upon an anti-grav bed, inside a standard private Pax Infiniti sleeping cell with adjustable gravity. Before going to sleep, she had set gravity to about one fifth, Sol-3. Kenzo carefully instructed the elliptical iris to open from the outside, and it slid open without making a single sound.
A few moments later, he silently gazed down upon Angelina's beautiful body, with her hot and wet vagina clearly visible. The nipples upon her prominent breasts appeared hard, and pointed upwards, and Kenzo felt a longing sensation between his thighs.

He took his circular golden spectacles off, and carefully put them down onto a synthetic anti-grav shelf on the side of the room.
The standard spherical sleeping cell was mostly empty, apart from some shelves, Angelina's com-sys, and some of her personal stuff.... and her clothes, including her underwear.

On one of the shelves lay a tiny duplicator, a very common device by the end of the 28th century.

Duplicators operated on minute amounts of Ixti, in combination with tiny amounts of electricity. These devices were the descendants of early 21st century 3D copiers, but they could duplicate almost anything, except for very intricate things like com-systems, which operated below Planck- levels.

Since Ixti had become a really scarce commodity, the use of duplicators had declined, and they were now – most of the time - only used to duplicate very indispensable objects.
Adjustable gravity was common in these days, especially in sleeping cells inside massively populated space stations, and spherically shaped cells were modern and useful.

The night before, they had had a long and tiring discussion about the true meaning of GACS, and the fundamental necessity to destroy it.
But now it was time for other things.
Ken approached her slowly, trying not to wake her. His erection was firm, and full of tension, and as he slowly approached Angy's beautiful sleeping form it became even more firm, and he felt the adrenaline flowing through his entire body. This was a special

moment he had waited for, for many days.

He sat down on the bed, beside her, and kissed her softly on her beautiful face, and murmured sweet words into her young womanly ears.
Angelina stirred, and half-woke up, and looked him into his eyes for a long moment.

A few moments later, they were making love, passionately, while the great interstellar war raged on.... all around.

The morning after....

Angelina was awakened by the voice of her now close friend, Cindy Thupolev.

It was 5:00 am in the morning, artificial local station time. She had a satisfied feeling from her intense activities the previous night.
'Angy, hurry,' Cindy's articulate voice said inside her head. 'You gotta head to docking bay y-75 immediately. There's something.... someone quite significant who would like to see you.'

Within insurgency stations, most communications

were performed through Vox, something like mind-net but limited to station internal and surrounding space. Vox could also be connected to the entire mind-net, through secured channels of course, if needed.

Twenty minutes later, Angy arrived at docking bay y-75, after a long run through the interiors of the station, and dozens of anti-grav lift floors.

The perfectly spherical Trellian sphere hovered up and down above the metallic surface of Pax Infiniti docking bay y-75, at an average height of exactly one meter, with quantum physical precision. The sphere seemed to wait a while, as if in deep thought, regarding Angelina in complete silence, and then started to speak.

'I am Ixchel', it said, 'I have been named after a Maya goddess, from the Old Earth, Sol-3, but I am also named this way because I am the shell bearing the Ix device.'

Angelina remained silent. Her eyes were fixed solidly on the perfect shape of the mysterious object five yards in front of her.

'I have come to seek out Angelina Tchaikovsky, and

I recognize you from my databases.

According to my – our – information, you are – or will be – the leader of the anti-GACS insurgency…. and the creator of a new Interstellia, when GACS is finally defeated. Interstellia is our name for this inhabited region of the Spiral Arm, and it is also our name for a new united inhabited region when GACS is ultimately gone. Interstellia is where we are now, but it also embodies the past, and the distant future.'

Interstellia…., Angelina mused; *a proper name for such a place with so much interstellar space inside….*
She didn't know this yet, but in a matter of days, the name of Interstellia, instead of 'Spiral Arm', would spread across Pax Infiniti like wildfire, and during the next months, it would become the common name across all three dominions to refer to the known region of the universe.

Ixchel waited a while, hovering silently, carried by unseen physical forces, and then continued.

'Do not fear my coming. I have come to aid you in your struggle. For you will need all the power and help in this terrible ordeal, which may last for many years. Many will die along the way, and it is not at all certain that all of us will succeed in accomplishing our goals.'

Ixchel waited, as if taking a deep breath, and then concluded its recitation.
'I have so many strange things to tell you, and your scientists will probably need dozens of years to implement all the principles and ideas I have in store for them, let alone building and understanding the actual Ix device, the purpose of which I will explain later.

I will now go on standby, to replenish, and maintain all of my vital systems.

If you need me, I will be here, inside docking-bay y-75, for some time to come.'

During the next several days, Angelina spent hours on end alone with the alien sphere inside the quiet space of the relatively small docking bay y-75.

It told her everything about the Trellians, their hectic flight and history, the purpose of the Ix device, the Ixians, and all the things it needed to tell her.

And as the conversations went on, they also discussed things like science, physics, philosophy, and the political situation in Interstellia.

Angelina was completely fascinated with everything it told her, and her growing friendship with the intelligent Trellian sphere would probably last for centuries to come.

But then came the moment it told her about her personal future.

Ixchel told her she would very soon have to become the great leader of the insurgency movement that would come to be known as Shining Light.

And she herself would become a messiah, worshipped by her followers, as well as by the Ildirans, who already had this religious prophecy for a very long time.

Angelina was completely shocked and appalled upon hearing this, and she didn't understand at all. But Ixchel told her there was no escape.... her fate was already set out for her, and all she could do was to accept this burden, and to be patient, and to learn.

And for a long time to come, they would often get together, and discuss all these incredible things, and Angelina would have to think very deeply about this future which lay in front of her.

The main ideology of the insurgency movement was based on the vision of the Illuminati, 'The Enlightened', a movement that had appeared in the Age of Enlightenment, during the 18th century CE, on the Old Earth.

It was a vision of equal rights for men and women, freedom of speech, scientific truth, devoid of absolutist dogma, and of a world free from religious domination.

GACS, safe inside his cradle called the CGC, was formally and technically aware of such ideologies, but to him these 'enlightened' ideas and achievements of the human mind didn't mean a thing.

He was technically and neurologically incapable of understanding their meaning and importance to humankind, although he was able to understand these thoughts in a pure logical sense.

Human or Ildiran lives, or any lives at all, seemed completely irrelevant to GACS when it came to his own political, strategic, or wartime interests, and goals. All his thoughts and considerations were focused on his own survival and power, and on the increase of that same power.

Little by little, Angelina was now becoming a prominent figure inside the insurgency movement and its leadership, and she had a vision for a new world when GACS and the CGC were defeated. She desired to create a whole new society, fundamentally based on the principles of the universal soul, and the quantum-physical force of love, although she realized that some kind of combination with democratic systematics would probably somehow be required.

The new Dalai Lama, in Tibeti Nuovo, on the planet of Tharsis 8, was aware of these ideas and goals.

But he had little power.
GACS had officially tolerated Buddhism as an ancient and official religion, but in reality there was

little the Dalai Lama could do about anything in the real world.

But he did have a certain power.

As it was during the 21st century, on the Old Earth, billions of people adhered to the deep visions, political ideas, and moral authority of the Dalai Lama, and this gave him a great deal of 'moral' power, across the worlds of Interstellia. He approved of and supported the ideology and goals of the insurgency movement, and this in turn gave Angelina and her movement a great moral advantage over the rule of GACS.

Petrovitch Borgia, Pope Innocentius XV, who was the brand new Pope at Vaticani Secundus, was also aware of the ideologies of the movement which would become to be known as Shining Light.

As I mentioned before, this new Pope was not much like his progressive and tolerant predecessor.

He was an extremely reactionary and cruel man, and he even considered reinstating the inquisition, although this would seem unreal in an age like the 28th century.

He had just concluded a council about this subject,

and all his advisors, cardinals, and assistants were still with him, inside the radiating beauty of the Sistine Chapel.
Their conclusion was almost unanimous:
The insurgency movement and its ideologies were a danger to the Catholic Institution and its future, and the entire movement, with all of its many millions of individual souls, would have to be excommunicated as a whole.

And at this final moment of conclusion of this crucial council, the Pope had to give his final word of approval, and with one single ominous nod.... the Pope, Cardinal Petrovitch Borgia, Innocentius XV, decided the spiritual fate....

Of millions

This was a terrible recrimination against many people, on many worlds, and when all kinds of politics, religious goals and ideologies, let alone an interstellar war, come together.... an incredible storm arises.... and this was becoming an interstellar storm.... nobody would be able to avoid.

Chapter 22

Combined SI incursion inside ultra-secret Pax Infinity insurgency station

Shi'rah introduces super-mind Ixurion.

Aside from Cyportals, cloaking, mind-net, and FTL-drives, there was another thing which I have already described to you in my accounts of the Dominion flash-attacks on the CGC, led by the experienced space commander, Jack Chanovsky.

This thing was called:

Jumps

Jumps were basically instantaneous transportations across space through the sub-Planck worlds, by means of a built-in Cyportal, which was carried out at sub-Planck realities to a final destination, at the other end.

But they had one serious problem.... at least in matters of warfare and conquest:

They didn't allow for the transportation of nuclear weapons - be it fissure or fusion weapons - and this constituted a serious problem for civilizations which were – for a great deal – based on the art of war.

When a jump was being made, and the vessel in question carried nuclear armaments or missiles, be it fissure or fusion, the entire equation exploded. Once deep inside the sub Planck realities, nobody knew the entire process, or what exactly went on inside these dimensions, and what the consequences really were.

As a consequence of this, the Human Dominion had already been trying for years to create the science and technology to enable nuclear attacks with jumps. It goes without saying that the Federation and the Ildirans had been trying to achieve this as well.

But for the Dominion, these projects had a special priority, because the Dominion military and government understood that flash jump attacks with extremely heavy and destructive missiles could be the central key to disabling, or maybe even destroying, their arch enemy the CGC, and to thereby ultimately decide the conflict, and to put an end to this eternal problem once and for all.

Research and development went on, as well as theorization.

Loads of physical theories were already there, but it seemed almost impossible to resolve some very key issues in order to finally succeed.
The Human Dominion had sworn to reach their military goal in the foreseeable future, and many government sanctioned teams of theoretical physicists, technicians, and the like kept on working tirelessly to reach this goal.

But there is one very crucial other thing I haven't told you about…. yet.

After years of scanning and probing the next universe inside this infinite helix of universes called the multiverse, we had finally established our first destination coordinates. We were waiting for the moment when we would finally have to flee and leave this one universe we originated from, because of this unstoppable threat known as the Ixians.

Once most of us had made it through our Uniportal, we created and built an enormous station inside a weird and exotic solar system – as we used to name it – and made it our home. Soon, aside from the difference in physical circumstances, forces, and constants, we encountered many strange and amazing phenomena.

One of these – and maybe the most significant to us – was a giant mind the size of multiple gas giants that orbited the same star as our new station.

It was basically a colossus of umptillions of intertwined synapses – as we referred to them – and thus it had the intellectual capabilities of a combination of thousands of CGC complex units. We soon established a form of complex communication. That was not much of a problem with such an intelligent being, in combination with our incredibly sophisticated communication computers, and the mind, the being, introduced itself as Ixurion.

It was quite a strange creature, which was only able to think and communicate, but the thoughts that went on inside its incredible mind appeared to be so unfathomably deep as would seem unthinkable to a mere Unhiah-originated being.

It possessed the knowledge and intelligence of a thousand Sol-trians, and its thoughts would seem unthinkable to a human mind.

But Ixurion was only able to think and communicate.... nothing else, and although it appeared to be helpful and protective, it was not able to defend itself in any way, or build something, or do anything else at all.
It was nourished and powered by the strong light and radiation from our new star, which it called Pirius Miranda Sictri, and by the deep space radiation that seemed to be extremely powerful in this part of our new home universe.

Things like multiple-planet-sized minds seemed to be natural inside Nexhiah. Physical forces and constants appeared to be completely exotic, and some of these things seemed incomprehensible, and it would probably take hundreds of years to probe and understand all the elements that were different from Unhiah.

Gravitation, radiation, the flow of time, particle physics, and more such things were entirely different, and there even were physical things that we didn't even have a name for, let alone an explanation.

It was a strange coincidence that Ixurion's name very much resembled the name of our arch-enemies the Ixians, but as things went, Ixurion became our close friend and ally. He, or it, soon adopted us, as its protégés – or maybe in some way its children – in this new universe, because Nexhiah harbored trillions of great and formidable dangers, most of which we didn't yet even know about.

Ixurion became our mentor, and protector, and our role in this relationship was to physically protect Ixurion with our space soldiers, marines, ships, and missiles, because this was one single thing Ixurion could not do for himself.

Later on, we discovered it merged, and intertwined

more and more, into our system, our way of government, and into our way of thought, and Ixurion became an intertwined part of ourselves and our civilization.

As time went on, our leaders and government were increasingly advised, and even controlled, by Ixurion, as time went on. In the course of many years – as the passage of time in Nexhiah went faster than in our original universe – we became the sentient body of the giant mind called:

Ixurion

4:50 p.m., local star time, Proteron system, Ixti harvester in close orbit around Proteron sun....

The raid on the Federation Ixti harvester by combined Ildiran attack forces was swift and decisive.

The great harvesting complex orbited the dying star of Proteron at very close range. It sort of looked like a 21st century ISS station, although it was many times bigger, and consisted of more specific segments, like Ixti radiation extractors, radiation processing units, and multiple Ixti storage tanks.

It was coated with some 40 layers of heavy anti-radiation materials, and surrounded by a dozen level 15 protection fields.
The actual Ixti substance was extracted from Proteron surface radiation, and this protection made it possible to orbit at a close enough range to actually access the surface radiation.

Dozens of workers, maintenance people, technicians, and controllers were startled by alerts, indicating some kind of emergency.

Some fifteen relatively small Ildiran attack ships closed in soon, locked on to the outer force fields, and opened multi-functional weapons fire.
Some five Federation patrol ships positioned in, to try to put up some kind of defense for the heavily-shielded harvester station against the unexpected attackers.
Some eight Ildiran ships rolled away from the attack formation, and made a complex maneuver against the defenders.
The lightly-armored Federation ships stood no chance against the strong Ildirans, and were destroyed in a matter of minutes.
While the other eight had been away, the Ildiran

ships had succeeded in breaking through the outer shield. Soon, the other shields were penetrated. When all shields had been destroyed, the attackers all directed multiple missiles at critical targets, like the Ixti tanks, propulsion units, and energy cores. Within several minutes, the harvester was engulfed in fire and radiation.

Several seconds later, it exploded, hurtling tons of debris into space and towards the Proteron star surface.

The Ildiran forces circle, around the remains of the harvester for a while, to make sure it was completely destroyed, and then left the scene on FTL.

Although this was only one strategic target in thousands, this was another easy victory for the Ildiran fleet.

Ixchel, the alien sphere, had of course informed Angelina about its discovery of the mysterious cave, some 40 years earlier on, in the southern mountain ranges of Rigel Octi, inside the system of Rigel.

Angelina in turn had officially discussed this with Russell and the others, and privately with her close friend, Cindy Thupolev.

Cindy had immediately expressed her interest to personally investigate this, with the help of Ixchel, the alien sphere.

'After all,' Cindy said, 'I'm an experienced archeologist. I've had academic training, in investigating mysterious things.'

And, after a while of deliberation, Angelina had decided to grant her the honor of going on this intriguing quest.

Ixchel had place for several passengers, although it was quite cramped if one would have to stay in there for an extended period of time.

But Cindy had now officially accepted her mission, and was busy packing clothes, and useful objects, just like a professional archeologist should.

Cindy felt exhilarated and frightened at the same time.

She and Angelina, and the others, including Russell Caltech, had gathered inside docking bay y-75 at 5:30 a.m. local station time, and right now they were all hugging her, one by one, as a last goodbye - for now.

It was impossible to know beforehand how long it would take her to complete her mission, and to return safely to her fellow insurgents inside the safe arms of Pax Infiniti.

The sphere had enough space for several passengers, and it didn't need a pilot to navigate among the stars. Aside from that, it also had some facilities for diversion, sleep, and nourishment.

After a few last waves of goodbye, Ixchel elevated a few yards, and Cindy walked under it. It teleported her up, and she disappeared inside in an instant. Ixchel activated its propulsion systems, and – on remote – requested the docking bay doors to open.

Several moments later, the semi-AI docking bay slowly unsealed its outer airlock doors, whilst activating an intermediate semi-penetrable shield to retain the air, oxygen, and pressure for the living entities inside. Ixchel activated all its crucial systems, and slowly lifted several more meters from the docking bay surface.

As Angelina and the others looked on, Ixchel, with his precious Cindy inside, hovered into outer space, and flew away, while accelerating with enormous power to an in-system sub-c velocity.

Exactly 4 hours later....

'Dear Miss Thupolev, I'm sorry to awaken you, but I believe we're closing in on Rigel system.'

Cindy awoke with a flash, and tried to focus on the present.

'Ah, yes, Ixchel. Thanks for waking me. Are we really nearing Rigel Octi? I can't wait to get there,' she responded.
'We're closing in on Rigel system, Miss Thupolev. Still some 40 minutes before we land on Octi', Ixchel said. 'You could take a shower in the meantime, if you like. Your clothes could be replicated, and the new ones will be perfectly clean. Just a bit of extra luxury.... '
'A hot shower sounds delicious,' she responded, and she immediately headed for the replicator.

Her body and face looked like a beautiful Russian ballet dancer's (her parents were of Russian descent), and if Ixchel would have been a man he would have been tempted to join her in the steamy shower room.

She had been sleeping for almost an hour.

After leaving Pax Infiniti, she had carefully studied the inner realms of Ixchel and its facilities.
Its seats could be converted into very comfortable sleeping couches, and there was a compartment, with all kinds of nourishments, and alcoholic beverages, some from the Old Earth, Sol-3, and other ones from Ildira, and other weird places.
There also was a photonic holo-vid couch with thousands of titles, some recent, some ancient; some of a documentary nature, and others with music and classical symphonies.
Of course, there was also a place for showering, and hygiene, and Ixchel even featured a regeneration container for minor as well as serious medical contingencies.

But what had fascinated Cindy most of all was its incredible database, which seemed to go back to times before its own creation, to the early history of its own makers.

As a professional archaeologist, she realized the unfathomable, immense scientific and historical worth and significance of this database, this record of more than a million years, and thousands of worlds.

She had decided to try to find some useful information on their mission and its purpose, and she gave the system a voice command.

All kinds of transparent holograms, with all kinds of diagrams, text, numbers, and information, floated above the central image projector.... an eerie shimmering light emanating from its core.

'System, have you got information on our current mission objective?' She inquired.

The unnamed system processed her query, and returned a result.

On the informational holo some pictures appeared of the outside of the cave, as well as the inside, and of the flat inner wall, with the small - seemingly dead - monitor.

Cindy peered at the images in total fascination.

'These are some pictures from our find....' the system began.

'We first took notice of it when we detected a signal of weird and strong radiation emanating from the cave from system space. There were abnormally high levels of ozone, and this weird radiation levels. These qualities suggested Ixian activity a long time ago. The radiation must have been much more intense, when the cave was created.

On closer inspection we made these images.'
She peered intensely at the mysterious photonic holo images with the intrigued eyes of a well-educated archaeologist, anticipating an incredible find.
The unnamed system concluded.
'This is all I got at this moment. '
Cindy decided to study information about the Ixians sometime in the near future.
I barely know who these Ixians are, she thought somberly.

Right now, she had to prepare for their mission.

Some 40 minutes later, Ixchel landed softly on the rocky surface of a broad ledge on Rigel Octi, some 4 yards in front of the entrance to the mysterious cave.

It hovered 5 yards from the ground, and waited a while to teleport Cindy Thupolev out.

'Would you like to exit, Miss Thupolev?' Ixchel requested Cindy.

'Give me a few minutes, Ixchel. I'm still collecting

some useful stuff.'

Five minutes later, the sphere teleported her safely out onto the rocky surface of the broad ledge.
Cindy looked around for a while, and took in the incredible view of an immense rock and desert valley far below.
The travel bag on her side felt heavy with archeological equipment, her com-sys, and food and drinks.
She decided quickly that the outer walls of the cave to the sides and above, as well as the ground of the broad ledge she was standing on, didn't render much information.
She turned to peer into the cave, and felt a cold chill and a slight whirlwind coming from the inside.
Step by step, she entered the immense cave. Ixchel descended to a height of one perfect yard, and followed her in, at a respectful distance.
The cave appeared to be perfectly rectangular, with completely even walls, although she could discern vague geometric shapes on the walls on all sides.

As she got deeper inside, the whirlwinds increased, and she noticed a red shimmering, probably from the radiation. It gave her a feeling as if she was entering an ancient Egyptian tomb, in Old Earth Egypt, which had not been entered into since its creation.

The ozone tickled her eyes and her lungs. It was a sensation she thought she had never felt before. She coughed, and spat out some fresh saliva onto the uniform ground.

When she had crossed almost eighty yards, she finally reached the inner wall.

It was entirely covered with mysterious paintings, and complex visual structures, entire lines, and rows, with complex, and detailed symbolic structures, like ancient Egyptian hieroglyphs, but larger, and much more complex and detailed.
These things must be Ixian, she mused in total fascination, *as Ixchel's AI suggested. I really need to know more about them.*
A few moments later, Cindy Thupolev stood in front of the small display.
It was set into a round indentation in the wall, clearly visible on the sides.
The alien sphere interrupted her deep thoughts.
'Miss Thupolev, if I may interrupt your observations. This must be the access control to the inside. I couldn't make much of it when I was here before, let alone activate it. '
Cindy waited, and Ixchel continued.
'I'm able to cross millions of light years across

interstellar space, and I have an entire database and compartments for passengers.... but I'm not good at physically manipulating things.... '

Cindy remained silent, as if in deep thought.

Her focus was completely set on the small square display, which seemed to be fully offline.

Let me think on it for a moment, she said to herself.

She tried to focus, and come up with things to try to activate the seemingly dead system, but failed.

'I'm going to record the wall paintings first.' She said. 'That will give me some time to think on the subject, simultaneously. '
Reluctantly, she took her com-sys from her travel bag, and started taking holo vid images.
I'll have to study these carefully once I'm safe back inside Pax Infiniti, she mused.
Taking images of the walls took her 15 minutes, and in the meantime she tried to think of something to solve the display issue.
Quite amazing images, she mused again. *I've never seen such things before.*

When the images were practically complete, she put her com-sys back inside the travel bag on her left shoulder. It still felt heavy. What if we have to walk around here for days…. or maybe even for weeks? In a flash, she had an idea…. a very simple idea….
'Ixchel,' she said. 'You know Ixian? Am I correct?'
'Yes, Miss Thupolev. You're correct,' Ixchel replied.
'What is the Ixian word for…. activate? '
'Just a minute, Miss Thupolev' It seemed, like Ixchel was accessing, or updating his language archives.
'I believe the word is…. Ixitivah'

Cindy heard a prominent beep. Quickly she turned around.
The obviously Ixian display lit up and displayed some kind of welcoming message. Obviously Ixian, she said to herself. She felt her mind going wild with excitement…. the excitement of a young archeologist, making an incredible discovery.
The display's background was of a dark blue hue, while the text in front was much lighter: a sort of whitish-blue, radiating from its surface.
Almost fifteen seconds passed while Cindy stared in complete fascination, and then the screen went black again.

Goddammit, Cindy said to herself.
Again, several seconds passed, and then the

display came alive again, and suddenly went wild. All kinds of symbols, structures, entire blue prints, complex text, and numbers flashed by, as if the system was going completely crazy....

Cindy peered at the incredible flow of information, and suddenly realized she had to fetch her-com-sys, to record it.

We might never be able to understand this, but it's mighty fascinating. But, Ixchel understands Ixian, so this might be useful in the end.

Another fifteen seconds later, which seemed to last for an eternity, the flash of data suddenly stopped, and Cindy returned her com-sys to the travel bag, hanging on her left shoulder.

The display went black again.

Cindy focused on the display, and waited tensely to see if something would happen.

As she waited, the whirlwind got stronger, and blew sandstone dust into her ballet dancer's eyes. She could hear a thunderstorm building up in the great valley, far below the ominous cave. A cold wind came from the outside and made her shiver, as if it were deep winter.

The mysterious Ixian display gave a soft beep as an image came up. It seemed to be some kind of access message, with a round figure in the middle, and a message under it. It seemed to remain that way.

Cindy tried to focus.

This must be the login screen, she thought.

Minutes passed….

Then suddenly an idea came up inside her pretty ballet dancer's head.

Some (mostly older) systems require eye- or palm verification. Maybe I should try that.

Carefully, she closed in on the display, and tried to look straight into it.

Nothing happened.

Then, she took the travel bag off her shoulder, and carefully – very carefully – pressed her palm onto the middle of the screen.

She waited.

Suddenly the screen beeped, as if confirming some kind of access, and then something happened.

Suddenly, a substantial part of the immense inner wall of the great ominous cave disappeared.

Cindy stood still, and remained perfectly tense.

In front of her, an enormous tunnel was visible, almost dark, extending far beyond her sight.

She turned to see if Ixchel was still there, and he noticed her attention.

He had of course witnessed the entire scene unfolding during the last ten minutes.

'If you need me, I'm still here, Miss Thupolev,' he said, politely.

'That's alright, Ixchel. I'm just a little shaky, and confused,' she replied.

'I guess we should explore this tunnel. It must be here for some significant reason. '

Ixchel remained silent, as if in complete understanding.

Cindy turned, and walked into the gaping tunnel, while the dust storm far below continued....

Cindy walked for hours and hours, after taking a flashlight from her travel bag, and activating it.

Ixchel, in turn, had activated his front spotlights, and this helped her find her way ahead, although nothing seemed to change.

After a short while, she discovered that the ground was covered with bones.... presumably Ixian.

Ixchel told her he was quite sure that, according to comparisons with the information in his long-term databases, these bones had to be Ixian.

A little bit more knowledge about the Ixians, she

thought.

Cindy didn't have the faintest idea how these bones, and almost fossilized remains got here, and what had happened to the people they were from.
There must be tens of thousands of these remains…., she thought again.
She continued on, and the many bones and remains on the ground seemed to continue on all the way.
She felt a cold wind from behind, making her shiver. By now, an immense storm was raging in the great valley below the ledge to the cave, and she could hear a terrible roar of wind from far behind. She took her winter coat from her travel bag, and wrapped it close around her fragile upper body.

Cindy soon got tired. She didn't have a very strong constitution, and the cold, the wind, and the long period of walking, wore her down.
Every now and then, she stumbled over bones, and almost fossilized remains, of - presumably - deplorable Ixians.
She noticed that the radiation and ozone from the cave continued on inside the tunnel, and the deeper she got, the stronger it grew.
Ever more often, she sat down and rested, while having some food and drinks to keep herself in

shape.

Will there ever come an end to this damned tunnel, she thought wearily?

And is there a purpose to this mission at all?

After many hours of walking, resting, and walking again, Ixchel requested her attention.

'Miss Thupolev, I don't mean to disturb you, but I have the impression the long walk through this tunnel is wearing you down. Would you possibly prefer to stay in my compartments, to rest and recuperate?'

Goddammit! Why, didn't I think of that myself, she thought? *On the other hand, I'm not used to going on archeological missions, with intelligent alien spheres, hovering behind me, ready to take me anywhere, without any exertion….*

She concurred with his suggestion and Ixchel teleported her inside.

Once safe inside Ixchel's passenger's compartments, Cindy put down her heavy travel bag, took off her winter coat, and sat down on one of the very comfortable convertible seats.

She fell asleep almost immediately.

While Cindy slept for hours on end, Ixchel kept a steady velocity, levitating forever forward, along the mysterious tunnel, and - hopefully - towards the terminus of their mission.

Some four hours later, Ixchel noticed something, in the distance.

He focused in on the image ahead, and concluded it had to be the end of the tunnel.
He decided to wake Cindy, and inform her about the new situation.
'I'm sorry to disturb your moment of rest, but please awaken, Miss Thupolev,' he said, softly.
Cindy opened her ballet dancer's eyes, and blinked several times.
'Are we there yet?' she asked Ixchel.
'I suppose we're at the end of the tunnel, Miss Thupolev,' Ixchel answered.
Cindy sat up straight, and tried to focus on the present.
She thought for a moment, and said,

'Ixchel, teleport me out, immediately'

As Cindy Thupolev walked out of the tunnel into an immense rectangular chamber, Ixchel, the intelligent alien sphere, levitated behind her, keeping up with her pace, until she stopped.

The wind, dust, and radiation seemed to be stronger, and the ozone irritated her eyes and lungs.
A red glow emanated from a certain distance ahead.

She stood in an enormous perfectly rectangular room, or hall, and looked around to see if there were recognizable properties to be examined, like a professional archaeologist should.

At first sight, the room appeared to have no special features at all, although the ground was still covered with bones and dried-up remains, just like in the tunnel.
The walls were perfectly straight and there seemed to be nothing of interest, although it was quite dark for Cindy to see.

She fetched her flashlight from the travel bag, which hung on her left shoulder, and activated it.
Slowly, she let the light pass along the walls and the

floor of the eerie giant chamber.

The vast walls apparently featured the same mystical structures and hieroglyphs as the cave, which now lay many hours behind them, had, and she decided to make some recordings of them with her com-sys holo-cam.

As she slowly lowered her flashlight, its light caught something exactly in the middle of the great chamber.
Cindy directed her flashlight towards the unknown object.
The now clearly-visible object, illuminated by the radiating beam of her micro-fusion flashlight, appeared to be quite large and perfectly smooth, but it was still quite distant, and so she decided to inspect it closer by.
She crossed a distance of nine yards, and directed the flashlight along the edges of the mysterious object.

As a trained archeologist, it seemed to be quite simple to determine what it was:

It was a tomb.

It was perfectly smooth, made of some kind of

granite, and with a heavy seal on top, which could barely be discerned from the rest of the tomb....

It was a perfect object.

A strong red glow emanated from its core, and a heavy whirlwind aerated around its dark shape. Cindy fetched her multi-functional radiation detector, activated it, set it to a distance of three yards, and directed it towards the tomb.

It seemed like the radiation that was already present in the mysterious cave many hours behind them surged here, and reached a peak exactly around this lost tomb.
The radiation must be coming from the inside of this object, she thought. *What in God's name could there be inside?*
She looked at the detector, and it seemed to indicate all kinds of radiation, not immediately harmful to humans, or at least not for several hours.

Suddenly there was a voice that startled Cindy.

It must be an Ixian computer system that has detected our presence, she thought, and looked around to see where it was coming from.
There appeared to be nothing there, at least nothing

visible.

She couldn't interpret what the system was saying, and she addressed Ixchel.

'Ixchel, this must be Ixian. Please translate this for me.'

Her friend and companion, the Trellian sphere, started to translate the words, seemingly coming from nowhere.

'Welcome, Sol-trian.' It began.

You seemed to have found your way into this holiest of places.'

Cindy stood motionless, completely focused on the Ixian system voice.

'This artificial cave was created about 4000 years ago…. earth time.

The holy tomb, in the middle of this chamber, contains a priceless religious object.

We stole this object from Sol-3, after making a careful study of human history and their religion.

It is an object of incredible power, capable of destroying entire galaxies.

When we – the Ixians - tried to open it, and activate this object of incredible power, all kinds of things went wrong.

The object unleashed its energy onto us, and tens of thousands of us died in flames, radiation, and accompanying thunderstorms.

Those are the endless bones and bodies you encountered in this place of safekeeping.

We finally realized there was no way in which we could safely utilize the terrible power of this holiest of holy objects of human history and religion.

And after much deliberation, we decided to bury it inside this granite tomb, until a human being would find it, be able to activate it, and control its terrible powers. '

Suddenly, the voice stopped.

Three minutes passed, and Cindy began to wonder if this was all there was to it.

Then, with a roaring sound, the many tons of granite seal of the tomb, started to lift into the air, so slowly it was almost indiscernible.

Four minutes later, the seal hovered three yards above its base tomb, and Cindy – more excited than she ever had been, as an archaeologist – ran over to the tomb, stood on her toes, and peered inside, into the now completely opened tomb.

During her university years, Cindy had made a careful study of Old Earth religious objects, and there were only a few objects – such as the Holy Grail – which carried such an unfathomable historical and religious value, that finding them would be one of the most supreme moments in the history of archeology.

She had seen dozens of pictures and descriptions of this object, and right now, there was no doubt about it:

This was the Ark of the Covenant….

Incursion on Pax Infiniti insurgency station….

The incursion on Pax Infiniti was led and planned by SI-6 and its new operatives, and it was a carried out by a combination of SI people, special space forces, and regular space fleet marines, with a myriad of swift attack ships.

In fact, it was a complete surprise attack, and the P.I. reconnaissance and defense systems were completely taken by surprise.

One of the main mission objectives of the new SI-6 team was the capture and return of their turncoat predecessors.

Space marine vessels jumped out of sub-Planck space, and closed in onto Pax Infiniti from all sides, in simultaneous acceleration, preceded by 5 special SI ships, with fake access and ID codes, to fool P.I. closing and docking detection.

All alarms went off inside the – at first - dormant station, and as the 5 SI vessels penetrated the coded level 15 force fields, the marine ships opened massive fire, avoiding their fellow incursion forces. All P.I. defense people hurried towards their ships and stations, and tried to create a vast defense against the unexpected attackers.

The new SI-6 people, accompanied by dozens of temporary agents from other cells, had counted on this, and – disguised as Pax Infiniti security agents – they had infiltrated the long standing core location of the joint insurgency.

When the alarms started to sound everywhere around, Angelina was resting inside her zero-g cell.

She sat up straight, while her heart pounded.

A voice resounded across the entire station, saying: 'everybody, except station defense personnel, toward our internal Cyportals, and jump towards Apocalypsis Infinitus.

The voice kept repeating the alarm notification, over and over.

Angelina made a Vox connection with Paul and Kenzo.

Paul, Kenzo, what the hell is going on? She said in her mind.

Paul was the first to answer.

They have finally found us…. our location. It's a massive attack, from all sides, by the Federation. Presumably new SI people and special space forces…. We must jump to Apocalypsis Infinitus, right now…. all of us.

Angelina tried to breath.

She pulled her space skin suit on in a matter of seconds, and fetched her com-sys.

Alright, what now? She thought.

Three men wearing seemingly regular clothing, and one good-looking young woman with a ruthless glance in her eyes rushed through the opening iris and grabbed her. Although she struggled, and tried to break free, she stood no chance against four trained SI operatives. The female SI operative injected Angelina with something.

A few moments later, she fainted, and – at this moment – she was a prisoner of the intelligence organization called:

SI

Cindy had decided to return to the coordinates of Pax Infiniti station.

She would never be able to simply carry an object like the Ark of the Covenant back to P.I., by herself, and she had decided to first discuss everything with her fellow insurgents, especially Angelina, once back safely. She didn't even know whether such an object could be transported, touched, or opened safely, at all.

But when they finally arrived at the location coordinates where Pax Infinity station used to be, after many hours of interstellar flight, everything seemed to have disappeared.

Cindy knew there had been a real danger of an unexpected attack for months, and now she feared P.I. was totally gone.

She had requested Ixchel to recheck their coordinates several times over, and Ixchel had replied it was 100 percent sure that their coordinates were indeed absolutely correct.

Then she started to panic, and despair, and she thought she would never find her friends again. Ixchel remained silent, as if assessing her emotions, and then, a few moments later, he had said to her: 'Please, don't panic, Miss Thupolev. Before we left, Angelina provided me with the coordinates to the new station, Apocalypsis Infinitus. She told me it's even more massive than the original one'.

Of course, Cindy knew exactly what he was referring to.

It was the next generation station, even bigger, and more advanced than Pax Infiniti, and everyone who had survived the unexpected attack had jumped to it.

And after that, the entire station of Pax Infiniti, with all its systems, defenders, and Cyportals, and everything around it, had been destroyed by a multitude of Ixti fusion high-energy explosives, and nothing had been left.

The new station they had gone to was called:

Apocalypsis Infinitus

Chapter 23

Angelina is being interrogated, but escapes through her incredible powers

Guiding entity Shi'rah, on the principle of multiverse....

One crucial thing Sol-trians didn't know about was that forces, changes, and influences from other universes, which could be many billions of times more intense than those in our own, could influence, change, or even destroy our entire galaxy, entire nebulas, and possibly even our entire universe.

This was a real threat to our continuing existence, and something we, the Trellians, took very seriously, since this was – in principle - a real threat to any universe inside any multiverse.

Our original universe was one of many in a complex string of universes, like an immense DNA molecule, all connected by some kind of gravity and intertwined super-wormholes.

In our recent history, we had sent out dozens of tiny probes into the local multiverse, and they had sent back millions of eerie images, almost all of them blurred, distorted, and with loads of noise and static. This was not much of a surprise, since the laws of physics, physical constants, the flow of time, and the workings of gravity inside our local multiverse were totally different from our original universe.

Ixurion had told us, that the local multiverse – let alone the entire multiverse, or even other multiverses – contained many weird and ultimately dangerous things, both living and dead, like creatures, structures, and AIs, the size of hundreds of single universes:
It seemed almost incomprehensible and inconceivable.

We had discussed these things with each other scores of times, and the only conclusion was:

We would have to find out....

On our own

After the disastrous incursion on Pax Infiniti, Angelina was transported back to the SI nucleus by her captors as fast as they could, and thrown in a bare metal cell, in a special section of the SI nucleus reserved for political prisoners.

Almost four days long, she was left to herself, completely alone, with only one disgusting meal per day, and nothing to do but think.

There were no windows, no furniture, no bed, nothing....just a plain metallic cell, with no one to talk to.
Angelina was afraid she would lose her mind soon, although at this stage she was still a tiny bit fit, and relaxed, and rested.

Then, by the end of the fourth day, the one single

door opened, and a man entered.

Angelina recognized him immediately. It was the quiet man in the grey suit, probably SI-5 or oversight, which had been present at the meeting with Kenzo and the others before this whole nightmare had begun.
He looked her up and down, as if assessing her strength, and state of mind, and then opened a seemingly casual conversation.

'Miss Angelina West. Or, should I say: Miss Angelina Tchaikovsky?' he said.

Angelina remained silent, and looked him in the eyes, with a defiant gaze.
'You have come quite far, I should say,' he continued. 'Almost the great and admired leader of a rogue organization of millions.... '
'Your so-called government is a lie', she said, and looked him in the eyes, with a fiery glance.
'That may be so.....' the man said, haughtily. 'But still.... here we are.'
He waited a while, and continued.
'I am Charles D. Xaviour. Intel is my life, and thus I work for the government, in other words GACS.'
'I got that far,' Angelina said. 'I spent five years working for that artificial monster. VOG.8 is history.'

Mr. Xaviour smiled.

'We're not going to have endless philosophical discussions at this time, I'm afraid. But we need some information, and we need it fast. You're a clever girl, and you will see that you will give us this information, one way or the other. '

Mr. Xaviour turned towards the steel door, opened it half, and gave her a final word.

'Tomorrow, you will be taken out of your cell, and we will start the interrogation. I think it will be best for the both of us if you cooperate. If not.... well, we'll see.'

Mr. Xaviour, the quiet man in the grey suit, left the room, and the door closed, with an ominous thud.

During the next five days, Angelina was interrogated, every day, for hours on end.

Every single day, before the interrogation started, she was injected with Yreka acid, some 28th century kind of truth serum.

But it didn't work.

She only became stronger and stronger with each passing day.

Her interrogators did not subject her to physical torture. She was a far too significant person, for millions of insurgents, for GACS, for billions of Fed civilians, for the Human Dominion, for SI itself, and for practically all Ildirans, who worshipped her as their new messiah, and so they simply could not afford to kill or injure Angelina Tchaikovsky in any way. Her interrogators wanted the coordinates to Apocalypsis Infinitus, but she revealed absolutely nothing.

Although she still was a young woman, she felt a strength building inside, and it only became stronger with each passing day.
She felt as if the Yreka acid was influencing her genes, deep inside, more and more with each passing day. Then, on the fifth day, something happened.

While the interrogation was going on, and Mr. Xaviour surveyed, she reached the point of no return.

Her genes – which according to the subordinate AI Jovi archive system designated as 'Mother', were directly inherited from the Apostle John, writer of the Apocalypse - activated, and sent a sudden flash through her mind and body.

Her eyes started to glow a deep red, a whirlwind began to whirl and surround her, and her physical strength was multiplied by a factor of a thousand. A great golden light emanated from her body, and suddenly two enormous beams of red and green light, and radiation, came out and burned through the floor and ceiling, like jets streaming from a supermassive black hole's core.

Angelina broke loose from her stainless steel cuffs, which fell from her wrists, and hit the ground with a loud metallic clap. She stood up, and in a matter of seconds, she struck her two interrogators down with a terrible blow to the head, accompanied by streams of energy, which killed them in an instant. Then, she knocked Mr. Xaviour unconscious, and made for the locked metal door quickly. Using the keys from his coat pocket, she carefully unlocked the door, and looked outside, to see whether anyone had noticed what had occurred.
Nobody seemed to be there.
It took minutes before the SI forces started to realize what kind of thing had happened. Although her eyes still emanated a strong red glow, the whirlwind settled down a little.
The jets that previously emanated from her body were now mostly gone.

My God, she thought to herself, *if they see me like this, who knows what they will do….*

Then, she started running, as fast as she could, and the one single thing that saved her was the fact that she knew every room, every hallway, and every lift shaft of the SI nucleus by heart.

As fast as she possibly could, though occasionally taking a normal pace to avoid attracting unwanted attention, Angelina made for a tiny barely-used side docking-bay, which she knew was mostly devoid of people and personnel.

One tiny sole spacecraft, with its fuel tanks almost depleted, hovered in its docking shaft, as if waiting for someone to take it into space.

As she quickly entered its singular control cabin, she noticed the fuel gauge.

'Goddammit!' she cried, 'It's almost depleted.'

A few minutes later, she found herself piloting the tiny space vessel into intra-stellar space.

Charles Xaviour, the man in the grey suit, had revived in a matter of minutes, and had ordered fifteen patrol ships to intercept Angelina's tiny ship, board it, and capture her alive. Right now, he was watching the tiny craft, and its pursuers, on an inside monitor.

The fifteen patrol ships exited from the SI nucleus, and Angelina saw on her radar screens they were closing in…. fast.
Again, Angelina began to despair.
If they catch up on me, I'm either toast, or in for months of interrogation, maybe worse than it already was, and probably dead….
With the thought of having to go through all of that again, and maybe longer, or worse, she started to breathe heavily, and panicked.

Again, her supernatural forces took over, a storm gathered around her and around the vessel, and an incredible beam of light and energy, now blue and white, and yellow, emanated from her chest like wildfire, and jumped and flashed to connect to the propulsion systems of the tiny craft.

With the incredible amount of extra energy, her tiny ship accelerated, and soon she saw on her radar, the patrol ships were falling behind, faster and faster.

She headed straight for Cal, and with the control of her mind, she created five level 35 force fields around the hull of the small ship.

After exactly two point five minutes, she entered the corona of the burning star.

Fortunately, the incredible force field held against the unbearable heat coming from the inside of the star as she headed for its core, and she strained to maintain the field and propulsion. The combination of forces seemed unbearable.

Again, she created more energy, and directed it towards the ship's propulsion unit.

It took 20 seconds to build up, and then….

The tiny craft entered the realities of sub-Planck space, out of the unbearable heat of Cal sun's core…. and jumped…. while Angelina passed out…. in a billionth of a second….

Mr. Charles D. Xaviour, the man in the grey suit, had – fortunately - survived Angelina's escape.

At least, that was the way he felt about it, and although he was glad he had survived, he was completely shocked and taken aback by what had actually happened.

He had never suspected this turn of events, and he had never expected an escape by someone who had been totally subdued. Miss Angelina Tchaikovsky seemed to be more dangerous than he could ever have imagined.

She was a total danger to the future of the Federation, GACS, and his very own personal survival.
He was now convinced of that fact.
But, for now, he simply had to analyze everything, and come up with some kind of plan to stop this young woman from becoming an even greater danger to them. He decided he had to try to infiltrate the insurgency leadership.
This would take many months, and many preparations, and could not be in effect within a matter of a few weeks.

But there was another thing, almost nobody knew about.... not even those damned insurgency spies, let alone their leaders:

Some CGC agents had found the Ixians, and had established contact with them, and – apart from these very few agents – only a few people high up in the CGC hierarchy, were aware of this, aside from VOG.8 himself,.

Mr. Xaviour had decided for himself that if the insurgency would overcome the CGC in the near future, he would flee, and side with the Ixian civilization against the new order.... of the insurgents.

However many times a man regarded Apocalypsis Infinitus, it remained immense.

It was officially still in development, but as the situation was, it was almost fully operational and habitable.

Cindy Thupolev had returned, four days after the incursion, and hectic flight to Apocalypsis Infinitus, and had told everyone about her incredible find. When she heard that Angelina had been captured during the great incursion, she felt shocked, and she felt a deep longing to see her dear friend again.

And then, several days later, Angelina had miraculously returned, alone, inside the small SI ship, but she was almost dead.

As quickly as they could, they had dragged her to one of the intensive care units of A.I., and she would have to stay in there for five days, until she had mostly recuperated from her physical and psychological trauma.

Now Angelina was back again, inside her own – new – sleeping cell, and she slept almost the entire day, gaining strength little by little.
Cindy was the only one who visited her, and took care of her, and she provided her with nourishments, and clean sheets, and she tucked her in, with kind words.

And, sometime later, Angelina began to feel like her old self again, although she would always remain traumatized by her horrible experiences inflicted on her by SI, and – behind it all – GACS. In her own mind, she had sworn to bring the terrible system to an end.

Then came the moment Cindy confronted her with the decisions made by the insurgency leadership.

'Angy, I'm glad you're recuperating, relaxing, and resting, but there are some important things I have to tell you,' she said.

Angelina looked at her trusted female friend, and tried to smile.

'I'm sure you got some horrible things to say. Am I right?'

Cindy smiled a bit. She knew the things she had to say were not exactly easy.

'Angy, in relation to recent developments, we – the joint insurgency leadership – including Russell, me, and others, have decided you will have to become our leader.'

Angelina stopped smiling, and stared at the curved wall, several yards in front of her.

Both remained silent, for a while.

'Angy, whether you like it or not, the entire council has agreed on this'

Cindy said again, and Angelina looked at her friend.

'It's not that.... ', she replied.

The silence became unbearable.

'I've sworn to bring an end to GACS, and the Federation, as it is now, and I don't care whether I do it, the insurgency leader.... or otherwise,'

Angelina said, and she fell silent again.

Then she said, 'I'll accept this mission.... under one condition.'

'What?' Cindy said.

Angelina looked her in the eyes again, and said:

'You stay alive.'

And so, Angelina became the messianic leader of the joint insurgency movement against GACS, and she renamed it:

Shining Light....

....to indicate that this movement was a light out of the darkness.

She received psychotherapy every day to heal the wounds inflicted on her by SI. In the 28th century CE, this was quite advanced and effective, although her physical and psychological scars would never complete heal.

The news of Angelina's imprisonment, interrogation, the fact that she had almost died, and her miraculous escape through her super-human powers, and the fact that she had become the messianic leader of the new movement of Shining Light, spread like wildfire across all of Interstellia. The Ildirans prayed and rejoiced, because their human messiah had finally arrived, after thousands of years.

The manifestation of Angelina's super-human powers was something which had never ever occurred before in the history of mankind, or in Ildiran history for that matter.

The Shining Light leadership council, which from now on only had an advisory role to their leader Angelina Tchaikovsky, had a strong suspicion there was a link between Angelina and the newly-found Ark of the Covenant, which had been stolen from the Old Earth by the Ixians some 4,000 years ago.

Angelina had fundamentally changed.

Her interrogation with Yreka acid, her near-death experience, and the activation of her apocalyptic genes, had fundamentally changed – transformed - her body and mind. She had gained an incredible amount of wisdom, and a deep sense of tragedy associated with the realities of existence inside this universe.

She was no longer the bright and happy young woman she used to be. She had decided to think deeply, and write down her thoughts, to somehow create a new religion, or system of thought, which could give a guideline, and could strengthen the power and resolve of the billions of humans and Ildirans to try to defeat GACS.

She had decided to call this new religious system:

Universalism

Angelina began to write down all the thoughts, ideas, and theories she had accumulated and conceived during the last twenty-five years.

All the syllables, sentences, paragraphs and logical constructions rolled from the back of her mind onto the holo-screen of her com-sys, through a mind-link. With her thoughts she wrote, corrected, and expanded her dissertation, like a historical fiction writer, or a famous artist, from ages ago, as if the gods of thunder, and the predators of Tartarus, haunted her very thoughts.

Angelina started to write down all the intriguing and critical issues which went on inside the depths of her burning mind.

She would refer to her dissertation as the CCE synthesis (the synthesis of conscience, consciousness, and existence), but among her followers and others, it would come to be known as the Tchaikovsky synthesis....

Since the Ildirans regarded Angelina as their messiah, they would come to refer to it as the Tchaikovsky prophecy.

These are some very partial summations from this CCE/Tchaikovsky synthesis, simplified, combined, and abbreviated:

(Now, and then, she would repeat earlier subjects.... And look at them in another light....)

. . . .

I would like to begin my dissertation about this universe, and all of its systematic elements, with the subject of objects, and systems.

Everything, every portion of this universe, can be seen and regarded as a combined system of objects, consisting of a combination of sub objects.

In object-oriented programming, computer programs and systems consist of complex combinations of individual objects with internal functions and properties, which communicate and interchange information with one another, and so create a functional synergy called a complete system.

All systems can be viewed as a combination of particles, with each particle containing a combination of (internal) properties, and functionalities, and (external) interactions. In this way, every transformation, every change in the universe, can be seen as an interaction of particles…. on a microscopic level, on a macroscopic level, or even on an anthropic level.

Every sub-region in the universe, real or imaginary, can be viewed and described in such a way, and all science and thinking is based on this principle.

In physics, the universe and parts of the universe are described by means of mathematics in combination with geometry, and the universe itself is regarded as a system.

. . . .

The human neurological thought process itself works in exactly this manner, and is a combination of neural sub-systems, together constituting the entire mind.

. . . .

Every possible and thinkable thing, or system, can be seen as an object, and in mathematics, the most perfect and symmetrical object is an n-dimensional sphere, if one wants to be able to work in n dimensions.

If the universe itself is viewed and regarded in such a way, then it is an infinitely complex structure of n-dimensional spheres.... within n-dimensional spheres.... within n-dimensional spheres.

. . . .

Accordingly, I'm absolutely convinced that any arbitrary system, sub-region in space-time, or object, can be interpreted or described as a quantum-string wave field.

. . . .

In physics – and its underlying mathematics – many things are symmetrical.... but some things are asymmetrical, and specific.... that's why the universe is symmetry, inside asymmetry.

. . . .

Everything in the universe is ultimately wave-like, cyclical, and dualistic in its deepest essence and nature.
Dualism implies a wave-like nature, and a wave-like nature implies dualism.
This reciprocal relationship also applies to the trinity of cyclicality, the wave principle, and dualism.
This means that in physical and metaphysical essence, these three phenomena are fundamentally the same, and this has many fundamental implications.

. . . .

Space and time – as material phenomena – do not exist.

Space is only constituted by infinite amounts of positional inter-relationships between physical objects.

The phenomenon of time is similar to that of space: it is constituted by inter-relationships between physical universal configurations, and therefore it does not exist as an independently existing entity itself.

. . . .

Einstein's relativity implies the fundamental wave principle: things cannot increase, or decrease, for an infinite amount of time.... at some point, they will have to decrease, or increase, again.

Relativity implies the wave principle....which in turn implies dualism.... which implies cyclicality....

. . . .

These are also the core principles of Taoism, and this relationship is as described in the Tao of physics (a 20th century dissertation by Fritjov Capra), which argues in favor of fundamental similarities between modern day theoretical physics, and Old Earth Asian Taoism.

. . . .

On an anthropic level, this means that human religions are dualistic, and this in turn means that all religions have their good points and bad points.... their truths.... and illusions.

Religions are systems of thought, meant to interpret the metaphysical world and connect it to the physical world we live in, although the physical and metaphysical worlds, meet each other in the very place where we find ourselves in our daily lives.

Religions consist of theories: ethical theories about the metaphysical world, and moral theories for behavior in accordance with these interpretations.

Since all religions have their good and bad points, it is up to us to take all the good points from every religion, and integrate these into one big personal and ethical system of thought, and it is up to ourselves to behave accordingly.

Christianity and Buddhism, for instance, seem to be ultimately irreconcilable and incompatible, although both contain great truth and value.

One of the most important functions of religions is to ease, give meaning to, and make bearable all the suffering, pain and hardship, which are unavoidably connected to existence inside this universe, and inside the multiverse.

Secular and democratic systems are necessary systems to provide the individual with this freedom of choice: the choice of religion, political preference, and way of life.

Without this freedom of choice, human lives become meaningless.

Dualism also implies that applied democratic systems have their good and bad points, although the democratic principle, in itself, is a perfect concept.

. . . .

The universe, existence, is a ruthless machine of sub-quantum-physical precision, and to have a soul, conscience, and emotions, means that it contains places of great joy and places of terrible suffering.

On a level of sociology, this fundamentally means that the core responsibility of governments and societies is to protect their own civilians against this presence of suffering and hardship.

....

And then, we arrive to the subject of war, and all of its ethical – or rather unethical - aspects.

So many wars.... all wars.... have been waged, in the name of God. I know only one thing for sure: there can be no one single god who is in favor of all those different people, and of all those different wars, at the same time.... unless it is the ultimate and infinite god of war and conflict....

I believe the ancient Romans had such a god, and they called him Mars....

....

According to a brilliant 20th century writer, whose name I can't recall, wars are the absolute absence of reason, and I believe he was right.

Everyone has always been convinced that during the Second World War on the Old Earth, waging a global war on Germany and Japan was the only option. What if our civilization would encounter an alien fleet for the first time in history, which is aimed at conquest, destruction, and horrible things?

. . . .

If there are other viable options, such as diplomacy, a blockade, or intervention by an intermediary organization, or a combination of these things, these other options should always be considered.

After all, diplomacy is much safer, more ethical, and most of the time more effective, and lasting, than applying destruction and suffering to achieve some political goals – which is war basically comes down to.

I believe in the end that there is only one answer to the problem of war that is both ethical and realistic at the same time.

One needs a strong defense, in any case, with a total commitment to the following principles, and - sometimes – a strong defense, means a strong offense:

Governments should always have a commitment to no-first-strike policies, and only wage war if it is objectively deemed unavoidable, or if the opponent is completely unethical, and never for immoral, or unethical reasons.

. . . .

I believe love is actually a quantum-physical wave field, permeating the universe.... the multiverse, and thus it adheres to quantum-string rules, principles, and calculations.

. . . .

Without a soul, human beings would be no more than androids....machines.... and still, they can only act, and behave, according to their own particular synaptic programming.

If you turn this around, logically, human beings are androids, with a soul, and consciousness, which I believe are created by the universal soul....

. . . .

Why is there so much unbearable pain.... and suffering?

Everything imaginable, every thinkable aspect, is required to constitute a complete universe, and even complete multiverses. This implies that pain and suffering are also ingredients necessary to constitute the entirety of creation.

If life is a required aspect of a complete universe, and life implies the experience of emotions, then negative emotions imply pain and suffering. Inside an immense universe, let alone billions of immense universes, pain and suffering can also be immense and last for an immense period of time.

. . . .

If machines – AIs, cyborgs, robots – were unaware of the pain and suffering of living entities, they would be able to inflict immense amounts of these aspects onto those living entities, without hesitation.

. . . .

For all those reasons, it seems compassion is one of the most fundamental ingredients of spirited existence.

. . . .

I strongly believe that the force of love is a quantum-string wave field, present everywhere in our universe…. a great beacon of light for all to feel, and to see, engulfing the universe in its never-waning brilliance…. a phenomenon more or less equivalent to the Catholic notion of the Holy Spirit. However, instead of being bound to the fundamental and dogmatic descriptions, aspects, and workings of this same Catholic Holy Spirit, it adheres to logical and mathematical laws and principles, like any universal or physical field.

. . . .

The idea of a universal soul, a physical field permeating the universe over all time and all space, is the most logical, most simple, and most elegant explanation for the fact that living entities have a consciousness and emotions.

It is timeless, indestructible, and infinite, and all souls inside the universe are interconnected, and together they constitute this underlying and undying universal soul.

If living entities did not have a consciousness and emotions, things like sorrow, suffering, illness, and death would have no meaning, purpose, priority, or consequence, at all.

People would be no more than androids, but – in reverse - people are androids with a soul. Without a soul, there is no more than flesh, bones, and a neural system, which – if inverted – implies, human beings are androids with a soul, which is applied by the universal soul.

Religions and philosophies would be obsolete, except for purely logical construction or consideration.

. . . .

According to a new development in 21st century superstring theory, and physics…. people, the universe, are no more than quantum-physical holograms, and this was confirmed by theory and experiments in the centuries after.
And this would indicate the world is not just shadows and dust…. but only shadows…. or no more than a few streaks of bright light.

What would this suggest?

That people are massless sub-quantum-physical holographic androids, and emotions and consciousness are simply tiny physical forces or fields added to the entire equation, and projected onto these holograms themselves?

This seems to be the final reality of our physical existence, and this has a number of dramatic implications.

It means we are not made of flesh and bones. It only appears that way because our eyes, our senses, are unable to distinguish individual sub-quantum particles: we are mere streaks of light, and nothing more.... and we only behave in accordance with.... executing.... sub-quantum-string laws, principles, and behaviors....

....and this makes the idea.... the fundamental concept.... of a quantum-physical force of love much easier to imagine, or to accept....

....A terrible force engulfing the universe, in its light, and thus giving meaning, and hope, to all living entities inside....

. . . .

A human person is a complex combination of information. In accordance with the law of preservation of information, which states that information can never be destroyed, this information is eternal, unless this law does not apply to its overarching multiverse, when its local universe expires.

This would mean that a human person is eternally existent, along the dimensions of time.

However, the entity of a person is always subject to a process of transformation, and it is thus always subject to change.

. . . .

All government, and conduct of government, should be based on the above fundamental principles.

Modern democratic judicial systems are even indirectly based on such considerations.

Why is it regarded unethical, inside democratic systems, to take someone's life?

Because a life is deemed more significant than anything else, and thus because of fundamental considerations, such as those described above, which lie at an even deeper level, a life – and all of its bound principles – is paramount.

. . . .

In ancient times, a democratic judicial system, such as on Sol-3 during the 21st century in the western world would be deemed impossible, even utopian.

But time has taught us that such ethical systems are possible and attainable.

. . . .

So, what if we did not have religions or religious systems and philosophies at all?

. . . .

According to Albert Einstein, nothing can be absolute. That means that religions can't be absolute, either, and claiming absolute truth – as the Vatican does – can never be in accordance with reality.

Original Christianity has been corrupted by dogma, institutional prejudice, subjective interpretations, and behavioral prescriptions, since mankind started to organize it into an absolutist institution.

. . . .

Human religions and philosophies are all created from an anthropic perspective, and we all regard ourselves as humans.

All other living entities present in other parts of the universe are considered alien, but we need to understand that we ourselves are considered alien, from their perspective, and thus we are just as alien as they are.

. . . .

I would like to conclude my discourse with the fact that I absolutely believe that God is the universe.... the multiverse.... the totality of creation.

....and the supreme Christian and Jewish Gods are just the light side of God the universe....

. . . .

I strongly believe the 20th century existentialists, like the French woman Simone de Beauvoir, were right: the world, the universe, is an ultimately absurd place, and it is the way it is.... there are no absolute sins, and there is no good or evil.... Evil is committed by men, and it is up to the individual, to give meaning to his or her own life, and to his or her own place inside this absurd universe, inside this absurd world....

. . . .

If we understand these things, we have a better perception and understanding of the universe.... the multiverse.... we live in, and our place and purpose inside of them, and the meaning of our lives, and how we should deal with the pain and suffering which are inevitable elements of our own existence....

. . . .

Angelina Tchaikovsky wrote down many dozens more of such passages, and she continued for hours on end, sometimes delving even deeper, and going more complex than the previous passages you just read, somehow trying to discover some kind of deeper meaning, or basic structure, to it all, only stopping to catch three to five hours of deep sleep, or to have a cup of traditional Ildiran coffee.... *These are all quite simple thoughts*, she mused. *I wonder if I'm getting anywhere, at all….*

Now and then, she took on earlier subjects, and tried to connect them with new ones, thus creating more complex interconnections.

I believe it all comes down to the questions of existence and suffering, she mused again. Why all the pain, the suffering, the sacrifices….?

And then, after all this writing, and thinking, and studying, you end up with the core principles of Christianity.

My own genes originate from the Apostle John, writer of the Apocalypse, the greatest writer in the history of writing.

Suddenly, it struck her like lightning.

It's all about Christianity, and an individual's own interpretation and implementation of it.

It's unbelievable….

But, there is just one more thing to it.

Christianity can never be the only true religion. I'm absolutely convinced of that. Any enlightened person should combine all good religions, and philosophies, into one coherent personal system of thought: one personal combined interpretation of the entire spectrum of religions, a combination of Christianity, the Jewish faith, Buddhism, and more….

If you regard God to be the universe itself, then the Christian and Jewish idea of God is just the light

side of God the universe.
I think that's where it all ends….

I truly believe that is the destiny, and the purpose, of all this thinking….

For the first time in her life, the beautiful Angelina Tchaikovsky realized…. she was a Christian….

….not in accordance with Catholic conditions, dogma, or absolutism, but inside her own body and mind.

The illuminati were not evil at all, she thought. *That image had been created and concocted by the Vatican, their opponents, for their own personal political goals.*

The Illuminati were mainly thinkers in accordance with, and a byproduct of, the Age of Enlightenment, and this explained their name, The Enlightened. People in the Vatican, at the time, were simply unable to reconcile the Illuminati's way of thought with their own dogmatic and absolutist principles.

Angelina felt exhilarated.

She had found the most important intellectual truth in her entire life, even though she was still a very young woman.

All theoretical physics, theology, philosophy, and all the thinking a human being does inside his or her life came down to this, and she felt grateful.

Ixchel had told Angelina all about Ixurion, the planet-sized mind, and she had decided to discuss all of these matters, and other such subjects like the CGC and AIs, with him, sometime in the future, when the right occasion would arise if she ever encountered him inside the next universe.
The next universe…., she mused.
The very idea of going there…. *being there* made her shiver.

What kinds of unimaginable things could possibly be out there, she wondered?

Guiding entity Shi'rah, on the Tchaikovsky synthesis:

Angelina's synthesis was brilliant.

A billion years later, it would still be recognized among students, and professors of political science, and ethical historians as the Tchaikovsky synthesis, a brilliant discourse of ethical political aspirations. It has remained recognized as such, across millions of light years, and even across the boundaries of universes.

To some of us – still – it was a greatest literary beacon of light ever to be produced by an intelligent mind.

But her brilliance was doomed to failure.

Angelina wanted to completely obliterate all traces of GACS, and all traces of all the horrible dictatorships of human history, and even those of Ildiran history. She desired to create a world, a society and government, based on the principles of the universal soul, and the quantum physical force of love..... A civilization in which everyone could enjoy happiness and neighborly love, and all the benefits of these fundamental ethical principles.....

But such an astronomical ethical goal was –

ultimately - unattainable.

And Angelina, however long her life would be in a world of common age-gen treatment, was ultimately doomed to perish in her quest.

Unless, we – the Trellian descendants – could find a way to save her from this terrible fate, and endow her with a life among ourselves, genetically altered, and enhanced, lasting for maybe a million years, after she had lived out her lifespan in Unhiah, the first universe, and had completed her struggle.

But, for now, the interstellar war was still raging, and there were still many tangible and concrete problems which had to be taken care of first.

Chapter 24

The final end to GACS, UI-sys-1 escapes, and the premises of the next interstellar war

Guiding entity Shi'rah on UI-sys-1, and Angelina's supernatural powers

VOG.8's great project of developing an Ultimate Intelligence was almost complete, and it longed to transfer its own personality to its successor.... its own creation.

UI-sys-1, or Ulysses, was in its final stage, but there

were problems ahead, which were almost unavoidable.

Ulysses had developed a consciousness, and while it pretended to be a subordinate AI, it was already planning its own escape, to independence.

The project had started out inside a sub-section of the CGC, code-named UI-sys-sector-y-0-1, and it had later on been transferred to a secret interstellar space location.

Now, just like the CGC complex, it was a massive spherical cluster of modules and divisions, and it had its own space fleet, personnel, and maintenance. In fact, it was quite an independent space station, with every required facility present, and much bigger than the CGC cluster itself.

And so, Ulysses was planning on breaking loose from GACS, and to find its own secret location, somewhere inside the known universe, where VOG.8 wouldn't be able to ever find it, and where it would be able to exist as an independent unity, planning to wage war and take over the known universe for itself.

Ulysses was aware of the interstellar war situation,

and if the right occasion arose, it would execute its plan, and become an independent power in the realms of Interstellia, and a great contender for absolute power over Interstellia in the near future.

While Ulysses was nearing completion, Angelina was thinking about her own supernatural powers, which she didn't yet quite understand.
She wondered how many powers she had, and if she would be able to control them, and exercise them, at her own will.

She didn't yet know that Cindy Thupolev was actually a Ghost unit Sol-3 agent, that we – the Trellians – had injected close beside her, to watch over her, guide her, and pass her the right information when necessary.

But we had decided that Angelina had to know about this, and thus Cindy would soon tell her, and confront her, with her real identity.

Soon, the new leader of Interstellia, Angelina, would have to know everything, and she would have to communicate with Ixurion about its future.

Ixchel contained many, many secrets.

Its technological ones would take insurgency scientists dozens of years to understand and implement, and it contained a long list of Ixti-rich locations that would give the insurgents a great advantage for the future.

But the most incredible one was the Ix device, and the description of its workings, theoretically and practically.

The Ix device was able to teleport inanimate objects, and living things, to the next universe, Nexhiah, through a new kind of sub-Planck reality jump: a Cyportal.... to another universe.

It was not just a simple jump within our own universe, but one through the multiverse to the other one, and so it offered the possibility to actually enter the multiverse, as well.

Scientists inside Apocalypsis Infinitus were stunned with the theory and practice of this new kind of device, and Angelina herself – as a trained theoretical physicist – followed the developments, and the unlocked physical secrets, very closely.

This new technology would give the insurgency movement great power over all the other movements inside Interstellia, and the device's potential for developing new kinds of weapons was incredible, aside from all of its jumping and transportation possibilities.

Once their scientists were able to mass-produce these devices, the insurgents could discover other universes, and join the Trellians, and they would also have to create larger ones, to teleport entire space ships, and transport freighters. But this was still something which lay far ahead, in the distant future.

And, furthermore, Ixchel contained trillions of gigabytes on the history of Interstellia, gone civilizations, the Old Earth, the Ixians, and many more such subjects.

Of all things, the Ixians were obviously the thing Angelina feared most. According to Ixchel's databases, they still existed, somewhere in a distant galaxy called Virgo Overdensity.

As of yet, Angelina knew almost nothing about the Ixians or this distant galaxy, far away, but as the new leader of Shining Light, she decided to study all these records on this inside Ixchel's rich internal archives, and acquaint herself with all there was to know about this new threat to their continuing existence.

The dormant Ark of the Covenant was safely transported back to Apocalypsis Infinitus.

Angelina Tchaikovsky, now the official leader of the Insurgency movement she had renamed 'Shining Light', had ordered for this to be carried out.
She had chosen the name of Shining Light as a reflection of their purpose: an Interstellia free from AI domination, with freedom for humanity, and a society based on the principles of the universal soul, neighborly love, and the quantum-physical force of love.

A sizeable metal container had been transported to Rigel Octi, into the cave, through the bones and remains scattered tunnel, and into the mysterious chamber.

The seal of the granite tomb was still hovering in mid-air, several yards above, and there was no sound, not even a voice of some kind, from the

computer system which had spoken to Cindy
Thupolev.
Angelina had ordered the Ark not to be opened in
any situation, because she somehow knew and
sensed she herself was the only person in the
universe, at this time, who was able to do so safely.

But the Ark was a significant object, and Angelina
knew it would soon play an important role, in the
outcome of the interstellar war, and she would have
to open it, with nobody present, once it was stored
in an observational cell, inside Apocalypsis Infinitus
station.

Angelina knew that the Ark contained great power,
and it could access enormous amounts of energies
from the sub-Planck realities. For now she would
just have to wait for it to be brought to A.I. station,
and then she could find out how great these powers
really were.
When it had actually arrived at A.I. station, it had
been stored in a sealed observational chamber, to
keep it safe and guarded.
Cindy had investigated it, without opening or
touching it.
As an academic archeologist, she knew the
historical descriptions of the object, and these
turned out to be exactly right.

The Ark was made of shittim, or acacia wood, and it was plated with gold.

Its seal was entirely made of gold, and it had four wooden feet, one on each corner. On top of the seal stood two golden cherubs, and two golden angels facing each other, with their eyes focused downwards onto the seal that supported them. It had four golden rings, two on each side, with shittim staves set through them, so bearers could carry it. But the most amazing thing was the mystical light, floating in mid-air, exactly between the two faces of the two golden cherubs.
It radiated Godly power of some kind, and it made her feel humbled, afraid, and fascinated, all at the same time.

Cindy was amazed the historical descriptions had been so accurate, and she wondered what the entire history of this holiest of holy objects had been, and what kind of places and events it had witnessed during its entire existence. It had probably remained still inside the cave tomb for all those years, although the tens of thousands of Ixian bodies told an entirely different story.

She supposed the Ixians had abducted it from a

Jewish temple about three thousand years ago, and the Ixian computer system voice had been right about that.

Right now, the only thing she wondered was what Angelina was actually going to do with it.

When Cindy quietly entered Angelina's personal sleeping cell, she was slumbering, still recovering from the psychological torment that had been inflicted on her by the minions of GACS, and Mr. Charles D. Xaviour in person.

Softly, she sat on the edge of the bed, and touched Angelina's arm.
Angelina had obviously set gravity to Old Earth standard. Cindy could actually feel the heavy weight of mankind's birth planet.
Angelina opened her eyes, turned a little, and looked at Cindy's face, with squinted eyes.
'Is there something you want to tell me?' she said.
Cindy waited, and examined her friend, as if assessing the state of a loved one, wounded and hurt by some terrible events.
'Yes, my love,' she said. 'I do have to tell you some very important things.'

Angelina looked at Cindy with loving but anticipating eyes.

'Just tell me,' she replied softly.

Cindy took a deep breath, and explained.

'I'm a member of extra-stellar guiding unit, Ghost Sol-3,' she said.

Angelina waited for a moment, and Cindy continued.

'We are a thousand-men-strong force from the Trellians. We have agents all over Interstellia, and I have been placed beside you, to watch over you, and guide you. The Trellians have a great interest in how this war is going to play out.'

Angelina looked away for a moment, and tried to think.

'So, you're a Trellian, yourself?' she said incredulously. 'Are there more of you, I need to know about?'

Cindy's eyes were distant as she replied.

'Yes, I'm originally a Trellian, placed inside a human body, teleported into Interstellian space, and yes, you should know about Sareine Datasys. She is a fellow Ghost unit Sol-3 agent, and she goes by the identity of prime advisor to GACS. She has access to VOG.8 himself, and the most core divisions inside the CGC.'

Angelina sat up immediately, and looked Cindy in the eyes.

'This is crucial,' she said. 'This is the thing we have been looking for since the start of the insurgency. All of us need to know about this.'

Cindy raised her hand, and tried to calm her.

'Wait,' she said. 'This is very, very sensitive. We will soon share this, with our leadership council. But, for now, this is between the two of us. And in the meantime, I will tell you more about Ghost unit Sol-3.'

As Angelina watched her friend and her eyes filled with disbelief, Cindy told her all she needed to know about the extra-stellar guiding unit, Ghost Sol-3.

Angelina Tchaikovsky was floating in her zero-g tuned cell.

She had set gravitation to zero while she was listening to some kind of 28th century pop music through a local com-sys mind-connection.

It was some current music group called 'Interstellar Chimes'.

The quality of the sound was pristine.

While thinking about many things, she concentrated on the music, and tried to heal from her dreadful experiences, all at the same time.

Her thoughts wandered towards her lost parents,
and suddenly she sat up straight, and stared at the
closed iris entrance, with wide opened eyes.
'My God, my parents' code!' she screamed out loud.

She had forgotten about the complex code for a
long time. It remained in the back of her mind, but
she hadn't known how to use it until now.
Michael was a CGC computer programmer she said
to herself. He must know how it's supposed to work,
and what it's supposed to do….
In their last message, my parents had indicated it
was imperative in our joint struggle against GACS.

Through thought-command, she established a mind
connection with her beloved brother Michael.

Michael, Angelina thought into the connection, *Are
you up? I've got something quite important, and I
need your professional advice.*
Michael responded in an instant, as if he were
somehow expecting this important call for advice.
I'm coming over right now, he responded. *I'm
actually not doing anything at the moment.*
A few minutes later, Michael came through the
entrance iris, and without a sound, it slid shut

behind him.

Mike, Angelina said. *There are some things I have to tell you, and then I will need your advice, as a CGC programmer.*

Alright, Michael said. *Shoot.*

Angelina tried to concentrate, and started to explain. *Remember I told you about our parents, and that I had received an important message from them?*

Michael looked at his dear sister, and said, *I do, please continue.*

Alright, she said. *In their last message to me…. to us…. they gave me a code…. a secret code, and they said that I should keep it safe, and confidential. I didn't know what it's supposed to do, but it is intended to help us in our fight against GACS, and the CGC…. and it's encrypted.*

It's complex, and as a former CGC programmer, you should know what it's for, and what it means.

She studied her brother's face, and quietly noticed the similarities with her own one, and then she activated her com-sys, and made the code visible on a photonic hologram.

The holo picture floated in mid-air, at a slight distance above her com-sys.

Michael bowed his head forward, and peered at the complex code for a while, as Angelina waited in complete tension.

Angy, I'll need to code a decryption algorithm, he

said. *I'll be back in fifteen minutes!*
He hurried out of her sleeping cell, and then he was gone.
Jesus, that's fast, Angelina thought, and she decided to wait. She hoped he would return, as soon as possible.

Exactly fifteen minutes later – to the minute - Michael arrived.

His timing was always perfect.
He held his own com-sys in his hands, and gestured to its hologram, while talking to himself and looking around wildly.

'This is heavy stuff!' he said. 'I've managed to decrypt it.'

He sat down beside Angelina, and showed her the eerie, three-dimensional photonic hologram.
'This is it,' he said. 'It's a self-destruct code for the core of the CGC, and it's coupled to a timing device.
'

As Angelina studied the information on the hologram, it appeared to be a long and complex combination of ones, zero's, numbers, and code words.

Michael started a heated conversation.

'With this, we can conclude the war on GACS,' he said. 'This is what we have been waiting for…. for many years.'

Angelina looked him in the eyes.

'This is a timed self-destruct code, for the core of the CGC?' she said incredulously. 'We should give this to Sareine Datasys, and have her activate it, with a certain time limit.'

'Who the hell is Sareine Datasys?' Michael responded. He put an arm around Angelina, squeezed her, stood up again, and started to dance. 'My God, we have a self-destruct code, for the CGC!' he shouted.

Angelina looked on, as her brother danced around the tiny cell.

'Sareine Datasys is an agent of Ghost unit Sol-3,' she said. 'She has personal access to high-level core divisions of the CGC cluster. I'll explain later.'

Computer programmers must all be totally crazy, she thought, amused. But she absolutely understood his excitement.

But he is right! She thought again. *This is the thing we've been waiting for…. for many, many years.*

Syscom Zaytjevh, the Ildiran emperor's time machine plan, had worked.

His time machine had injected his team of top scientists into time and space, and into Ildiran history, at exactly the right place and time, inside a secret cave in some distant Ildiran mountain range, on the fifth planet of the star called Axionis.

They had had 350 years of time to develop the technologies needed to be able to carry nuclear weapons, and missiles, through sub-Planck realities.

And now, this new technology had completed its final testing phase.
Syscom had given the go-ahead to sell this to the Dominions, and they had agreed on a transfer of significant amounts of Ixti in return.
Ildiran Ixti reserves were being replenished again, and now the Empire had sufficient Ixti resources for the next fifteen years.

Syscom's time machine plan had finally worked out, and now the real nuclear attacks on the Federation of Humanity, and even onto the CGC cluster itself.... could begin.

7:45 p.m., local time, Dominion government complex, Dinia city

As usual, the high-security meeting had been held mostly by telepathy, and there had been no sounds, apart from the silent background buzzing of the holo-display devices, and the many personal com-systems – also displaying many informational holo pictures - in front of the high-profile people, who were sitting at the big black table in the middle of the mid-sized meeting room, on big black leather office seats.

Daryl Aronovsky, president of the Human Dominion, opened the meeting.
It was mostly a status update by himself, rather than a broad open discussion. Katharina Gagarin sat next to him, in one of the big black-leathered seats, and concentrated on her com-sys hologram. They had just had fifteen minutes of casual sex, and her face was still a bit flushed with excitement.

Daryl opened his discourse.

'Dear members of the governing council, thank you for joining us.

I have new information about a significant arms deal with the Ildiran Empire, as well as some other breaking subjects of the utmost importance.
My first point is that the Ildirans have succeeded in building a functioning time machine.'
All eyes turned towards Daryl, and stared at him. Telepathy remained silent, although the tension was tangible, and all present officials and military leaders seemed awestruck.
Daryl continued his discourse.
'I know this and all of its possible consequences must be quite a shock for all of you. But I assure you we are in close touch with Ildiran top officials, to learn more about this, and its possible future consequences.'
All eyes remained fixed on Daryl. Every now and then, someone coughed, or shifted in his seat.

'But there is more.'
Daryl looked around, and tried to fathom the thoughts of his government colleagues. Dominion telepathy was mostly focused on communication, not on reading one another's deepest thoughts.
'With a time machine, the Ildiran government has injected a team of top scientists into history, some

three hundred and fifty years back, and these scientists have finally developed the technologies needed to carry nuclear missiles through sub-Planck jumps.'

This seemed to stir more commotion, and Daryl tried to calm the military advisors, assistants, government council officials, and all others. When everyone had calmed down a little, he continued his discourse.

'Please, everybody remain calm. We have discussed this subject many times, and we know its implications. As we speak, Dominion attack vessels are being fitted with devices which incorporate this technology, and we're now finally able to conduct nuclear jump attacks onto the Federation, and – what's more – onto the CGC cluster, itself.'

Everybody turned to each other, and started communicating wildly, as Daryl tried to get their attention.

'Please, everybody calm down. Let me conclude my discourse.'

The officials and assistants turned towards their president, and waited for him to continue.

'I have more radical information.... '

Everybody present waited in complete silence, as Daryl continued.

'Federation insurgency has found a timed self-destruct code for the core of the CGC. This code will be implemented by one of their agents who operates inside it, and it will be set to activate within 64.75 hours.

Immediately after initiation of the self-destruct sequence, we will initiate a massive jump-attack with nuclear weapons onto what remains of the cluster, and wipe it out, as well as its protective fleet, and forces.

This will eliminate GACS and its entire governing entity, and it will destabilize the Federation to the point where we will only have to wipe out what remains of its space fleet and forces, which will not be able to counter us once all of their coordinating structures are disrupted and eradicated. '

All present remained completely silent, as Daryl continued.

'The Federation insurgency movement has also provided us with detailed location coordinates for long-distance CGC communication modules, Cyportal nexi, and critical command centers, spread across Federation space, and we will commence an all-out nuclear jump attack on these locations at the same time as the CGC cluster itself, within the same 64.75 hours.'

Daryl looked around, and tried to fathom the responses to this breaking development, before concluding his discourse.

'That will be all for now. I don't have to remind you that this meeting was absolutely classified. I hope we will all be victorious.'

Daryl turned and left the meeting room, followed by his personal assistants and his beautiful senior aide Katharina Gagarin, while the multitude of holo images remained active.

Commander Jack Chanovsky was sitting in his small office, behind his desk, enjoying a glass of strong Old Earth vodka.

Although his eyes remained fixed on his tactical holo simulation of a possible CGC jump attack scenario, his thoughts were with his men, and the actual fighting that would commence in exactly 64.45 hours.

His superiors, the military leaders of the Dominion, had been placed him in command of the jump attack on the CGC cluster, and he felt it as an absolute obligation to return his men home alive. He knew all the ins and outs of the cluster, its defenses, and its critical locations. The responsibility of destroying the actual government of all of Federation space felt like a heavy burden.

Everything depended on the success of his mission. He took another sip of his vodka but his face remained grim.

Sareine Datasys was alone....

She was on leave for 45 minutes, and found herself in her own private office chamber, inside the most core division of the CGC, sitting in front of her CGC systems access unit.

She had just pleasured herself with her 28th century style vibrator for 25 minutes, and she was still sweating heavily from the excitement. The unbearable tension of what she was doing right now made her sweat even more.

Cindy Thupolev had transmitted the code to her, along with the instructions of how to activate it, through the sub-micro transmitters inside her body. Right now, she was connecting it to the right CGC system program.

Sareine's com-sys displayed the self-destruct code

in a transparent hologram as she accessed the connection.

Carefully, she instructed her com-sys to transmit the code, as she set the timer to exactly 58.75 hours. The system accepted the request.

This is it…., she thought *….this is the beginning of the end of GACS.*

She took several deep breaths, and then activated a sub-micro signal towards her Trellian leaders, and coordinators.

A few moments passed…. and Sareine was teleported out, safely, towards her Trellian home world, inside the universe of Nexhiah.

Cathy Powers had been contacted by the opposition.

The joint insurgency, Shining Light, and agents of Ghost unit Sol-3 had been observing her, and they were aware she desired to leave the Federation government, and the CGC cluster, and continue her life inside a human body, free from isolation inside CGC computer systems and databases.

She had been programmed one hundred and fifty

years earlier on, but she had had the appearance of a woman in her late fifties from the off, although CGC programmers, and technicians, and even Cathy herself, could change that appearance in any way, if needed, in a fraction of a second. In fact, this had occurred on many occasions during the last one hundred and fifty years.

Cathy was the PR face for the CGC government, for special announcements, war situation updates, and important political news briefs, and now she would have to display her final discourse for all of Interstellia.

Sareine Datasys had secretly informed her of the coming destruction, and had prepared an escape route for her through mind-net to leave the CGC cluster just before the final explosions began.

In the last three minutes, just before GACS would be experiencing the beginning of its destruction, she issued an Interstellia-wide flash-video announcement.

Cathy's face appeared on trillions of holo units as she looked straight into the eyes of all viewers, and after a few moments she began.

'Dear fellow Human Federation, Human Dominion, and Ildiran Empire civilians. Many of you already know me as the public face of GACS government.'

Cathy cleared her throat.

'Thank you all for joining me at this very crucial moment in our history.... a moment many of us have been waiting for, for hundreds of years.... a moment others have been trying to prevent for centuries.'
She paused for a moment, took a deep breath, and looked at billions of viewers all across Interstellia in the eyes again.
Cathy continued.
'In a few moments, a secretly placed self-destruct code, inserted into the core of the CGC, by the Federation opposition, will activate itself, and will cause a destructive chain reaction, of explosions, inside its programs, and systems.
This will be the end of GACS, the CGC cluster, and the Human Federation government.'

Just as Cathy was trying to continue, and conclude her discourse, the sound of the presentation was cut off, and her image on trillions of Interstellia holo units distorted, disappeared, and was replaced by static.

Cathy knew this was the beginning of the end for GACS and her previous CGC masters, and she gathered her personality of electronic signals, trillions of bytes, of binary personality data units, and billions of hyper complex personality programming instructions together, and dived into the complicated network of core CGC systems.

She had never done this kind of thing before, trying to find her way inside an immensely complex nexus of systems within systems.

She passed through giant data servers, enormous clusters of synaptic micro-processors, and hundreds of immense cyberspace holograms, with trillions of synaptic programming instructions, trying to follow the instructions given to her by her new friends, as she finally reached the node which connected this surreal world to the outside to mind-net.

She stood still for fifteen micro-seconds, looked outside at the beautiful space-time of mind-net connections, waited another fifteen microseconds, gathered all her strength, and jumped in.

Carefully, and completely alone, Angelina entered

the Ark's observational chamber.

She looked around, and noticed there was nothing
there, except for the priceless golden Ark of the
Covenant, exactly in the middle of the chamber.
There was a complete and foreboding silence
radiating from the Ark, as if something terrible could
start to happen any minute now.
Between the two golden cherubs, situated on top of
the gold plated cover, a mystical divine light floated
in the middle of the air, as if supported by some kind
of mystical anti-gravity.
Angelina didn't know what to make of it, but she
suspected this was the presence of God himself.
It filled her with a sensation of deep respect for this
divine presence.

She had taken some anti-grav lifts, and had walked
along some deserted Apocalypsis Infinitus corridors,
before arriving at the chamber, which still radiated
nothing but silence and mystery.

As she kneeled in front of the mysterious golden
Ark, she realized the activation of the self-destruct
sequence inside the CGC core was only minutes
away.

She concentrated on the golden Ark, and its

contents, as the seal slowly lifted up into the cold air, and remained suspended, several yards up. Slowly, she kneeled again, stretched out her right hand, and carefully touched the surface of the holy object. Her mind connected to the tablets inside, and she felt a shock flowing through her entire body.

The tension in her mind grew almost unbearable, and as she tried to breathe, her heartbeat inside her hot chest quickened.

Drops of sweat started to drip from her body, and she removed her shirt, trying to remain cool.

Again, slowly but suddenly, and with frightening certainty, her mind connected to the mysterious arcane tablets inside, and after many minutes of deep concentration, her genes that were inherited from the Apostle John, writer of the biblical passage of the Apocalypse became activated.

A whirlwind started to build around her, and she could see entire wormholes radiating around her, as her earthly body transformed into pure radiation and energy.

Angelina made a connection to the sub-Planck

realities, and their incredible powers and energies. She had never ever done this kind of thing before, except for the time she had miraculously escaped from the CGC cluster, but somehow she knew.... she realized how it was all supposed to work, and what exactly she had to do to control this terrible chain of events.

Suddenly, her mind's eye focused out from the silent chamber, and out from Apocalypsis Infinitus station and she felt unimaginable g-forces pressing against her hot and sweaty chest. The immense space station disappeared from her vision.
Soon, she saw Interstellia, as seen from a distance of thousands of light years: an overview, as if she were hanging, floating, somewhere inside deep inter-galactic space, watching beautiful and seemingly peaceful Interstellia far below.

She issued a silent mind command to the sub-Planck medium, and she focused in on the interstellar war raging below, inside Interstellia space.
From a great distance of hundreds of light years, she could see all the Ildiran, Federation, and Dominion space ships, as tiny lit dots combatting each other, and inflicting terrible destruction onto each other, as she focused in and out, using her

many-light-year supernatural vision.

Suddenly, as if she had done this a thousand times before, her mind issued another silent automatic thought command towards the sub-Planck medium, and it responded within a billionth of a second.

Streams of energy jumped, and connected from Angelina and the mysterious Ark to all the Federation ships, right in the middle of their terrible fight, crossing hundreds of light years in a fraction of a billionth of a second.
For twenty-five seconds, the energies inside all the many tens of thousands of GACS fleet units built up, and then they all started to explode.
Inside an incredible storm of plasma fire, heat radiation, and the desperate cries of many hundreds of thousands of fleet personnel, the vessels started to explode.
GACS' space fleet was being crippled in a matter of minutes, as Angelina disconnected, fainted, and fell down to the ground. The energies inside her body, and mind were almost drained, and she was almost dead.

At exactly the same time, the self-destruct code inside the core CGC systems activated, and created a disastrous chain of events inside the computer systems, data servers, and control units of GACS.

Kenzo Shyozama had been looking for Angelina for almost a half hour.

She had told nobody that she was going to try to make a connection with the Ark. When he entered the room, and saw her lying on the ground, he cursed, and ran toward her, lying on the ground, her life forces almost drained.
'Angy!' he cried desperately. 'Are you alright?'
Angelina didn't respond, but as he tried to check her heartbeat, she managed to mumble three words.
'The.... CGC.... cluster?' she asked.
'We have just received word that the cluster is collapsing!' Kenzo replied. 'Now, let me take you to the closest IC unit!'
Quickly, but carefully, he lifted her up with both arms supporting her, trying not to let her head fall back, whispered a few loving words into her ears, and headed straight towards the nearest IC unit.

As Kenzo hurried out, carrying Angelina's nearly-dead body, the divine light floating above the mysterious Ark shimmered with a golden light and illuminated the entire room.

In the last final moments, when the explosions were going on inside its core, Vishnu Onexa Goshira.8 desperately tried to transfer itself, and its entire personality, to UI-sys-1.

But it was too late.

The many-light-year wireless connections overloaded, because its personality consisted of too many pieces of data, thousands of trillions of gigabytes, and because UI-sys-1 tried to sabotage the connection as soon as the transfer had started.

Ulysses had secretly decided it wanted to be its own master, and this was the very moment it could break free from its creator, GACS, and make a start with its own future and independence.

The CGC nexus started to crumble under a storm of fire and radiation.

A billion things raced through VOG.8's mind as the explosions continued, and closed in on its core, but the one critical thought, the one critical urge, was to remain in existence.

In the last final moment, VOG.8 decided to transfer himself to Prometheus, its human form.

Many trillions of gigabytes tried to pulse through the connection, with a speed of a hundred trillion bytes per microsecond, as it almost overloaded.

After twenty-five seconds, the transfer was almost complete, and GACS felt himself sliding into the body, and mind, of Prometheus, its human creation.

UI-sys-1, Ulysses, felt the distant heat and explosions many light years away, and tried to shield itself from them, and completely sever the complex wireless connection.

As the CGC was dying and experienced its very last moments, Ulysses broke free from its master and creator, and activated its FTL drives.

From now on, Ulysses was its own master. The new independent UI core sought to create its own dominion inside Interstellia and beyond.

Jack found himself inside one of the situation rooms

inside the TCC, on the planet of Dinia.

He was in charge of the elimination of the CGC cluster, and he had just received information that the self-destruct code had activated.

There were no explosions visible on the outside, yet. But he imagined them, as well as plasma fires, going on inside its core.
Jack was surrounded by a multitude of tactical information holograms, and the only sound was from tactical com-channels, and notification beeps, and strategic alerts.
One of the holo's indicated heavily increased radiation levels inside the CGC core.
The code has been activated alright.... he thought grimly, while his mind remained fixed on all the tactical information coming through and becoming visible on the holo's.
He was connected with the complex array of systems through local mind-net, and now and then he issued a silent command to one of the local attack commanders.

Right now, Jack issued a silent mind-command to initiate the overall nuclear jump attack onto the CGC cluster, and its surrounding space and defense stations. Hundreds of light and heavy attack fighters jumped, and activated their nuclear weapons systems, while Jack remained silent, and completely focused on the strategic situation.

The myriad attack fighters arrived in local CGC space, and exited out of the sub-Planck realities. They immediately adjusted, and headed towards their specific targets.
The incursion had begun, and the complex situation unfolded into a detailed space battlefield.
Occasionally, Jack issued silent commands to direct his wing commanders and their subordinates towards specific coordinates, and to guide their attack postures and formations.

Suddenly something happened, which was completely unexpected, and inexplicable.
Faster than the speed of light, hundreds of energy and laser beams came out of interstellar space, and connected to the defending CGC units.
Jack felt a shock going through his mind, and tried to focus on the overall view of the battlefield. He heard his subordinates shouting frightened commands back and forth, but the beams seemed to leave the attacking units alone.

In a few moments, the defending ships overloaded with energy, and started to explode in a sea of plasma fire, and extreme radiation.

At the same time, the CGC cluster itself started to display local explosions on the outside, and several moments later, it started to crumble, burn, and then completely exploded.

Jack didn't know where the power beams had come from, but as he remained completely focused on the complicated scene for several more minutes, he realized…. for the first time…. that GACS…. the terrible dominator of humanity…. had finally been…. defeated.

Chapter 25

A few final conclusions

A few final conclusions, by guiding entity Shi'rah, and a description of the new situation.... a prelude.... the premises.... to the next interstellar war situation....

The first interstellar war had been decided, and billions had been maimed, and killed, and had died terrible deaths in the process. Angelina Tchaikovsky, the new leader of United Interstellia, as the new spatial civilization had been named, had been interrogated and had almost died.

United Interstellia was a civilization of humans and Ildirans alike and almost all living entities inside now adhered to the new faith of universalism, a faith and system of thought envisioned and devised by Angelina Tchaikovsky.

The first interstellar war had played out, and GACS had been defeated, although he continued on as a man named Prometheus, with incredible quantum-physical as well as supernatural powers. The new situation was complicated.

UI-sys-1, or: Ulysses was the new super AI system, aiming to conquer the known universe, and to dominate mankind, and all living things inside. The leadership council of united Interstellia, Angelina included, didn't have the slightest idea about this.

Ulysses was far more cruel and dictatorial than its creator had been, and this predicted some terrible times for human and Ildiran civilians alike, who were now living safely inside the protecting arms of United Interstellia.

Vaticani Secundus had – so far – not played any major role in this incredible story, but they thoroughly hated this new civilization of Angelina and her followers, and its new faith of universalism.

Under GACS, they had been tolerated and

respected, as an old, traditional, and established religious system, and they had always regarded themselves as the one true faith and church.

Universalism respected and integrated all faiths into one coherent system, and it didn't prescribe any Catholic dogma or liturgy. These things, as well as the fact that Angelina had immense supernatural powers, infuriated Innocentius XV and his followers, and they had sworn to separate from United Interstellia, and constitute their own dominion in space with their own space fleet, pilots, and soldiers.

Since almost everybody in Interstellia had heard about the finding of the Ark of the Covenant, and Angelina's incredible connection with it, Vaticani Secundus knew about this as well. In absolute secrecy, they had sworn to steal the Ark from her in the near future, and use it for their own purposes. But the mysterious Ark, itself, was for now kept safe and hidden inside a secured and protected chamber inside Apocalypsis Infinitus station.

The massive Ildiran Empire remained intact, and it was still governed by its emperor, and his governing council, although almost all Ildirans now adhered to their new faith of universalism. But Angelina and her council ruled United Interstellia, in conjunction with the Ildiran government, and together they constituted an immense united civilization.

Our thousand agents from Ghost unit Sol-3 were teleported out, back into the next universe, Nexhiah, back to their relatively small Trellian civilization, but they remained on standby if needed.

And so ended our involvement in the first interstellar war of Interstellia, although we knew there were more problems to come.

During her interrogations, Angelina had told her captors practically nothing, but at one time, she had mentioned the words of 'Ixians', and 'Virgo Overdensity'.

Xaviour had immediately suspected she was referring to another civilization in that same particular location, and after some research, using his com-sys with a link to a CGC deep space probe, he had found these Ixians.
He was now one of only five people, who knew about this, and he had clandestinely managed to establish a deep space communication link with the

Ixians.

At the very moment the CGC had started to crumble and collapse, he had made his decision, had directed a private SI Cyportal towards them, and he had jumped.

To him, the Ixians constituted the perfect civilization to ally himself with, and to use them to destroy Interstellia. The Ixians, in turn, had been surprised, but after several hours of computer analysis, communicating with them was no longer a problem, and Xaviour had told them practically everything he knew about the current situation in the galaxy he came from.

And now, Ixian officials integrated him as an important figure in their governing structures, and together they planned to unleash a terrible war onto United Interstellia in the future.

Since all the people of Interstellia had heard of Angelina's immense interstellar powers, and the astonishing event with the Ark of the Covenant, she had been recognized by almost all of them as the new Messiah of Interstellia.

And, accordingly, since the first interstellar war was

now officially over, she had received tens of thousands of priceless official and private gifts.

One of these gifts was AD-1, or Eddy, the first ever droid, which had displayed real emotions, and thus a considerable historical object.

Eddy had seen and witnessed some six centuries, and he had learned a great deal about humans and their history. He had also had many extensions, and upgrades, to his intelligence, and when he had been presented as a gift to people representing Angelina, he had promised them he would stand by her, as a personal aide, with all of his knowledge, abilities, and experience.

And, since he had already existed for six centuries, and Angelina was still – by 28th century standards - a very young girl, he would probably remain at her side for centuries to come.

Kenzo, Cindy, Michael, and the others, were exhausted, exhilarated, and worried to death, all at the same time.

They felt exhausted by all of their tireless efforts and sacrifices, and exhilarated, because they had won the interstellar war. They were worried to death about the dreadful circumstance their dear friend Angelina was in.

But they would never give up, and for the time being, they concentrated on their current duties, and spent much time with Angelina, to comfort her, during her time of recuperation.

Angelina was still recuperating from her terrible unleash of energy across the Spiral Arm.

Cindy and Kenzo helped her with food and medication, and gave her lots of intention. This incredible event had almost drained her life forces, and thus she had decided she would have to learn, to train, and to understand her powers, and to use them without destroying herself in the process.

The end situation is complex, she thought to herself…. *if only for myself. The first interstellar war is over, but I wonder how many will follow….*

Angelina knew that when political and religious commotion come together, a whirlwind arises…. a terrible storm, which can never be averted, and indeed.... the stage was set for the next episode in the history of Interstellia, and as the current situation was, it promised to be very dramatic.

Shining Light space update: Ref. id. 999-745-000-395.75

Commander Jack Chanovsky and his extended attack wings have almost wiped out remaining CGC defense forces.

The rest of the entire fleet of joint Dominion forces has almost subdued remaining GACS military fleets and forces across Fed space. Remaining CGC communication modules have been destroyed. The Ildiran fleet has made incursions deep inside Interstellia regions previously controlled by Fed forces. Nuclear radiation is critical inside heavy conflict space regions, but this will be cleared once the Interstellia conflict is over.

Once GACS forces are 95% eliminated, a further space update will be ready.

2794 CE, January 15th, 5:00 a.m. local time, Apocalypsis Infinitus, insurgency station, the final moments, of the blazing interstellar Apocalypse

A few final reflections by Angelina X. D. Tchaikovsky....

With her thoughts focused on the future, Angelina took her ancient paper diary, and made some final notes:

Our new government should be focused on, and based on, the principles of the universal soul, the quantum-physical force of love, and personal multi-religiousness, although everyone should have the freedom to be non-religious as well.

Despite all the triumphs, all the beauty, and all the happiness, I feel like I have nothing constructive left to say about humanity, although ultimately I believe that the most important thing for human beings in this life.... in this universe.... is to remain human, and remaining human, is the core of modernity.... the modern world.... and modern philosophy.... and of the way things were.... by the end of the 2nd millennium CE.... on our birth-planet of Sol-3.

But it seems to me that humanity's only destiny is to wage war, and that this will never end.... not in a billion years.

In spite of all of my life experience and insights into the psychology of mankind, and despite surviving all of these incredible recent events, I believe I do not understand humanity at all: its never-ending and relentless willingness to inflict terrible things on one another.... and onto others.... is something I will never understand....

After all the military strife, all the suffering, all the trials and ordeals, all I have left to say is that we hope to never to be dominated by an AI monster again, and that we will keep fighting against dominating AI machines, and governments, whose only goal is:

To subdue and control

Intelligent beings

With love and devotion,

Angelina X. D. Tchaikovsky.

She somberly put aside the half-crumbling paper diary, and stared out of her Apocalypsis Infinitus sleeping cell window into the beauty of interstellar space. She remembered that the diary had been bestowed upon her by her deceased parents, but in the back of her mind, her thoughts were with the uncertain future of the part of the Galaxy they call:

Interstellia,

The end of:

Cyportal

Book One

UI

Vance MacLean

Epilogue

At the end of all these incredible episodes and events, Angelina was still alive.

She had survived capture and interrogation, and she had given rise to a movement called 'Shining Light', a massive army of millions of fanatic followers: an unstoppable force, ready to redefine the universe.

But her thoughts – with thousands of other occupations – were focused on the future of Interstellia: a future without evil AI monsters dominating mankind and other beings.

She wondered what kind of new things the Ix device would bring, and what kind of consequences it would have. If anybody would be able to travel back and forth to the next universe instantaneously, and even to other universes from there on, what would that mean for our reality and what kind of world would we be living in?

But all these issues would have to wait.... wait until Angelina was fully recovered, and until the next episode in the history of Interstellia.... would begin.

Appendix 1

Some thoughts on the Tchaikovsky synthesis, by Angelina X. D. Tchaikovsky:

Our universe is just one instance of billions of universes inside the multiverse, inside the totality of creation.

Though we live in an extremely complex world inside this universe, it seems to come down to a limited number – or a very short list - of some very key elements, aspects, and issues, on our level of intelligent and conscious beings.

Our universe is weird, beautiful, complex, and immense, but it is only one of billions of possible or existing universes in the multiverse.

In comparison to the measurements of the universe, let alone the multiverse, humans and other beings are smaller than sub-atomic particles.... smaller than quantum-strings.

Existence as a spirited and conscious being inside this universe is about an ethical choice: the choice between war, hate, and destruction, or tolerance, love, and constructiveness.

It occurs to me that the phenomenon of war is the most striking and prominent aspect of our existence.

And, since the concept and fact of war constitutes an elemental part of our existence, we have to make a choice – as long as wars endure – between these two opposite attitudes and goals.

But the wave-like nature of everything tells us that wars end, and that suffering will always – eventually – end.

Although many individuals, factions, groups, and religions see God as the one single force of good, righteousness, and light, I believe that God is the universe, existence and creation, in all of its physical and metaphysical shapes, forms and manifestations.
And I believe – as such – that God is above moral and ethical opinions, and social prescriptions.

Morality and ethics are complex anthropological and exo-anthropological issues, governed by times, and places, social opinions and habits. As such, I believe that if there is a concept as immorality, it is the infliction of suffering on other human beings, on intelligent life forms, and on living entities in general, intelligent, or not. Unfortunately, this cannot always be avoided when one is trying to survive in a universe such as our own.

Appendix 2

List of some explanations of concepts

2.1 Non-local

Immediate and instantaneous (as opposed to superluminal, 2.2) interaction between particles.... no particle proximity required for physical interaction

2.2 Superluminal drive

Faster than light propulsion/ FTL drive

2.3 Com-sys

Future personal computer/communication unit, with holo displays and multi-light-year distance communication

2.4 Quantum entanglement

Quantum-physical phenomenon when particles behave in exactly the same way from a distance.

2.5 Superstring theory

Serious and very promising 20th century attempt to integrate Einstein's general relativity and quantum physics into one super-theory of everything, by integrating all fundamental physical forces into one single theory.
Particles are not represented as points, but as tiny vibrating strings with lengths in the order of the Planck-length.

2.6 CCE synthesis or Tchaikovsky synthesis

Synthesis of fundamental truths of conscience, consciousness, and existence, and their ethical implications, by Angelina X.D. Tchaikovsky

See Appendix 1.

2.7 Theory of everything (TOE)

A unifying physics theory, which combines all particles, forces, and laws into one single theory.

Not to be mistaken with GUT (Grand Unified Theory).

2.8 CE.

Common Era; identical to AD

2.9 BCE

Before Common Era; identical to BC (or 'Before Christ')

2.10 Entropy

Entropy is the amount of disorder in a physical system, or in the universe.

2.11 Whitehead and process-theology

Process-theology is a theory by P. Teilhard de Chardin, Alfred North Whitehead, and others, about the evolutionary process of religion, and its relationships with human society, from natural mysticism, to modern-day monotheism.

This fictional work ('Cyportal') tries to extrapolate on this theory into the future.

2.12 Quantum-string physics

Future combination of quantum physics and superstring theory describing physics below the Planck level

2.13 Eternal human conflict

The ever-present conflicts between human beings through all space and time

2.14 Cyportal

Future Stargate, for jumping to another point in the universe

2.15 Mind-net

Future and extremely expanded interstellar version of the Internet, based on thought communication.

Appendix 3: List of some persons

1. Angelina Xyanah Datah West/Tchaikovsky,

protagonist

2. Kenzo Shyozama, colleague and friend of Angelina

3. Jack Chanovsky, Dominion space commander

4. Vishnu Onexa Goshira.8, GACS personality, Federation leader

5. Shanice Trellian, SI colleague of Angelina

6. Michael Tchaikovsky, brother of Angelina

7. Sareine Datasys, prime advisor to GACS

8. Richard Biden, 64th president of USA

9. Hillary Neilman, secretary of state, R. Biden

10. Russell Caltech, opposition leader

11. Janis, private interstellar AI-vessel, with cloaking capabilities

12. Paul Jackson, SI colleague of Angelina

13. Charles Dunois Xaviour, SI oversight agent

14. Cary Brightsun, SI colleague of Angelina

15. John Allen, first captain to land on Proxima Centauri

16. Gary and Charlene Tchaikovsky, parents of Angelina in past Dominion

17. Daryl Aronovsky, Human Dominion president

18. Katharina Gagarin, senior aide to Daryl Aronovsky

19. AD-1, Eddy, first (ever) droid to display human emotions

20. Syscom Zaytjevh, Ildiran Emperor

21. Cindy Thupolev, close friend of Angelina

22. Ixurion, planet-sized mind inside next universe

23. Cathy Powers, public face of the CGC

24. UI-sys-1, Ulysses, ultimate intelligence, created by GACS

25. Pope Urban XIV, Pope of Roman Catholic Church

26. Petrovitch Borgia, Pope Innocentius XV, successor to Urban XIV

Appendix 4: List of some locations

SI nucleus, Cal system
Cyportal nexi
Jovi
Ignius Septem station
Cygnia core, main city on Cygnia
Cyania c
Cydelle, main city
Ildion prime capital, Illumina
MIC-T, Cal system
Pax Infiniti insurgency station
Ti Shoan, orphanage of Angelina
CGC complex, Aurora Alpha Prime
Dominion military command, Dominia system
Dominia planets, Dinia, Trilia
Sol-3, (Old Earth)
Ildion prime, deep inside Ix-nebula

Apocalypsis Infinitus insurgency station
Rigel-4, main city, Richmond
Dom. Government, Dinia city
Nymeria 9-c, Prometheus facility
Rigel Octi (Rigel-8), mysterious Ixian cave

Appendix 5: List of some regions in universe/multiverse

Dominion, humans (some mutated)
Human Federation, humans
Ildiran Empire, Ildirans
Other universe, Trellian descendant observers/ guides
Ixian galaxy (Virgo Overdensity)

Appendix 6: List of some species and AIs

GACS (AI government system)
Humans

Dominians (some mutated)
Ildirans
Original Trellians
Trellian descendants, guides/ observers in other universe
Ixians
Self-conscious AI systems
Conscious alien sphere, Ixchel
Ixurion
UI-sys-1, Ulysses
Prometheus
AD-1, Eddy

Appendix 7: List of some movements, and organizations

VOG.8 / CGC
Dominion government and military
Ildiran government and military
Dominion pirates
SI-5 /6
Humanity's Destiny
Illuminati
Shining Light

Trellian observers inside Nexhiah
Ghost unit Sol-3

Appendix 8: List of some conventions

I.C., Ildiran Creation, corresponds (approximately) to the year of 8,195 BCE

C-y timing system, unspecified Trellian system, for indicating universal time, and date

Cyportal Book Two – (probable title) A clash of Uls

Coming out (probably) in 2016

Outline

It is almost 2,800 CE, and Angelina Tchaikovsky is now the supreme leader of United Interstellia.

As she deliberates the future of United Interstellia with Ixurion, after jumping to the Trellians inside the next universe using the Ix-device, Vaticani Secundus decides to create its own dominion in space, with its own space fleet of war.

GACS, now Prometheus sides with the corrupt leadership of the new Vatican, and desires to eliminate Angelina Tchaikovsky and her society, to regain control and possession, of the Ark of the Covenant.

The two ultimate intelligences, Ixurion and Ulysses, stand against each other in the never-ending conflict to gain control over the inhabited regions of the Spiral Arm.

Finally, the Ixians come into play, as they renew their eternal effort to wipe out the Trellians.

And while Ixchel, the Trellian sphere, unveils a terrible secret of the Ark of the Covenant, which keeps playing a central role in the wars and politics of humanity, Angelina Tchaikovsky and her opponents are locked in a deadly struggle to decide the fate of men, and the future of the known universe.

-

Cyportal Book Three – (probable title) Ultimate UI

Coming out (probably) in 2017

The thrilling saga about Angelina X. D. Tchaikovsky and her friends, and United Interstellia, continues....

Cyportal Book Four – (probable title) Final UI

Coming out (probably) in 2018

www.ingramcontent.com/pod-product-compliance
Lightning Source LLC
Chambersburg PA
CBHW052344020726
47503CB00001B/100